I owe my inspiration for the Tinman Series to the late, great Donald E. Westlake. I only knew the man through his writings but he showed me a new path, and sent me on my merry way.

Much gratitude is due the curators and staff at the Nevada State Museum in Carson City.

My appreciation goes out to Gene for living such a colorful life and for sharing it with me.

I thank the city of Reno for being such a wonderful character to write about.

Most importantly, I owe all my success to Peg.

Books in the Tinman Series

Posse of Thieves

Shady Deal

Coming Soon

Calling the Shots

SHADY DEAL

Marc J. Reilly

The Thieves Press

Cover Photo by ljupco/www.123rf.com

Title Font by Daniel Hochard/www.imagex-fonts.com

Printed in the United States of America

First Printing, 2019

ISBN 978-1-947107-01-4

The Thieves Press
www.crookbooks.site

"Credo Quia Absurdum"

THE IRREVERENT
CONCEPTION

THEY USED TO CALL HIM DOG. It was on account of his last name being difficult to say, and spell. No doubt conjured up by a drunken Hun, hundreds of years ago. Otto Scheidegger, aka, Dog. Even the cops had it in his file. He never really minded his handle, that is until a certain beautiful, red-headed moll, who he affectionately nicknamed Dizzy, recently dubbed him, Shady.

He smiled at the thought of her, some four months ago when he'd first blown into town, over drinks at Harold's Club where she worked as a dealer, her looking at him with that little luscious pout of hers. "Dog," she had said, "is not befitting of a big-time heavy like you. And I for one, will not utter such drivel."

What a dame. Big words and all. So now he was Shady. And it fit like a glove.

At the time he met her, he was hooked up with another woman and had no chance to explore a potential relationship. Now that the first dame was permanently out of the picture, if Dizzy did her job well when things got dicey after tonight—and he knew they would—he might just have to give her a little token of his affection. His hands sweated up at the thought.

He drummed his fingers on the dash of his 1953 Vauxhaul Velon. The boxy car was four years old but still had that new smell to it. Just the way he liked things, new and fresh. It had plenty of giddy-up, but he had never used it on a caper. This was his casing car. Anybody looking at it would just think he was another straight, out for a late-night cruise, trying to get away from the screaming wife and kids.

Anyone choosing to investigate closer would take one look at the driver and know, instinctively, this was the face of trouble. A crooked slit for lips, thin, sandy hair, gray eyes that only sparkled at the suffering of others, sharp angles forming the cranium, like it was hewn from brittle slate, an ugly scar stretching from chin to shoulder. His frame was tall and lanky, but his taut body belied powerful muscles that could rip a man apart. In a war-era movie, he would have been the Gestapo interrogator who tortured for the pure joy of it. An Oscar shoo-in.

Just thirty years old, Shady had been a danger to society since shortly after he was spawned. His father had come to the New World from the Old Country, and was born and raised in a little town on the border of Austria and Germany. A place called Braunau am Inn, infamously known as the birthplace of Adolf Hitler. Shady liked to brag about it.

His father settled in Wisconsin in a German enclave on the outskirts of Wausau. He was fifty-five with five grown children and a dead wife when he was remarried to Shady's mother, a frail woman, thirty years his junior. Shady was born the following year. The only income the family had was from his father's bootlegging and gambling. Shady's earliest memories are that of watching the booze drip from the still's copper tubing that snaked around the kitchen.

When Shady was age eight, his father died. His mother retreated into some dark recess of her mind, and Shady was left to his own devices. At age eleven, he was arrested for running a gambling den in the back of a neighbor's barn. He had roulette and dice tables, and a running card game. Buy-in was ten chips for a penny. Kids raised the money by collecting deposits on bottles. When the cops found out he was being raised by a single mother they let him go. He was back in business the next day.

He got his first gun when he was ten. A .22 rifle. His only buddy, Billy, had also recently acquired a small caliber hand gun. One day they were out by the Wisconsin River, where the railroad tracks run alongside. There was a car parked nearby but they thought nothing of it. They were idly shooting at anything that moved and were not aware of a man fishing down by the banks. One of the potshots came a little too close and he climbed up the bank.

Smiling, he admired the rifle and asked if he might see it. Shady, too young to suspect anything, handed it over. The man removed the bolt and threw it into some brush. Then he hitched the barrel under a rail and bent it in two. He handed it back to Shady and told him he should learn to shoot better. He sauntered to his car, grabbed more bait, and climbed back down the riverbank.

After the man had gone, Shady borrowed Billy's handgun and shot out the car's headlights, windshield, radiator and tires. He and Billy managed to escape but a complaint was made and the police put out a search for them. It was the first time he made the news on the radio, and he was thrilled.

He shot his first human when he was thirteen. By now, he'd graduated to a double-barreled shotgun, and with his own hands built a little row boat for duck hunting. One morning, he set out with his gun. His boat was chained to a little scrub tree on the bank of the river. As he approached the spot he heard loud whacking and saw a guy with a rock trying to break the lock.

Shady dropped in a couple of rounds, and called the man out. He snarled back at him, but started down the swampy edge of the river. As he was disappearing around a bend, he turned and shot Shady the finger.

A familiar light filled Shady's head, blinding rational thought. He lifted his gun, the guy turned to go, and Shady gave him both barrels in the back. It flipped him completely over in the air, like some sort of gymnast going for a ten. He hit the water, and staggered off. Shady just watched him go. He wasn't going to hunt him down. Too swampy. For a couple of weeks he listened to the news on the radio. Nobody was reported being shot, and they never found a body. Shady hoped he'd offed the guy, but with no proof, he never included it in his tally.

He killed his first human for sure when he was fourteen. He was working for a brushing crew where a utility company was clearing trees for a power line. His crew was compiled mostly of kids like himself, delinquent and wild. Like gypsies, they went wherever the company was cutting timber, and cleaned up the brush.

One day, Shady's hatchet broke and he went into the tool shed to fetch another. One of the adults on the tree-felling crew was in the shed at the same time. He was a fat, ugly, slob of a man who had taken joy in tormenting the youngsters. Shady hated him and envied his power as an adult. They got in each other's way, and the guy pushed Shady across the shed into a bunch of tools.

Shady was an aggressive, smart-mouthed kid. He cursed the guy and he rushed him. Shady grabbed a pick handle and swung for the fences. It caught the man clear on the skull, just above the eyes. The top third of his head slid over two and a half inches. He froze for a split second, suspended between life and death, and wilted. A sure kill if there ever was one.

Shady went before a local judge who claimed he was quite familiar with the dead man and it was no great loss to society. Shady was released with not a slap on the wrist. It was his fondest boyhood memory. He saw it clearly as one of the better things he'd ever done in his life. He nailed the son of a bitch, and he was gone. Problem solved. It didn't get any simpler than that.

At sixteen, he migrated to Chicago. Fascinated by the city he haunted North Division Street where many of the strip joints, cat houses and speakeasies were located. He was in a bar when he heard a wise-guy looking for a handgun. Guns were a hot commodity in the city, and hard to come by. Shady quickly realized a profit could be made. In Wisconsin, handguns were aplenty. Soldiers back from the war would sell their .45's, .38's and 9mm's cheap for drinking money.

He took a bus back to Wausau and quickly bought a gun and returned to Chicago where he sold it to the guy at a good profit. The guy was so impressed with the merchandise, he told Shady he could find buyers whenever he could produce. Once a month for a year, Shady returned to his stomping grounds, bought up any available guns and sold them in Chicago.

His reputation grew until he was approached by a mob who specialized in bank heists. The leader, Fat Tony Albano, immediately recognized Shady as a man with thieves' blood and took it upon himself to teach him a trade. Shady was an apt student, and soon learned all the tricks of the honored occupation that had been chosen for him. As a budding yegg, he successfully tackled the tricky task of sweating dynamite to extract the nitro. He discovered how to punch and peel most safes. And it was found he had an uncanny knack at manipulating tumblers and opening jugs without force. Within two years, he became the mob's top peterman.

Unfortunately, Shady discovered Fat Tony was skimming the hauls and shorting him. The next heist, he gained access to the bank, and after the rest of the gang had entered, he locked them inside and tipped the bulls to their presence. The entire mob was arrested. Shady, free and clear, headed west as a freelancer.

He never thought what he'd done had broken any criminal code. He was the wronged one. Fat Tony had stolen from him and so he had to pay. Simple as that. The yegg did all the work anyway and, in Shady's mind, he should rightfully get the lion's share. This wasn't the way mobs worked, but it's how he felt.

This attitude is in part what had caused his recent breakup with long-time partner, Johnny "The Quill" Zelmanovich. It's why he was also now turning off Caliente Street onto Haskell and flipping his lights off. He crept the car along, passing a small alleyway to his left, running between a bakery and some store frontage on Caliente.

Halfway between the intersection of Arroyo and the head of the alleyway, he pulled the car to the curb. A little over three hundred yards to his left sat the back of the Washoe Super Market, it's front bordering on S. Virginia. In between his car and the market was nothing but a small field and large parking lot. There was no sign of life, but he knew it wouldn't be long. This was the night his plan had called for, and he was certain to have company.

The problem with Johnny had begun when his name had come up after a heist and a federal complaint was filed. Shady wasn't fingered, but they had to put several states between themselves and Tennessee.

They landed in Reno, a town known to be loose, and a place where someone unlucky enough to get pinched could easily fade the beef if they had enough fall dough to pay a fixer. Shady always had money stashed away in various places around the country, but he was a smart crook, and had no intention of getting arrested and giving his hard-earned money to some bent judge and lawyer just to beat a rap.

Shortly after they landed in Reno, it became clear they would have to part ways. The way they worked was Shady handled all the locks, safes and alarms. Johnny did the heavy lifting and worked out the plans. Early on, Johnny's capers were perfect. It's how he got his nickname. The Quill. His plans were clear and pure. Pure gold. But lately, Johnny had taken to the needle and was getting sloppy. And dangerous. Most importantly, it was costing Shady money.

The first three heists they pulled in Reno were total busts. Two safes in the State Department of Agriculture, which Johnny had assured were filled with payroll, were empty. Even more galling was the Sunderland Building job. Housing Reno's revered Sunderland Shoe Store and Paterson's haberdashery, the three-story men's emporium with Mezzanine lounge should have yielded a pile.

Shady had successfully drilled the safe only to find the deposits were made on a slightly different schedule than The Quill had figured. Once again, a total waste of energy. They finally scored when they hit the Miner's Tavern. A tipster had pointed Shady to the bar, and this time, he had been the one to lay out the plan. They made off with $6900, and when it came to the split, Shady demanded he get two-thirds, claiming Johnny was not holding up his end. Johnny made a stink, but Shady convinced him with a gun butt to the head.

When Johnny came to, with $2300 in cash strewn over his body, Shady was gone and the partnership officially dissolved. The moll Shady had been shacking up with, Peggy Nell Dansen, had witnessed the breakup and decided Shady was not a safe guy to be around anymore. She took off with Johnny, and Shady learned they had hooked up with the O'Boyles, a husband-and-wife team who had gone to ground in Reno after a botched burglary of a First State Bank in Shannon City, Iowa.

The couple had the feds after them, all over $421 in silver, $400 in cash and $4000 in practically useless traveler's checks. Another Bonnie and Clyde wannabe. They were no more than rank amateurs to Shady, and he put Johnny's new partnership out of his mind. Until he got wind they were planning on pulling a heist, which Shady had earlier blueprinted, and shared with Johnny.

It was Peggy who tipped him off. After their breakup, she'd come back to his apartment to collect some of her things. As she was crowing about how much better life was without him, she let it slip. She didn't give any details and Shady didn't need any. He had mapped the whole thing out, and knew without any doubt the caper was going down. The whole plan hinged on it being the night before Mother's Day. Heavy shopping would have occurred before the holiday, and with the banks closed on Sunday the deposits would have to wait for Monday.

From earlier observation of the store's patterns, Shady had estimated the take would be upwards of $20,000. He and Johnny had planned on doing it themselves with help from an inside man. Now the O'Boyles had hijacked the plan and Shady felt it only right that he hijack the heist.

In his rearview mirror, he saw a car turn onto Haskell. He quickly tilted the mirror at a downward angle, and hunched in his seat. He watched as the car's lights were extinguished as it turned into the alleyway. He was able to make out two women in the front seat, with other bodies in the back. He smiled. The women were the wheelman and jigger. The men would do the actual job.

If he was pulling this heist he would have circled the block and surrounding area at least five times, looking in cars, house windows, anywhere prying eyes could be. He sighed and hoped the rookies would be capable of knocking off this lead pipe cinch.

It was a new experience: casing a heist without actually being involved in it, knowing every move as it was happening without making it happen. He wondered what poor slob they recruited to be the inside man, who had been sitting in a damp, hot boiler room most likely since Friday night.

The plan had begun when Shady was searching the town for likely scores, a python looking for rabbit holes. He'd wandered into the market which had many departments, and he guessed the daily take must be impressive. He chatted up a cashier and she told him the store had so much difficulty hiring stocking people they were ready to kidnap someone off the street. She even jokingly offered him a job. That was the hook.

Upon further examination of the building, he realized the necessity of having an inside man. The only practical entry point was the rear door, bordering on the parking lot. He could see it from where he sat. There was no outside handle, being secured from the inside by a padlock. All the other doors were on S. Virginia. Far too visible for illegal entry.

The plan therefore hinged on getting an inside man hired shortly before the heist, then have him hide somewhere in the guts of the building. On the night of the caper, he would open the rear door from the inside. It didn't take Willie Sutton to fill the position. Even a straight could be taught to open most padlocks with a pair of pantyhose and a rubber mallet. He figured they must have gotten Newmann, an ex-convict and part-time meat cutter, whose house, Shady had discovered, was where the gang holed up.

His attention was drawn by the sight of two shadows moving low and fast out from the far corner of the bakery where the alleyway ended. The dark form leading the way was lugging a heavy bag. He recognized the skittish movements of his old partner bringing up the rear. All hopped up while on a heist. Stupid. Couldn't wait for the boost until later.

Shady supposed the two women would wait in the alleyway. He wondered if a cop meandered by how they planned to explain away two women sitting alone in a car in a deserted alleyway at two in the morning. Two dumb ducks in a pond. He mentally crossed his fingers. Just let them pull off this one job right.

He saw the two shadows melt into the wall next to the rear door. A few moments later the door swung open, light spilling out into the night. Shady exhaled. Morons. There was a lot of shuffling and waving of arms, then the shadows disappeared inside. The caper was on. Time to go.

There was nothing more he could do but head off to Newmann's house and wait. He eased his car down Haskell, and right on Pueblo, where he switched on his lights. He crossed over Forrest, and caught a glimpse of the Redfield mansion two blocks down at the corner of Mt. Rose. It was the site of a famous burglary, and Shady had earlier scoped it out. Wondering if possibly the time might come when it could be hit again.

It was only a ten-minute drive down Plumas to the hideout, and having heard about Mr. O'Boyle's skills as a yegg, he knew he would have a lengthy wait.

There were purportedly two safes in the market, and though Shady had not had a chance to see them, he figured they were probably installed when the store had its grand opening some eighteen years ago. Most likely old Diebolds, single hinged, rotary combination lock, no relockers. Shady would have opened both in thirty minutes or so. He figured maybe an hour or more for these numbwits.

He had scoped out Newman's house earlier and knew the main feature was both a plus and a minus. It was isolated. Reno was still a young city and there were few neighborhoods so far west of downtown. Where houses did congregate, they were spread out, with lots of space between. This was a good thing if the gang decided not to play nice. There would be little chance of neighbors hearing gunshots, even police officer Robert Hastell who lived four doors down.

When Shady learned about the cop's house, he wondered just how idiotic this crew could be. Sleeping amongst the sharks is never a good thing for crooks. But for what he had to do tonight, it wouldn't affect him.

On the other hand, the isolation of the house was a bad thing regarding his car. So when he pulled into the driveway of the ranch-style house, he continued into the scruffy backyard and tucked in as close to the rear wall as he could. He was counting the mob would be as dumb as he thought and never look behind the house when they returned.

He slid out and sidled up to the back door. The lock was easy to pick, and a few seconds later he was standing inside the small kitchen.

He wandered into the various bedrooms and bathrooms and found little of interest except the $4000 in traveler's checks the O'Boyles had stolen. Even with his low estimation of the husband-wife-team, Shady was stunned they would still have the useless paper in their possession.

In the living room, he found a fairly rare 9x19mm Parabellum Luger, fully loaded, just sitting on a bookshelf. He slipped it into his suit jacket. Nice gun to have around, or just look at. He had a fond spot for anything German.

Under a couch cushion, he uncovered a .45 Colt M1878 double-action revolver, fondly referred to by connoisseurs as a "Frontier." Also loaded. It was an older gun, but handsome nonetheless, with plenty of kick. He thought about pocketing it as well, but decided he might have a little fun first. He removed the cartridges, dropped them in his jacket pocket, and replaced the gun where he'd found it.

Strewn carelessly around the living room floor was a collection of burglar tools. Shady never kept the tools of the trade anywhere near his person, unless he was on the job. He wondered again how these bunglers were not already locked away.

Most interesting was an oil painting perched on the mantel over the fireplace. Paint still wet. Depicting three burglars slipping down an alley on their way to pull a heist. They carried acetylene torches and tank and the whole thing was surprisingly realistic. And to Shady's way of thinking, amazingly stupid to have displayed. Nothing like advertising what you are. Even a cursory visit by the law would have been a disaster. Shady checked his watch. By now, even a dumb yegg would have managed to get into the safes. He hoped so. It was dangerous just being in this place.

He unconsciously patted his chest where his own gun, a snub-nosed, .38 Colt Banker's Special, sat cradled in a shoulder holster, and settled down to wait.

Twenty minutes later, headlights flashed across the living room curtains and approached the house. Shady slipped his gun out of its holster and nestled it in his lap. He knew Johnny always carried a .22. But he wasn't worried about any popgun. Newmann he'd seen around Reno and considered him too stupid to be much of a threat, packing or no. The O'Boyles were the unknown factor.

A car door slammed. Then another and another. Muffled laughter. Peggy was the first to come in. Her squeals of joy cut short in a choked gasp.

"Evening Peggy," growled Shady.

"Dog!"

Shady gestured her toward the couch. She scampered over, hands cupping her crotch.

"Honey, I gotta pee, real bad!"

"Squeeze tight."

Mrs. O'Boyle, a hatchet-faced woman with hair cropped like a man, strode in like she was the head honcho. She spotted Shady and her eyes narrowed, but with no fear.

"And you must be Mrs. O'Boyle. First name happen to be Bonnie?"

"Lily," she snapped. "Who the hell are you?"

"Tax collector."

"You don't look like no tax collector," she hissed.

"And you sure as hell don't look like no flower," said Shady, fixing his gun on her head. "Down on the couch."

The three men entered. Mr. O'Boyle had a large canvas bag over his shoulder, and Johnny was cradling another in both arms. Newmann was last, dragging the third, much heavier, bag.

Johnny saw Shady first and froze. "What are you doing here, Dog?" asked Johnny, like he might cry.

"It's Shady, now. You know that. And you know why I'm here. Drop the bag and slide over your piece."

Johnny followed directions while Shady focused in on O'Boyle. "Is he packing, Johnny?"

Johnny's eyes flickered nervously. He went to O'Boyle, reached inside his jacket and pulled out a Walther P38. He slid it over to Shady's chair, next to the .22. Shady emptied out the shells from both and tossed them into the kitchen. "Newmann?"

The big lug shook his head so violently Shady knew he wasn't lying. He asked him, "Why's your bag so heavy? You got a dead body in there?"

Newmann shoved the sack onto its side and rolls of coins spilled out. Shady couldn't believe his eyes. "You bozos took the time to grab the coinage!" He laughed and laughed, pointing a finger around like enjoying the clowns at a circus.

After catching his breath, he rose from his chair and approached Mr. Boyle, whose face had turned fuchsia. "You must be Mr. O'Boyle."

"William."

"Well, Bill O'Boyle, you must be the brains of this crack outfit. I can see it in those keen eyes. Yeah, I seen eyes like yours before. At the monkey house at the zoo." Shady squawked in his face.

"Honey, I swear I'm gonna pee my panties!" squealed Peggy.

Shady waved her out of the room and she hopped down the hall to the bathroom.

"And you must be Johnny's old partner," said O'Boyle.

"Yep, me and Johnny go way back, don't we Johnny." Johnny hung his head and wouldn't meet his eyes. "And we have a little problem. You see, Billy Boy, my old partner came to you with a blueprint of mine and you and your dyke stole it."

Shady heard something behind him. He glanced back and saw Peggy fumbling around the bookshelf. "You looking for this, darling?" He pulled out the Luger and waved it in the air.

Peggy sighed and grinned nervously. "Didn't mean nothing by it."

"Sure. Now here's what's about to happen. I'm going to collect my plan fee and then we're going to say ta-ta and you can only hope we never run into each other again. Newmann, grab O'Boyle's sack and haul it out back to my car. You got one minute."

Shady caught a look between Mr. and Mrs. O'Boyle. The fun should start any minute. "So Newmann was the sap you found to sit in that boiler room all night and day, huh? And how did those two Diebolds treat you, Billy? Any troubles?"

O'Boyle sighed. "Look, we didn't know Johnny got that plan from you. We thought it was all his idea."

"Bullshit," said Johnny.

Shady laughed. "No in-fighting boys. Gang's got to stick together." By now, he could see Mrs. O'Boyle's hand under the sofa cushion, but he diverted his eyes, waiting for the moment. Newmann rushed back in and stood waiting for further orders.

Shady said, "So, Johnny, I figured the haul to be twenty large. Was I right?"

Johnny forced a nod.

"I wonder what would be fair as my fee for that beautiful plan. The first sack looked to be about half the take so I'm at fifty percent. How much more you think I deserve?"

Mrs. O'Boyle rolled to her left with the Colt in her right hand. Before she could draw a bead on Shady, he had the drop on her. He closed in and placed the barrel of his gun in her ear.

"Say did you know that some lilies are poisonous?" asked Shady. "That's right. Which gives me an idea. You go ahead point that gun over at my old partner and give him the tried and true. Two in the head and one in the heart, just to be sure."

Johnny looked up at Shady, his face dripping. "You wouldn't do that."

"Well, sure I would. But it's not going to be me. Your new partner's gonna do it. And in exchange, I leave half the money. What do you say, Missus? You up for that proposition? Lose a partner, gain ten G's. After all, you're obviously smarter and got way more balls than your husband. And you know as well as I do, cash is hard to come by. Partners are disposable."

The purple veins in Mrs. O'Boyle's head swelled. Her eyes turned pitch black as she raised the gun and turned it on Johnny. Trembling, he covered his face with his hands. Grip steady, dead aim, she pulled the trigger and the empty chamber went click.

"Now how could I forget. That thing doesn't work without these," said Shady, pulling out the shells. "Hey, Johnny, that was pretty funny. Like you thought your hands were gonna stop a speeding bullet. Just like Superman."

Johnny collapsed. Mrs. O'Boyle stared at Shady. "You bastard."

"Pleased to meet you," said Shady, and he snatched the gun from her. "Either way, you lose. And in consequence that means my percentage goes up. All the way up. Well, that's not quite true. Newmann, reach in that sack and peel off two grand."

Newmann did, and handed the sheaf over. Shady split it in half and handed a stack to Newmann. "This is for you. Not your fault you got stuck with these bums, on top of having to hide out in that boiler room."

"Thanks Shady. You're square with me."

Shady, turned to Peggy, clinging to the edge of the couch, legs curled up under her tush like crocodiles were floating through the carpet. "And of course I owe all this to you, dear Peggy Nell."

"No you don't Shady. Please."

"Sure I do. If you hadn't tipped me to these maroons stealing my action, I never would have known." He flipped her the remaining wad of cash and it wafted over her.

The O'Boyles and Johnny pinned her to the couch with their angry eyes. She curled up like a child ready to be spanked, and whimpered. "Now you're gonna have to take me with you Dog. You know that."

"It's Shady. And I don't know nothing about that." He hoisted Johnny's sack and said, "Don't look so glum everybody. You guys get all the coin. Go buy yourselves some penny candy."

As he started for the kitchen, Peggy leapt from the couch and rushed him. He swatted her away and she crumpled to the floor, a strawberry forming on her cheek.

He turned to the others and said, "By the way, I think your pretty painting is dry now."

Outside, he moved fast. As he backed past the O'Boyle's car, he shot out the radiator. There was no movement at the front door as he pulled away.

The most important part of any heist is the plan to get away. Even though Shady had not technically pulled the job, he was now in possession of the loot, and the cops wouldn't care if he actually pulled the caper or not. But he was prepared.

At a dive motel on East Fourth where he had earlier rented a room, prepaying for the week, he put the cash inside two suitcases and stashed them in the closet. Under the bed, were his burglar tools which he had moved from his apartment. He hung the "Do Not Disturb" sign on the door and drove into downtown.

He didn't like it, but there had been no other way to hijack the money except on the night of the heist. If he had waited until afterwards, the gang might have split up the take and gone their separate ways. But Shady knew once the heist was discovered he would be top on the cops' list to question. Now it all came down to Dizzy.

It was shortly before 4 a.m. when he entered Harold's Club and wandered to the 21 tables. Saturday night, the place was humming. This was a good thing. He stopped in front of a full table where a tall, buxom, redhead was dealing. He waited for a seat to open up, and slid into the play. He smiled at Dizzy and gave her a quick wink. She nodded with a grin and dealt out the cards.

He stepped out of the casino as the sun was just rising. He got in his car and headed for his apartment on Airport Road. He figured he'd have a chance to get a little shuteye before the bulls showed.

He was right. They didn't roust him until 10 a.m., and by noon, he was officially arrested and sentenced to a "ten day or less" vagrancy charge. It was a bum rap and everybody knew it. But the cops were able to get away with it because the judges backed them up if there was reasonable suspicion the person being held was involved in a crime under investigation. Shady denied any involvement, claiming he'd been at Harold's all night. The cops were in no hurry to check his story, and that was okay. With the O'Boyles and Johnny no doubt gunning for him, he was safer inside than out.

Eventually, the cops got around to interviewing the dealers at Harold's, and sure enough, one of them, well-known around town, swore up and down Shady had been playing Blackjack all night. She even rattled off some of his hands and how he made a boner move on this deal and should have held on this hand, and on and on until the cops begged her to shut up.

Four days after being arrested, Shady walked out of the jail with no more than a $25 fine for failing to have registered with the police as an ex-convict. As he was paying his fine, the detective who had led his interrogation told him it was a crying shame they didn't have any other suspects. Until they did, they'd be keeping a close watch on him.

Shady told him he ought to keep a lookout for a couple named the O'Boyles who were wanted in an Iowa bank heist. When the cop asked him why he was providing such information, Shady said he liked Reno and was doing his part as a reformed citizen to clean up the riff-raff. The cop was still laughing as Shady hit the streets.

After retrieving his stash at the motel, he only had one loose end to tie up, and he knew it would give him great pleasure. He drove to a dingy hotel on West and Lake. It was early evening when he climbed to the third floor. He knocked once and the door flung open, like she'd seen him coming.

They stood looking at each other for several seconds, both beaming like two teenagers hooking up after school, with the parents still at work and the house empty. Shady opened his arms and Dizzy fell into them.

"So I did okay?" she asked.

"Darling, you're a gem! It must have been some performance."

Dez broke the embrace and twirled around. "Well, I am an actress of the highest degree. Next they'll be inviting me in front of the Academy of Motion Pictures." Her green eyes sparkled with mischievous glee. Then she got serious, her voice hushed like the place had ears. "And it wasn't any picnic either. They really grilled me. Course my local rep didn't hurt. Hell, Nick Abelman and Bill Graham practically raised me. Those names still hold clout you know. But even with that it was dicey, like you said it'd be. Those dicks don't think very highly of you, you know."

Shady grinned. "The feeling is mutual. Gotta drink for a thirsty fella?"

She ran to the bureau, pulled out a bottle of rye, and filled two glasses. They toasted.

"So what now Shady?" asked Dez breathlessly. "Are we really going to do like what you said?"

Shady moved in close and started running his hands up and down her long sides. She twitched and giggled as his fingers ran dangerously close to private areas.

"Well I don't know about you, but I know what I'm up for," said Shady, pulling her across the room to the bed.

It was several hours until both were too exhausted to perform any longer. They lay side by side in the small bed, smoking. Both seeing different visions of their future in the drifting haze.

"Seriously Shady," said Dez. "You gotta know by now, I want to run with you."

"You think you got what it takes?"

Dez crushed her butt in the ashtray and leaned into him. "I handled those bulls didn't I? And I can handle a gun if that's what you mean. I'm not scared of anything."

Shady chuckled. What a dame. "Let's you and me get some grub and talk about it."

"Someplace fancy?" Dez shrieked.

"You name it," said Shady. "But I'll expect you to get all dolled up. I want everyone to see what a dish I got."

"You're on!"

"And make sure you show off those gams."

Dez giggled, grabbed three possibilities from the closet and raced into the bathroom. "You get dressed and have a drink. It won't take me but ten minutes."

Shady quickly dressed. He pulled out an envelope from his inside jacket pocket and laid it on the top of the bureau. He'd already prepared it in his motel room, and now he took a pencil from the bedside table and scratched out a note on the front. He looked at himself, cocked his hat just right and left the room.

Dez stepped out of the bathroom in a sky blue, off-the-shoulder, sequined sheath dress with slits up the sides. Her ginger hair swept down across one side of her face like Elizabeth Taylor. A faux diamond necklace graced her neck.

"What do you think of this one," she said coyly. "Shady?" She saw the envelope on the bureau. She read the note, then squeezed it against her face and let it sop up the tears. A knockout, down for the count.

A little over a half hour later, Shady was approaching the California state line on Interstate 40. He turned on the radio and caught a news report out of Reno. The reporter breathlessly describing a 100-mph car chase on Boynton Road, ending at a roadblock at the intersection of Peckham Lane. The chase involved 12 police cars and 15 officers, including one FBI agent. Two guns were found in the car, a .22 revolver and a Walther P38. Arrested were Johnny, the O'Boyles, and Peggy Nell.

Shady smiled. He was glad Newmann had parted ways with the rest of the gang. He wondered if any of the other four had enough fall dough to pay a fixer. Probably not. Which meant they were going away for a long time. This was good news. It meant he wouldn't have to be looking over his shoulder for some time to go. The smart thing would have been to kill them all, so he'd never have to worry. But at the time, he was having too much fun watching them squirm.

Either way, life was good. He was flush. Wide open California just ahead. And Reno, he liked what he'd seen. Good times, fat safes, and always a helpful, warm body if you felt the urge. Yeah, he had a very good feeling he'd be visiting again sometime.

ONE

"YOU'RE BEING WAY TOO SERIOUS, you know that don't you?" asked Peach. "This is supposed to be the fun part. Actually, it's all fun if you look at it the right way."

Tinman sighed. It had only been a few months since he had changed careers from pool hustler to burglar, and it was true. He had yet discovered the right way to look at it. His instincts told him this was Serious Business. But his brother, Peach, kept veering him away from that notion. Whatever he did was a lark and Tinman was both irritated and in awe of his nonchalant attitude towards what should cause heart palpitations in most normal humans. He and Peach were fraternal twins but there was a vast chasm between their personalities.

He shook the nerves from his wide shoulders, remembering he was still in training. The final exam had not been passed out, so there was time to improve his skills.

After the abominable basket burglary of last year that netted them little but pain and suffering, Peach decided to start Tinman's training at the very beginning. Baby steps, he said. They began with Rudimentary Casing of a Standard Residential Property. Peach gave him a B on the course because an A would have meant he picked the right house to case. Which he didn't. Never much of an overachiever, except with pool, he was satisfied with his grade.

The next course was Basic Lock Picking. It's all a matter of touch, Peach kept saying. You have to believe the lock is already open, was his mantra. Locks are meant to be opened with keys, was Tinman's response after he failed to open even a basic Kwikset entry knob that he worked on for three days.

When he later snapped Peach's favorite double ball pick in two trying to open a wafer lock, he received a D on the course and it was decided Peach would handle all the mechanics from then on.

Tinman was grateful for the D. He knew he didn't deserve it. He also determined to raise his GPA by doing better in the next course: Following a Mark From the Source. Peach said this was the first technique he'd ever learned in how to locate a likely score. Now, as a true professional, he rarely used it, but he felt it was good practice for Tinman. Also, it was supposedly as easy as falling off a log, if for some odd reason one happened to find themselves balanced on a log. Which Tinman wasn't and had never been and he was finding this course just as difficult as the previous two.

The problem was, he now found himself in a foreign land. A world where only straights ventured, and where no faint-hearted burglar would ever tread. It was an alien experience in a truly scary place. Costco.

As a scratch cooker, he was no stranger to shopping. He bought most of his food at the local WinCo and considered himself a Professional Shopper. He was, however, new to the concept of Mega-Shopping.

When they first walked into the Mega-Store, he was immediately cowed by the sheer size. He lost Peach twice en route to their destination, until he decided to surreptitiously hang onto the tail of his shirt. Sure, there were some funny looks, but it was better than a kiddie leash, right? The second thing that flummoxed him was that nothing in the store was recognizably food. The Mega-Packs and Mega-Boxes and Mega-Containers somehow managed to depersonalize everything that was near and dear.

Mostly, the thing that twisted his brain into knots were the shoppers. It was a Sunday, Mother's Day, a day of repose if ever there was. But in this cavernous hall, devoid of beauty, a hostile army of rabid buyers patrolled every aisle. Some pushing two, three, four carts piled high with Mega-Everything. Tinman wondered if he'd missed the announcement of Armageddon. People looked desperate to stock up their bomb shelters before the shelling began. Better pick up a Mega-Bin of those Clorox Toilet Wands, honey. You never know how long the siege may last.

It was unnerving, and the last place Tinman wanted to be. He didn't have a mother, but he wished he did, so he could sit on her lap and have her rock his fears away. Instead, he had his brother, who at that moment was softly whistling, his head slowly panning the scene, waiting for the right mark to wander into his flytrap.

They were in the Home Improvement department, surrounded by boxes claiming to hold garbage disposals, faucets, toilets, ladders, pressure washers, wall sconces, cabinets, generators (for when the invading force shuts down the grid), solar power panels (same idea), everything but the kitchen sink—no, they're right over there, stainless steel or fireclay.

Amid this domestic olio was a display area with several safes, some commercial, some domestic. The assignment was to locate a customer who was buying one, follow them home, case the joint, break into the house and relieve the safe of its contents.

Simple. But to Tinman, strange. In his former occupation, he never went looking for a sap. They came to him. All he had to do was wait in his office, a pool hall, until the right mark stumbled in, and the game was on. This was different. And it was taking some getting used to.

"Seriously. Stop doing that," scolded Peach, not for the first time.

"What?" asked Tinman with feigned innocence.

"Pocket pool, that's what," said Peach. "People are gonna think you're some kind of perv, scoping out little girls."

"I have an itch," said Tinman, quickly removing his hand from his pocket.

With no further incriminations forthcoming, he looked at his brother and saw he'd stopped whistling. His eyes locked on a couple, coming their way. Oddly, their cart was completely empty, as if they were on the hunt for one thing only. An anomaly too strange to be believed in this bizarre bazaar. (When's the last time you got to say that?)

Tinman saw Peach rub his left eye, then stick both hands in his pockets. It was "office," a form of communication among criminals, using verbal or non-verbal signals as code. As kids, they'd learned it from their adopted uncles, Catfish and Bones, two old grifters who now specialized in pickpocketing, or as old-timers call, "being on the whiz."

The use of office is more commonly known to straights in the game of baseball. All that slapping and scratching and ear tugging coming from the dugout is not, in fact, the manager suffering from a bad case of fleas. It's a highly developed code meant to relay information. For example, depending on who's at bat and what pitch is coming, the shortstop will signal to the second baseman who should cover second base. An open mouth means he will cover it, and a closed mouth signals the second baseman to cover.

In this case, Tinman knew the office meant Peach had spotted a likely target and it was time to put on their cover. Right. Here we go. Mother's Day shopping.

Tinman tagged along as Peach meandered to a display next to the safes featuring Bathroom Accessories. To Tinman's eyes it was a macabre Tower of Babel, boxes and boxes stacked precariously high into the sky, reaching out to heaven, with a brushed nickel finish toilet paper holder perched on top, as an offering to their irascible God.

Tinman heard Peach say, "I think this is the perfect thing! What mother would not want this?" Tinman realized this was part of the cover. Okay. His turn. "Sure," he said, "What mother could resist?"

He decided it would be a good idea to know what he was talking about, so he focused on the box Peach was eying. Ancona Comfort 10S Electric Towel Warmer and Drying Rack. $249. A must have!

It took every ounce of his strong will not to snort, laugh, howl at the moon, or climb to the top of the unearthly Tower of Toiletry and demand to know what planet he'd landed on. Instead he said, with a mischievous smirk, "I'm thinking we get her two. One for each bathroom."

To his consternation, Peach said, "Good idea. Now we have to decide if we want the in-wall timer or the kind that has a plug coming out of it."

Tinman stared at him. This was getting out of hand. The couple was closing in and he had no idea what Peach was talking about. He figured the best thing to do was boop it back over the net, while still sounding natural.

"Well, brother, that is a very apt question indeed. It never occurred to me we would have to make such an intricate and elemental decision regarding this sublime towel warmer. I must, however, defer to your better judgement."

Peach did one of those slow head turns of incredulity you only see in the movies. Tinman shrugged nervously. As an unapologetic, self-taught, wordsmith, he sometimes got into trouble in this semi-literate world.

Peach jabbed him under the ribs as the couple stopped in front of the safe display. The middle-aged woman was very short, abnormally thin, with unnaturally large breasts, bleached blonde hair, surgically pouty lips and too much makeup. The man was tall, fit, tanned, casually dressed in expensive clothing and clearly hated being among the Costco rabble as much as Tinman. His rose-tinted, Oscar de la Renta aviator sunglasses still on, saving him from having to look at the lowly proletariats in the harsh fluorescent glare. They were hard enough on the eyes as it was.

From his days hustling pool, Tinman's skill at reading marks was equal to Peach's. Both silently came to the conclusion the man was a dentist and the wife didn't work. There was also the hint of some kind of conflict. The dentist seemed perturbed and frustrated but felt the need to hide it in front of his wife.

"Ohmigosh! Look at all of them!" squealed the dentist's wife. "This'll take forever!"

The dentist chewed on his tongue, then said, "Suzanne, This is not necessary."

"Yes it is, Thomas!" said Suzanne. "You've never given me such an expensive Mother's Day gift and I'm going to make sure it's safe for ever and ever."

"You're overreacting. As usual," said Thomas, obviously hoping to start a spat which would cause them to leave the store and delay the purchase.

His ruse didn't work, because Peach jumped into the play. "Miss, I wonder if you could help us," he said, flanking Thomas and cutting into Suzanne like on a dance floor.

"Excuse me!" said Thomas. "This is my wife. You can't possibly think this is someone who works here?"

Peach responded to Thomas without looking at him, his eyes working Suzanne. "Not a chance. She just looked like a woman who has good taste. I'd like to pick her brain."

"My brain?!" chirped Suzanne, obviously not used to anyone wanting to know what she thought. "Of course I'll help! What's the problem?"

"My brother and I are thinking of getting one of these towel warmers for our mother."

"Two of them," said Tinman, hoping his efforts might bump up his grade a little.

"That's right," said Peach, wishing Tinman had kept his mouth shut. "Do you think a mother would like something like this?"

Suzanne made a big deal of expertly examining the towel warmer box with her uneducated eyes. Thomas, resigned to buying a safe, was now eyeing the cheapest ones and grumbling under his breath.

"I think," said Suzanne finally, "if you really want to impress your mother, you should go to a fancy jewelry store and buy her the shiniest necklace you can find. That's what we mothers really want." Thomas looked over and she smiled sweetly and batted her fake eyelashes. He harrumphed and turned back to his price comparisons.

"Say! We never thought of that, did we Dan?" said Peach to Tinman who looked around then realized he was Dan and nodded, then remembered the question and shook his head, no.

Suzanne said, "Your mother will love you even more than I'm sure she does now. Jewelry does that to a woman."

"Thanks so much for the suggestion!" said Peach, beaming at Suzanne who blushed, though it was hard to see through all the rouge. "I know just the place."

He shook her bony hand gently, turned to Thomas and said, "Thanks for letting me borrow her for a minute."

"My pleasure."

Suzanne winced and Peach, ever the gentleman, quickly covered. "By the way, I have a little experience with those safes. My ex-wife was a locksmith."

Tinman choked down a guffaw and waited for the couple to shoo Peach away. To his surprise, the ex-wife bit gave him credibility. The couple swallowed the baloney easily and were happily waiting for more.

Peach went on. "And my ex would tell you the ones on this end are not what you're looking for. Not if you want real security."

This caught Suzanne's ears. "That's exactly what we want! Right honey?"

Thomas, staring bullets at Peach and wishing (not for the first time) he'd gone for his concealed weapons license, forced out a crocodile smile and said, "Of course, we are very security conscious. But no need to go overboard."

"Got you there," said Peach. "But these three are all fire safes, not meant to keep a burglar out. A good crook can open one of these in a few seconds using a magnet."

Suzanne gasped and clutched her breasts. Thomas was shocked but, given his status as a well-educated professional, felt the absolute need to hide it.

"What would you suggest?" asked Suzanne.

Peach slid to the left, past the cheap hundred-dollar specials, and landed in front of an impressive floor-mounted, Cannon 7.7 cubic foot safe with electronic lock. It stood about 2.5' and weighed 175 pounds.

"Now this one is going to give any self-respecting burglar a real migraine." Suzanne giggled. Thomas stared reproachfully at the price sticker: $579.99. Tinman was so irritated at Peach's upselling he could only bob his head up and down like one of those toy birds perpetually dipping their beaks into water they can't possibly drink.

Peach continued. "This baby features six, count 'em, six, four-inch active locking bolts. Yep, that's quite a safe."

"We'll take it," said Suzanne.

"We will not!" declared Thomas.

"Well, that's my two cents. Have to be going," said Peach, and he half-bowed to Suzanne. "Thanks so much for your suggestion. We're taking our mother out to dinner tonight and we need to get hopping if we're going to find that special piece of jewelry."

"Oh, I'm sure you will," said Suzanne, so proud of her brain being picked successfully. "My Thomas is taking me to dinner as well! After our boy gets home from college. He's at UC Berkeley. Where are you taking your mother? Perhaps we're dining in the same restaurant."

"I doubt it," said Thomas, holding a grudge against both the price sticker and Peach.

"Not sure. We always let her choose," said Peach breezily, shrugging off Thomas' antipathy. "But it sure would be something if we met up again. Think of that."

Suzanne did, and thought it both funny and profound and was still tittering and pulsating when Peach walked off with Tinman in tow. Tinman, trying for some extra credit, turned and waved. Suzanne waved furiously back. Poor Suzanne. She doesn't get out much.

Tinman saw the exit doors first and dropped Peach's shirttail. He scooted in front and when he reached the great outdoors he sucked air like a death row inmate who just escaped from the gas chamber. Peach strode past and headed for his car. Tinman caught up and spun him around by the shoulder.

"What was that all about?!" he demanded.

"Huh? That's how it works. Now we wait and see."

"I'm talking about the upsale! Why did you pooh-pooh the cheaper models? Christ, what if they actually buy the fancy one?"

"That's the whole point. It's a new model and I'd like to have a crack at it. Those others were just too boring."

Tinman blinked hard, sighed, and continued to the car. Twenty minutes later, Suzanne and Thomas emerged, a bedraggled employee trailing behind pushing a heavy cart with a large box. Peach had moved into a corner area of the parking lot, away from most of the cars. He watched the couple through his zoom camera as they made their way to a black Cadillac Escalade.

"Now, we'll see how much of a cheapskate Thomas really is," said Peach.

The Costco grunt stopped the cart at the back of the SUV and, unaided, wrestled the box inside. Peach adjusted the zoom lens and examined the box.

"Damn, he bought the next model down."

"What a shame," said Tinman happily.

"Yeah, this one only has four locking bolts," said Peach. "Still it'll be more of a challenge than one of those First Alerts, or god forbid a Sentry Safe."

"Perish the thought," Tinman said, wishing it had been a Sentry. He was certain he'd mastered the magnet trick and it would have been an easy A.

Peach said, "So let's see who can guess where they live. Given he's a dentist and they have this inferiority complex around other professionals, I'll say he's probably planted in one of the old money estates west of Plumas. Could be on Manor Drive, or a crossroad like Nixon, even Mark Twain."

Tinman disagreed. "Too many neighbors. Not like in the old days. I can't see this guy liking to hobnob, except at the country club. I think he's an isolationist. Better to hide the boopsie wife away so she won't make him look dumb in front of his tennis pals."

"You don't see him at one of those new developments down south? The ones that are eating up all the old ranches."

Tinman shook his head. "Those are for new money from California. Like you said, this guy wants to look like he's got lineage. I'm going to say down old route 671. One of the side roads off Lakeside, or Holcomb Ranch Lane."

Peach grinned. This was why he kept the faith regarding Tinman's ability to be a first-rate burglar. He might not be able to pick a basic lock, but his brain was hardwired for crime. "Sure, I can see that," said Peach. "We'll find out soon enough."

The Escalade slid backwards out of its parking spot and started for the exit road. Fifteen minutes later, Tinman's guess proved to be right. Keeping a loose tail, they followed it from Costco, to Kietzke, down Moana, left on Lakeside and right onto Faretto Lane, a dead-end road featuring a handful of luxurious estates, most built some decades ago. Each was surrounded by a gigantic yard, and from the height of the fences, all the residents obviously valued their privacy a great deal. An ideal setup.

Except for casing it. That might be tricky. When the Escalade turned onto a private drive, Peach turned the car around and following Tinman's instruction quickly backtracked a quarter mile and turned left on Evans Creek Drive. The houses here were deceptively constructed by the developers not to look like cookie-cutters, when in fact they were. Strictly for the dwindling middle class they were butt up, and laid out in pretty circles where they could all stare at each other.

For casing purposes it was perfect. From several points along the drive they had a clear view of the estates on Faretto. At a spot where several vacant lots were being prepared for construction, Tinman told Peach to stop. They were directly behind Suzanne and Thomas' house.

The Escalade was backed up to a three-car garage. Thomas had paid for towering fences on either side of the large lot to protect against his prying neighbors, apparently thinking the enormous length of his backyard provided sufficient privacy from the rear. He was wrong.

Peach reached under the seat of his 2004 Taurus Wagon, a perfect casing car if ever there was one, and pulled out a clipboard. He dropped it in Tinman's lap, said, "Come on, you take notes," and climbed out.

Tinman scrambled after, asking, "What kind of notes?"

"We're site construction inspectors inspecting these sites for proper drainage. So like that, those kind of notes."

Tinman stared at the clipboard and drew a blank. He decided doodling might serve the same purpose. Peach paced around the vacant lots with his camera. At the rear of one, a rented mobile office trailer had been brought in for the construction company. He took pictures of the trailer and of this and that, but mostly of the layout of Thomas and Suzanne's house. Occasionally, he took one of the two of them, as well.

The poor kids were having a spat outside the garage, with Suzanne obviously demanding the safe be installed posthaste. And Thomas no doubt claiming if he lifted the safe himself he might never perform another root canal. Suzanne won and Thomas went to work.

"Okay, make a note of this," said Peach. Tinman hurriedly crossed out his doodle. "The safe is going in the upper left back corner room. From the looks of the curtains, that's gotta be Suzanne's bedroom."

"Separate bedrooms?" asked Tinman.

"Would you sleep with a guy who's had his hands in other people's mouths all day?"

No argument there.

"There is a security system, but the weak link is through the garage, and that's a snap. Will people never learn? It's a shame, you know."

Tinman didn't know any such thing. And he found it increasingly disconcerting his brother would prefer his job be a lot more difficult than it was.

"What kind of sports car do you think is behind one of those garage doors?"

"Why a sports car at all?"

"You didn't know? Sixty percent of all dentists either have, hope to have, or used to have a sports car. It's that inferiority thing again. Like an oral fixation. I say a Porsche 718 Boxster. Professionals can't resist a Porsche. What do you like?"

"Datsuns," said Tinman, proud owner of a 1978 Datsun 280Z, with stolen registration tags and nonexistent insurance.

"I'm talking about the dentist."

"Oh. I'll say that new Audi R8 Spyder. That's his style."

"Nice! 5.2 Liter, all-wheel drive, V10, zero to sixty in 3.9. Make him feel more like a man. You might be right. Twice in a day, wouldn't that be something?"

Tinman certainly thought it would be nice, given his average was hovering at a middle C. He prayed an Audi was behind door number two—or three. Just so he was right.

"Let's blow. We have stuff to do. What time you got?"

Tinman didn't wear a watch. "I'll say just after two."

"Plenty of time before junior gets home."

"You mean we're pulling the job tonight?!" asked Tinman.

"When else?"

TWO

THREE HOURS LATER THEY WERE READY. The time had been spent preparing at Tinman's extremely humble abode. He was now living in the small manager's quarters of the All Inn Motel, a permanently closed fleabag of which he had recently come into possession.

They were dressed in black coveralls over their regular clothing and wore black crepe shoes. Peach was a stickler when it came to the proper work attire. Clothes can leave distinguishing fibers and lead to a conviction if the burglar is still in possession of the garb should he be rousted. Therefore, all clothes were immediately discarded after a job.

Shoes were highly important. He always used the type they had on tonight. They had virtually no tread, lots of people wear them, and they were difficult to trace. Just in case the cops did get an impression, he always purchased them one size too large to throw off any height and weight estimation they might make.

After the basket debacle, where these particular shoes caused Tinman quite some grief, and almost got them both run over by a truck, it took some time for him to agree to wear them again. With gentle coercing and a fair dose of logic, he finally came around.

After a quick bite, Peach chose the items he might need on the job. Tinman watched eagerly as he sifted through his impressive collection of burglar tools, fully expecting tonight's job would require some serious firepower. The tools were stored in a large metal case, specially designed to perfectly fit in the wagon of his car. The lid slid back toward the front, and like a roll top desk disappeared by wrapping around the far end.

His tools included the mundane, such as cold chisels, drills, pry bars, drift pins, electric saws, cutting torch, slap hammer, acetylene torch and tank. As well as the exotic, like cystoscopes, burning bar, electric blasting caps, condensed explosives, loiding tools, and an extensive collection of lock picks that would make a locksmith weep with envy.

Much to Tinman's chagrin, Peach selected only a very small bag of basic tools: pick set, two electronic gizmos, pry bar, and something that looked suspiciously like a metal coat hanger. After poring over a thick catalogue with pictures and diagrams of various safes, and a quick search of the internet, he was ready to go.

Tinman thought him woefully ill-prepared, but Peach said, unfortunately, that was not the case. Then he complained people did not take crime seriously enough. "These days, with all this high-tech security stuff available to screw up our play, what do they do? They go to Costco! Everyone's too cheap to keep up with the times. How am I supposed to get any real practice?"

A few minutes before five, their ride for the night arrived right on time. The driver's name was Tek, a boy of sixteen, born with thieves' blood and undergoing extensive training at the hands of the Posse—Peach, Bones, Catfish and Tinman. The car was a non-descript SUV, technically owned by Tek's mother, a part-time stripper and full-time divorcee who robbed her ex-husband blind when he went to jail for embezzlement.

Tek had shown great aptitude with basic burglar tools and was a gifted computer hacker, but Peach told him to be a well-rounded crook he needed to understand all the various jobs and positions. His pay would be a flat rate of $500 for driving, even if the job was a bust. He did not qualify for any percentage of the take, because as Peach explained, he had not fully graduated his training and plebes don't get a cut. Period. Percentage no, Tek jumped at the chance to work.

Peach never drove his car to a job. Mostly because it contained all his tools of the trade, and being in possession of burglar tools anywhere near a heist was a quick way to get a five-year vacation on the state's tab.

It was a companionable drive across town ending at the vacant lots on Evans Creek Drive. Tek drove onto the dirt lot directly behind Thomas and Suzanne's house. He stopped next to the door of the construction trailer, with the car blocking any view from the road. Peach hopped out, used a diamond pick and tension wrench to pick the simple lock, and he and Tinman slipped inside. Tek quickly pulled away.

Inside the trailer, they had a perfect view of the backyard. They had to wait two hours before they saw a slick little Subaru WRX pull up the driveway and stop around back.

"The kid likes sports cars, too," Peach commented.

"If daddy's paying, who wouldn't," said Tinman.

"True. Hey, looky here. Junior's getting baked before dinner."

Tinman grabbed the camera and watched as the college student huffed away on a joint. "I hear it helps the appetite," said Tinman.

"I'm sure it doesn't hurt dealing with Thomas either."

Junior finished his blunt and stepped out of the car. He stretched, braced himself, and walked to the back door like his feet were sticking in hot tar.

"I don't envy a kid like that," said Peach. "Having to deal with parents and all."

"Especially those parents."

"Good point. But I mean any parents. You ever think what it would have been like?"

"Only in my nightmares," said Tinman, abruptly ending the question of what if. He lived in the now, and had little patience for hypotheticals.

Half an hour later, the family emerged with junior's arm firmly around Suzanne's hip, hanging on for dear life, and Thomas leading the way with a no-nonsense, let's get this damn family dinner out of the way, attitude. They piled into the Escalade and drove off.

"Let's go," said Tinman.

"We follow the plan," said Peach.

Tinman grimaced, knowing he just lost any chance of acing this course. He was so out of practice. As kids, he and Peach had pulled off many thefts. Back then, it was just a lark. Still, he had always been the one to insist on the cardinal rule of following the plan. And Peach always screwed it up, acting impulsively, trusting in his charm and devil-may-care attitude.

Now Peach was a professional, and Tinman's chosen career as pool hustler had reached a glorious peak only to come crashing down like a moon shot gone bad. In the interim, he had forgotten his past and the lessons he'd learned as a teen.

To wit, the best way to stop yourself from making on-the-spot judgements is to make a firm plan and don't veer from it. And if your driver is supposed to wait at Audrey Harris Park in-between the turnoff for Evans Creek Drive and Faretto Lane, that's what he does. And if the driver's assignment is to wait for the marks to leave and follow them to where they are dining, then report back to the inside men before they move on the target, that's what you do.

They hadn't had a lot of time to plan for this heist, but as Peach said earlier, "It doesn't take long to figure out what to do with a woman who's begging you to cure her insomnia."

Tinman was still deciphering the metaphor. It had been a long time since he'd dealt with women, as well. Twenty minutes later, Peach got a message from Tek on his digital pager. It was only a name, but it was full of information—Gas Lamp.

"Sweet," said Peach. "At least Thomas has good taste in restaurants. You know the place, down on Pueblo and Holcomb. It's got all those cool murals around the outside and the whole building is like one big painting."

Tinman despised all the murals springing up around town, brightening up the lovely seediness he had grown up with. But he did know the place. Fine dining.

"That's at least a two-hour meal," said Peach. "Tek did good. I tell you that kid is really coming along. He's top of his class."

Great, thought Tinman. The kid's the teacher's pet and I get a ruler on the knuckles.

Peach sent Tek a message reading, "One hour."

"An hour?!" cried Tinman. "You really think we can crack that monster that fast? And what if you were wrong about where they installed it. What if we can't find it?"

Tinman stopped ranting long enough to notice Peach had slipped on his black ski mask and nitrile gloves and was disappearing out the door. He caught up to him at the edge of the backyard, next to the long, eight-foot high fence that stretched to the front yard. Keeping low, they scooted along it until they were at the back of the house.

Peach pointed to a motion-sensor light hung above the three-door garage. Tinman nodded, having already been trained in the procedure. They ran over and the light clicked on, flooding the area. Tinman hoisted Peach up and he unscrewed the bulb.

Back on the ground, Peach pulled out the coat hanger from his bag, and straightened it out, leaving the hook at the end. Tinman picked him up so his head was level with the top of the center door. Peach shoved the hooked end into the gap between door and jamb and fed it through. After a few seconds of manipulation, he yanked hard and dropped to the ground. They lifted the door enough to slip through and eased it back down. The whole process took twenty seconds.

Peach grinned. "I could've used my code catcher to get the RF code for the garage door opener, but actually it can take longer to find the right code than it does to release the emergency lever with a hanger. And there's always the chance you tap into the neighbor's garage door and accidentally open that, and now you have trouble. Simplicity is always the best policy."

The automatic light clicked off and Peach switched on his flashlight. Tinman followed suit and they scanned the garage. In the middle was an older model, Lexus ES sedan, Suzanne's designated car. On the far left sat a late-model, Audi R8 painted in factory Vegas Yellow.

Peach examined it. "It's a Coupe, not the Spyder, but we still have to give you that one. Good hunch."

Tinman smiled. He was finally right. Oh happy day. He had little time to bask in the glory, because Peach was back to business.

He was in front of the door leading to the inside of the house, a security panel mounted next to it. He held one of his gizmos, and was turning a small dial. After a few seconds he pushed a button, a light on the front started blinking, and he handed it to Tinman. He picked the lock to the door and swung it open.

Tinman held his breath, waiting for an alarm, even though he knew if there was one, he wouldn't hear it, only the monitoring company and the owner of the house would get a notification. Peach looked at him with a bemused smile.

"Don't sweat it, brother. That thing you're holding is a jammer. It sends out radio noise to block the signal from getting through the sensors to the control panel. Even though this door is tagged, it's like we were never here." He turned and strolled into the house, still chatting away like he was talking about the best way to bake ziti.

"If we'd felt like taking the time and doing the heist in a few days, we could have used my USRP N210. What a honey. Most of these rinky-dink systems are wireless now and use unencrypted radio frequency signals from the sensors to the control panel, even if they're not armed. The N210 can monitor the signals from 250 yards away. And get this, no line of sight needed. All we'd have to do is sit out in that trailer and anytime Thomas, Suzanne or even junior opened a tagged window or door, we'd pick up the commands that are sent to the control panel. With that info we just walk up and replay the commands, or passcode if we happened to pick that up, and bada bing, bada boom, we're in. Even more fun is to set the system to display a bunch of false alarms until the homeowner and security company thinks it's a glitch, and ignores the alert while the house is being cleaned out. Hah! What a kick."

They were through the gleaming, commercial-sized, rarely used kitchen, and the for-display-only living room, and heading up the stairs to the bedrooms. "Either way," continued Peach, "for our purposes tonight, the jammer was enough. Simplicity itself. People think technology has put guys like us out of business. Just the opposite, the more comfortable they think they are the more burglary becomes a possibility. I hope you're taking notes."

Tinman was still relishing the fact he had guessed the right sports car, and was not, therefore, taking notes. Still, a feeling of pride rushed through him when he once again realized how far his brother had come. From stick-up guy to high-class jewel thief. What a success story.

"Wow, Suzanne sure knows how to hire the help. This place is spotless," said Peach. "You'd be surprised how many women don't know how to hire good help."

He stepped into Suzanne's girly-girl, pink bedroom, complete with stuffed animals on the bed protecting it from any hostile intruders with slobbery fingers—namely Thomas. He slid open the double doors of the monstrous dressing closet and spotted the newly installed safe in the far corner. Well, not really installed. It was designed to be floor-mounted, but Thomas was obviously no handyman and had simply plopped it in a corner and washed his hands of it.

Peach knelt in front and opened his bag. For Tinman, this was the moment of truth. If Peach had neglected to bring along the correct tools, he would certainly gain crowing rights for having pointed it out—maybe even a gold star!

"I hate to even do this, but it'd be wrong of me not to try. Seeing as I'm trying to teach you the right way to go about this. Still I really hope they're not as dumb as I think," said Peach. "It'd be more fun to crack it the honest way."

"Yeah, a real blast. Are you messing with me on purpose?"

"Why would I do that? All I'm saying is, I hope they changed the factory default. Believe it or not, this one happens to be, 1, 2, 3, 4, 5, 6. Pretty imaginative, huh?"

"You're wasting time," muttered Tinman.

Peach turned the handle on the safe and it clicked open. "Damn. I knew it would be too easy."

Tinman gaped and sputtered. Peach smiled and said, "You have to realize, nothing works more in our favor than people feeling secure. A straight thinks it's common sense that if there's an alarm system, fancy door locks, and an impressive looking safe, any thief is going to look elsewhere. But a pro's common sense tells him such a person is a much better target than, say, someone who lives in an area where they have to be alert. They may only have a padlock protecting their place but if they're aware of the risks and keeping an eye out, it's a much more dangerous score. You see? It's all in how we look at how they're looking at it."

Tinman nodded his head slowly, letting it sink in, knowing it was probably the most important thing Peach would teach him. He asked, "So what do we got?"

Peach pulled out a packet in a clear plastic envelope. "Well look at this. It's the manual to the safe. Good place for it, huh?"

He quickly examined a stack of personal papers, and shoved them aside. The only thing left was a black, rectangular presentation box, with a thin, gold foil border and snap closure.

Peach opened the front panels, revealing a glimmering necklace and earring set. The featured stones were rubies with a particularly large one in the shape of a heart as the centerpiece for the necklace. Small diamonds made up the chain, and encircled the large pendant ruby, and the medium-size ones in the earrings.

Tinman felt a shudder move from his toes to the peak of his head. He whistled softly. He was now a bona fide burglar, and the feeling left him breathless and heady.

Peach grabbed his loupe from his bag and examined the rocks. Tinman said, "Pretty big score, eh? Even for you I imagine. So, how much do you think your fence will give for it? I mean, these are not your run-of-the-mill rocks, right?"

Peach leaned back. "No wonder he didn't want to buy the safe. Probably worth more than this."

"You're wrong!"

Peach shook his head and said, "Wish I was. This here is synthetic corundum. It's the same chemical compound of actual rubies, but they make this crap in a lab. The diamonds are colorless zircon. It's not synthetic, like cubic zirconia, and its dispersion is close to diamonds, but still not worth anything to us, or a fence. What a bastard you are Thomas. You don't do this kind of thing on Mother's Day, it's unpatriotic."

He carefully placed the necklace and earrings back in its box and sealed it. Then he positioned everything in the safe exactly the way it had been, and shut the door.

Tinman's euphoria had turned to rage. It was a corundum conundrum. And he felt like driving to the Gas Lamp and punching Thomas in the nose. Or maybe shove his dinner up his nose, then punch it. Yes. Better. Particularly if it was pasta.

"Now he's pissed me off," said Peach, "Time to find the husband stash."

"Exactly," said Tinman, not knowing what he was talking about, but dutifully following him out of the room and across the hall.

Peach sensed his confusion and said, "You know, like when we were kids and hid nudie magazines from Dez. Deep down, husbands are still bad little boys. They never get it out of their system. They have to hold on to their little secrets so they don't feel so trapped. I suspect Thomas has more than one secret he needs to hide from Suzanne."

As they stepped into Thomas' bedroom, Peach continued. "Secrets aside, in my line of work, I've also discovered a lot of wealthy people who can't figure out why they get paid so much, like movie actors, politicians, lawyers, and especially dentists, are afraid they'll be found out. So, they always keep a cash stash buried away."

Tinman caught on. "Like Linus with his security blanket."

"Bingo," said Peach. "Okay, game on! Let's see who can find it first."

"You sure it has to be in his bedroom?" asked Tinman.

"Not positive, but damn close. People have an absolute need to keep their valuables near them, especially at night."

Tinman searched his mind for clues. Thomas would have to be careful both Suzanne and the maid would not be able to find it. The room was sparsely decorated and furnished with a king bed dominating. Under the mattress was too obvious. Peach was busy with the drawers and the socks and underwear, so that avenue was taken.

He stepped inside the large walk-in closet. The man had more shoes than Imelda Marcos. No point in checking inside all of them. Too accessible. What if Suzanne sent them out to get resoled or something inane.

A shelf ran around the top of the closet holding carefully stacked sweaters and sweatshirts. There was nearly a two-foot difference in height between husband and wife. Thomas might take advantage of this. He checked behind the stacks of clothing and found a small flat box covered in gift wrapping. On top a card read, Do Not Open Until Christmas. He sighed and replaced the box. He noticed a partially used roll of wrapping paper and a small tape dispenser tucked against the wall.

Why would he keep the wrapping paper if the box was already wrapped? Unable to immediately grasp the intricacies of a dentist's mind, he was about to leave the closet when the answer came. The gift thing was a blind, a cover. He was planning on wrapping it again. And again.

He wheeled around, grabbed the box and ripped off the paper. Inside was a manila envelope.

"You win," said Peach, looking over his shoulder. "Nice job. The way you figured that out and all." As twins, Tinman and Peach had a disturbing habit of reading each other's thoughts.

Tinman grinned with unconcealed pride, and opened the envelope. Inside were some folded letters and two stacks of hundred-dollar bills with rubber bands around them. He handed one to Peach, and the two did a quick fan count.

"I'm looking at five large," said Tinman.

"Three plus here. Not bad. Let's see what other secrets he's got."

Tinman unfolded one of the letters and handed Peach another. They both scanned the contents. "Son of a bitch," said Peach. "He's boinking his hygienist."

Tinman handed his letter to Peach. "She's the one who got the real rocks. Look how she says she's going to thank him for the pretty necklace."

Peach said, "Pretty kinky. Maybe I made a mistake overlooking hygienists, but who'd a thought they could be so creative?"

"Maybe we should leave these inside the safe for Suzanne to find."

"Nah, I don't like leaving traces, even for a good cause. Better yet, we just take the whole box and let Thomas think she found it. He'll think she's holding it over his head, like a guillotine waiting for the right cross word to set it loose."

The brothers locked eyes, the mirth inside begging to be free. Tinman was the first to give, with Peach immediately following. Both giggled like prepubescent boys who just stuck a "Kick Me" sign on the back of the school bully.

They were still chuckling when they hit the kitchen. Peach said, "We still have thirty minutes before our ride shows. Gives us plenty of time for the best part of our job."

One of the reasons Peach loved his work so much is it gave him the chance to learn more about people. He loved people and always wanted to experience a little of how they lived. He didn't want to be like them. He never wanted to be anybody but himself, even when his life was in shambles when he was younger. He just wanted to be in their body if only for a short time and see what made them tick.

"Let's start in the basement, work our way up. I'm dying to see how he did his game room."

"I'd rather not," said Tinman, fully aware of his brother's idiosyncrasies, and wanting nothing more but to be safe and secure in his dumpy apartment, not wandering around some mansion, imagining what it was like to be a philandering dentist.

"You really have to learn to enjoy the whole process, like eating a whole sandwich and not throwing out the crust. That's the best part. Hey! I got an idea. Let's go for a spin in the Audi. I know you can't resist that."

"You're insane."

"Here's the spare key hanging on the fridge. And check this, Thomas has a little note wrapped around it saying for emergency only. What a piece of work."

"Let me see that." Tinman looked at the little note and his innate sense of chivalry swept away any doubt. "Let's do it. For Suzanne."

Peach smiled. "Take that little note off real easy."

Tinman did and Peach wrapped it around a key he'd taken from his bag. "I always carry a few dummy keys around for this very purpose. Never know when you might need a sweet ride. If they ever discover it, which I doubt seeing the little lady is not allowed to touch daddy's toy, they'll just think it was a bad print. Let's go."

In the garage, Peach tossed the key to Tinman and said, "You're the better driver," then hopped in the passenger's seat of the Audi.

It was true. Back when they were younger and on the road, with Tinman riding high at the top of his game as a pool hustler, he had saved Peach's butt with his driving skills. Peach, the law on his heels for a busted armed robbery, had shown up at the pool hall where Tinman was working. Tinman had hustled him out the backdoor and into his 280Z, and proceeded to outmaneuver three cruisers on the prowl. In doing so, he saved his brother from certain prison time. They'd parted ways shortly after, and it was nearly twenty years before they would see each other again.

A semblance of sanity crept into Tinman's mind as he pulled down the front drive. "What if one of the neighbors sees us?"

"Definitely don't wave. They'll know for sure it isn't Thomas. He's not the type."

Tinman nodded, almost certain the knotty logic somehow unraveled itself into the truth. They turned right onto Holcomb Ranch Road, a twisty affair that wound around and past several horse farms and old money estates. The peaks of Slide Mountain and Mt. Rose were lit up by the moonlight.

"Still snow on the mountains. Can you believe it?" asked Peach.

"You've been away too long. There's almost always snow in May. Hell, after this past winter, I hear they're talking about keeping the skiing going until July 4th."

"Dumb sport," said Peach. Tinman grunted. They both agreed trying to stay in one piece while hurtling down an icy mountain was not their idea of a good time. Peach went on. "I bet you miss tooling around town in the Z, what with those iffy tags. That's a situation we have to, uh, what's the word?"

"Rectify," said Tinman.

"Really? That sounds so gross."

"We're talking about the DMV."

"Right. Good word for it."

Tinman loved the handling of the car as he smoothly maneuvered around the sharp bends going exactly the thirty-five-mph limit. "Uh, what are you doing?" asked Peach. "This car has 540 horsepower and you're coaxing a nag along. Open it up."

"We're on a heist! What if we get pulled over?"

"Have you really forgotten that much? Cops only come down here if one of these people have a problem and invite them over. Otherwise, they don't want to have any idea what illegal stuff the rich are doing. They pull over one of these people for speeding and it costs them their job. Christ, you're the one who taught me that kind of stuff!"

Tinman crinkled his eyes. There was that twisted logic again and Peach was right. At one time, he owned that way of thinking. What happened? There was no time to dwell on it as he shifted down to second, stomped on the pedal and shot off into the night.

Twenty-five minutes later, they slinked out of the construction trailer and into the back of Tek's SUV. They waited until they got back to Tinman's room before they did the cut. Tek was thrilled to get the half G for such an easy gig, and promptly took off to meet some girl he was attempting to woo. He'd never had much interest in girls until Peach arrived in Reno. Under his tutelage, however, he had learned much more than just criminal skills, and was anxious to try out some of the lady slayer techniques he'd recently picked up.

Once Tek was gone, Tinman started whipping up some dinner while Peach split the take on the small card table, one of the few pieces of furniture. A previous owner of the motel had built the former manager's quarters on top of the L-shaped building. It sat above where the two lines of the L met, and was accessed by an outside staircase. It was one large room with various areas segmented into kitchen, bedroom and living room. There was also an attached bathroom. After Tinman moved in, he built a little sun deck and in good weather spent much of his time outside watching the trains start off on their journey over the Sierra Nevadas.

"After Tek's fee, we cleared $7600. Not bad for our first official team haul," said Peach. "Here you go partner, $3800. That'll get you back on your feet."

Tinman laid down his wooden spatula and reached for his stack. He peeled off $800 and tossed the remainder on top of Peach's pile.

"That's for the floater to cover the taxes on this dump," said Tinman. "We're even, unless you're looking for interest."

"Do I look like a friggin' loan shark?" cried Peach, his voice full of indignation and hurt pride. "And there's no need for you to fork all that over now. Don't leave yourself so flat. You've been broke long enough."

Tinman waved him off, and turned back to his wok. "I want to make sure we're straight, in case nothing else comes my way."

"What is this nothing I'm hearing?! We're just getting started! And I have a serious hunch we're due for a major score real soon. I gotta nose for that kind of thing."

With his back to him, Tinman said, "Face it, Peach. I'm not cut out for this kind of thing. I barely scraped by with a D minus tonight. I shouldn't even get a cut."

"Oh yeah?! You pegged Thomas' car, and you sniffed out the husband stash. Not to mention you proved the Audi R8 Coupe can indeed go from 60 to 124mph in 8.1 seconds. I'm seeing you as a strong middle B. Definitely."

Tinman idly tossed his ingredients in the wok, not willing to commit to something he didn't really believe. Peach sidled up, and draped an arm over his shoulder.

"Let's get this clear. It's not about you actually learning how to do what I do. It's about you knowing what I'm capable of. This way, you're armed with all the info you need in order to come up with the master plans. That's the whole point of this training. Now look, I need you. I told you that. You got the brains and the imagination, I got the know-how. We're a team."

Tinman couldn't stifle a smile. It was just that way with Peach.

"Okay. Now, sorry to do this, but I gotta cut and run," said Peach.

Tinman was surprised. "What's the rush? I'm making a pork stir fry. We could maybe do the crosswords together."

"Another time. I, uh, got an event. I'm sort of the guest of honor."

Tinman could only imagine. Probably twin, Scandinavian sisters with a mutual yen for the criminal sort. Or a topless women's basketball team inducting their new mascot. It was better he not know. He might get jealous.

"Hey, we should call Dez before I go," said Peach. "Wish her happy Mother's Day."

"She's not our mother. And you know she hates when you call her that."

"That's the fun of it."

"Pass."

"Spoilsport. So tomorrow, you still gonna canvas that neighborhood we picked out?" Tinman nodded. Peach said, "Good deal. Call you around three. See what you found." And he was gone.

The rice still had fifteen minutes to go. Tinman plodded to his easy chair and grabbed the crossword puzzle he was working on. He was uneasy. His estimation of his performance today was a far cry from Peach's. Brains and imagination. Pshaw.

He settled in and grabbed a pencil. Seventy-eight down, five letters: One in a cap in a corner? Blank, U, blank, blank, E. Tinman sighed and filled in the word—dunce.

THREE

PEACH WAS ALONE IN A CORNER, his back to the large gathering. He was wearing a pink robe, and a hat that closely resembled Fred Flinstone's lodge hat for the Loyal Order of Water Buffaloes. His right shoe was missing and his pant leg was rolled up to show his bare foot and calf. He was poring over a manual, an index finger scanning the lines of text, his lips mouthing the words, his mind desperately trying to remember everything he would need for the Great Test.

Like Tinman, he had never attended much school and had never graduated from any institution of learning, be it higher or lower. Right now, he felt like he was the dumb kid in the class who had been sent to the corner to ponder his mental inadequacies.

There was so much to learn! Granted, he had been lax in his studies. To his credit, he'd been busy training his brother, but he knew there would be no excuses if he screwed this up. He'd be out. No second chances.

In fact, if one was invited to become a Clamper, member of the Ancient and Honorable Order of E. Clampus Vitus, and one refused, they were never invited again.

Since he'd returned to Reno, Peach had been hanging out at Floyd's Fireside Chat, an old-time bar on Kietzke, proudly known by its unofficial nickname, The Cleanest Dive in Town. He had taken to the cozy atmosphere, the friendly patrons, and the spirited conversation. So when Stan, the owner, and an official Clamper, had invited him to join the Ancient and Honorable Order, he jumped at the idea.

He was still wondering why he had jumped so quickly. He had never belonged to any organization and was never a member of anything, except a prison population. But the Clampers appealed to him with their love of Western history (even though he didn't know any history and had never been a huge fan), and their unwavering loyalty to fellow brothers of the Order. As an orphan, he was always on the lookout for instant family and this seemed an easy way to conjure one up.

To enter into Clamperdom the initiates must have an interest in history (still working on it), a sense of humor (covered), good character (sticky wicket that one), a willingness to participate in the order (done), a flare for the ridiculous (why else would he be wearing Fred Flinstone's hat), and an appreciation of absurdity.

The last requirement was the most important, as the Order's motto was, Credo Quia Absurdum, very loosely translated as, Take Nothing Seriously Unless it is Absurd. Which was perfectly acceptable to Peach whose life philosophy had long held the whole world and everybody in it was absurd.

He was therefore completely taken by this organization whose very existence was based in the absurd. It was purportedly founded in the United States by Ephraim Bee, a bar owner in West Virginia who was fed up with the elitist ways of the various other fraternal organizations of the times, the Freemasons, Odd Fellows, etc.

In retaliation, he claimed that in 1845, the Emperor of China had commissioned him to spread the Ancient and Honorable Order into the New World. It required no societal stature to belong and collected no dues, so it was a way for blue collar men to have their own organization without needing means or coming from a wealthy family.

The Order spread to the west and became wildly popular with the miners, at one point boasting membership in some boomtowns that equaled all the members of the traditional fraternal organizations combined. The Order died out when the mining faded but was revived in the 1930's by Three Great Revivifiers: Carl Wheat, Leon Whitsell, and George Ezra Dane. And in modern day it still boasted over forty charters and some fifty thousand brethren.

All members and officers of the Order are of equal status and held in equal indignity (a notion any good closet communist could appreciate). They are dedicated to the Care and Protection of the Widow and the Orphan—especially the Widow (a goal Peach very much subscribed to).

A meeting of the Clampers can only be called any day before or after a full moon (which shows just how user-friendly the group really is). A gathering of Clampers mostly involves drinking and telling stories of the Old West. It has always been a matter of conjecture as to whether the Clampers are an "Historical Drinking Society" or a "Drinking Historical Society." Their underlying theme, however, is to spread a sense of community and belonging. What was so absurd about all of this?

Well, according to Peach's manual, some Clampers claimed their former members included Solomon, Julius

Caesar, Henry VIII, Sir Francis Drake, George Washington, and even Adam.

Peach had to think on that one. He figured since there were no other men in Eden to initiate Adam, and Eve couldn't have done it because no women were allowed to join, The Original Man must therefore have been the first Clampatriarch. Momentarily pleased with this brilliant deduction, he was quickly nonplussed by the dubious claim Ronald Reagan was also a former Clamper. Inconceivable.

The problem with Clamper history was nobody seemed to agree on anything, so everyone was right, and wrong, depending on how you felt about it. Which of course made finding the correct answers to the questions just a wee bit difficult don't you think?

As he huddled in the corner and pondered this mystery, he thanked his lucky stars Tinman hadn't asked where he was going, or to come along. Even if Peach had managed to smuggle him into this secret gathering, he certainly wouldn't have wanted his brother seeing him in such a nervous state. After the ribbing he'd been giving him over his burglary training, he knew he'd be a perfect candidate for verbal torture.

A horrible blare from a hostile horn sounded and Peach's stomach catapulted to his throat. It was the Bray of the Hewgag, blown by the Grand Musician (a loose term for anyone who, despite their level of inebriation, happened to still be able to blow through a horn). The initiation had begun.

A hushed solemnity fell over the besotted, boisterous crowd. All the men were dressed in red shirts and vests, adorned with funny badges, pins and medals. Many sported beards, fake and real, with black miner hats perched on top. In front of the bar's pool table, stood the Clampfunctionaries, who would lead the proceedings.

They included: the charter's Clampatriarch with a fake, white beard stretching to the floor, the Sacred Staff of Relief in one hand; The Noble Grand Humbug; The Grand Musician holding the Horrendous Hewgag horn; The Clamps Petrix and The Clamps Matrix; The Roisterous Iscutis; The Royal Platrix; The Clamps Vitrix; Damfool Doorkeeper Number One, with the revered Blunderbusket, and Damfool Doorkeeper Number Two, proudly holding the Sword of Mercy Tempered with Justice. (Hey, don't blame me, I didn't make this stuff up.)

Peach felt a hand on his shoulder and knew it belonged to The Grand Imperturbable Hangman. He wore a large, bushy, fake mustache and carried The Chain of Punishment. As a PBC, Poor Blind Candidate, Peach would be under his control throughout the initiation. In prison, he had to get used to being under the control of a lot of people so he didn't mind, but he couldn't figure out the whole blind thing.

The Grand Imperturbable Hangman said, "Is the Poor Blind Candidate, who so ignominiously perpetrated this foolish decision to consecrate one's being in the sudsy golden nectar of the Ancient and Honorable Order, disorderly prepared for the ensuing absurdity?"

Peach worked through it. Given all the big words, he briefly wondered if his brother had something to do with the script. He figured the answer should damn well be, yes, or the whole shebang was going to stop right here and now. So he said, yes. With conviction. Which must have worked, because everyone bellowed, "Satisfied."

Peach breathed a sigh of relief. Question Number One—Easy A!

The Hangman strapped a bandana over his eyes. Right. The blind thing. Then he poured a cup of sudsy, golden nectar (Miller Lite) over his head as a symbolic beginning of his baptism, and they were off and running.

Peach had been forewarned that this Clamper charter was very old school and attempted to follow the traditional ceremonial procedures whenever possible. The Noble Grand Humbug rapped his scepter and demanded there be order in the Hall of Comparative Ovations (the bar). Nobody was out of order before he demanded order so nothing very exciting happened.

There was a lot of mumbo jumbo essentially announcing an initiation was about to occur which everyone knew but decided to humor the old humbug with appreciative grunts and burps. Next the Clampatriarch made sure the PBC had relieved himself of enough "treasure" to cover tonight's event.

New candidates were always responsible for funding their initiation, and since there was little expense involved outside the cost of drinks for the membership, the money was immediately deposited in the bar's till. Peach had already forked over three C-notes when he arrived, which the membership agreed was sufficient to cover their drunks.

Once this essential step was covered, the membership rose and showed their fealty to their patron. "HAIL VITUS, NOBLE CLAMPATRON."

They then proceeded to chant various mottos and passwords which were so secret and ridiculous as to be completely omitted in this narrative. Throughout, the Grand Musician blared on the hewgag until The Roisterous Iscutis, suffering from a blinding hangover, told him to knock it off, and he did, for which Peach was also thankful.

The Noble Grand Humbug then made a Grand Clamplamation. "Semper ubi sub ubi."

"Dorkus malorkus!" responded the brethren.

"Illegitimi non carborundum est!" roared the Noble Grand Humbug.

"Gustatus similis pullus!" cried the brethren.

Peach was led around the room, stopping at various brothers along the way who lectured him on the rules and policies of the Clampers. Most made little sense, which was only proper and fitting. Peach was struck, however, by the absolute loyalty he was required to give to his fellow members and they to him. It gave him a warm feeling to know he was part of such a tightknit group.

The Clampatriarch went on a long blather covering the history (true and false) of E. Clampus Vitus. When he ran out of drivel, and the membership ran out of patience, he asked Peach if he understood and believed everything he had heard.

Peach was still hung up on the Adam thing, but thought it best not to rain on everybody's parade. To do so would have been akin to Original Sin. And whatever the heck that was, he vaguely recalled it gave Adam a whole lot of grief. To play it safe, he said, "I do," hoping it would do the trick.

"Satisfied," responded the membership.

Score! Thought Peach.

The next and most important section was a series of physical tests. First, The Soul Cleansing Ride. Peach was placed in a wheelbarrow filled with cold, wet, sponges. As the brethren chanted, "THE HEWGAG BRAYS, BEFORE OR AFTER THE FULL MOON," Peach was given a ride down The Rocky Road to Dublin. Actually a ladder placed on the ground with the wheelbarrow banging up and down over the rungs. With the exception of now having wet underwear, he got a real kick out of it.

He was next asked if he believed in The Ascension of Man. Peach had never been a big fan of flying. Particularly now, what with all the increased security. One could never be sure anymore if that fake ID you were using was going to pass muster. It was a pet peeve, though, and this was not the moment to bring others down with his own hang-ups. Instead, he said, "You betcha!"

He was quickly picked up by several hands, forming a sort of human trampoline. The brethren chanted, "CREDO QUIA ABSURDUM," while Peach was flung up and down into the air, higher and higher until the horns on his Fred Flintstone's hat were rapping on the ceiling.

With no time to recover, he was required to perform a sensual dance with the dreaded hewgag accompanying. He did a damn good job of it. He was unabashed in his hip grinding and pelvis shaking and could have gone on for much longer. Unfortunately, several of the brethren suffered choking fits while attempting to laugh and swallow beer at the same time. The dance was cut short over safety concerns.

Peach was moved to the center of the room. The Clampfunctionaries encircled him as the brethren chanted a nonsensical dirge. This was the moment of truth.

The Noble Grand Humbug waved his scepter over Peach's head and asked, "Under fear of imperious, impregnating death, the Poor Blind Candidate will answer the following questions in all simulated, extrapolated truthfulness and incriminating candor. Are you of such good character as to be worthy of joining this magnificently, malodorous ménage of malingerers?"

Yikes. This was the biggie. Peach had struggled mightily over how he would answer. He wasn't exactly sure what constituted good character in the world of straights, but in his estimation, he surely had one. He had never double-crossed a fellow partner in crime. He had never shorted anyone while cutting up a take. He no longer used guns on a job (a good thing, because the Clampers didn't approve of guns, a fact Tinman would appreciate). And he never knowingly stole from someone who couldn't afford it.

"Absolutely!" he said, and held his breath.

"SATISFIED," spoke the brethren.

Whew. The rest was going to be cake.

"Will you feed the hungry?" asked the Noble Grand Humbug.

Peach wondered if this was a trick question and if he said yes he'd have to pay for everybody's dinner. He decided it was a fair price to pay for brotherhood, and said, "Yes."

"Will you clothe the naked?"

Another trick question. "Male or female?"

Apparently, the brethren felt this was a very apt question because, as one, they broke into laughter, snorting and spitting out beer through their nostrils. When they could breathe again, they all shouted, "Satisfied."

What an easy test. Didn't even have to answer the question.

"Will you take care of the orphan?"

Peach had always taken care of himself, which should count for something seeing he was an orphan. "You know it!"

"Will you be a husband to the widow?"

"If she's game, sure."

The Grand Noble Humbug lifted his scepter. The Hangman rattled the Chain of Punishment. Then he removed Peach's blindfold.

"I will now instruct you in the Order's secret signs and passwords. You must swear never to repeat or share these profound secrets to any man, woman, or child, be they living or dead. Do you hereby swear?"

Peach loved secrets and almost always had one. He didn't always keep them because what's the fun in having a secret if you can't tell at least someone. But the gravity of the situation was overwhelming. He decided then and there he would do his darndest to keep the Order's secrets. "I swear."

The Hangman recited several passwords which Peach knew he would never tell another soul because they were so confusing he forgot them as soon as they were uttered.

There was one series of signs used when a Brother was trying to find out if a certain other person was a fellow Brother. The Brother places his thumbs to his ears and bends his fingers into a semi-circle, then waggles them around. If the other person is indeed a Brother, they respond by closing a hand into a fist and striking their chest.

It was the symbol of the Well Jackass and Peach filed it away as important, and something he would probably need.

"There is one final sign, the most important and secret of all. The symbol of the Ill Jackass. The Sign of Distress. If you find yourself in deep doo-doo, it will at all times and places bring Brother Clampers from far and near to your assistance."

The Hangman showed Peach the sign, which Peach repeated to make sure he got it.

The Clampatriarch laid a hand on his shoulder and intoned, "There is one other secret you must know. The meaning of our name, E. Clampus Vitus. There may come a time when some lowly peon will ask you the meaning of these mystical words. You must answer thus, I do not know. For no one has ever uncovered the mystery of our sacred name and only a true Brother will know this secret answer. Do you understand?"

Peach, trying to get his head around the fact nobody here actually knew what club they belonged to, said, "I don't know."

Satisfied, The Clampatriarch continued, "Damfool Doorkeeper Number One and Damfool Doorkeeper Number Two will now escort the newly ordained to the Impenetrable Portal. The Clamps Petrix and The Clamps Matrix will light the way. When you have safely traversed the ungodly path to unholydom and reentered the Hall of Comparative Ovations, you will be stranger no more, nay, you will be Brother Peach."

He rapped the Sacred Staff of Relief on the floor three times. "Take this holy relic as protection for your final and most dangerous task."

Peach took the staff gingerly. Damfool Doorkeeper Number One beckoned with his Blunderbusket, and with the Sword of Mercy Tempered with Justic, Damfool Doorkeeper Number Two pointed at the exit of the bar. Peach gulped and walked to the door, with The Clamps Petrix and The Clamps Matrix lighting the way with candles.

The procession marched through the parking lot and along the sidewalk on Kietzke. Several cars honked and somebody tossed a half-full can of beer, but other than that, there was little danger to be had. The group approached the front door of the bar which actually did have a porthole mounted in it. Stan, the owner, had earlier told him it came off a Thai merchant ship, and one of the Brothers installed it for Clamper ceremonies.

Peach peered through the glass and the brethren peered back. Damfool Door Number One rapped on the door.

"ENTER," came the roared reply from within.

Peach stepped inside and the place went nuts. Everyone leapt up and slapped him on the back and spun him around and shoved a mug into his hand. He downed it in one giant gulp.

He soon realized his newly adopted family could really plow through the beers. Over the next hour or so, he had to twice replenish the charter's treasury, and realized belonging to a family did not come cheap.

At one point in the festivities, the Noble Grand Humbug, now several king-size sheets to the wind, approached Peach and slurred, "By the way, palsie, as our newisht Brother you are hereby appointed Chairman of the Most Important Committee. Sooo get to work you swlacker."

"But, er, what exactly is this committee up to and who are the members?"

"Membershlip of one. You. Task. Thatsh for you to figure out." Then he passed out and slipped gracefully off his stool, landing softly on another brother.

Peach had never really been in charge of anything except himself, and the thought of taking on such a weighty job made his head spin more than the beer.

His phone rang and he stepped into the backroom where the pool table was. The call was from Tek.

"Peach! We got a lead! On Crookslist! I told you it would work."

Tek had convinced Peach to open an account on the underground website, Crookslist. It was only accessed through something called the "darknet" which was kind of like the internet but reserved for people very much outside the law. He had agreed to go along with it if Tek managed the account.

Crookslist was an online job board for thieves, where an undesirable could post their approximate location, if they travel for work, and their specialty. If someone was putting together a string and needed a certain specialist, the two parties would hook up. If the heist was successful, the site requested a five percent cut of the haul. The payment of said cut was based on the honor system, so Peach figured the site wouldn't last long.

"You're kidding?" said Peach. "Who's it from?"

"That's what's interesting. It's from a guy who doesn't have an account but is piggybacking off some other guy who's a longstanding member. His username is Jingles, ever hear of him?"

"Sure. We crossed paths at the pen. He going in, me going out. He's a forger. Specializes in fake IDs, passports, birth certificates. Supposed to be one of the best."

"That's him," said Tek. "But the posting says this is coming from another guy who claims he knows you."

"Oh yeah? What's his name?"

"Won't tell. Just says you snore louder than he farts, and he'd like to play a little cat's cradle with you. Think it's a hoax?"

Peach grinned. "No hoax. He's an old cellie of mine, I just can't believe they let him out. Even more, I can't believe he's still alive. Send a message. Tell him my fingers are itching for a string to play with, and get his number."

"He already gave it," said Tek.

"That's unusual, no?" asked Peach.

"For sure. But I think he's got a timetable. I got the message alert ten minutes before I called you, and he says he'll only be available at the number for the next few hours. Then the post is null. What do you think it means?"

Peach's grin turned to a full smile. "I think it means high times ahead, little brother."

FOUR

SHADY DROPPED THE CELLPHONE ON THE DESK, leaned back in the office chair, and smiled. Fifty years had turned his sandy hair white, the chin-to-shoulder scar had faded becoming smoother, paler. His frame, still muscular and dangerous, now carried dead weight. His eyes, however, had not changed, still glistening gray with the same malevolency.

His release from prison had taken many years of study, careful planning and self-control. It began shortly after he'd been arrested for the first time in his long criminal career. It was over the heist of a jewelry wholesaler in Maryland. The charge was grand larceny and arson. The arson was a bogus charge but it was the one he'd received the most years for.

The safe had required a burning bar using magnesium rods. His rookie partner, in charge of the extinguisher, had panicked when sparks caused a small fire. The place burned to the ground, and his partner got pretty charred up, but lived. It was just an accident, but they tagged Shady as an arsonist, with a separate charge of grand larceny. Thirty to life.

What angered him most was he wouldn't have even needed to be working that safe if he'd gotten his share of the haul from the Redfield heist. That should have set him for life. It's why he spent year after year plotting his freedom. Payback was due.

The plan to get out of prison came when he heard about the "silver tsunami" the prisons were experiencing. With the advent of the "tough on crime" and the "three-strikes-you're-out" policies, the prisons were filling up with older inmates. The number of prisoners age 65 or older had increased by 63 percent, while the overall population of prisoners grew only 0.7 percent. The cost to house and care for them was three times more than younger inmates. Prisons had to build wheelchair ramps, add special shower handles, and provide staff who changed inmates' clothes when there was an "accident."

Some states were realizing they would soon have to build full-blown geriatric facilities. The prisons were required by law to allow access to medical care, and 90% of the prison hospitals in the country were ill-prepared to provide for geriatrics.

Some enlightened systems realized it was far cheaper to dump elderly prisoners into society, and let their families and social services absorb the costs. The legislators, however, were under pressure to keep their constituents safe, and the two groups often butted heads. Eventually, in some states, a partial compromise was reached, allowing for some selective release of prisoners deemed low risk for recidivism. Maryland was one of those states.

The decarceration of OPs, older prisoners, was a highly controversial program, and there were many hoops a prisoner had to jump through.

Shady found it simple to fake various geriatric ailments: dementia, arthritis, incontinence. His body was in surprisingly good shape, but he worked hard to hide it. He exercised by night and tottered around the prison by day, bent over, muttering to himself. The most difficult thing was to not kill or maim the younger inmates who preyed on the elderly. To appear helpless and at risk, he was forced to take their abuse.

It had all been worth it when a young law student working with the Project for Older Prisoners, POPS, was assigned his case. The project had been created by a law school professor, and was a compassionate, well-thought-out, regulated solution to the problem. Except for someone as conniving as Shady.

The project worked by assigning a volunteer law student to a candidate. The students were learning pro bono work and were idealistic and naïve. POPS required a four-step protocol, including extensive interviews, before a prisoner could become qualified for early release.

For Shady, conning his young handler was the easiest part of all, as the law student eagerly soaked up all the bullshit he fed him. The fact the kid's grandmother had dementia helped to tug the heartstrings. He highly recommended Shady as a low risk to the public.

Two years after he entered the program, and several years before the end of his sentence, Shady was approved. His supervised release was contingent on his good behavior. A week ago, he had hobbled into a halfway house using a walker. The next morning, he strolled out the front door, stole a car, and drove to Tucson where an ex-con he knew, Jingles, had been persuaded to help him.

There was every reason to smile. And, he'd just been the recipient of some unexpected good luck. Luck was something he never counted on, but didn't spit on when it came his way.

While Jingles had been working on his new ID, Shady had mentioned he was looking to put a string together for a very lucrative job. Jingles was not a heister, but he suggested a computer service. He claimed he got much of his work for fake credentials through the site. Shady was skeptical. He knew computers left trails, no matter how secret the connection might be.

With a little urging, Jingles agreed to let him use his account. After a few dead-ends, he stumbled upon his old cellie, Peach. To his delight, he was located in Reno, just a short distance from where he intended to even the score from the Redfield heist. It couldn't be a more perfect set-up.

Peach was a good kid, with genuine thieves' blood, and a sharp brain. He also had a good heart, which equaled sucker. It would be that much easier for Shady to take care of his business with a little free help. He was also pretty certain Peach would not make a fuss when the cross came down. He hoped not. Peach was a good kid.

Shady examined his new credentials. Unfortunately, the disagreement over payment for the documents had come before Jingles could complete the birth certificate and passport, but he did have a driver's license and some temporary credit cards that would float long enough to pay for his expenses to Nevada.

He knew the phone would do him no good, as it could be tracked. He'd found no gun in the house which was very disappointing. Still, he had a clean car for the time being, thanks to his old buddy. He pulled off the latex gloves he'd been wearing and shoved them in his pocket.

He started for the garage of the little clapboard house. As he stepped over Jingles' body, he shook his head. He would have had to lose him anyway, to cover his tracks and the new ID, but it was a shame they couldn't first come to an arrangement regarding payment. It's always better to have proof of birth when assuming a new identity, and good old Jingles really had a knack. His work was always the quill.

FIVE

"GRRROWFF!"

"Sshhhh!"

Tinman was in an upscale neighborhood, bordering on the Hidden Valley Country Club's golf course. Peach had chosen this neighborhood for canvasing because he said houses on golf courses were perfect targets. He had been wandering around for over an hour and had located a large estate he thought might be of interest.

He was in a cable guy's uniform that Peach had mysteriously produced, saying he had a buddy who owed him some favors. His buddy's name was apparently Clive, since that's what the name tag said. He had been lucky so far, and had not yet been required to say his name was Clive, which he was thankful for.

"GRrrap, GRRrap!"

He was not thankful, however, for the mongrel who appeared in the neighbor's fenced backyard as he was studying his target house.

"Ssshut UP."

"Grrrrrrrrrrr."

Tinman sighed and was about ready to call it a day when a woman in a robe appeared at the backdoor of the cur's house.

"You're late!" she said.

"Uh," said Tinman.

"What are you doing back here? I told them to have the man come to the front door."

"Er."

She leaned back and appraised him. "They finally sent me a big boy, huh? Well, get in here. I don't have all day."

Tinman eyed the fierce little rat dog. The lady snickered, and said, "Inside."

"Grrrrrrrr."

"Get the hell in here or I'll kick your puny butt into your throat!"

Tinman scrambled for the fence gate then realized she was talking to the dog, now dutifully scurrying between her shapely legs.

"You, too!"

This time, he knew for sure she meant him. He stepped through the gate and slipped by the lady who refused to budge, intent on having their bodies brush on his way past.

The kitchen was vast and well-appointed, as was the lady, given the size bumps he brushed against on his way in. He was struggling to come up with a cover story when she broke into his desperate thoughts.

"I specifically ordered a FedEx man," she said. "What's with the cable getup?"

"Um."

"It doesn't matter. Here's the game. I'm going to be Isabelle. My old college roommate. That bitch. This is payback for all the boyfriends she stole. And you are, Clive?"

"Sort of."

"Mind if I call you Ajax?"

"Well."

"That means powerful eagle." she said, parting her robe a tad to show the hint of a bright, red teddy. "Do you think you can be a powerful eagle?"

"Uh, Isabelle—"

"Not now!" She snapped her robe shut. "I'm Mrs. Jenkins to you. Wait for the game."

"The game."

"I'm getting to it! And please stop doing that. That's Isabell's job." She pointed to Tinman's crotch where he was busy scratching the pesky itch which was more pronounced than yesterday. He quickly removed his hand and grinned sheepishly.

"So, you were supposed to be a delivery man, but now you'll be a cable repairman. You'll go back outside and wait at the front door. When you knock and I open, I'll have just finished taking a shower. I'll have a towel wrapped around me. You say you have to check a cable outage. I'll go to the TV and bend over with my back to you. A primal desire wells up. You can't control yourself. You sneak up behind and take me. Well, Isabelle. And I want you to really ravage her. Sink those powerful talons in and take her like the little tramp she is. Now I was all set, but of course you were late, so I'll have to prepare again. I'll just wet down a little and throw on a towel. Well? What are you waiting for? Out! Wait three minutes, then knock."

She shoved him outside. As the door clicked shut, he swam up out of the murky fog into the light of reality. The coward in him told him to run. The powerful eagle wondered, what's the harm? It had been a helluva long time, and how often does lightning strike? Not often, not ever, unless of course it was your job. He briefly wondered if the call boy firm was hiring.

He knocked on the door. The lady opened it wrapped in a towel. He assumed that meant she was now Isabelle. This was his cue. He was just about to fire out his line, when a car pulled up the driveway and a young stud in a FedEx uniform jumped out and bolted to the door.

"Mrs. Jenkins," panted the delivery stud.

"Who are you?" asked Mrs. Jenkins—Isabelle now on hold.

The stud eyed Tinman suspiciously, not sure how to proceed. Tinman looked to the sky, wondering how the weather was doing up there. Hoping lightning would strike twice, this time for real.

"I'm from RandyMan, ma'am," spoketh the stud.

Mrs. Jenkins' eyes popped. First from the truth being revealed, and second at the sight of the lump in the stud's pants. "You're from RandyMan?!" she screamed and pointed at Tinman. "Then who are you?"

Tinman gulped. "Ajax?"

"Agh! You pervert! How dare you! Get off of my property!"

Tinman and the stud quickly turned to go. "Not you!" cried Isabelle, grabbing the stud and tossing him inside. "Clive, you are one depraved lowlife!" She slammed the door.

Tinman slumped and walked down the drive. When he reached the end, he heard, "Psst," from behind a bordering hedge. An old lady popped her cotton tip head up.

"Two in one day, oh?" she said conspiratorially. "What a hussy, ick. I'm tempted to tell the good doctor, what would he say, eh? Of course, he's probably bopping his nurse, so what the hell's the world coming to, huh?"

"I'm just the cable guy, ma'am," said Tinman, praying this day would soon end.

The old lady examined his name tag. "Clive, hm. That must be tough, eh? What are mothers thinking when they do that to their boys, huh?"

"Um, I'm investigating a cable outage but I went to the wrong door."

"Pandora's Box, eh, that's what you knocked on, humph. Well, my cable's fine. I just finished Days of our Lives, uh-huh. Do you follow it?"

"My days are confusing enough. The outage must be at that house," said Tinman, pointing at his target.

"Mr. Clarkson, ah, he's a lovely man."

"You know him?"

"No."

"Oh."

"Nobody does, hah!" said the Q-tip. "He never leaves the place, only the first two days of the week, Monday and Tuesday, hmm. Always leaves the same time, right before my show comes on and right after it's over, see? Nobody knows where he goes, no. They say he's a miser, stinking rich, keeps it all stashed away in there, so he can touch it, play with it, heh. Say, you're not such a bad looking specimen, hmm. Maybe you can come over and check my connections. At least my husband's dead, uh-huh."

Tinman's phone rang which proves beyond a shadow of a doubt, prayer does work. "Hello?"

"Heya, brother," said Peach. "How's tricks?"

"Help."

"Huh?"

"Help! My, uh, truck broke down corner of Skokie Way and Sleepy Hollow Drive. I need immediate roadside assistance."

"I thought your cabbie buddie, Garshasp was your ride today."

"NOW."

"Okay, okay. Give me fifteen. By the way, I got great news. Our lucky day is right around the corner."

Tinman watched the Q-tip licking her lips, and shuddered. It would have to be one heck of a lucky day to wash the taste of this episode from his mouth.

Six

"I THOUGHT AJAX WAS A SOAP!" said Catfish, barely recovering from his laughing fit over Tinman's excursion into deepest suburbia. His distinctive Chicago accent always made him sound like a tout in a Damon Runyon yarn.

Bones, his longtime partner, said with his Alabama drawl, "Sure. It's stronger than dirt. That's why housewives turn to Ajax when they need their pipes cleaned!"

Tinman knew it was better to let them get it out of their systems. Even at his expense.

The Posse was at McCue's, the only place left in Reno that somewhat resembled a pool hall. Peach was chatting up Amber, the bartender, who had blackmailed the owner into giving her complete control of the business. She was in her 40's and plump in all the right places. Not that it made any difference to Peach who felt that all women were beautiful—one just had to dig deep enough.

Tek was leaning over his laptop, hacking a wormhole in an online app site. His income came from siphoning small amounts from online purchases, and he was very excited about this new addition to his financial portfolio.

Tinman wished he could get everybody's attention as a plan was hatching. He felt a great urge to come up with a perfect scheme to heist Mr. Clarkson of Hidden Valley. When he was top dog he never worried about making his brother proud, but now their positions were reversed, and he was struggling to find his way.

He paced, listening to Catfish and Bones who had moved from Ajax to Mr. Clean and were mangling the words to the old jingle.

"Can he clean my underwear?"

"No not even on a dare!"

Tinman retreated to his table. An Olhausen Grand Champion. It was left covered unless he uncovered it. Amber made no exceptions. McCue's had started out as a real pool hall, but as the players dwindled it crept ever closer to being just a bar that happened to have some pool tables. The felt was quality—five years ago. Tinman had offered to re-felt them at no charge. But the owner wouldn't even swing for the cost of the cloth. Still, with no other hall left in Reno, this was home.

Not for long, Tinman kept telling himself. Some months ago, Peach had reminded him of his childhood dream to have his own pool hall. He later fueled the flame by presenting him with a beautiful Brunswick he absconded from a retirement home which he decided didn't need a pool table anymore. The table now lived in the old office of the All Inn Motel. Tinman's private pool room, affectionately known as the Clubhouse, was strictly reserved for members and honored guests.

Nearly every night he showed up for work at McCue's, hoping the tide would turn and the high rollers would emerge yet again. The good times would return and he would be the confident killer once more. Instead, he was barely able to clear five bills in a month hustling dumb teenagers and drunken tourists.

Somewhere in his addled, crisis-stricken mind, he believed it was all a matter of environment. The game would rise from the ashes if only someone could present Reno with a genuine pool hall. A hall that represented all that was beautiful and pure about the world's greatest game. No corners cut. Top-of-the-line tables. Simonis cloth. Perfect lighting. No pinball machines, air hockey or shuffleboard. And no juke box.

Pure pool. That was what Tinman now ached for, as he had when he was a small boy sneaking into some of the great halls Reno once boasted, like the Silver Cue.

But this dream took money. It's why he was working so hard on his training, and beating himself up unmercifully when he screwed up. He knew he would never be able to fully become the heister his brother was, but for now, he had to succeed, or fade.

As he idly rolled balls across the table, his analytical mind isolated the various problems associated with burglarizing Mr. Clarkson. Each ball represented a variable, a twist, a problem. Their routes across the table were possible actions, the holes solutions. As collisions occurred, the causality proved or disproved the theory.

"Can he make my shit not stink?"

"Yes but then you'll need a drink."

Like two ten-year-olds trying to out fart each other, the old guys hooted and howled. What a team. Catfish, the consummate conman, who had watched his action fade along with the big con. Like Tinman now, he was forced to reinvent himself and work as a stall alongside Bones when he was picking pockets. Tinman knew it must have been a struggle to make such a change, and it gave him hope he might work through his metamorphosis with equal grace.

Bones was a class cannon, the most elite of all pickpockets. One of the last, if not the last, who turned bodily theft into poetry. Born to a half-white, half-Chickasaw mother, his white father left when he was two months old. His grandfather on his mother's side, a proficient cannon in his own right, taught him the trade.

Like Catfish, he was one of those rare animals who once they hit a certain age seem to freeze in time. Due to murky circumstances the two ended up assisting in the raising of Peach and Tinman. Both owed quite a bit of their criminal aptitude to the old grifters. Dez, the lady who kept them mostly fed and housed as kids, filled in the gaps.

Bones and Catfish quickly ceased their shenanigans when their favorite section of the news came on. CRIME WAVE.

"Good evening to you! Scott Frenley here with all the crime we can muster! Only one story tonight, but it's a real tearjerker. Yesterday, a man walked into an Umpqua Bank and demanded the contents of the safe and all the safety deposit boxes. Quite a tall order given he was armed with nothing but a pocket knife! Ooh. I'll bet those tellers were scared right down to their skivvies!

"Despite his lethal arsenal, the bank robber was quickly subdued. He later told officers he'd attempted the robbery so he could go back to prison. Recently released from a twenty-year sentence, he was feeling a little homesick. It just goes to show you, folks, there's no place like home."

Catfish clicked the remote and Frenley went away. A moment of somber silence.

"I feel sorry for the guy," said Bones. "Being inside that long does strange things."

"I've known guys like that," said Catfish. "Hey Peach, let's hope this old cellmate of yours don't have the same plan. Hate for us to go down just so's he can get back inside. Got no longing for the pen."

"No way," said Peach. "He's good people. Straight up. Let me tell you some more about him."

"No," said Tinman.

When Peach picked Tinman up in Hidden Valley, he was all atwitter over his old cellie coming to town. It was not the lucky news Tinman had been hoping for. He had the feeling Peach had given up on him being the planner, and was going to replace him with this new guy. He knew his only chance was to come up with a perfect blueprint to heist Mr. Clarkson.

Peach said, "Let me just give you a little more skinny."

"We'll meet him tomorrow," said Tinman. "I need a huddle. I have an idea about this deal in Hidden Valley."

Peach, Catfish, and Bones meandered to his table. Tek clicked his laptop shut and closed in with the others.

Tinman began, "The main problem is this guy never leaves the house, except on Mondays and Tuesdays for about an hour."

"In the sunshiny daytime," noted Bones. "With lots of people strolling round,"

"Daytime is not necessarily bad. People don't expect anything to be going down," said Peach. "Tek, bring up the satellite on this place. I'd like a better look."

"Check."

Tinman continued. "In order for this to work, we'll have to split up. There are two secondary problems that have to be isolated. Isabelle and Q-tip. Isabelle's house borders the target, and Q-tip is nosy."

Tinman rolled the nine ball and the eight ball near each of the two side pockets. He pointed at the eight ball with his cue. "I'm the natural to take on Isabelle. I show up to apologize. Get down on my knees, like that."

"You might give her ideas," said Catfish

"Yeah, she might think you're proposing," tittered Bones.

"Or muff diving," said Catfish.

"No thanks." said Tinman. "The apology will do the trick for the time we need." He stroked into the eight ball and it sank in the left side pocket.

"What was the address?" asked Tek. Tinman told him and Tek went back to work.

"Which leaves us with Q-tip," Tinman continued. "We'll need someone to flirt her up. The cover can be a door-to-door salesman, or someone looking to move into the area. Catfish, I'm thinking you're the guy for that."

"No can do," said Catfish promptly. "Not my type. She's old."

"So are you."

"Sure, but I'm in denial."

Tinman sighed. "Fine. Peach has to be free to do the heist, so it'll have to be you Bones."

"Uh—no. I may be a thief, but I have scruples, and I will not give up my virginity for all the money in the world."

"You're not a virgin."

"Prove it."

"Are you two purposefully trying to sabotage my plan?" asked Tinman.

Bones and Catfish gave him their most angelic looks, and his eyes moved to Tek. "What about you, Tek?"

Tek gave him a horrified, incredulous look. "Hey! I really am a virgin! Would you actually want that old thing to be my first?!"

Tinman thought. Hmm. Maybe not. He wouldn't want to be responsible for some childhood trauma that came back to haunt the kid.

"What about Plan B?" asked Bones.

"Huh?"

"Surely you got one," said Catfish.

"Of course I have one!" declared Tinman. "The first one was just to see if you were all paying attention."

Eight eyeballs, at full attention, stared back. "Plan B, er," said Tinman.

"I got the house up," said Tek. He spun his laptop around so everyone could see the satellite view of Mr. Clarkson's house and the surrounding area.

"Easy access from the golf course," said Peach. "No house bordering on one side. I can see why you like it. What about the security system?"

"I couldn't get close enough," said Tinman. "You and I do a dry run tonight."

"Tek," said Peach.

Tek zoomed in and slowly moved around the house until landing on a panel mounted to the side. Peach leaned in and examined it.

"No need for a dry run," said Peach. "I can take this box easy. Sorry to interrupt. Okay, Plan B."

Tinman chewed on his lip and paced along the table, his eyes scrutinizing the balls. Plan B beginning to formulate.

He was about to explain when Peach said, "What do we know about this guy other than what Q-tip told you?"

"What more do we need to know?!" asked Tinman, anxious to get on with his new amazing plan. "He's some rich miser who sits around and plays with his money."

Peach hitched up his cheek. "Sometimes secondhand info is not always reliable. Tek, see what you can find out about this guy."

"This is the perfect mark! What's the point in digging deeper?" demanded Tinman. "Do you want to hear Plan B or not?!" Peach waved his hand, giving him the stage.

"Tomorrow," began Tinman, "Bones and Catfish follow this guy to wherever he goes. Bones forks his leather. Now, we wait until night, then we have Tek call him. Think you can find a number for him, Tek?"

"Already got it. Old guy still has a landline, can you believe it?"

"Has to, for the security system," said Peach.

"Wow, I hadn't thought of that," said Tek, going back to his search. Neither had Tinman, but he wasn't dumb enough to admit it to the teacher.

"So Tek calls," continued Tinman. "Says he found the wallet. Offers to give it back for a reward. But the guy has to come pick it up. We send him to the Meadowood Mall. Give him the runaround for an hour. That place it so confusing it'll be easy. Meanwhile, Peach and I do the heist. No more worries about neighbors or bright sunshiny day. Mission accomplished."

He held his breath, his mind surprised at how good his impromptu plan actually sounded, but still fearful his Posse may find some obvious flaw. Catfish gave Bones a sidelong look. Bones raised one eyebrow. Peach stared into space. Tek clacked away on the keyboard.

"Using a fixed pattern to force a schedule on the mark. I like it," said Catfish sagely. "Just like in a con."

"Or a jug mob on the whiz," said Bones.

Tinman half-exhaled. The other half still waiting on his teacher.

"That's good stuff. Simple. Clean. It's a go for me," said Peach.

The other half of the exhale oozed out, allowing in a sweet tasting breath of fresh air filled with newfound hope.

"Yeah, that plan's the dope, except for the fact the guy's in arrears," said Tek.

The breath Tinman had just inhaled suddenly turned toxic. He sputtered, desperately trying to expel it before it contaminated his body and mind with everlasting depression.

"Kind of like what you were in not too long ago, right?" Tek asked, oh so innocently.

He was referring to the situation Tinman found himself after Dez, former owner of the motel, had dumped the dive on him, leaving him with a large tax bill. When the basket burglary went bust, Peach loaned him $3000 to cover the fees. It was a low point in his life, and he was oh so glad Tek had brought it up.

"Are you sure?" he asked without hope.

"House is due for tax sale soon. Mortgage company is after him too, but the county gets first dibs. Looks like he was fleeced by an ex-wife and then booted from IGT. Older engineer. Probably couldn't keep up with the technology. These damn digital slot machines. Wasting good tech on something so stupid." He clicked shut his laptop and wandered off.

Unceremoniously, but without rancor, condescension, or contempt, Bones and Catfish rocked back from the table and sauntered to the bar. Sometimes it just goes that way. When it's not right, you walk away.

"Gee, I hate seeing anybody lose his home, you know? I wish I could think of a way to help him out." said Peach with not a hint of irony.

"Yeah. Tough luck," said Tinman.

Peach sidled up. "Good plan, man. Just wasn't meant to be. I like that about life. Never know what banana peel is gonna trip you up around the next corner. It's so fun!"

Tinman wished he could join in this profound celebration of life, but circumstances restrained his enthusiasm.

"Don't sweat it, brother," said Peach. "Just think, if we had gone through with it, we woulda had to reschedule our meet with my old cellie. Right there, see how wacky life is? But somehow it all works out. And you gotta believe me, this is the one we've been looking for. This guy is our lucky charm."

SEVEN

"OTTO SCHEIDEGGER, AKA SHADY. THAT'S YOUR MAN," said Special Agent-in-Charge Franklyn Tilston, commander of the Fugitive Apprehension Unit. He was a large, black man who climbed the ranks of the FBI to become leader of this elite unit. He wore his position proudly, and couldn't stand the man sitting across his desk.

"Is this a crock, or what?" asked Special Agent Deke Wolff, the guy Tilston hated. Deke had started out adult life as a burglar and was arrested in his mid-twenties. He skipped bail and remained free for three years. The FBI was impressed with his caginess and ability to elude capture. After he was finally rearrested and did three years of his sentence, he was approached and offered a deal to work with the FAU in exchange for a suspension of sentence.

"Shut up!" demanded Tilston, who loathed the fact the FBI would sink so low as to work with ex-convicts and criminals. His driving hope was to rid his unit of Deke and replace him with someone more befitting of such a noble undertaking. It's not that he was a bad agent. In fact, he was Tilston's best. He thought like a crook and often outguessed whatever fugitive he was after. This irked

Tilston even more and made him more determined. When this recent case came up, he knew it might be his chance to oust him.

"The guy is like eighty something!" said Deke.

"Besides the point. He walked away from a halfway house in clear violation of his early release."

"Says here he had dementia. Has anyone tried canvassing the neighborhood? He's probably out picking flowers in the park."

"I don't think so. The old-age thing was a ruse to get out of prison early."

"But he is old!"

"He's also smart. Spent most of his life on the outside. Suspected in dozens of heists but never got one pinned on him until this thing in Maryland."

"So why don't they take care of it?" asked Deke.

"They believe, as do I, that the fugitive has crossed state lines and is out of their jurisdiction. Now it's a federal case. Ours."

"Sounds to me Maryland doesn't want to cover the overtime running down a geriatric, so they pawn it off on us. I'll give you ten to one odds he's a mile from where he disappeared."

As soon as Deke spoke his last sentence, he wished it back. He'd recently gotten into a lot of trouble over his gambling habit. It didn't matter to the bureau that online poker is legal in some states. No. It only mattered that it was illegal in the state Deke was caught playing. On the bureau's computers. During work hours.

Tilston bristled and bore down. "It would behoove you, Agent Wolff, to keep your trap shut and listen to what I have to say."

Deke hated this guy, but he hated prison more. After his last snafu with the poker, he was on a very thin thread indeed. Another violation or show of insubordination would send him back to complete his sentence. He settled into his chair.

Tilston continued, "The day our fugitive disappeared, a car was stolen a short distance from the halfway house he was assigned to."

"Some punks out for a joy ride. It'll turn up in Baltimore or some such."

"It was discovered two days ago in a Tucson neighborhood. What do you think of that smart guy?"

"Hell of a joy ride," said Deke, hiding his embarrassment. In hopes of a rebound he added, "Still, there's no proof it was our perp."

"A mile from the car, a man was found strangled in his home. And before you make a bigger fool of yourself, the man was Charlie Flanders, aka Jingles. A top-notch forger and known associate of Shady while in the Maryland Penitentiary."

"Oh."

"Yeah, oh. We're not sure if Shady managed to get fake ID before he killed Jingles or not. But a car was missing and we have an APB out."

"Any leads on where he might be looking to hole up?" asked Deke, the hunter getting interested.

"I have a gut feeling this guy is not out to hide away in a hole until he dies. He's up to something. He may be putting together a string for one last heist. Retirement money. Our techs are searching the darknet for any recent activity on Crookslist and some of the others, but nothing's come up yet."

"Family?"

"None. He was born in Wisconsin and left when he was a teen. Never looked back."

"Who would?"

"I was born in Wisconsin."

"Sorry for that. I mean, you know." Deke's main flaw was he had a big mouth and had never learned to tame it. "What about old cellmates?"

Tilston slid over a sheet of paper. "He was known to work mostly in the West. California, Arizona, Nevada, sometimes Oregon. The Maryland job was out of the ordinary and I have to assume that's why he immediately left the area after he escaped. No contacts. No safe haven."

"What's his MO? Mostly small-time stuff?" asked Deke.

"No. He's a real pro. A mechanic. Stuck strictly to safes and was very good at it. There are also rumors he didn't like to leave loose ends. Mainly his partners."

"Not a good guy to team up with, huh?" said Deke. "Anything stick out with the cellmates?"

"All of them hated him, and he them, except one. Did three years with Shady and never had a problem. They were practically inseparable. There were even some suspicions Shady was acting as a mentor."

Deke chuckled. "Ah, prison. Still the best schooling an up-and-comer can have. Which one is he?"

"Third down from the top. Troy Harrigan, aka Peach. No recent arrests. Whereabouts unknown. However, in his file it says he was born in Reno."

Involuntarily, Deke's fingers began to itch. Just the mention of the gambling town got him revved up. "Never been. Town have any connection to Shady?"

"Yes," said Tilston, watching Deke's reaction. "1957 he was suspected of involvement in a supermarket heist. Not enough evidence to hold him and he walked. They eventually found the gang, but the money was missing. Every one of them swore it was Shady who set up the deal, but he was long gone."

"He crossed them," said Deke knowingly. "A real sweetheart. Anything in Reno after that?"

"Nothing substantiated. There were a few high-profile heists over the years, unsolved, some of them had Shady's signature all over them, but no proof."

"Sounds like he went back to the well. Crooks are superstitious. If a town was good to them once they consider it safe territory."

"So, Special Agent Wolff, in your expert opinion, do you think Reno would be a good place to start your search?"

Deke spotted the trap in the nick of time. Tilston had been gunning for him since they met. No wonder he hadn't stuck a rookie on this dead-end case. "California's a better bet," he said. "Easier to get lost. But I defer to your expert opinion. Where would you like me to start?" Back at you, jerk.

Tilston had seen the glimmer in Deke's eyes as he caught onto his little ploy, and it pissed him off. Still, he knew his man. "I leave that entirely up to you. I'm sure you'll get your man."

Damn. Outfoxed. "Who's my second?"

"You're solo until you locate the perp," said Tilston. "I'll assign you backup for the apprehension."

Deke wondered who they would have tailing him, watching for him to slip up. No matter. Deep down, he was still a crook. He'd find a way to get his man while having a little fun of his own. Game on.

He rose, gathered up the files, and nodded at his boss. Before he could escape, Tilston said, "Best of luck, Wolff," and shot him a wide, mirthless smile. Deke clamped his jaw shut, and left.

Tilston picked up his cell phone. "Did you get all that?

"Yes sir," answered a curt female voice.

"You can come in now."

From a side door, a young woman appeared and marched to the front of the desk. If she didn't look so sincere and have FBI credentials in her wallet, her overplaying of an agent would have been perfect for a Saturday Night Live skit.

Tilston beamed with pride. This was his incarnation. Probationary Agent Mandy Leadbetter. Raised by a father who was a lieutenant in the Boston Police Department, Tilston had recruited her out of college and pruned her into the kind of agent he felt the bureau desperately lacked. Analytical, hard-working, honest to a fault, absolutely no sense of humor, and obedient. The perfect machine. Not hard on the eyes, either. And single. He was hoping she would be Deke's replacement, then perhaps their relationship might expand further.

Mandy stood at attention, feeling slightly uncomfortable under the appraising stare of her leader. Her brunette hair was, as usual, pulled into a severe bun so that her eyes seemed to stretch outward, giving her a slightly Asian look, even though she was anything but. Her perfectly tailored clothing showed no obvious female attributes.

Long ago, she learned women went a lot further if they emulated men. No make-up, lower vocal range to an alto, hips as stationary as possible when walking. A sports bra took care of the boobs. She didn't want to be a man. She just wanted what men have. And the sacrifices were well worth it.

There were only two men she knew thought she was beautiful. Her father, who had told her, like all fathers do, or should. And the man staring at her now, who had not told her, but despite her façade, she was a woman through and through, and could tell.

Her boss's attraction was not flattering, as he wasn't her type. What her type was, she had not yet discerned. She would, however, utilize him for her purposes. Ambition had a firm hold.

After achieving all she wanted, then she could worry about a man. She wasn't fretting success in that department. Not many men had seen her naked, but she had, every day, and it made her smile knowing what was hidden underneath. One peek at that, and she'd have men crawling all over her.

Tilson ogled her, imagining the hidden wonders. A mystery he was determined to uncover. Wife or no wife, there are some things a man has to know.

"Do you understand why you are here?" he asked.

"Your conversation made it apparent you do not trust Agent Wolff. You believe he is not capable of apprehending the escaped fugitive and you want me to undergo a separate search, knowing that I will succeed where he will not."

"Wrong."

"Wrong?"

"Right," said Tilston. "Agent Wolff's ability to execute his duties is not in question. He's the best we have. But it is true I don't trust him. You're too new here to know why."

"I don't understand."

"I just said that."

"Um, right. Sir. Please elaborate."

"Come closer." It's not that he wanted to make sure she heard him or that he needed more privacy, he just wanted to smell her. But she would never know that. To her it was just an order from a superior. One of the perks of being in charge.

Mandy played along, leaning in conspiratorially, knowing damn well he was a closet olfactophiliac. Tilston breathed in heavily, like he was going to entrust her with the nuclear codes, while actually drawing in a big whiff of her musky scent. Heaven.

"Now then," he began huskily. "A few months ago, Special Agent Wolff was found using company equipment to access an illegal online gaming site. Any other inappropriate behavior will lead to his immediate dismissal."

Mandy nodded gravely, even though she had absolutely no idea where this was going.

"Exactly," said Tilston, so happy his prodigy was quick on the uptake. "It is no secret in the unit that I do not approve of Agent Wolff. I am therefore determined to rid the bureau of him. Which comes to you. I want you to follow him on his assignment. Strictly undercover. He will begin his search for the fugitive in Reno."

"But sir, he didn't seem convinced that was the correct place to begin."

"All a blind. He's going to Reno. He can't resist. And when he's there, he won't be able to resist the urge to gamble. When he does, you get proof of that, preferably photos, and contact me immediately. I'll take care of the rest."

Mandy leaned back. Not at all pleased. Her father and three brothers were all cops. Growing up, she had learned the cardinal rule. Always protect your kind. Even if a brother in blue is doing something untoward or illegal, you never rat him out. Tilston was asking her to be a snitch, and it really grated.

Even more galling, Agent Wolff was the best of the best. What did it matter if he gambled a little? In their field of work, one had to have a release, a way to let the stress of the job fade away. What if the bureau told her she'd lose her job if she continued pole dancing, her chosen form of relief? Would that be fair? It was done in the privacy of her own home. In front of her own mirror. Purely for her own satisfaction. Did her pole dancing somehow interfere with her job performance? Certainly not. This assignment was wrong, and beneath her, and even if it hurt her advancement, she simply could not accept.

"Naturally, once Wolff is gone," said Tilston, oblivious to Mandy's ethical turmoil, "I'll be making a very strong recommendation that you take his place as Special Agent."

"Sir!" cried Mandy. "Thank you so much! You can count on me!" Hey, when someone offers you a promotion and more money, integrity goes out the window, right, Judas?

"Good," said Tilston. "Now, he has never met you so it shouldn't be too difficult to stay off his radar. Report downstairs and they'll set you up with some disguises."

Mandy snapped to attention. Tilston nodded, and she spun on her heels and left. He watched her go, loins stirring. He rearranged himself and got back to work.

EIGHT

TINMAN COULDN'T STAND IT ANY LONGER. He'd gotten to bed late. After the collapse of his master plan, he felt the need to take out his grief on the pool table, running rack after rack, late into the night, proving he was still good at something.

It was closing in on noon and he was still half-asleep in his single bed. His mind assured him there was plenty of time before he had to face the day. Peach wasn't picking him up for the meeting for a couple of hours. His body, however, had different ideas. At least one specific part. The itchy part. Way down yonder. The place where no woman had ventured since time immemorial.

Which was exactly the point. How could there be anything wrong down there? He barely used that area, except for the obvious human requirements. Still, it had woken him up, or rather his fingers did as they strained to do their jobs, craving the need to scratch and prod and chase the irritant away. As he rose to full consciousness, dread quickened his heartbeat and shortened his breath.

Like most people who grew up with little access to hospitals, doctors, even Band-Aids, Tinman was a hypochondriac. Some people like to flaunt their imaginary illnesses but he thought it a sign of weakness, so he was a closet hypochondriac. Still, any itch, twitch, blotch or glitch in his physical state of being, gave him a bad case of the jitters.

As he pondered what horrific ailment may have attacked his otherwise hale body, he remembered his last bout with the mysterious blob on his left foot. How he had fretted and worried only to have Peach reveal the deadly growth as a harmless wart.

A self-deprecating grin forced its way onto his face. How silly and frail humans were. Magnifying miniscule maladies into malevolent malaise. His grin widened as he admired the number of syllables and alliterations he'd managed to meld. Only a wordsmith gets a kick out of stuff like that.

He hopped out of bed, chuckling at his own foolishness. He hit the shower, washed his body from toe to head, and halfway up found a bump on his left nut. Then he stopped chuckling. His heart threatened to have a seizure, and the lungs figured this was a good time to check out while the going was still good.

Two fingers were assigned the odious task of rechecking. It was still there. He didn't want to look. First of all, it was difficult to bend over that far. Second, he was afraid he would bang his head on the shower head, get a concussion, collapse to the tile and die! Oh my! (Forgive him. That's just the way it is with full-blown hypochondriacs.)

Bottom line, though, if he saw it, it would be real. No more convenient use of denial. He would put a face to the evil thing and it would haunt his dreams. If only his fingers discovered it, then its existence was still subject to debate.

He bent over and looked. The eyes officially confirmed its presence. Damn it. Why did he do that. Now what?

Even if he had the money, and inclination, to get health insurance, he would never let anyone poke and probe and know things about his insides that he could never fathom. In his estimation, going to a doctor was a form of rape, an involuntary baring of one's insides to a perfect stranger. He would not be a party to it.

So what, then? Water. The perfect healer. Yes. Water would take care of it. Hot water. Burn and melt the nastiness into oblivion. Gingerly cupping his now contaminated privates in one hand, he turned the knob to full hot, and let 'er rip.

The itching stopped. For now. But his nuts looked like overripe strawberries. Either way, Round One was over. Time would tell.

Usually, after his shower, he did an hour of exercise: a combination of yoga, tai chi and jumping jacks. But the morning's trauma had sapped him of energy. As he was dressing, he realized it might be a good idea to constrict the little red buggers so they wouldn't flop around so much. He was a boxer guy, but underneath his pile of underwear he found an old pair of tighty-whities. They were a little stretched but they did the trick.

After his normal breakfast of hot five grain cereal and fresh fruit with dabs of yogurt, he plopped into his easy chair and grabbed his worn 1972 edition of the New Webster's Dictionary and Thesaurus of the English Language. He'd read it three times in his life and was a third of the way through his fourth go around.

Inharmonious: adj. lacking harmony, discordant, jarring.

How fitting to describe the moment, his state of mind, his current life. He closed his eyes and prayed Peach's cellmate would bring the promised good luck. His dream of owning a pool hall was now just whimsy. The newly discovered ailment may well require drastic measures. That meant money. Lots of it.

Peach showed up a little after two. "What's wrong with you?"

Sometimes it really sucked having a twin. "Nothing! Why? Does something look wrong?"

Peach knew something was wrong, but Tinman was stubborn and no amount of cajoling or probing would force it out of him if he didn't want to tell. "Not really. I was just asking. Ready to go?"

As they drove east on Fourth, Tinman asked, "So where is this meet?"

"A little joint on Kietzke, near the corner of Mill. It's called Floyd's Fireside Chat."

"Why would you possibly pick that place? It's a dump. Used to have a Chinese laundry attached."

"Yeah, then it became a barber shop. But the bar bought it and expanded so now they actually have two addresses, one for each room. There's a pool table in where the barber was. I think you'll like it."

Tinman groaned. "A lot of bars have a pool table."

"But this one is pretty decent. Can't remember the brand. You'll recognize it."

"So you picked this place because it has a pool table. I thought we were having a meeting."

"They have other tables too."

"How nice."

Peach turned left at Sutro and said, "It's actually really cozy. It's been my favorite haunt since I got back into town. All the people there are my brothers."

"I didn't know we had so many siblings."

"Not brothers like you! But in some ways it's the same."

Tinman was wearying of the conversation. Unfortunately, Peach continued. "And it's not a dump. It's a dive. There's a difference. This place is always really clean. And you know what, they have this front door with a ship's porthole mounted in it. They say it's from a Thai merchant ship."

Despite himself, Tinman was curious. "You're joking."

"Who would joke about something like that? Remember as kids, maybe eleven or so, there was that story in the paper about a Thai sailor who fell off a boat somewhere in the Pacific Ocean? He was out there for hours until a sea turtle popped up and gave him a lift. Rode him miles through this heavy fog, just the two of them, until a ship saw them and rescued the guy. I remember thinking how nice that was of the turtle. You know, he didn't have to stop for the guy. Turtles don't owe nothing to nobody."

Tinman felt there was no need for a rejoinder. Peach continued. "Wouldn't it be something if the porthole in the bar was from the same Thai ship this guy fell off? Maybe it was broken and he was just taking a peek outside, seeing how the ocean was doing, and it popped open and out he went!"

"The guy was Korean," said Tinman, suddenly remembering the article.

"You're lying!"

"Why would anyone do that?"

Peach thought about it, realized no one would lie about another guy's nationality, and spent the next few minutes getting over his disappointment that the porthole could not have been the one the guy fell out of.

"What's this guy's name?" asked Tinman.

"How should I know? I thought he was Thai," said Peach.

"No! Your old cellmate!"

"Oh. Well his real name is German, I think, but now you got me second-guessing myself. Could be Polish. Definitely not Thai, though, or Korean."

"Just give me his name!"

"I can't. Too hard to pronounce. And spell. Except for someone like you. People just call him Shady."

"A name that inspires trust."

"Right! You'll love him. So, anyway, when we were setting up the meet, I mentioned this place, and he knew of it. I told you he did some jobs around here way back when."

"This joint has been here that long?"

"Since the early 60's."

Peach hung a right on Kietzke. Across the street, sandwiched between a gigantic Dodge dealership and an Arco gas station/Mega-convenience store, sat the bar. An oasis threatened by an ever-encroaching desert of capitalism.

The building was painted brick, the color falling somewhere between pumpkin and atomic tangerine. The wall bordering the street was curved. A rustic, wooden door with a brass porthole sat at one end of the arc. On the roof was a classic, cocktail lounge style sign. Math nerds would say the shape was an irregular hexagon, but to most it looked like a squared-off pineapple with the top sliced off. Inside read, FLOYD'S FIRESIDE, with Floyd stacked on top of Fireside. The 'Y' in Floyd's was in the shape of a martini glass complete with olive. Perched on top of the sign was another giant martini glass, this time in neon.

Tinman immediately warmed to the place. He loved the old seedy Reno of yore and wished it had never succumbed to the maddening charge of so-called change for the better. On the side of the long, narrow building was a teensy parking lot, besieged by giant, new Dodge vehicles, staring greedily at the few empty parking places. The dealership had long wanted the land the bar sat on, but the place had stubbornly thrown back all forays.

Peach pulled into the lot and they hopped out. Tinman started for the front door, but Peach explained it was only used for certain ceremonies. Then he stuttered, and said, occasions. Tinman watched, waiting for more Freudian slips, or even a coherent explanation (who has ceremonies in a dive bar?) but Peach grinned and stepped in through the side door.

Inside, Tinman found himself at the end of a long bar stretching off to the left. Across from it was a fireplace with protective glass front and a decorative grill. Over it, hung a custom-made velvet painting depicting the bar's bar, with caricatures of six intoxicated patrons, and an equally intoxicated bartender.

To the left was a brick wall, part of it poorly mended with an odd alignment of bricks. An adjoining wall was covered in old wallpaper that was obviously original to the place. The repeating pattern depicted a bare breasted woman floating in the clouds. Her identical twins floated here and there, spattering the wall with cream-colored, D-cup breasts.

In front of the fireplace, were four small tables, currently empty. Apparently, no one had anything worth chatting about. Across from the front door was an ATM machine and juke box. A neon sign with the letters ECV hung near the television set.

Staring at a soap opera were two regulars. Both turned and looked when Peach and Tinman stepped in.

"Hey Brother Peach," said the first.

"Hey Brother Ernie."

"Long time, Brother Peach," said the second.

"Too long, Brother Will."

The bartender appeared. "Brother Peach! Good to see you."

"Feeling is mutual, Brother Stan."

Tinman feeling like the bastard child at a family reunion, was about to say so when he saw the regulars staring at him and mumbling. Will elbowed Ernie who placed his thumbs to his ears and waggled his fingers. Tinman raised his eyebrows, not sure if this was an insult, or if the bartender should flag the two guys.

Peach jumped to the rescue. "No brothers! He isn't one of—uh—Meet my real brother! Name's Tinman."

Ernie stuck out his hand, "Any real brother of Brother Peach is a brother of ours, almost."

Tinman shook, then moved on to Will, and finally Stan. He was starting to believe this was a practical joke set up by Peach at his expense. It was all too weird. He decided to see if he could uncover the ruse.

He gestured at the porthole and said, "Where did that come from?"

Stan said, "From a Thai merchant ship, same as this," and he pointed at a brass bell perched behind the bar.

Hmm, thought Tinman. If it was a ruse, they were well-rehearsed, he had to give them that.

"So, Stan. We're having a little meeting with some pals," said Peach. "Mind if we pull a couple of tables together?"

Stan waved his hand good-naturedly and went back to polishing glasses. Peach arranged a couple of tables in the corner with the amazing floating boobs as background, and said, "Let me show you the pool room."

On the way, Tinman noticed the carpet pattern was neon colored planets and stars, like a psychedelic solar system. It reminded him of the horrifying moment in the planetarium some months ago when he and Peach were being chased by a maniacal security guard while attempting to steal back the blasted baskets. It gave him a shiver and he decided not to look down anymore, at least while he was in the bar.

In the backroom stood a 4x8 pool table. A sign demanded there be no attempts at massé or jump shots. Tinman grinned, that was meant for people who didn't know how to do those difficult shots, and ended up tearing the cloth. To him, they were just another necessity in his arsenal.

The table was a Global. A respected brand, founded by a Scandinavian couple in the 60's. This particular model was a solid specimen by all accounts. Even the cloth was in good shape. It was properly placed in the room so no need for a midget cue. The levelness was true. Decent lighting. All shockers to Tinman.

Despite the carpet, the mysterious brotherhood, and the strange regulars who made funny hand gestures, he was beginning to like the place. He was not a bar person, but made a note to return and try out the table.

They ordered two draft beers and retreated to their tables. Tinman, who was sitting directly in front of the mended part of the brick wall, asked, "What's with the wall?"

"That's where a car ran through it, a few years back. Ran right off Kietzke, across the parking lot and pow. Good thing the place was closed, huh?"

Tinman lifted his chair and moved it three feet to his right. He wasn't superstitious but sometimes lightning does strike twice. Once he was settled into his new spot, he said, "Why do we need two tables?"

"I invited some other people," said Peach. "Shady said he was looking to put together a string. I told him I could drum up a few more bodies besides me. Here we go now."

Bones and Catfish turned the corner. Peach called out for two more beers.

"I should have dressed up," said Catfish, examining his surroundings.

"Maybe worn a tie," Bones agreed.

"It's not so bad once you get used to it," said Tinman. "Just don't look down."

They did. Bones said, "Kind of makes you feel like God looking down at his creation."

"If God created that, he must have been on mushrooms," said Catfish.

"That would explain a lot," said Tinman, who had always felt a little disdain for whoever, or whatever, dreamed up a world where nothing made sense, and then forced little ants like himself to traverse the madness.

Peach returned with the beers and settled into his seat. The four shared a sip and pondered the mystical taste of mass-manufactured beer.

"This guy of yours," said Catfish, "you personally vouch for him?"

Tinman noticed Catfish was wearing one of his fake mustaches. It was his trademark, and where he got his moniker, for always wearing a disguise while working a con, the whiz or a heist. Tinman realized it was for protection should Shady turn out not to be on the up and up.

Peach said, "Of course! I shared a 9x12 with him for three years. Not much a guy can hide under those circumstances."

Catfish and Bones nodded, temporarily giving Peach the benefit of the doubt, yet fully aware there was a helluva lot someone could hide from another no matter what the circumstances. Just look at husbands and wives.

"So, we're all here," said Tinman. "Except for your guy."

"Actually, we're still missing one more," said Peach.

"Christ, you didn't invite the kid, did you?" asked Tinman.

Peach didn't need to answer because Dez appeared, and a hush fell over the crowd. She was tall, with natural, ginger red hair, green eyes and her original gleaming teeth. Even as a septuagenarian, her figure was the sort that would drive most happily married men to infidelity. There was something about her, though, that spoke of ruthlessness. It took a strong man indeed to stare her down when she was preparing to strike.

"Why in the hell did you tell me to get all dolled up?!" asked Dez, looking around the place. "I could have stayed in my bathrobe."

Peach pulled out a chair. "I just wanted my friend to see you in all your glory."

Flattery got you everywhere with Dez, especially when it came from Peach's mouth. As is often the case, the wayward child is the most beloved and this was true with Peach. He was the favorite. Tinman was too absorbed in pool to care much, but every once in a while, he had to bite his lip when the two fawned over each other.

Dez did a full turn showing off her floral print, belted dress with mock neck, from Nordstrom. Her hair was swept to one side and held in place by a crystal hair comb. Diamond stud earrings completed the presentation.

The men at the table all politely applauded. Ernie and Will's mouths were filled with beer so they pounded their mugs on the bar instead. Dez acknowledged it all gracefully, like any good diva.

"I have to pee like a racehorse," she said, dropping all pretense. "Where's the can?"

Peach pointed the way. "Around the corner there."

"It better be clean," she said to Stan on her way past the bar.

"Cleanest dive in Reno," said Stan, admiring her tush.

"What a woman," Catfish murmured. He had always had a thing for Dez and vice-versa. The problem was neither of them had the selflessness to endure a real love affair. As a solution, they tacitly agreed to conduct a near fifty-year fantasy affair, replete with flirtation, innuendo, and, for titillation, the occasional brushing of private body parts. For two hustlers, it was a match made in heaven. No guilt, obligations, restrictions or any of the other pesky drawbacks that come from being in love.

The others all privately agreed with Catfish. But for different reasons. At some point in each of their lives, Dez had come to the rescue, saving them from catastrophe. For the twins, it had come shortly after they were born.

As family legend has it, a young, unwed barmaid gave birth to them on top of a pool table in the now defunct Colony Club which sat next to Harold's Club. Bones and Catfish happened to be in the wrong pool hall at the wrong time, and assisted in the delivery. The mother was close friends with Dez who was then a dealer at Harold's. When the mother promptly skipped town shortly after the birth, Dez felt obligated to take over the raising of the orphans.

She would not reveal the identity of the mother, explaining it would serve no purpose tracking down a lady who had turned her back on them. The logic made complete sense to the boys and they never thought of her again. Their surname, Harrigan, was concocted by Dez and the sham doctor who provided the birth certificates.

Dez never professed to be a good mother, and she wasn't. She kept a roof over their heads, barely, and provided foodstuff that Tinman cooked. She only worked as a dealer when she really needed the money. Her chosen career was in poker. As she struggled to perfect her play in all-night games, the boys were given carte blanche. Enrolling them in school was too much paperwork, so she took it upon herself to teach them street sense. She called it home-schooling, the law considered it contributing to the delinquency of minors, and truancy.

Whether they realized it or not, their life growing up was difficult. When the cards were cold, she packed them up and moved a block or two to another seedy motel. When she was on a roll, they might not see her for a week. The brothers never thought of their life as bad or out of the ordinary. They knew nothing else, and took it as a matter of course this was the way a family lived.

There's no denying Dez was partly responsible for the way they turned out, but neither resented it. They both loved her and were grateful to her for raising them. By the time they were teenagers, Dez was a "DP" or dangerous player, and began to make a very decent living. Now in her seventies, she was at the top of her game and almost unbeatable.

"Yeah, she's quite a woman," said Tinman, breaking the reverie. "But why in the hell did you invite her? You think she's going to be part of this string?"

"Course not," said Peach. "It's just they're around the same age and I thought it might be nice. You know. They can swap old war stories about the good old days."

"That's what Bones and I are here for!" said Catfish brusquely.

"I'm just trying to add a little spice to her life," said Peach.

"What are we, milquetoast?" asked Bones.

"Touchy, touchy. I'm not stepping on your toes, guys. It's just Shady's been inside so long, I thought he could use a little reminder about what the opposite sex looks like."

Peach looked around for a response and saw all of them staring at something behind. He turned, and there was Shady, hovering at the edge of the corner, his steely, grey eyes probing the foreign landscape. He was wearing worn, dark dress slacks, and an equally worn, single-breasted suit coat over a pale, button-down shirt. The collar of the jacket was turned up. From fifty paces a cop would recognize him as a no-goodnik.

"Is it good to see you!" shouted Peach, jumping up and escorting him to the table. "Everybody! This is the guy."

Catfish and Bones studied Shady intently, like they knew him, or knew his kind and what it meant. They nodded slightly. Shady reciprocated, and his eyes fell on Tinman.

"Is this it?" asked Shady.

"Well, sure, you said you needed four guys," said Peach.

"The two old slugs," said Shady. "Do they come with their own walkers?"

Catfish slowly rose. "We can borrow yours." Bones rose up next to him.

"Guys. Let's not start this way," said Peach. "Shady you want a beer? Sure you do. Oh, nearly forgot. There's someone else I want you to meet. Not for the string, you know, just someone I thought you'd get a kick out of. Here she is now!"

Dez swirled into the scene. Shady turned. They both froze.

"Dizzy," said Shady, his whole demeanor changing. The lines in his angular face softening. Eyes that had never shown any emotion moistened. "It's been a long time."

"Too long," said Dez, slinking toward him.

"You mean that?" asked Shady.

"Oh yeah. I've been waiting a long time to do this."

Shady never saw it coming. The fist, shoulder height, caught him just below his left cheek. His head snapped back, he lost his balance, toppled over the tables, and slammed into the brick wall, right where the car had plowed through. One of the bricks slid out and landed on the carpet, square on top of Saturn.

Ernie said, "Childhood sweethearts?"

Will concurred. "Probably stood her up at the junior prom."

NINE

"HOW DID YOU FIND OUT ABOUT HIM?!" Dez was bearing down on Peach.

"Huh?"

She spun to Tinman. "Did you have anything to do with this?"

Tinman sputtered, still trying to wrap his brain around the whole "Dizzy" thing. She snapped her head to Bones and Catfish who held up their hands, palms out, surrendering before any shots were fired.

Without knowing the lay of the land, no one was willing to help Shady up, so he was slowly helping himself up.

"I want to know how this guy got here!"

"His name's Shady," said Peach.

"I gave him that name! How do you know him?"

"He's my old cellmate. But how did you—"

"You were in prison?!"

"Didn't I tell you? Must have slipped my mind."

Her eyes widened as the truth hit hard. "That means you shared a cell with your own father!"

"My huh?"

"What?!" croaked Shady, slumping back to the ground.

Silence. Ernie and Will turned off their soap, preferring the real-life drama.

Dez' face slowly turned the color of her hair as she realized after all these years, carefully nurturing the lie, she'd managed to blow her own cover.

"So that's the guy," said Catfish. "Not what I imagined."

"Yeah, I thought he'd be, I don't know, special," said Bones.

Tinman always thought the tale of their birth was like a coloring book with some of the sections conveniently left uncolored. Now, as he watched the cartoon unfold, everything was suddenly in bright technicolor. He looked to his brother who for the first time in his memory was completely at sea. He grabbed his shoulders.

"My huh?" murmured Peach.

"You okay?"

Peach nodded, but Tinman knew he was not. He spun to Dez. "Out with it, old lady. All of it."

She backed away.

"It's high time," said Bones.

"I'll say," said Catfish.

Tinman looked to them, his eyes sparking. "I'll deal with you guys later."

"Hey, what could we do? She swore us to secrecy," said Catfish, Bones bobbing his head.

"We'll discuss this later." Bones and Catfish nodded emphatically. People tended to do that when Tinman has that certain look.

Back to Dez. "The truth. And if you lie, even a fib, you'll regret it."

"What do you want me to say?!" she squealed. "That creep is your father. At least I'm pretty sure."

"Pretty sure?"

"Well, around the same time I, er, knew him, I also, um, knew this craps dealer."

Shady hoisted himself up. "You were sleeping with another bum? Same time as me?"

"Shut up," said Tinman. He shoved him and he dropped into a chair. The stare-down ended with Shady giving first. He knew the time wasn't right, but, son or no, payback was due.

Tinman went back at Dez. "So you're not sure?"

"Ninety some percent. As you kids started getting older I started seeing sides of him in you. Same thieves' blood. That's when I decided it must have been him."

"Now I know why I am the way I am," said Peach, emerging from the fog, "What a relief!" He smiled at Tinman, then saw he was not feeling the same relief, and the smile vanished.

Tinman continued. "But you are sure you lied to us for fifty some years saying you weren't our mother."

Dez looked to Bones and Catfish for help, but they were equally as stony. "I didn't want to be responsible for how you turned out, okay!" she squeaked.

Ernie and Will nodded at each other. Perfect sense.

"Wow, I was right all along," said Peach. "Calling her mom and all."

"Yeah, brother, you were right."

"But the father thing's a little weird, no? I mean I spent three years in a cell with my dad and never knew it. Is that coincidence or irony?"

"It's bullshit," said Tinman.

"I agree," said Shady. "You should've told them Dizzy."

"Another word out of you and I'll bury my high heel up your nostril," said Dez. "How did he get here anyway?"

"He just got out," said Peach lowering his voice. "He was looking to put a string together. He found my number and I mentioned this bar for a meet, and he said he knew all about it. So that's why he's here. Simple as that."

Her eyes smoldered. She snapped her fingers to get Stan's attention. "Bartender. When was this place opened?"

"Early 60's," said Stan, busy wiping the bar.

She turned to Shady who had little droplets of sweat forming under his nose. "Knew all about this place, huh? You walked out on me in '57. You came back to Reno and didn't look me up? Didn't you?"

"Urrm."

"I was practically starving trying to raise your boys and you didn't try and find me?!"

"How was I to know the punks existed?"

"That's not the point! I was going to be your moll! You said I was different than the other gals. Special."

"You are, Dizzy! You've never left my mind, all these years, not for a minute. I swear."

Their eyes locked. Tinman was amazed to see Dez soften. He couldn't see the attraction. But there's no accounting for taste, especially with women.

Peach said, "You actually jilted my mother?"

"Sorry kid. I didn't know."

"Didn't know what? That she's the hottest thing on two legs?"

"Why thank you Peach," said Dez.

"You're welcome, mom. By the way, sorry I didn't get you anything for Mother's Day."

Her bottom lip quivered. "You didn't know."

"No. I didn't. Your loss. In fact you missed out on a lot," said Peach, and looked to Tinman. "Let's get the hell out of here." He started for the door with Tinman right behind. "Brother Stan, I'll take care of any damages."

"Don't sweat it," said Stan.

"Peach, wait!" called Shady.

"Get back here, this instant!" demanded Dez, but they were gone. She looked at Bones and Catfish. "What am I supposed to do now?"

"Ask your boyfriend," said Catfish as he headed for the door. Bones followed, deftly picking Shady's wallet as he passed.

Dez suddenly felt alone, for the first time in a very long time.

"Good looking boys we made there," said Shady. "Must have got that from you."

Dez nodded sadly. "And smart. Must have got that from you."

"The one, though, Tinman is it? He's got an attitude."

Dez squawked harshly. "He's the one that reminds me most of you. When he gets that look. Like you're expendable."

Shady closed in. "I always loved when you used big words, remember?" She half-turned away. "Look, I was a fool, what more do you want?"

"For you to get out of Reno, and not come back."

He knew she didn't mean it. The tone was all wrong. He needed her on his side if he was going to get Peach's help. The plan was everything. Despite all the drama, nothing important had changed.

He started sliding his hands up and down her long sides. She twitched and giggled as his fingers ran dangerously close to private areas. It was the same electricity she'd felt so many years ago. The juice had been turned back on.

"You got a place?" asked Shady. She shrugged. "Maybe we get a bottle, have a few laughs, catch up." She nodded. He put a hand around her waist and led her to the door.

As they disappeared, Ernie said, "I win. What did I tell you? True love always prevails." He held out a hand and Will slapped five dollars in it.

"Yeah, only in real life though," said Will, and he turned the TV on to catch the end of their soap.

Ernie scratched his jaw and said, "You know, that scene was pretty good. We should jot it all down. Send it in to these TV people. They could make an episode of it."

"Nah," said Will. "Too real. Audience would never believe it."

Ernie pondered this profundity, took a sip of beer and burped.

TEN

"DO YOU STILL THINK WE WERE BORN ON A POOL TABLE?" asked Peach.

"Who knows," said Tinman.

"I hope so. I always liked that part of the story. Especially the bit where supposedly I came out right after you and shoved your head into the three ball which sunk in the corner pocket and that's where your name Trey came from. Is that your favorite part?"

"Hardly."

"I wonder if that's true?"

"It's true," said Catfish, who had let himself and Bones into the Clubhouse, and were peaking around the corner at the pool table where Tinman and Peach were sequestered.

"We still members here?" asked Bones.

"Of course!" said Peach. "Why not?"

"Because they've been lying to us for as long as Dez!" Tinman roared.

"Really?" Then he thought about it. "I guess that's true. So what's up with that, guys?"

"It was necessary," said Catfish. "She was scared, you know. She was going to abandon you two. We just couldn't have that," said Catfish. He had grown up as an orphan on the streets of Chicago and the sincerity of his plea came from personal experience. "You'd have ended up as wards of the state. Think what that would have been like! Growing up in foster homes, maybe worse. They might've split you up."

"So, we made a suggestion," said Bones.

"You two came up with the idea," stated Tinman flatly.

"We suggested it, yeah," said Catfish. "It made her more comfortable thinking you weren't really hers. After a while, I think she came to believe it."

"And you decided it really didn't matter to us, is that it?" barked Tinman.

"Would it have made a difference?" said Bones. "You both turned out alright. We made sure of that."

Tinman was so furious he could find nothing to say. Peach's face was scrunched up, like he'd eaten a sour apple.

Bones laid a hand on each of their shoulders. "Fact is, we started taking to the idea of being your uncles. With Dez not wanting the responsibility, we were free to raise you how we wanted. We were selfish. I'm truly sorry for that."

Catfish piped in. "We had no right. Just neither of us ever had any kids."

Peach laid a hand on top of Bones'. "Way I see it, you did us a favor. You saved us from the state, and in a way, from Dez. What do you think, Tinman?"

Tinman was in no mood to forgive anybody, but his logical mind told him it was not these two who deserved his wrath. He shrugged, and everyone breathed a little easier.

Peach broke the uncomfortable silence. "I'm hungry. All this drama really drains a guy. Anybody else hungry?"

Grunts all around. Peach turned to Tinman and said, "Maybe we could whip something up for lunch."

"We?"

"Actually, you. Feel like cooking?"

Tinman headed for the door. Everyone followed, traipsing outside and up the stairs to his little apartment.

Tinman examined the contents of his refrigerator. He was listless and his brain was on hold. "I haven't had time to do any shopping since Sunday's score."

"We're not picky, right guys?" asked Peach. Bones and Catfish readily agreed.

Tinman surveyed the fridge again, and started idly tossing things on the counter. To everyone's delight they realized he was fixing his famous grilled sandwich. He had always been the cook of the family, and this was an all-time favorite.

It consisted of two slices of nine grain bread, each coated lightly on one side with olive oil. Swiss cheese went in first, topped with grilled onions. Slices of fresh tomato were next, followed by one thin slice of grilled ham. Each sandwich then received an over easy egg, cooked so that only a little wet yoke was left. Another slice of Swiss cheese topped it off. It was sealed by the second piece of bread and lightly grilled to melt the cheese.

As Tinman cooked, alone in his own thoughts, Peach began his interrogation of Bones and Catfish. "So the part about Tinman sinking the three ball is really true?"

"It's all basically true," said Bones. "Just replace Dez with the mystery mother and there it is."

"Did you know her before it went down?" asked Peach.

"Nah," said Catfish. "We had just blown into town for the first time. Reno was one of the last in the country still working the big con. There were still two big rooms in operation, using the old Rag stock swindle. We hooked up with both mobs and signed on as ropers. We weren't having too much luck until Bones spotted a juicy mark, an out-of-state businessman at a convention. He was taking a break in the pool hall so we followed him in. It was right next to Harold's so a lot of gamblers cooled down in there. Catch their breath before losing the rest of their money. We weren't there more than ten minutes watching our mark, when in comes Dez."

"What a mess she was," said Bones, smiling at the memory. "She was so fresh at having babies she hadn't prepared for nothing. Like she thought that big lump was maybe from eating too much pasta. A good dump would take care of it."

"Pure denial. That's for sure," said Catfish.

"Even still, why would she go to a pool hall?" asked Peach.

"Looking for Bill Graham," said Bones. "He and the other guys that ran the town back then had always looked out for her. I guess she thought he'd know what to do."

"Makes sense," said Peach. "She always talked about Graham, and the others, Abelman, McCay. She told us when she ran away from home as a teenager and ended up in Reno they took her under their wing."

Bones gave Catfish a sidelong look. Catfish shrugged and nodded. Bones said, "Since we're clearing the air here, you should know the whole truth. Dez was born in Reno. Her mother was, well—a working girl. At the Stockades."

Tinman froze. Peach spun to him. "Did you know this?" Tinman shook his head.

Bones hurried on. "So anyway, Graham and McCay ran the Stockades. The way Dez tells it is her momma placed her in Graham's arms soon after she was born, then skipped town. So you see, Dez never knew her momma, or her poppa."

Peach thought about this. "Kind of explains her feeling about having us."

"Maybe it does at that," said Bones.

"She never worked that side of the road did she?" asked Tinman, his back to them.

"Hell no! She was the darling of the town. Her benefactors wouldn't have stood for it," said Catfish. "And after you two were born, we kept very close tabs on her. Only thing she ever wanted to do was play cards."

"No surprise there," said Peach, "But anyway, she's looking for Graham, he's not there and then what?"

"Her water broke," said Bones. "Made quite a mess. Everyone, including our mark hightailed it out of there. Just me and my buddy left with the little lady."

"And between the two of us," said Catfish, "Bones was the only one who had ever birthed anything. And that was a goat back in Alabama!"

"Pig."

"Oh right. Still."

"Yeah, still. It was pretty hairy," said Bones. "Once Tinman was out we thought the worst was over, then we see this other head coming on through. Man, Peach, there was no stopping you. Never saw anything in such a rush to get into this godforsaken world. 'Bout knocked your brother clean off the table. Damn good thing he hit that ball."

"True enough!" said Catfish. "But after you were out, Dez went a little nutso. Saying she wasn't cut out to be a mother, too young, no father, yada yada. All good points, but off the mark. You guys were here and that was it. What were we gonna do? Stick you in a box and send you down the Truckee?"

"Didn't turn out so bad for Romulus and Remus," said Tinman, flipping the grilling sandwiches. "Where would Rome be today?"

No one had a clue, so Catfish continued. "So anyway, we talked her off the ledge, and then Graham shows up and he talks to her some more. He likes our little ruse, and he was the one who really convinced her. She didn't know us from Adam, right? But he was close, you could tell. He arranged for the sham doctor to make up the fake certificates. The back story was created. It was easy in those days. And, ta-da, you became orphans. Simple as that."

"Gee, I love family history!" exclaimed Peach.

"What about Shady?" asked Tinman, holding plates of sandwiches like ransom.

"We never laid eyes on the bum before today," said Catfish. "That's on the square."

"And she never mentioned him, or the craps dealer as being the father?"

"We tried to get a name out of her," said Bones, "We were hoping to shake the guy down for some scratch to help her out, but she just wouldn't give."

Tinman sighed and nodded. He handed them each a plate with a sandwich and said, "Let's eat out on the deck."

"Fresh air. Good idea," said Bones. He and Catfish grabbed their plates and went out onto the rooftop deck.

Peach anxiously awaited his plate. Tinman said, "You knew all along, didn't you?"

"What are you talking about?" He waited, but Tinman stared him down. "Okay, yeah, not about Shady, I swear, but about Dez. At least I was pretty sure."

"How'd you find out?"

"One day, when we were around twelve, I almost got arrested for shoplifting at the new mall, Park Lane Center."

"They'd just opened it. You were trying to boost some clothes. Socks, I think."

"Right, my feet were cold. Anyway, I had the store call Catfish, told them he was my uncle. He paid off the security guys so they wouldn't call the cops. When we got back to our motel, Dez was there, but you were at some hall. Catfish had me wait outside and the two had a go-around. At one point, he told her she had a responsibility to her own flesh and blood."

"Did she know you knew?"

"Later, I think she guessed. That's why she'd get so pissed when I called her mom."

"And that's why you kept doing it."

"You got it! Sorry I didn't tell you. I didn't want it to distract you, screw up your game."

"Appreciated."

"What are brothers for?" said Peach with a smile. "And, you know, for parents, they're not exactly what you would call perfect specimens, but it's better than no parents."

"I liked it the way it was. Thanks," said Tinman and handed Peach his plate.

They were both settling down in their respective chairs on the deck when an SUV pulled into the parking lot of the motel. Tek hopped out and bounded up the stairs three at a time. He screeched to a halt in front of the Posse, took one look at the plates and said, "Where's mine?"

Tinman's shoulders drooped. "I'm all out of everything."

Tek shrugged like he wasn't really hungry. "I'll live."

Though he would never admit it, Tinman was a mother hen to his gang. He grabbed a table knife and cut a quarter

126

of his sandwich off. Peach did the same. Bones and Catfish followed suit. When the semblance of a full sandwich was compiled, Tek grabbed it and took his place.

There was no talking as they all devoured their sandwiches, but quite a lot of happy moans and smacking of lips. When finished, they kicked back and watched a train as it slowly picked up speed for its climb over the mountains.

"So, is anyone going to tell me how the meet went?" asked Tek. "What kind of job does this guy have? You think it's going to be a big haul, like you thought?"

"We had to cut the meeting short," said Peach. "Personal business."

Tek wrinkled his forehead and said, "You guys got personal business?" Like it was akin to wearing women's underwear.

"Not until today, we didn't," said Tinman, sharing Tek's appraisal.

"Oh," said Tek, completely in the dark, and quite happy to be there. "Well, I did like the website requested. They want you to send a thank you message to anyone that hooks you up with a lead. So I sent Jingles a little note."

"That was nice of you," said Catfish.

"I try. But the strange thing was it looked like Jingles' account had some kind of block on it. I thought the message went through, but then it kicked back with some response asking for me to verify my account and location."

Peach sat up. "You didn't do that did you?"

"Hell no," said Tek. "In fact I deleted our account. Just didn't seem right. Maybe they're doing site maintenance and they screwed up the binary code. I'll wait a couple of days and check again."

"You did good," said Peach. "If I have to, I'll just give Jingles a call, thank him personally. That was his number we used when I called Shady wasn't it?"

"Yep," said Tek.

Peach nodded and stared into space. A puzzled look in his eyes.

"So are you going to meet up with Shady again?" asked Tek.

"Not sure, little man," said Tinman. "Things didn't go so smoothly at the meeting. We might have seen the last of him."

"Oh, no. We'll be seeing Shady again," said Bones. He flipped Shady's wallet onto the table.

"When the hell did you fork his poke?!" asked Catfish, grinning widely.

"Sorta plunked into my hands on the way out of the bar," said Bones. "Just curious to see who we're dealing with."

"Thank you," said Tinman.

Bones winked. "My pleasure."

Catfish rifled the wallet. "No cash to speak of, but that's normal after being in for so long. But look at this. Your guy's only been out a week and he already has a new name, and plastic." He flipped a driver's license onto the table and a couple of credit cards. Tek, a decent forger in his own right, snatched them up and pored over them.

"He must have got these from Jingles," said Tek. "That's why he went there first. The cards are stolen. Different name than the license. Probably just for temporary use. But, man, this license is top-notch. Where's the birth certificate?"

Catfish turned the wallet inside out. "That's all she wrote."

"That's weird," said Tek. "When you pay the kind of money it takes to get a license like this, you always get a matching birth certificate. This kind of ID is meant to last, not be a use and burn."

Everyone thought about this. Tinman said, "Expensive work, huh?"

"A ton," said Tek.

Tinman locked eyes with Catfish. After a moment of telepathy, Catfish said, "Wonder where a guy just out of stir comes up with so much cabbage?"

A concerned look crept over Bones. He cocked his head to Peach.

"He must have had a stash," said Peach. "He always talked about his stashes, all over the country. Fall dough."

Tek was confused. Peach explained. "It's an old term, for when you get picked up by the law. Also called case money. You always have to have some tucked away to cover the lawyers, and payola if needed. Whatever it takes to stay on the outside."

"I suppose that must be the case," said Bones.

"Yeah," said Tinman. "Let's hope, for good old Jingles' sake."

"What do you mean?" asked Tek.

"Nothing," said Tinman.

Peach frowned and opened his mouth, preparing to press the issue, when Tinman's cellphone beeped. He flipped it open and stared at the text message on the little screen. "It's Dez. Says, HELP, COME QUICK."

"Help?" said Bones. "You sure that's from the Deziree Hartman I know?"

"Sure doesn't sound like her," said Catfish. "What could make her stoop so low?"

Everyone pondered this mystery. Peach said, "What happened after we left the bar?"

"Nothing. We left just after you all," said Bones.

"And Dez was still there with Shady?" asked Peach.

"Sure, but I don't think they were exactly there together," said Catfish.

They all wondered about this a while longer. Tinman dialed Dez' number. He waited while everyone waited with him. "No answer."

"Maybe she doesn't need help anymore," said Bones.

Everyone but Tek thought that was a very good assumption. Self-satisfied smiles all around. What a lovely day it was. The minutes ticked by.

Tek couldn't stand it any longer. "What if you're wrong and she does need help? We need to go find out!"

The notion came as a surprise. Bones and Catfish looked at Tinman who looked at Peach. Then they all swapped looks.

"You think we really have to?" asked Tinman.

"The question involves ethics which is not my strong suit," said Catfish, sagely.

Nods all around. Ethics not being anyone's strong suit.

"Maybe she just slipped in the bathtub," said Bones. "That's quite common among old people. Or so I'm told."

There was a consensus that indeed this was a common mishap among older people.

"Why would she have her phone in the bathtub?" asked Tek.

Nobody had a good solution for that, so they sat and thought about it for a while.

"Damn," said Peach. "I hate mysteries."

This was mutually agreed upon, and they took a couple of minutes to discuss what a drag mysteries were on the brain, and how they prevented one from thinking about more important things. This segued into a chat about magic, and it was revealed that almost everyone at the table hated magic tricks about as much as mysteries.

"It's just unfair. The magician knows the trick behind the trick and they refuse to pass it on," said Catfish. "It's like some superiority trip, lording over everyone, knowing they're the only ones in the know. And people pay good money to see this junk. Like they enjoy being the patsies."

"Enough!" cried Tek. "I'm going to help this lady out! With or without you guys."

"What do you owe her?" asked Tinman.

"She was a good sport at the Christmas party when I took her for $50 on that bet where I said I could open her door without using a key."

"That's true," said Peach. "Dez never welches on a bet."

"That is a good human quality," said Bones.

Tek was halfway down the stairs when he yelled, "Are you coming or not?" The guys sighed, and heaved their contented bellies up from their chairs.

"Shotgun," said Catfish.

"Damn," said Bones.

When they reached the bottom of the stairs, Peach veered off. "I'll follow in my car. I gotta make a call."

Everyone grunted and climbed into Tek's SUV. As it pulled out, Peach walked behind the motel, where his car was parked next to Tinman's illegally registered Datsun 280Z. He continued on until he was near the train tracks, the slow-moving train still building up steam. He took out his phone and dialed Jingles' number.

After a few rings, the call was answered, but there was no voice. Peach waited. Then he cupped a hand over his mouth and said, "Is this Jingles?"

A muffled voice said, "Yeah, who's this?"

Peach said, "It's Shady."

There was a sharp intake of air, then a long pause. The voice was more intense, as it said, "Where are you?"

Peach hung up and looked at the train sliding by. A long line of open hopper cars approached, their sides covered in bright graffiti. He waited until they were directly in front, then he chucked his phone into the back of one. He was deep in thought as he found his way back to his car.

ELEVEN

THE IVORY TOWER WHERE DEZ LIVED was a far cry from the seedy motels she and the boys used to live in. Perched right on the river between the Virginia and Sierra Street bridges, the gleaming white high-rise was L-shaped, with the large patios and floor-to-ceiling windows of the luxurious condominiums overlooking a central swimming pool, mounted on the roof of the ground level clubhouse. This was The Palladio.

Peach arrived shortly after the others. The doorman knew them and let them in without a call from Dez. Peach, as always, tipped him heavily for breaking the rules.

She was on the top floor, corner unit, one of the largest in the building. She worked from home, holding illegal, high-stakes poker games six nights a week. Sunday was reserved for counting her booty. In her golden years, her game had reached new heights, and she could easily afford her posh digs.

The Posse converged in front of her door. Peach used a rake pick to open the lock which took about three seconds. The doorman was key to security here, so the developers had skimped on the interior locks. Before he opened the door, he said, "If she doesn't need help anymore, I'd prefer to make this quick."

All agreed, and they stepped in. The color scheme was mostly tasteful greens and cream. A Chesterfield Grand Sofa, upholstered in emerald velvet, dominated the living room. A beautiful oak poker table sat prominently in a corner. One wall was all windows, with sliding glass doors leading out to a huge balcony. Strewn here and there were various articles of clothing.

Dez was on the balcony, dressed in an Oriental silk robe decorated with dragons, looking out at south Reno and the mountains beyond. Shady, sporting only his worn boxers, stood behind with hands on her shoulders.

"Well knock me over with a feather," drawled Bones.

"Please tell me my eyes are lying," said Catfish.

"Maybe that's why she needs help! That guy's going to push her off!" said Tek. Nobody moved, everyone but him wondering what that would be like. "Who is that guy anyway?"

"Shady," said Peach.

"What's he doing here?"

Before Peach could explain, they all watched as Dez slowly turned into Shady's arms. The two faces met, kissing like a couple of newlyweds.

"I feel sick," said Tinman.

"Get in line," said Catfish.

Dez broke the kiss, her eyes straying over Shady's shoulders. She whispered something in his ear, and he plopped down in a lounge chair and picked up his highball. She lashed the belt of her robe, straightened her hair and slid open the patio doors.

"Bones, Shady wants his wallet back."

"Does he now?" said Bones.

Dez closed the patio doors, but her back remained pressed against them, like the plush carpet concealed mini-landmines. "Please."

The effect on the guys was as if she had sprouted wings. This was a word she never uttered. Bones pulled out the wallet and walked to her. "You okay?"

"Never better," said Dez, but he caught something he'd rarely seen. The last time was when he used his long, delicate fingers to ease Tinman and Peach out of her. It was buried deep in her iris. Just a flicker. Fear. She whipped open the patio doors.

"I told you it would work!" she cried to the back of Shady's head. "You said they wouldn't come! But I knew. Pissed off or not, they'd still come to my rescue."

Shady lifted a palm to the sky. She placed the wallet in it. His fingers clamped down hard, squeezing her hand and the wallet tightly together. She yanked away and turned back to the Posse with a nervous grin. "Anybody want a drink?"

"You know better than to cry wolf when it ain't so," said Bones.

Tinman started for the door with the others quickly following. Dez dashed inside, flanked them, and ended up in front, splayed out like Da Vinci's Vitruvian Man in drag.

"You can't go!"

"And why is that?" asked Tinman.

"He needs your help! Isn't that enough? After all, he's your father."

Tek cried, "Wait a minute! Shady's your father?"

"You said you weren't sure about that," said Tinman.

Dez bit her bottom lip, then recovered. "Do it for me then. For your mother."

Tek said, "And she's your mother?! Aw, man, you people are hurting my head."

"I know how you feel kid," said Catfish.

"Get out of the way, Dez," said Tinman.

She stepped aside. As he reached for the handle, she grabbed his wrist. "Then do it for yourselves. I know what you and Peach are up to. Working for dribs and drabs. He says this is a big score. It could set all of you. Bones and Catfish could retire."

"And do what? I like picking pokes," said Bones.

"Me too," said Catfish.

She stamped a foot, then launched one last desperate volley over the broadside. "You could get that pool hall you always wanted, Tinman."

Tinman paused. Dez always knew how to hit the soft spot.

"You knew about that, huh?"

"I am your mother!" Tinman's mouth parted in awe of her chutzpah. "Well, I did raise you!" Even Peach had to snicker at this one. "Hey! I was around a little." Catfish and Bones met her look with bemused smiles. "FINE! I picked up on it. Okay?"

Peach jumped to the rescue. "Did he tell you what the job was?"

"No," she said, showing her irritation. "But he's a pro. If he says it's a big job, it is."

"She's got a point there, brother. Shady doesn't mess with little stuff."

Dez, feeling Tinman soften, piped in. "It could be a good thing, the whole family working together. Like a family should."

"Can it with the family business!" said Tinman.

"Hey, hey, don't talk to your mother that way," said Shady, who had drifted inside and was now standing behind the Posse. Tinman turned to face him with a mixture of incredulity and fury.

"Shady, I asked you to let me handle this," said Dez.

"Did I ever listen to you before? Go get ready. You got a game tonight."

"The hell with that! I want in on this!"

"Go—get—dressed," he repeated, his voice barely a whisper.

To everyone's amazement, she obeyed. They'd never seen her take orders from anyone, and Tinman grudgingly admired Shady's control over her. When she'd disappeared, Shady beckoned everyone in, like the place was his.

Nobody moved. He sat on the arm of the sofa, "Look, fellas. We got off on the wrong foot. But, hey, none of us knew we'd be walking into the middle of a soap opera. Reminded me of that show we used to watch in the pen. Remember, Peach? Two o'clock sharp." His chuckle sounded like a clogged toilet gasping for air.

"Sure do," said Peach, stepping closer. "And, I, for one, am glad to see you."

"Likewise," said Shady. "Even if you are my stinking flesh and blood." He laughed again, the gurgle turning into a choking fit. Peach slapped him on the back and he caught his breath. "Ah, just too much smoking. Nothing much else to do in stir."

"Speaking of which, I figured you still had at least a five-spot to go."

"Decarceration. Prisons are so full they're getting rid of as many older prisoners as possible. Costs an arm and leg to keep the old fogies. So, they look for guys they figure are no longer a threat to the straights and their precious little kiddies and wives, and they boot them to the wind." His chest heaved up and down with silent laughter. "I think maybe the system made a mistake with me! Whaddya say?"

Peach smiled but didn't laugh. "No probation or supervision, huh?"

"Nope. Just swung open the gates and shoved me out."

"That's some story."

Shady's eyes narrowed, but he fought back the suspicions, and smiled. "Yeah."

The room echoed with silence. Tinman was prepared to leave, but the thought of a big score won out. "What's the caper?"

Shady approached. "Got things to talk about first. Want to make sure you're the right guys. And I don't talk in front of kids. So come on, punk, whoever you are, beat it."

"Go to hell old man," said Tek.

Shady's temper flared and he closed in quick and hard, cocking one arm for a backhand slap. Tek straightened up, defiantly sticking his chin out to receive the blow.

Tinman snatched Shady's wrist and said, very quietly, "You touch him, you swallow teeth. Then I twist that chicken neck of yours until you choke on them. Understood."

Their steely, gray eyes met. A flicker of recognition from both, like they were staring into a mirror.

"Tinman's right. The kid's with us, dad," said Peach, lightly laying his hand on Shady's shoulder.

Neither approved of his use of the word dad. But his hopeful smile diffused the moment, and Tinman and Shady separated.

"He's a good kid," continued Peach. "He's got our blood. I vouch for him."

"And I'm the goddamned one who hooked you up with Peach you jerk," said Tek. Bones grabbed him by the shoulder and pulled him back into cover.

"That so?" said Shady.

"Yeah, it is. And why can't I get ahold of Jingles anymore? Crookslist says his account has been flagged."

Shady suddenly decided he was thirsty. He headed for the patio where he'd left his drink. Over his shoulder, he said, "No idea, kid. But I'm sure he's out enjoying all that money I paid him for my fake ID."

"Why didn't you get a birth certificate?"

Shady paused on the patio to take a long gulp. The kid was becoming a problem, and his hands were tied. The thought made him clench his glass so tight his fingers turned white. He drained his drink, and walked back inside. "The cost of the driver's license was all the dough I could come up with."

"It's always a package deal with a quality forger."

"I guess Jingles felt like doing me a favor," said Shady, with a crocodile smile.

"Where'd you get the money for the driver's license?" asked Catfish. "Save it up in the pen scrubbing dishes at a quarter an hour?"

"You're a smart guy, aren't you?" said Shady. "Peach'll tell you. I always have a stash here and there. I stopped along the way. Picked up a little scratch to get me through 'til the job goes down."

In the bedroom, Dez suddenly broke into a spirited rendition of "Luck Be A Lady." Shady looked around at the others and said, "Frankie does it better." He smiled and the moment eased. "We need privacy. You got someplace we can go?"

Tek said, "The Clubhouse!"

"What I am dealing with here, Spanky's Gang?"

The humor fell flat. Peach said, "You'll like it dad."

"Please stop doing that," said Tinman.

"Yes, please," said Shady.

"What's wrong with it?"

Shady said, "Nothing. I just, er, need to get used to it."

"Well, how you gonna get used to it, if I don't call you it?"

As if on cue, Shady and Tinman simultaneously let out a long, deep sigh. Their eyes met. Shady said, "Maybe there is a little me in you after all."

"I doubt it," said Tinman. "We've got cars outside. After we talk, then we decide if we want to do this thing with you. Capisci?"

"You the boss, huh?"

"You could say that," said Bones.

Shady saw complete agreement in everyone's faces. "Okay, boss man. Let's go."

He gathered his clothes and dressed. Then they all left.

Dez twirled out of her bedroom, dressed to the nines in a champagne, half-sleeve, Lela Rose taffeta gown from Neiman Marcus.

"Ta-da!"

She held her arms out in pose for a brief second, then they flopped to her sides. "Dammit. Men."

TWELVE

SHADY DEMANDED HE RIDE WITH PEACH, so the others rode in Tek's SUV. Peach couldn't get a word out of Shady until they pulled into the parking lot of the All Inn Motel, and they saw Tinman talking with a short, stout man next to a shopping cart piled high with empty aluminum cans.

"Who's the bum?" asked Shady.

"That's no bum," said Peach. "That's Rudy. He rents out the end unit."

Tinman first met Rudy when he had to leave his nice apartment and move into the abandoned motel, which Dez won in a poker game. Rudy was the general of a small army of can collectors. He ruled the dumpsters of Reno and any collector who wanted to work his turf had to pay a tariff. Tinman had immediately admired his initiative and they worked out an agreeable arrangement, so Rudy would not be homeless.

Peach and Shady walked over. Rudy said, "Hey, Peach!"

"What's shaking?"

"Just paying my dues to your brother here." He continued counting out a jumbled mass of small bills and placing them in Tinman's open palm. "That's May."

"Thanks, Rudy," said Tinman, pocketing the money.

"Au contraire. You're the one keeping me out of the elements."

Shady snorted and the other three looked at him. Rudy shrugged and said, "Let Dez know the game this week has been moved from Saturday to Sunday night."

"I'll tell her," said Tinman. "How she been doing?"

"Holding her own. Her game is sharpening up, having to go up against people who are playing for survival. Ciao for now." He saluted, and pushed his cart to his room.

Tinman turned to Peach. "I have to hit the john, I'll be there in a few." Ignoring Shady, he spun on his heels and marched to the stairs.

Shady ignored him back. "What does that bum have to do with Dizzy?"

"I tell you he's no bum. In fact, he and his gang saved Tinman and me from a homicidal security guard during a heist gone bad end of last year."

"When I ask a specific question, give me a specific answer!"

"Sorry, dad. After Rudy saved us, we invited him to Dez' place for the Christmas party. Naturally a game was going, and he sat in. It was a sight to see, I tell you. He beat the pants off her. After that, they hit it off and he invited her to his game. Told her it would tighten her play. It's held up the road, under the highway. They play for cans."

"Cans?! What in the hell is Dizzy messing around with that trash for?"

"Like Rudy said, these players are more cutthroat than any at her regular games. They live off the money they get recycling cans, so they don't give them up easy. She says since she's been playing with them, her game has improved twenty-five percent."

"Yeah, well, that's gonna stop. No broad of mine is going to associate with lowlifes."

This struck Peach as hysterical. He was still laughing when he led Shady into the Clubhouse. The office section of the motel was now arranged like a lounge/bar using tables from the motel rooms. A few liquor bottles and a cooler of beer sat on the counter. A parted, red velour curtain hung in the entrance to the old mini-mart. Behind it sat a beautiful Brunswick pool table, the gift from Peach to Tinman.

Catfish, Bones and Tek sat in a semi-circle at one of the tables, all facing the door.

"What's so funny?" asked Bones.

"Shady says he doesn't want Dez hanging out with any lowlifes," said Peach.

Spontaneously, they all cracked up. Shady's face flushed. Since he left prison he'd been yearning for a gun. He was naked without one, and it was moments like this a piece came in handy. He would get one as soon as the opportunity presented itself.

Peach noticed Shady was not enjoying the joke, and broke off the laughter. "Have a seat, dad. This is the Clubhouse. Comfy, no? Want a drink?"

Shady didn't answer. He was stalking the place, looking for hidden traps. At the pool table, he appraisingly ran his hand over the cloth.

"That's right, you used to play a lot when we were inside," said Peach. "As I recall, you weren't so bad."

"I can handle a cue," said Shady. "Better than anybody here."

"I won't argue that, but my brother's not in the room."

"I heard all about him. Mothers always talk up their kids. Don't mean nothing."

Catfish, Bones and Tek stifled laughs. Tinman strode in.

"There he is now, my son the two-bit pool hustler. If I'd raised you, I'd a broken both your arms before I let you take up such a dirty occupation. At least Peach has a respectable job."

Tek shot to his feet. "Shove it up your ass, you old fart!"

Shady sneered at him. "You following in his footsteps, huh?"

"I'm not good enough," said Tek, spitting out his words. "But he's the best ever."

"We'll have to see about that."

"Rack 'em up," said Tinman.

"Business first," said Shady. He jutted his chin at Catfish. "Dizzy says you used to be a bigtime grifter. Your specialty three card monte? Fleecing pensions off little old ladies? Or was it the Hype? That's always good for a sawbuck."

Bones drained his beer, grabbed the bottle by the neck and flipped it over, sending suds drifting to the ground. Holding it like a weapon, he said, "Well my specialty is not killing people. But I'm a firm believer in broadening one's horizons."

Catfish put a hand on his arm. He looked at Shady with the eyes of a man who had earned respect from heavier gees than him. Two old-timers in a showdown over pecking order. No words needed. Shady flinched and everyone in the room caught it.

"No offense," said Shady. "I known a few big players. They always been straight up."

Catfish sized him up like only an expert confidence man could. His veiled eyes bore into him, reading him like a mark, locating the weakness that exists in every man. His head slowly shook back and forth.

"You're lying Shady. You never knew any class grifter. We don't get our hands dirty."

The slight momentarily revived Shady's bravado. "You think a lot of yourself, don't you? Do you kiss yourself in the mirror every morning? You grifters are all the same, think you got something over on the rest of us. Well, I'm not impressed."

"By the time I was twenty I was roping for Brickyard Jimmy, the Honey Grove Kid, the Indiana Wonder, among others. Hear of them?"

Shady certainly had. The names were legendary. Any criminal of that era knew of them. He flared his nostrils and shrugged like it was no big deal. He immediately regretted it. It was one of the few times in his life he looked stupid, and he knew it.

"So you have," said Catfish. "Oh good. That means you really are in the rackets."

The jab enraged Shady. But as much as he hated it, he knew he couldn't mess with him. In fact, he would have to be careful. He had the grift sense. Knowing what somebody was really up to.

He gave a half-nod to Catfish as an acknowledgement of respect. He turned his sites on Bones, believing he would be easier prey. "And I got a beef with you."

Without answering, Bones got up and headed for the office counter.

"Hey, I'm talking to you!"

"I need another beer." Bones shuffled by a table and his foot caught the base. He half-stumbled into Shady who instinctively grabbed his arm and steadied him.

"What you need is a wheelchair," said Shady. Bones waved a hand in dismissal. Shady continued. "So you're the dip, huh?"

"He's no dip. He's a class cannon," said Catfish.

"Call it what you want. I think it stinks."

Bones cracked his new bottle of beer and glided to his table like a dancer. "Well I am truly sorry you have such a low estimation of my chosen occupation."

"It's as low as it goes. Takes no skill to snatch a wallet when someone's unaware."

"So you mean if you had known I was a cannon, I would not have been able to pick your pocket."

"Exactly. And if you ever try picking my wallet again, I'm gonna smash those long, pretty fingers of yours so you won't be able to hold your own tool to take a leak."

"I'll remember that. Next time." Bones pulled out Shady's wallet and flipped it at him. Shady's hands fumbled, and it fell to the floor. He couldn't hide his amazement, and it gave everyone the giggles. Again, he longed for a gun.

Peach slapped him playfully on the back. "Don't take it personally, dad. Bones just can't control those fingers of his."

"I can see that. And I admit he's pretty slick. But they're both useless to me. A conman and a cannon. What good are they on a heist?"

"You kidding? They've been on jobs with us. They make excellent jiggers, wheelmen, diversions, backup. Look how long they've been in the game. Who better to trust?"

Shady grumbled, and cocked his head at Tek. "And him?"

"He's a computer genius. He's also enlightened me some on these new wireless security systems. These days, you can't do better than having a tech whiz on the team."

"Mebbe you're right. I been in so long. Things have changed. Okay. And you and I are the yeggs. What does he do?" Shady shoved a finger at Tinman.

"He's the blueprinter, the brains."

"A pool hustler!" Shady stomped around the room, hooting and guffawing. Everyone quietly watched. He stopped in front of Catfish. "Get with me on this old-timer! You sure as hell know what it takes to pull off something really big."

Catfish smiled. "I do. Him. Because if he says it's a bad deal, then I, along with the rest of the guys, are out. And you can get yourself another string."

Shady found the same silent answer from the others. His eyes came to rest on Tinman. "I'm talking about a big-time heist here. A once in a lifetime haul. You really think you're capable of doping out a scheme from start to finish, including the getaway? Hey, you listening to me? You look half asleep."

Tinman sighed. "That's what happens when I get bored."

Shady's eyes widened, his narrow lips curled back, baring his teeth. "No son of mine talks to me like that."

"Look old man, until I see a DNA match, I'm still betting on the craps dealer. So knock it off. You got no hold over me."

Shady was not used to not getting his way and his blood pressure was causing his face to flush. He took a minute to get his temper under control. He had to work with this guy or find another string, and everybody he used to work with was in prison or dead. Some of them he put there.

His lips relaxed into the semblance of a grin. There would be time later to teach him a lesson. He hissed, "You're a real smartass. But I like that. You got gnads. Yeah, I think I'm warming to you kid."

"Shucks. My plan backfired."

It took Shady completely by surprise and he practically blew snot from his nose. "What a card! Peach, did you know your brother was so funny?"

"He has his moments."

"Sure he does! If I'd have known about you two, nothing could've kept me away. What they call fatherly instinct."

"Like Papa Bear," said Tinman. "Who, if he's a grizzly, has a nasty tendency to eat his little baby bears."

"Aw geez," said Shady. "Gimme a break."

"No. Now get on with it. What's this big score of a lifetime you think you have."

"Know I have, punk. How many of you ever hear of a guy named LaVere Redfield."

"Tinman and I saw him plenty of times when we were kids running around the casinos while Dez was working," said Peach. "He was the crazy rich guy used to walk around dressed like a pauper but with bags stuffed full of cash and silver coins. Gambled it away like monopoly money."

"Crazy like a fox, Peach," said Catfish. "You know where that guy made his first fortune? He out-conned a great conman. C.C. Julian. In the 20's, he set up an oil scheme in Southern California. The original Ponzi. Made millions. By the 30's the scam fell apart, brought down Hollywood stars, politicians. It was huge. He went on the lam, left the country. The state set up a board of three trustees to manage the few actually producing wells. LaVere was one of them. He was only in his 20's. Made him a rich man. Poor Julian died of an opium overdose in Shanghai. But every conman back then heard about LaVere. The mark that got away."

"He used to own most of the land around here, as well," said Bones. "Fifty thousand acres or more, the whole one side of the mountains looking out west from Reno."

"That's the guy," said Shady.

"And he happens to be dead. Thirty years or more," said Tinman. "So let me guess, Shady. You think he took all his money to the grave, and the big plan is to rob him six feet under. Shouldn't be too hard to dope out a grave robbery. I'm up to the task."

"You're not as funny as you think."

"You are."

"Think so? Let me finish the story. Then we'll see. I first got wind of Redfield in '52. A bunch of rookies heisted his house."

"The river rock mansion, on Mt. Rose and Forrest. Looks like a church," said Tinman.

"That's right. Redfield was a hoarder. Liked his money close. Kept a fortune in there. So this gang of losers including two soap salesmen, a janitor, a bricklayer and some French floozy who was having a fling with Redfield, break in there and make off with over a million and a half of cash, jewelry and signed stock securities. At the time, it was considered the country's largest burglary."

"They don't sound too stupid to me," said Bones.

"Yeah, well, every one of them got pinched right after the heist. Idiots. Rookies never plan for afterwards. Make a note of that Brains," he said to Tinman, who sloughed it off. "Redfield stuck in my head, though, and in '57 when I was pulling a job at the old Washoe Super Market, I did a little casing of his house. But I had to leave town right after the heist, due to circumstances."

"And that's when you walked out on Dez," said Peach.

"Which is between your mother and me. And as I said there were reasons. Anyway, the Redfield thing never left my brain, and lo and behold, I get contacted by a guy in the fall of '61. Newmann. Had a few dealings with him, first time in Reno. Seemed like a straight up joe. He's teamed up with another guy, Chester Greenauer."

"Funny name," said Tek.

"Yeah, and one I'm not likely to ever forget." The guys looked on as he forcibly controlled himself, like someone who's over their drinking limit but desperate not to throw up all over the place. He swallowed hard. "So this bum and Newmann have a job in the hopper. All they need is a jugger. The target is the Redfield house, and as much as I now hate this Chester guy, it was him who came up with the angle. The whole deal looked sweet, so I'm in. Holy Christ, get me a beer. I'm dying over here."

Nobody moved. They were so absorbed in the story, and the request was so out of the blue, it didn't register.

"Hey! Is that too much to ask? I'm offering to let you in on a major haul!"

Peach caught on first. He grabbed a beer from the cooler and delivered it. Shady took a long time to drain it, savoring every drop. When he was finished, he leaned back and his eyes glazed, like he was preparing to nod off.

"So what was the damn angle?!" said Tek. "God, you take forever."

Despite himself, Shady grinned. "Sorry, I know how the younger generation is. No patience. Teach him some of that Peach. Otherwise, he'll never be a true heister."

"Sure, dad. But to tell you the truth, I'm getting a little impatient myself."

Shady sighed. "The angle was this. Rumor around Reno was Redfield had a tunnel built from his castle to a house sat right across from it on Forrest."

"I know it. Little place. It's made of the same river rock," said Tinman.

"That's right. Everyone thought Redfield owned the house and was using the tunnel to visit his various lady friends who he stashed there, to keep out of sight from his wife."

Tek cried, "So these guys, Newmann and the bum, found the tunnel!"

"Wrong. One night they broke into the place and it was empty, no tunnel. But Chester gets the idea to rent the house."

"To make their own tunnel," said Tinman.

"You're not so dumb after all."

"Coming from you, that means a lot."

Shady's chest heaved up and down. "Yeah, I love you too. So anyway they dig their tunnel right under Mt. Rose. Took 'em three months. They're ready to bust up through the floor of the garage. All they need is me for the jugs. It was a risk coming back here. After the Mother's Day heist, the dicks had me on their radar. But this was the kind of score that could've set me for life."

"Could have?" asked Catfish.

"Should have. We pulled the job middle of December. A thing of beauty. Two, thousand-pound jugs. Old models. I punched the dials and peeled 'em like a couple of bananas. And we hit pay dirt. Stacks of hundred and thousand-dollar bills. Jewelry. Silver dollars. A coin collection. And a big old pile of signed, negotiable bonds. Most for an outfit called Pacific American Fisheries. None of us knew anything about coins or their value, but all told, we were guessing the total haul was over two million."

Tek whistled and said, "Probably worth five times that now. So what happened?"

"Make note kid. For the first time in my life, I trusted someone. My mistake. With Redfield being so known, we knew the town was going to be smoking hot. Every bent guy in fifty miles was going to be rousted. I couldn't afford to stick around. Newmann also had a record, but he was local and already set up an alibi. He figured he could wait out the heat as long as he didn't have any of the loot near him for the bulls to find. Chester was the only one who had a clean record."

"So he held the take," said Catfish.

"Yeah. We decided I'd leave town that night. Chester would lay low for a month. After that, we'd meet up on the California border, near Boomtown, and do the split."

"What about the tunnel?" asked Tinman. "As soon as the cops found that, they must have locked right in on Chester."

"You really do know how to think. Don't you? And you have a point, except for a few things. Before we left the house, I jimmied the door with a crowbar, so it looked like that's the way we came in. Also, the tunnel came up in a corner of the garage where Redfield had piled all kinds of junk. When we went back out, we covered the hole good. Would have taken a month emptying the whole garage to find it. On top of it, Chester's lease on the house was under a false name, he never stepped foot in it again."

"That's pretty good," said Tinman.

"Like I said, Chester was no dummy. We also caught some good luck. Didn't know it, but while I was cracking the safes, a neighbor came to visit. He must have knocked, but we didn't hear. But he left footprints in the snow. Cops figured they were ours. Sent them on a goose chase. It was maybe the most beautiful job I'd ever been in on."

"What went wrong then?" asked Tek.

"When the cops kept drawing blanks, Redfield got upset. He talked to some of his pals, heavies in Reno, Joe Conforte and others. Asked them for justice. Chester spread it around town Newmann was behind the whole thing. A couple days later, they found him, strangled, stuffed inside a barrel of cooking oil."

"Chester pulled a cross," said Catfish.

"You got it," said Shady, his face hardening. "I catch wind of what happened to Newmann, and I know I gotta move fast. I slip into Reno, trying to find Chester. He hears I'm in town and drops a dime to the cops and the heavies. Tells 'em I was the yegg on the job. I had no choice. I headed south, and didn't stop until Mexico. Hung out there for six months before I could go back to work."

"What a jerk!" cried Tek. "Didn't you keep looking for him?"

"Every second kid, but he went to ground. Easy enough to do with all that money. What should have been my money."

"You mean a third of it, naturally," said Bones.

"Sure, yeah, that's what I mean."

There was a long silence as everyone digested the story. Tinman wandered around the room, hands in his pockets, eyes on the floor.

"That's a real tearjerker," he said. "But what's it got to do with anything? Even if you could find him, there's no way he still has any of the haul. That's over forty years ago."

"I already know where he is. And you're right, it's long gone," said Shady. "Except for the coin collection."

"Slim pickings," said Catfish. "For such a big haul."

"That's what I used to think. But I studied up on coins some when I was in stir. Those coins in the safes were rare silver dollars. Worth a pretty penny now I'm betting. The coin collection, however, was in a case with each coin in a sealed packet. His prize pieces. That's why he got so pissed off. It wasn't the securities or the cash, it was the collection. Probably worth upwards of a million dollars, maybe more."

Everyone but Tinman started buzzing. He stopped the chatter. "You're a good storyteller, Shady. I'll give you that. But I'm not buying the idea this collection exists or that you know where Chester is. You've been in prison for twenty years. How could you possibly find out anything?"

"Didn't have to. He found me. About ten years after I got popped, I got a letter from him. Tracked me down in stir. Didn't see that one coming did you?"

"Why in God's name would he do such a thing?" asked Bones.

"To rub the salt in deep. Sent a picture of an estate he bought with the loot. North Shore, Tahoe. Every few months, new pictures. His car, boat, pool table." The pain from the torture was evident, and no one could blame him for the hate that oozed out.

"That's really low," said Tek softly.

Shady came out of his daze. "Yeah But he made a mistake. He figured I'd die inside. He was wrong. Now it's payback time."

"Pictures of boats and cars don't help us. What about the coin collection?" asked Tinman, sounding a little less sure of himself.

"Two months ago, I received another letter. Take a peek."

He reached in his shirt pocket and pulled out two folded snapshots. Everyone gathered around. The first was of a classic old Tahoe mansion built in the 20's or 30's when land developer Norman Bilitz was luring in all the wealthy barons. The second was of a leather case, opened, displaying rows of coins in sealed, acrylic coin slabs.

"What do you think of that smart guy?" asked Shady with a self-satisfied grin.

"How do we know any of these are worth anything?" asked Tinman, examining the photo of the coin collection, his nose inches from it.

"Because I say so!" roared Shady leaping out of his chair. "Christ almighty, you're stubborn. I suppose you still doubt I was even in on the heist!"

He and Tinman faced off, neither willing to give.

Peach slipped in, forming a triangle of faces. "My fence could tell us all about them. But he's mobile, and doesn't do house calls on spec. If you know what I mean."

Shady's breathing slowed. He pursed his lips "Tell you what, you and I are going to go for a little run. When we get back, I'll do a little show and tell. Your brother will have all the proof he needs, and your fence will pay us a little visit. Guaranteed."

THIRTEEN

"I NEED YOU TO LEND ME A PIECE," said Shady.

They had barely left the motel in Peach's car, but it was the most pressing issue in his mind. He looked at Peach and saw there was a problem. He was not in the mood.

"I'm asking a simple favor."

"Gee, I'd sure love to do that for you dad, but I don't pack anymore."

For Shady, it was like he said he'd had a sex change. "What kind of stupidity is that?"

"Well, I got to thinking, and there's quite a big difference between armed robbery and burglary. If you get nabbed. Having a gun can add a lot of time."

Shady was amazed at the naiveté. "You got it all backwards. With a piece, if the job is beefed by some nosy guard, the chances of not getting arrested are much better. Because now the guy is on the ground bleeding and has no chance to call the law. Christ, didn't I teach you anything when we were inside?"

"Sure you did. And I see your way of thinking, but Tinman, he thinks different."

Shady snarled. "Yeah, he does. But does that mean you have to?"

Peach's brow furrowed. "Well, we're partners."

Shady could see the bond between the brothers was going to be difficult to break, and it irked him to no end. He needed Peach doing what he was told.

"I think your brother is a pain in the ass."

"Yeah, I got that impression. I think he feels the same way about you. I mean the two of you didn't exactly rub noses like the Eskimos do when they like someone."

Shady stared at him. It had been awhile since they'd shared a cell and he'd forgotten Peach's tendency to not take anything very seriously. It was time to squelch that side of his personality.

"You're a fool to team up with him. He's not our kind. And you don't owe him nothing."

"Actually, I do. Pretty much everything. I can't tell you how many times he saved my butt when we were kids. And he practically supported me when he was riding high as a hustler. And of course, he's the one that inspired me to learn a real trade. If it wasn't for him, I'd still be sticking up convenience stores."

Shady did a slow burn. There was no way out of it. He was forced to work with both brothers. Either way, he had an agenda, and nothing was stopping that. They passed a little bar on Fourth, with a lone pickup truck outside. Dilligas Saloon. The sign also advertised, The Hole in the Wall Grill, specialty, Indian Tacos.

"Pull over," said Shady. "It's time father and son share a beer."

Peach's excitement was palpable as he veered his car into the parking lot.

The old pickup truck had seen better days. The bumpers were dented, and the passenger window was partly open, and at a funny angle, like it refused to go either up or down anymore. It sported two bumper stickers: I'd Rather Be Fishing With Bunny, and, If Guns Are Outlawed Only Outlaws Will Have Guns.

The saloon was the classic cowboy design. Long wooden bar in the railroad car style, pool table, pinball machines and a small dance floor, for two-stepping. A bartender was playing on his smart phone. The only patron was a grizzly man of about fifty, sharing a private conversation with his beer. He was wearing a shirt that announced, Come on In. House Protected by a Conservative Gun Owner.

Shady smiled. This was exactly what he was looking for, and he felt right at home.

* * *

"So what do you guys think?" asked Tinman.

"There's got to be something to it," said Tek. "You could see how pissed he was at this Chester guy. Who wouldn't be?"

Tinman nodded. Up until hearing about Chester's taunting, he'd felt no sympathy or kinship with his supposed father. He still didn't like him, but nobody should be treated that way. He began pacing. He was hungry for a big heist, but something was holding him back. "I think you're right. Whatever he went to get, I'm sure it will prove there's some truth to his story."

"But you think he is not telling the whole truth," said Bones.

Tinman shot him a look. He hated when people read his mind, but when you're right, you're right. "That's it, yeah. I don't buy this decarceration stuff. Tek, research what's involved with releasing older prisoners. Any supervision, stuff like that."

"On it."

"When you're done, see what you can find out about Redfield, and any heists of his house. Let's see if we can trip him up with the facts." He bent his head and continued wandering. He couldn't put his finger on it, but his instincts told him to back away, despite the possible rewards. There was more to Shady than he was showing and he was starting to be a real pain in the balls. On cue, his left testicle started itching again, which reminded him of why he needed money. He didn't know how much it would cost to have his nut cut off, but it couldn't be cheap.

"Maybe I'm overthinking this. He's offering to let us in on something big. I should just keep my doubts to myself."

Blank stares from the old guys, patiently waiting for him to come to the correct conclusion. A trick they both used when he was younger. How he longed for the heady days when the only thing he had to rely on was a keen eye and steady stroke.

"What is it about that guy?" he asked. "He walks in a room and your skin starts crawling. Maybe it's the father thing. I'm holding a grudge and it's keeping me from seeing straight."

The blank expressions were still there. "I could use a little help here!" cried Tinman.

"As far as the heist," said Catfish, "that'll be up to you to decide once you see the proof, and case the thing out. What I think, though, is if you decide to move forward, keep an eye out for Imogene."

"Oh my, yes," said Bones. "Sweet Imogene. She who dances down the primrose path, must die by the primrose path."

Tinman waited for more, but the two old guys just stared at each other with knowing looks. "So who the hell is Imogene?"

Catfish took the stage. "Ever hear of a guy named George Remus? He started out as a mouthpiece in Chicago representing bent guys like us. But when prohibition started he saw how much money his clients were making and decided to go into the rackets himself. He finds a loophole in the Volstead Act. Learns he can buy up distilleries and sell bonded liquor to himself for medicinal purposes."

"It was beautiful," said Bones. "He moved to Cincinnati where eighty percent of the country's distilleries were, and snapped up most of them. Then he hired people to hijack his own legal liquor so he could sell it on the black market for a lot more."

"How much more?" asked Tek.

"He made over 40 million dollars in the first three years," Bones answered.

"That's like over 500 million today!"

"Yeah, and all tax free," said Catfish. "And people loved him. Who wouldn't. If you were lucky enough to be invited to one of his shindigs, you'd most likely go home with a new car as a party favor. He was that kind of guy."

"What the hell's he got to do with this Imogene?" asked Tinman.

"She was his wife," said Bones. "Supposed to have been a real looker. Apparently, Remus said she was the only person he truly trusted."

"Yeah, so much so that when the dicks finally caught up with him and tossed him in the can, he stashed most of his fortune with her," said Catfish. "The law knew there had to be money, so they planted an undercover fed in the same prison as Remus. Name was Franklin Dodge. Well Remus spills all. Tells him about the money. Sucker. And get this, Dodge up and quits the bureau. Starts wooing Imogene.

Convinces her to liquidate all of George's assets. They clean up. Over 100 million bucks."

"And they left Remus flat?" asked Tinman.

"Oh no," said Bones. "They were very generous. Gave him a single C-note in return."

"Whoa, that is nasty," said Tek. "Sounds like my mother. That's exactly what she did to my dad when he went away for embezzlement."

"Gets nastier than just that," said Catfish. "When Remus found out, he goes bonkers. He only spent two years in the pen and when he gets out he goes after them. To shut him up, Dodge and Imogene try to have him deported. When that went south, they hired a hitman to kill him, but the clown bungled it. Finally, Imogene files for divorce. On the day of the trial, Remus runs her car off the road and puts a couple of bullets in her."

"Serves her right," said Tek. "But now he's back in jail."

"Nope. He was acquitted," said Bones. "Claimed temporary insanity. Most people, however, thought the judge sided with him because of how bad Imogene treated him. She who dances down the primrose path, must die by the primrose path. Those are the words that saved his neck."

Tek analyzed the anecdote, and said, "No way. Shady wouldn't double cross Tinman! Actually, he might. But not Peach. He's his son, too, and he really likes him!"

Tinman ignored it. He knew with criminals, blood didn't hold as much weight as money. "What tipped you to think he'd pull a cross?"

"Grift sense, what else?" said Catfish. "Are you losing your touch?"

Tinman didn't need to answer. The gnawing feeling he'd been having over Shady was gone. He had sensed the same thing as Bones and Catfish, but his judgement was clouded, causing him to ignore the source. Subconsciously he had given Shady the benefit of the doubt. It was the damn father thing. The thought irritated him, and he committed to never let it happen again.

"Now how do you feel about this thing?" drawled Bones.

A dangerous smile slashed across Tinman's face. "I need this heist. If dear old dad wants to try and hustle the Posse, he better bring his A-game. You up for that guys?"

"I was born to play," said Catfish.

"I can think of no better fun," said Bones.

"I'm in," said Tek.

Tinman smiled. "To start, it's better if we're not all sitting around here with bated breath waiting for him to come back. Let's scatter. When I get anything, I'll let you know. Tek, keep me posted on that research. I want to know who we're really playing with."

* * *

Shady rapped his knuckles twice on the bar and the bartender, without looking away from his phone, said, "Who's there?"

Shady grimaced. "The grim reaper if you don't get two beers right now."

A look to Shady and the bartender's smirk quickly disappeared. "Sorry, what'll it be?"

"Draft."

The bartender filled two mugs with suds and slid them onto the bar. Peach dropped a few bills, and said, "You wanna sit at a table?"

Shady ignored him, walking over to the redneck. "Mind if we join you?"

The redneck shrugged and Shady sat. Peach stood behind, forming a triangle. Shady said, "Why is it so empty in here?"

"It's early. Place fills up after eight," said the redneck.

Shady said, "You and me have something in common."

The redneck cocked his head, and Shady said, "Your shirt. You're a gun-loving American just like me."

The redneck's smile was wide. "Goddamn right! Never leave home without one. Normally, I'd have it right here on my hip, but this damn place won't let you bring 'em in. Used to. But some fool shot up the juke box last year and ruined a good thing for all of us. Now I feel naked as a newborn. Man ain't no man if he isn't carrying a piece of iron."

Shady nodded and drained half his beer. "I wish I could teach that kind of thinking to my boy here. He's got some kind of moral issues."

The redneck scrutinized Peach, like he was on display at a freak show. "You some kind of pussy, son?"

Peach grinned. "Oh no. And the problem isn't moral. It's about practicality."

The redneck snorted. "How practical is it if some nutcase terrorist busts in here and you don't have no gun? What are you gonna do? Throw your beer at him?"

He thought this was the funniest thing ever and he choked and sputtered. Shady joined in, then said, "You're just what I'm looking for partner. Someone good with words. Look, I gotta take a crap. See if you can talk a little sense into him."

"Well, I'll give it a crack. He's not queer or anything is he?"

"Nah," said Shady. "Just gun shy."

"Okay, you go drop a load and I'll hammer on his brain a bit."

Shady asked. "Bartender, where's the can?"

The bartender immediately looked up from his phone "Past the grill. On your left."

"The grill open? I'm getting hungry."

"Cook's late. Won't be open for another hour."

Shady shuffled through the long, empty bar. As he neared the kitchen, he looked back and saw Peach and the redneck debating head to head. The bartender, lost in cyberspace.

He darted into the kitchen. His eyes scanned the room and landed on a row of cooking utensils. He chose a metal pasta ladle with a pronged scoop. and walked to the outside door. He opened it a couple of inches, saw the parking lot was still empty and slid out, leaving it ajar.

It took him thirty seconds to cross the lot to the redneck's truck, slip the ladle through the partly open passenger window, pop the lock, and open the door. A quick search in the glove box proved fruitless, but under the front seat, he located the handgun he knew would be there. His educated eye told him it was a Jericho 941, semi-automatic, chambered for the .41 Action Express cartridge. It packed a punch and it made Shady's heart thump a little harder, like seeing a dear old friend for the first time in years.

He slipped it into the inner pocket of his suit coat and patted his chest. Whole again. He glanced at the pro-gun bumper sticker and mumbled, "God bless America."

Back in the kitchen, he quickly replaced the ladle. As he started out to the bar, a young, Mexican man bustled in. He froze, then quickly went on the offense.

"What you doin' here, man? Qué haces?! Huh?"

"Just looking for the bathroom Pablo," said Shady with a sneer.

"My name no Pablo! Dees booshit. And dees no baño! Is cocina! Comprende?"

Very slowly, Shady inched in close. "No speaky Spanglish." The cook flinched. Shady shoved him aside and walked into the bar.

The redneck and Peach were whooping it up. The bartender was still making love to his phone. The boost had gone unnoticed.

"There you are!" croaked the redneck. "I'll tell you what, this boy of yours is a hoot!"

"Yeah, he's a real card."

"I tried lecturing him on guns, but somewhere we took a wrong turn and ended up discussing the weaker sex. And this kid has got some juicy stories, I can tell you that!"

"I'm sure he does," said Shady. "Time to go."

"But dad, you didn't even finish your beer," said Peach. Shady just kept looking at him. Peach turned to the redneck. "Nice meeting you, pal."

"Likewise! Stop in anytime. I'm usually here."

Shady laid a hand on his shoulder. "Thanks again, partner. Where would guys like me be without guys like you."

"You can say that again!" said the redneck. After his new buds left, he stared into his beer and wondered exactly what the comment had meant. After a moment, he smiled and said aloud to himself, "He was just talking about being good neighbors. Helping one another out when they're in need." He nodded, feeling oh so pleased over his good deed. "Bartender! Hit me with another one."

* * *

As freezing cold water shriveled his manhood into oblivion Tinman tried to remember the last time he took two showers in one day. The chattering of his teeth distracted his brain, but the answer he arrived at was, never. He also could not remember taking a shower at night. He'd decided to take one the moment after everyone had left, and the little red alien residing on his left scrotum decided to make its presence felt in a big way.

The itching was so severe, his first notion was to grab his favorite kitchen knife and do the deed, consequences be damned. Better to be a eunuch than live with the horror of itchy balls. Before he could act on his madness, however, cowardice got involved in the debate, and in the end, won the day.

He therefore resolved to allow water—the Almighty Healer—have one more crack at his malady. This time, however, he decided hot water didn't do the trick. Ten minutes into the cold shower, and about five before hypothermia set in, he examined his affliction and noticed it had increased in size. Then he realized it might be an optical illusion since the sack it was living on had shrunk to a quarter of its normal breadth, and now resembled an albino prune. Due to this variable, he decided it was too soon to come to a definitive conclusion regarding the success of his latest attempted cure.

One good thing, the itching had subsided. Of course, now he was shivering uncontrollably, his teeth clashing and clanging into each other, his entire body quaking on the verge of succumbing to shock. It was a small price to pay, he thought, as he wrapped himself in a towel and slapped his quivering skin.

"What a stupid day," he said aloud to the empty bathroom. The bathroom seemed to agree, his voice echoing off its tiles.

He looked in the mirror. "And there's still hours to go. What else can go wrong?"

The mirror didn't know the answer, staring dumbly back, waiting for the punchline.

As Tinman looked at himself, an image of Shady formed. He found it very difficult to believe he was actually his father. They had nothing in common. Okay, sure, they were both tall with similar builds, had the same color eyes with the same cynical look in them, both pigheaded, suspicious of others, and quick to anger, but did that really prove anything? Probably.

But what about Peach? He wasn't anything like Shady. That should be proof enough that neither of them were really his.

A terrible thought suddenly arose, and he raced from the bathroom. He grabbed his dictionary and started flipping over large sections until he arrived at S. His fingers scanned the entries, seeking a word he'd discovered on his last complete reading of the tome. He found it at the end of the section.

Superfecundation. n. the successive fertilization of two or more ova from the same cycle by sperm from separate acts of sexual intercourse.

Egads. Could it be true? Was he the product of Shady, and Peach the result of the fling with the craps dealer? Technically they would still be fraternal twins, but only half-brothers. Is that why they were so different? It would make perfect sense.

He slammed the book shut, unwilling to accept the possibility. Peach was the only family he ever had, or wanted. He was his brother. His full brother, and he could not have it any other way. He could accept the other family revelations, but not that. Never that. It would be like cutting him in two, leaving a half-empty soul.

The phone rang. He lunged for it, desperate for any respite from the war raging in his mind. It was Tek. "Yeah, what do you got?"

"Okay. Everything Shady says about this decarceration adds up."

Tinman was surprised and said so. Tek cut him off with one word, "Except. It doesn't make sense he's out on his own this quick. The early release program requires a minimum of one-year regular supervision, like parole. And the ex-con is required to reside in whatever halfway house assigned to them for at least two years."

"Any exceptions?"

"Not that I can find. But I guess it's a possibility."

"That's good stuff. Maybe Shady was such a pain in the butt, they cut him loose early." Tek laughed. Tinman added, "You just keep digging my man."

He hung up, a thin smile easing onto his face. He always hated mysteries, gaps in a story, hidden facts. But now he was at least certain of one thing. Actually two. Shady was on the lam, and he was a consummate liar.

FOURTEEN

PEACH WAS LIVING HIS DREAM. Tooling around with his very own father! Unlike his brother, he'd always wanted one. When he was a kid watching other kids play with theirs, he was envious. Now he had one and he was happy. He could care less what they did together, as long as they were together. If Shady had said he wanted to play chicken with a speeding locomotive, he would have jumped on the tracks first. Anything, just to be with dear old dad.

"That sure was fun sharing a beer with you," he said. "Or at least half of one. So where to next?"

"I need to go to church."

Peach didn't see that one coming and it struck his funny bone. He laughed and laughed until he realized he was the only one in on the joke. He looked at Shady who had not changed his dour expression. Hmm. Sometimes dads can be hard to figure out.

"Sorry, I didn't know you were religious. What faith are you? I mean do you need a special church, or will any do?"

"Methodist," grunted Shady. "And make it snappy. It's important!"

"Okay. But I admit I've been a little lax on the churchgoing. I'll have to think about where one of those might be."

"The one downtown."

Peach used to know everything there was to know about Reno, but things had changed. He told Shady so, hoping to get the benefit of the doubt. He was wrong.

"For Christ's sake kid, it's the oldest church in Reno! I doubt very much they got rid of it for some high-rise."

"Oh! That place! Sure. When I was a kid I hid out there once when the cops were after me for boosting some food."

"Shoplifting is for punks."

"I agree," said Peach quickly. "I was just hungry."

"No excuse." And that was the end of that father/son chat.

They drove in silence until Peach blurted out, "Sure would have been great growing up with you!"

"Why's that?"

"Well, I learned a lot from you in stir, but think how much more I'd know if I'd have been raised by you. Only dads can teach certain lessons."

Shady didn't answer for a moment, then a melancholy grin appeared and he said, "They can be helpful at times. Most important lesson I ever learned came from my pa."

Peach was all atwitter. This was what he'd been waiting for! To learn more about his father, and his roots! He could barely contain his enthusiasm. "You realize, your father would be my grandfather!"

"That's usually how it works."

"So tell me about him! Tell me these words of wisdom he passed on, so I can learn this important lesson too!"

"Well, my pa, your grandfather, was a bootlegger and a gambler. Died when I was around eight. Rotted lungs.

Stomach full of holes. But before he went, I guess I was seven or so, he taught me something. It started one day when I was at the local Catholic school. My mom sometimes made me go."

"That would be my grandmother!" Peach crowed.

"You catch on quick. Now shaddup and let me finish! So I'm in class and I'm hating it. There's this smartass young priest doing the teaching. I tell him he don't know shit and he takes offence. He hauls me into an empty room. I can see he's going to go after me with the belt, and I'll have nothing to do with it. So I throw a chair at him. One of those little kiddie ones. It whaps him side the head and I take off. When I get home, I tell my pa. Well he sees red and goes off to the school and tells this little piece of shit priest not to mess with his kid. Says he's the only one allowed to punish his own flesh and bones."

"And you learned you were right to throw the chair and defend yourself!"

"Knock it off. That's not the end of the story." Peach grinned nervously and Shady continued. "So my dad says everything's jake. Tells me to go back to school the next day. The first thing this priest does is haul off and beat me with the belt until I got welts all over. I go home and try to hide 'em from my pa. But he sniffs it out and goes real quiet. Without a word, he takes off for the school to teach this priest a lesson."

Peach waited for the finale but Shady was staring off into space. Finally, he said softly, "So did he teach him a lesson?"

"Huh? Oh, yeah. Sure did," Shady said, and burst into laughter, his head nearly banging into the dash as he rocked back and forth. "He beat the living daylights out of the jerk! When he was through, the priest was crippled and scarred for life. Jaw permanently deformed, and one ear torn off! What a scream!"

Peach was having real difficulties seeing the humor in all of this, but he knew it must be in there somewhere. After all, if his father thought it was funny, then it must be so.

"That's great, dad," said Peach. "But where exactly is the lesson in all of that?"

"Well, after my pa nearly killed the priest, word spread and he got quite the reputation. Nobody would mess with him. They all said he was as meaner than a crosscut saw. I idolized him for that. I saw how power comes with reputation. So if you want to make it in this world, you have to be as mean as a crosscut saw. End of lesson."

He looked at Peach with a grin, like he was the Oracle of Delphi revealing the mystery of life. "You let that sink in boy. You'll never go wrong."

Peach had no words to say, but he knew what he was thinking. His dad was a whackjob. And this made him feel guilty because sons don't think their fathers are whackjobs. Sons love their fathers unconditionally, and understand their wisdom comes from years of experience. You don't question, you just believe, and have faith. Right? At least that's what his romantic image of the perfect father/son relationship was. He looked at Shady who was staring back with his steely, heartless eyes, the ugly scar on his neck glowing with the passing of every street lamp. Peach grinned. As they say, you sho' can't choose your family. You just have to learn to love them.

"You letting that pearl sink in?" asked Shady.

"Sure am dad! That's a real beaut! By the way, where did you get that scar?"

"None of your damn business! Lesson two. Respect your parents' privacy. Christ Almighty, don't you know nothing?!" Peach's face turned red, and Shady said more quietly, "Are we there yet?"

"Right around the corner. I'll park here."

Shady was right about the First United Methodist Church. The city had not replaced it with a high-rise. Barely.

A stone's throw from the Truckee River, and on the edge of Reno's original gambling district, the church used to be a towering beacon for all the sinners stumbling out of casinos looking for sure forgiveness. Now, if your eyes were drawn upward to the two commercial towers sandwiching it into the narrow slot corner at First St. and West, you were likely to miss the statuesque church done in Gothic Revival, with its impressive bell tower, and ornate wrought iron gates gracing its broad side.

The painted plaque in front of the enormous wooden doors declared the church's motto, "At the heart of the city with a city-wide ministry." A larger sign, like the kind used at old movie theaters to display upcoming movies, announced the latest sermon. This week's feature was, Open Hearts. Open Minds. Open Doors. Peach tugged on the decorative metal handle on the front door.

"It's locked."

"Churches don't lock," said Shady.

"Apparently, this one didn't get the memo."

"You got a pickset?"

"Back at the car. But is that such a good idea? I mean, being a church and all."

Shady looked at him like he wanted to disown him. "Haven't you been listening to what I've been saying?"

Peach figured he must be referring to his quaint story about his dad committing first degree manslaughter on a priest. But he wasn't sure what that had to do with breaking into a church to do god knows what in broad daylight. Okay nightlight. But it's pretty darn bright downtown no matter what time of day it was, and it just didn't seem like that slick of an idea. Filial respect be damned.

"It seems a little hasty, let's see if there's another door." The suggestion didn't go over too well with Shady, so before he could make a fuss Peach scooted around the side of the building where another, smaller door stood. A sign read, Office, but the door was locked. Peach pushed the doorbell button.

"Why in hell did you do that?!" cried Shady.

"To see if anyone's home. That's what they're for you know."

"Don't be a smartass! I told you I need to be in there alone!"

Peach didn't have time to answer, because the door swung open and a matronly woman appeared.

"The early evening service is over," said the matron. "Come back tomorrow."

She started to close the door when Peach said, "Ma'am, I can tell in one glance you are a caring, compassionate woman."

The matron was not buying it, but she showed some small appreciation at Peach's attempt. He leaned in closer, blocking Shady's view, and said, "My father is old. He doesn't have much time left. He's been in the hospital. When I was visiting him, he told me his wish was to go to church one last time. So, I snuck him out of the hospital and now all I need is a church. It's the least I can do, for all he's done for me."

The matron was hooked. She peered over his shoulder and whispered, "He does look pretty bad. I'm surprised he's still walking." She pursed her lips, making a decision.

"Alright, I'll let you in. But only for a short time. I don't get paid for overtime, understand."

Peach gave her his best smile and she melted. She waved them in and they entered a small sitting room. On one wall was a Plexiglass window like the kind they have in banks. Peach decided that's where the donations were deposited. Behind the window was the tiny office for the church, and Peach suspected the lady spent much of her life stuck in the little cubicle. The far wall was made up of several large, wooden doors leading to the inside of the church.

The matron walked quietly to the center door, and using a key from a large ring unlocked it and swung it silently open. She disappeared and lights turned on inside. She reappeared and waved them in. As Peach passed, she put a hand on his arm.

"Should I get him a priest, to give him comfort?" she asked.

"No! No, I don't think that would be a good idea."

"That's right," Shady growled. "I want to be alone." And he stepped inside.

The lady frowned and Peach whispered, "He prefers to go mano a mano with the big guy. Especially at a time like this."

The woman's eyes widened, completely understanding. "Then I will leave him to it. I have some things to do in the office before I leave. You can wait out here." She softly closed the door, and shuffled across the room and through another door.

Peach smiled as he explored the sitting room. He was never a big fan of churches or religious people, but their blissful innocence sure came in handy at times.

"Psst!"

Peach looked through the Plexiglass and saw the woman as she settled down at her desk. Hmm. If not her, then who?

"Hey, dumbo!" a gravelly voice whispered.

Peach turned and there was Shady, half his head stuck out the parted church door. Peach waved. Shady jammed a finger at him, then pointed at the floor in front of him. Peach got the idea and strolled over.

"What are you doing out here?" asked Shady, his face brimming with anger.

"You said you needed to be alone."

Shady's head drooped. "That did not include you."

Peach beamed. So that's how it worked. It's an unspoken thing between fathers and sons. Even when the father says he wants to be away from everyone else in the world, he doesn't mean his son. Peach filed it away, not wanting to make the same mistake twice. Shady grasped his wrist and yanked him into the church.

"Sorry about that," said Peach. "I'm still catching on to the ins and outs of father and son relationships."

"Huh? Eh, whatever."

"I did a good job getting us in here though," said Peach, hoping for a brownie point.

"Yeah, yeah, it was good. But don't you ever again say to anybody I'm dying! What are you trying to do, jinx me?"

"No, I, uh, just—"

"Shaddup. I need you to get up there."

Peach looked around the church. It was lit with globe chandeliers hung on long chains attached to the broad dome ceiling. The tall windows were of intricate stained glass, portraying the Gospel Writers, the Holy Trinity, the Christian Graces and the Eight Disciples. In the nave, were rows of pews with a small balcony. The chancel held the altar, the pulpit and the lectern. A giant arched window displayed the Holy Family in multi-colored glass. At the bottom, was written, That Ye Love One Another.

The whole place gave Peach the creeps. So many faces staring at him, all looking like they had never so much as swiped a stick of gum. So damn holier-than-thou. And they looked at him like they knew exactly what he was up to, even if he didn't. He felt a slap on his head, and snapped out of his daze to look where Shady was pointing.

Which was at a long rank of shiny, metal organ pipes many feet high and vertically mounted onto a windchest. There were several other ranks distributed around the front of the church, but this one was the largest and was placed above and to the left of the lectern, over top the door they'd come through.

"Am I allowed to ask why?" asked Peach, sort of guessing what the answer would be.

"You need an answer for everything, don't you?" snarled Shady. "Up there is where my stash is. The proof your damn brother wants."

"You hid your stash in a church?"

"No better place in the world. They almost never tear them down, and they like leaving things just the way they are. Tradition, you know."

"Sure," said Peach as he peered up at the prize. "But how did you get up there?"

"Same way you are. I'd do it myself but you've got a lot fewer years on those legs."

Peach mapped out his route, figuring if he started on the low bannister that ran around the altar, then climbed on top of the lectern, he could reach the bottom of the windchest, which if it was supported well should hold him long enough for him to pull himself up and swing his legs around and get in a sitting position.

His experience as a cat burglar served him well, as it's exactly what he did. As he perched above, he said, "How weird is this. When I was a kid, running from the dicks, I hid behind that very lectern. And all along, your stash is right over my head. Way back then, we were connected and didn't even know it!"

"Life is full of wonders."

"Isn't it?! I'm always telling Tinman that, but he sometimes doesn't buy it. I can't wait to tell him about this, then he'll have to—"

"Stop! No more talking!"

"Sorry, dad. So, where is it?"

"You're not there yet."

"I thought you said it was in one of these metal pipes."

"I didn't say anything! I pointed! And I was pointing at those wood pipes, in the row behind the metal ones."

Peach leaned around the end of the row of metal pipes and spied the rank of square, wooden pipes. To get there he would have to hang onto the last metal pipe in the row and swing his body through the air and hope he landed on the little ledge on the other side. First, he would have to stand up. Which he did. Safely. Then his sweaty hands slipped on the pipe, which caused his left foot to slide off the ledge, and left him in a very precarious position.

Down below, he saw Shady instinctively throw his arms into the air, like he was hoping to catch him should the worst befall. Peach figured his eighty-year old arms would do little to slow his progression, but it warmed his heart his father cared so much. For a fleeting moment he kind of looked like Moses, on top of whatever that mountain was, raising his arms to God, asking for something. Peach never could remember that part. But still, it was a beautiful image.

Just then, the inner door to the church opened right under where Peach was dangling in space. The matron peeked in. Shady, his arms still thrust up, shot her a look.

"Oh dear, excuse me," spoke the matron.

"You got a problem?"

"Heavens no! I was just looking for the other man."

"Him? Oh, uh, he had to take a dump."

The woman's face blanched. "I'm sorry I asked."

"I'll bet."

"Well, then, I'll leave you to it. Him! I mean him." Then she crossed herself.

"That'd be good. He and I are in the middle of something here."

The woman bowed her head, crossed herself again and backed through the doorway. Peach grinned at Shady and he snapped his fingers and urged him on.

After regaining his footing, Peach's planned maneuver around the rank of metal pipes to the wooden pipes went smoothly. Once there, he looked around and could see no place any stash of any consequence could be hidden.

Shady called up, "Third one in from the left. See the little slots at the bottom?"

Peach could see them, and suspected it must be where the air escaped to make the pretty sounds. "Uh-huh. Sure. But—"

"Hey! What did we say?"

Peach zipped his lips and Shady said, "Reach in that slot and feel around. It'll be laying on the bottom so you'll have to use two fingers to fish it out."

Peach quietly followed directions and his fingers landed on something hard and plastic. He strained to get a claw grip on it, and snaked the thing out. It was a single coin, encased in a plastic sleeve. He gave Shady a puzzled look.

"Don't give me that stupid look. And don't get too fond of it! Toss it down." Peach dropped the coin into Shady's eager hands. He held it up to the light, the gleam reflecting off his eyes.

"Now we go see that pigheaded brother of yours. And we call your fence. With this beauty, I'll make true believers out of both of them."

FIFTEEN

PEACH WAS FAIRLY CERTAIN HIS FENCE was not going to drop everything and come running over an old coin. He was more than certain Tinman would not be bowled over by it either. He didn't say anything, however, because Shady was looking so pleased with himself, almost smug, and he didn't want to ruin his moment.

Instead, he drove silently back to Tinman's motel, his mind trying to take care of one problem at a time. He couldn't think of any way to sway Tinman, so his brain was thinking of what valuable thing he could pick up quickly that would entice his fence.

His fence had a unique approach to the business. His office was a state-of-the-art RV driven by a burly white guy who looked like the quintessential RVer. He was the perfect cover as they drove from place to place, responding to calls from bent guys with stolen goods. The setup was very effective as it was nearly impossible for the law to get a fix since they were always on the move. Also, the fence almost never left the RV, allowing his driver to be front man, dealing with RV park owners and the like. There were various reasons for this arrangement, but the biggest was the fact he was an illegal immigrant and preferred to remain invisible.

Jahllo was of Arabian descent, and claimed to be from a royal family. This gave him excellent overseas connections to people who are too rich for their own good, and who loved snatching up valuables from the states, particularly if they were sparkly, or had any historical significance.

Jahllo was rightfully proud of his business, claiming to be the only mobile fence in the country. He once told Peach he was thinking of franchising the idea. They had done business several times, and both were pleased with the arrangement, even though Jahllo was a real horse trader. To get the best price one had to be a hard haggler.

The biggest problem in recent years, was Jahllo had naturally become quite popular in criminal circles and his services were in high demand. With this success came a certain pickiness. Now to get him to come, you had to have something juicy.

"Before we go see your brother, I need to get a room," said Shady out of the blue.

"But dad! I thought you'd be staying with mom."

Shady winced. "I'll shack up with her at first, but you never can trust women to behave and mind their own business. In which case, I'll need some other place."

"But it's Dez! You said yourself she was special, different from other girls."

Shady let out a half-snort. "That's what you say when a dame's upset. Am I right?"

Peach frowned. "I don't know."

"Let me explain. We were born to be father and son. It was planned or something."

"Destiny?"

"Like that. And Dez turned out to be the one to make it happen, but it could've been any moll. Back then, all of them had the eyes for guys like us. If you were bent, you had 'em falling all over you. Just so happened Dez was the one that fell on me."

Peach didn't like one word he was hearing. It was like having someone drag the needle across your favorite Led Zeppelin album, while it was playing. His stomach tightened up. For the first time since he'd arrived, Peach caught a glimpse of Shady bathed in a harsh light. And it hurt his eyes.

Shady sensed trouble. "Don't get me wrong, kid. Dez is tops in my book. I'm just saying, any woman, don't matter who it is, can only go so high. Not like you. Different animal all together. We're a team, right? So, come on, let's get me a room."

Peach momentarily shook off his funk, but the memory of it lingered. "Okay, Shady. But I'm sure Tinman can put you up. Some of the rooms are still livable."

"No," said Shady flatly. "Where you staying?"

"The Morris Hotel."

"That place still around? I remember it in the 50's, and it was already twenty years old. Used to be a class joint. Okay, if you say it's still standing, that'll suit."

Uh-oh, thought Peach. "I'm thinking somewhere else might be more comfortable."

"You got a problem having your old man sacking out same place as you?"

"Not at all! It's just the place is now for people who have an alternative way of looking at stuff. Make sense?"

"Not a bit."

"Right. Well, it's a place for Burners."

"Druggies, huh? I thought you knew better."

"Oh no, not druggies. Well, sometimes, but they're more like modern hippies."

"Freaks."

"In a manner of speaking. But really nice freaks. And creative. In fact, their big thing is every year, come September, fifty thousand of them, give or take, all meet up in the middle of the desert for a week, just north of here. Called Black Rock."

"And what do they do—Commune?" said Shady with a sneer.

"Somewhat. They dress up in costumes, and dance and, you know, party. But mostly they build all kinds of giant art. And one of these giants is a huge wooden dude. He's The Man. At the end of this week in the scorching desert, they burn this guy. And that's why they're Burners. I hear it's something to see. I'm hoping to go this year."

"You'll do no such thing," said Shady, immediately feeling really strange for having said it, but nevertheless feeling some primal need to do so, and continue with, "No son of mine is going to lower himself by associating with scum."

Finally, the teenage rebel in Peach woke up, and he felt like telling his dumb dad to go to hell and mind his own business. But then he figured his dad's old-fashioned attitude suited him just fine—given the alternative of taking him to the hotel. Still, he wasn't going to let the old codger diss his newfound friends.

"They are not scum! The guy that owns the hotel used to be a heavy in the microelectronics biz. I've only been there a couple weeks, but it's like one happy family."

"You've been brainwashed."

"Naw. But let's take a pass on that place, and I'll think of another. You're from a different generation. You wouldn't understand."

Shady huffed and puffed. "You don't think I'm with it? That's what they say, right? With it! Well, listen up, kiddo, I been through the 60's. I'm no babe in the woods."

"Wow! You were a flower child?!"

"Don't be an idiot. I said I went through it, not that I was of it. But I seen enough to swing. Drive on."

The Morris Burner Hotel, located on the corner of Record and Fourth, was brick and had three floors, the guest rooms were on the upper two. At different times, the bottom floor had housed a flower shop, an upscale clothing store, a tire outlet, and a boxing gym. It was a last relic of one of Reno's many booms. This one built out of demand for temporary residence for soon-to-be divorcees who had come to get the "Reno Cure."

It looked very much like it had when it was constructed in the early 30's. One notable exception was the addition of a marque-style sign over the entrance, with "BURNER" emblazoned in psychedelic neon.

Shady noticed a small sign taped to the front door that read, "No freaking out. Breathe in, breathe out. Until you reach the playa." He shook his head, like preparing to deal with a bunch of kindergarteners at recess.

Peach knocked and a pretty face parted the curtains on the front door. Her hand appeared and waved excitedly. The door swung open.

The weekly event going on was Tutu Tuesday. Nothing in Shady's life had prepared him for such a thing.

They stepped in. The pretty face belonged to a young woman wearing a bright pink tutu, and nothing else. She threw herself into Peach's arms and spun him around. Then she dragged him into a large room off to the side which used to house the boxing gym. Shady, suddenly afraid to be alone, scuffled after them.

The room had been converted into a small stage with a dance floor. It was packed with men and women, young and old, all dressed in brightly colored tutus, and nothing else. Okay, some of them were wearing LED fiber optic tiaras, but purely for effect.

On the stage, a DJ was playing horribly loud music, and the crowd was eating it up. Like whirling dervishes they spun uncontrollably around and around, never once crashing into any walls, furniture, or other dervishes.

The young girl with the pretty face (and a very nice rack, thought Shady) screamed at the top of her lungs, "Hey everybody, Peach is here!"

A huge roar went out, "PEEAAACCHH!" They gang rushed him and he disappeared inside a giant pulsating ball of flesh and tutus. It hopped around and around until suddenly exploding like a giant nova, all the glowing pieces of the star scattering far and wide, populating the empty galaxy (or dance floor if you're not digging the astronomical simile). Norm could only dream of getting such a welcome at Cheers.

Peach spun out of the ball laughing hysterically. He crashed into Shady, still standing in the doorway, mouth agape.

"Sorry dad! They missed me. So what do you think of my adopted family? Fun huh?"

Shady looked fearfully over Peach's shoulder at the writhing crowd. His instinct was to pull out his newly acquired gun and shoot as many of the freaks as he could before they turned on him. Before he could act on this thought, another pretty young woman sporting even a nicer rack than the first slid over and wrapped herself around him.

"Who's the sexy old guy, Peach?" said the sexy young woman.

"Hey, Sirius. This is my dad. He's looking for a room if you got any."

"Absolutely. Follow me, hot stuff," she said huskily into Shady's ear. She bent low at the waist, stuck her head out and shot out of the room with a "WHEEEEEEEE!"

Peach casually followed with Shady behind, constantly checking over his shoulders for any more sneak attacks. He whispered to Peach, "Her name is really Serious?"

"That's right." Then he sensed Shady's confusion and said, "But not Serious, like as in being serious. That'd be kind of funny, huh? Given who she is. But it's spelled different. It's actually the name of a star. The Dog Star. It means the scorcher. She thinks she was born there and sent down to earth to bring joy to all men."

"Hooker, huh?" said Shady.

"No way! She's not that sort at all. She's just full of love. Isn't it great?"

Shady didn't answer. He was too busy watching flashes of Sirius' naked butt as she bunny hopped up the steps to the second floor, her tutu hiking up with every bounce.

When they reached the landing, she started her tour, pointing out available rooms on the way down the long hall. "You have several to choose from. All specially designed by fellow Burners, and all with their very own unique vibe and aura. So just let go. Your heart will choose. This one is the Enchanted Forest Room."

Shady peered in. The room featured flowing white muslin draped here and there, with two mannequin legs, in a corner, splayed and turned upside down, the feet reaching for the ceiling. The central focus however, was a naked, life-size statue of what appeared to be the body of a man, with the head of a deer, or elk, not sure, but there were antlers.

A set of bunk beds filled one wall. "This is a shared room, but no one's chosen it yet, so if you want it, you get first dibs on top or bottom bunk. Bathroom is at the end of the hall. We all share. Onward! Here is one of my favorites, the Goddess Room."

It featured an enormous mural of a woman's head, her white hair shooting off in all directions, like she'd been struck by lightning. She looked a little like one of the Gorgon sisters, probably Medusa, since the other two were immortal, and this one had her eyes closed like she was dead. Shady quickly passed.

"Over here is, The Booby Bar. All the decorations have been repurposed from the original Booby Bar that was used at Burning Man for several years. I don't know why, but this room always titillates me. Tee-hee."

Shady wasn't surprised. The walls were covered with posters, paintings, and figurines, all depicting boobs in various shapes, sizes and colors. He slowly panned the room, landing on Sirius who had slipped inside and was posing in a corner like a statue, her arms over her head like a belly dancer, boobs jutting out, body and face perfectly still. She couldn't hold it for long, though, and soon started giggling and bouncing from one foot to the other.

"Got ya! Didn't I?! But I don't actually come with the room. Tee-hee," she squealed, and squeezed by Peach and Shady, her boobs flattening out on Shady's chest. Shady was feeling a little faint, but he dutifully followed his guide to the next room, entitled, Down The Rabbit Hole, exactly where he thought he was. It was one giant black and white op art mural. Before Sirius could finish her spiel, Shady was weaving, and Peach had to keep him from falling.

As they approached the next room, Sirius started walking on her tiptoes and spinning around like a ballerina. "Now, if you so choose, you are welcome to share my room, it's right next to Peach's, The Sparkle Pony Room."

Shady shot Peach a look. Peach shrugged and said, "I always wanted a pony."

Sirius grasped Shady's hand and pulled him into her gaudily painted room. "This is my haven. The Kitty Kat Pussy Playground!"

She flopped herself on the bed piled high with stuffed cat dolls. She struck a fetching, come-hither pose, and purred, "Meow. Does daddy want to sleep with kitty tonight?"

Shady involuntarily backed out of the room, his brain ready to explode from an overdose of foreign stimuli. He heard laughter from down the hall. A long line of tutu clad Burners were coming toward him, doing a Disco-inspired version of the Conga. He was trapped.

He turned to run, and saw what looked like Jeremiah Johnson—complete with thick, bushy beard—dressed in a bright yellow, sequined tutu. He was happily huffing away on a large spleef. He smiled at Shady and cried, "Who wants a shotgun?!"

It was a gift from heaven for Shady. A shotgun is exactly what he needed to fight his way out of this insane asylum. With the handgun he was now clutching in his pocket, he should be able to take out enough to clear a path to freedom. He raised his hand like he was asking the teacher to go to the bathroom.

Jeremiah beamed and took a giant hit from his joint. He ran over to Shady and planted an open mouth kiss, injecting high-octane smoke into his lungs. Pulling away with a big smack, he said, "I hope the beard didn't scratch too much. Happy Daze!" And he skipped away, joining the

Conga dancers. The head of the snake had reached Shady, and it began to encircle him in a sea of tutus.

Peach appeared at the doorway of The Kitty Kat Pussy Playground with Sirius riding piggyback, her boobs divided by his neck, draping over his shoulders.

Peach said, "So what do you think, dad? Pretty with it, huh?"

Shady said, "Help," and crumpled to the floor.

* * *

"Geez, I wish you hadn't scared everybody like that," said Peach.

"Me! Scare them?!"

"Sure, they thought maybe your heart gave out while it was trying to choose the perfect room. Anyway, I know another place we can try."

"NO," said Shady. "I'll stay with your mother."

Peach smiled contentedly, and Shady caught a glimpse. "You did that on purpose, didn't you?"

"Huh?"

"Never mind. Just get me to your brother's place. Then you call your fence."

Peach pulled the car onto Fourth. Besides Shady's two measly coins, he still hadn't come up with something he could use to entice Jahllo. He set his mind to the task as he drove to the All Inn Motel. When they got there, Tinman was not in the Clubhouse or his apartment. Shady was furious for having been stood up.

But Peach assured him he could find his brother in no time, and off they went to search. McCue's was dead, and Amber said she hadn't seen Tinman, or any of the Posse for that matter. Peach didn't tell Shady, but he had a feeling Tinman was doing this on purpose. He wanted to make Shady come to him. It was one of the things he admired most about his brother: his ability to mess with people, and not have them catch on. It was the hustler in him, and Peach was always trying to emulate the trait.

It was pointless searching the bars, because Tinman rarely went in them. He was known to fly one of his kites at odd times, even in the middle of the night if the wind was right. But the sky was calm which ruled that out. Then it dawned on him.

"He's at the ballgame," said Peach. "Baseball, that is."

"Why in the hell would he be at a baseball game at a time like this?!"

"It's baseball season."

"I know that! Why now?"

Peach was still confused. "Well, the Aces, that's our triple-A team, went to the post last year. They were really good. And they started out this year looking good, so that's why he's at the game. To see if they stay good. Now does it make sense?

Shady nibbled on his tongue. He didn't want to blow up on Peach. Not yet. He needed him, even if he was a lot weirder than he seemed when they shared a cell. "Just get to the ballpark, will ya? And please stop talking. I want to think."

Peach was fine with that, since he also preferred to think. He had the germ of an idea about what to present Jahllo, and he wanted to flush it out.

* * *

The Aces were losing. It suited Tinman just fine. It meant many of the fans left early in the bottom of the sixth, including the wench who had absconded with his favorite seat for the last two seasons. Money issues caused him to forego the purchase of season tickets, and now Seat 1 in the sixth row of Section 110 was in the possession of a little old lady who dozed through most games. Life was definitely not fair.

But now she was gone, and Tinman slipped away from the cheap section, and reclaimed his prized spot. At least for a few innings, he was back in the driver's seat. The El Paso Chihuahuas were at bat in the top of the seventh and hitting just about everything the Aces could hurl at them.

He did not know the score of the game. He cared little about the standings, the rivalries, or the overall sport for that matter. His love of baseball came purely from the pitching. His fascination began after he discovered the use of spin in pool. He saw the similarities between the effect a pitcher's release has on a baseball, to the English a pool cue has on the cue ball. The game held little interest but he never tired of analyzing the pitching.

That's why he cherished this particular seat. Right behind home plate, it had an unimpeded view of the ball as it left the pitcher's hand and sailed through the air en route to the catcher's mitt. He could care less what team was pitching, or what pitcher was on the mound. He sat through the games mesmerized by the paths of the pitches and the spins that caused such reactions, caring little whether the hitters hit or not, or if hits produced runs or outs. When a game was over, there was a fifty-fifty chance he would actually know who won.

He came to the game because he needed a distraction from the stupid day he was having, and he wanted to mess with Shady. The old fart would expect him to be waiting like a good little boy, and he was determined to prove him wrong. He'd learned long ago, the importance of keeping people off-kilter.

He knew Peach would eventually find him, and that was fine. He was still curious about what Shady had to show, he just didn't want to appear too interested. The pitcher for the Aces threw a snapdragon curveball, and Tinman rewound the pitch in his mind and studied how it was done. Then The Feeling broke into his thoughts.

He first felt The Feeling before he learned to talk. It was a supernatural connection he held with his brother. When Peach was nearby, the energy of the universe shifted, and he would know beyond a shadow of a doubt he was right around the corner.

It was so strong right now, he didn't even have to turn around to know Peach was about to say—"

"Hey, brother!" Peach flopped down in the seat next to him. Shady harrumphed as he sat beside Peach.

"I told you to wait for me," barked Shady at Tinman.

"How are they doing?" asked Peach, knowing Tinman wouldn't know, but hoping to ward off a public scene.

"What do you have to show me?" asked Tinman to Shady without looking over.

Shady leaned forward and locked his eyes on the side of Tinman's face. It had absolutely no effect. Finally, he reached in his pocket and pulled out the coin. He looked around like he was holding the Crown Jewels which had just disappeared from the Tower of London. Normally, he would never act so dumb, but, hey, he was stoned. No one was paying the least bit of attention to him, so he placed it flat on an open palm and surreptitiously slid his hand out low in front of Tinman. "It's one of those rare silver dollars I told you about. Picked it up as a keepsake during the heist."

Tinman glanced down, then rolled his eyes. "If this is all you have, it could prove inimical to our proposed collaboration. Don't you think?"

Shady's face went blank, like he'd wandered into a church where everyone was speaking in tongues. He didn't know how to answer. How many people would? He closed his hand over the coin, and sat back.

There was a long pause where Tinman enjoyed the silent war going on in Shady's ignorant mind. Shady shook his head rapidly, like trying to come out of a bad dream. He let out little frustrated bursts of air. Peach was having trouble keeping the giggles at bay. Shady was oblivious as he leaned over and whispered in his ear.

Peach whispered back, "Don't ask me, he's the one reads the dictionary."

Shady exhaled sharply, leaned forward, and cocked his head to Tinman. "I don't see why it would prove that," he said in answer to Tinman's question, and sat back, feeling quite pleased with himself for dodging the intelligence bullet.

Tinman admired the half-ass attempt but wasn't willing to let him off so easy. "You think two coins proves this heist is worth my time? Are you trying to inveigle me?"

Shady's marijuana-addled mind finally exploded. He let out an involuntary yowl like a newborn who's suddenly realized they had arrived in the cold, hard world, and the comfort and protection of the womb was a thing of the past.

The guy at bat whipped his head around, as did the umpire. Several players climbed out of the dugouts to see the source of the disturbance. Everywhere Shady looked, the field, the stands, the Jumbotron, he was the center of attention.

When it became clear he was not going to make any more weird sounds, play resumed. Through clenched teeth, he hissed, "Peach, Your brother is too blind to see what I've got. Call your fence. If he's as good as you say, he'll know what's what."

Peach was okay with that, because he'd finally figured out what to use to lure Jahllo. "Sure thing," he said and started to go. He stopped, and bent down to Tinman. "I, uh, lost my phone and haven't had a chance to get another. Do you mind?"

Tinman handed over his throwaway and said, "I don't think you'll have much luck. Either way, ditch that thing when you're done. We'll both get new ones."

"Check," said Peach and climbed up the stairs, whistling, "Take Me Out To The Ball Game." Several people in the stands joined in.

Deciding he had to do something to break the impasse with Tinman, Shady took a few moments to rally his THC infused brain cells. He hated the guy, but needed him.

"You really read the dictionary?" he asked in what he thought was his nicest tone.

"That's right."

"Must be working on the I's."

"That's very insightful of you."

Shady sighed. "Must get that from your mother. She always used big words back in the day. I liked it coming from her."

This surprised Tinman but he refused to show it, merely grunting. Shady tried a new tack. "You know your brother is living in a nuthouse."

"I'm the one introduced it to him."

This surprised Shady but he refused to show it, merely snorting. Never very tactful, he had run out of tacks, so he clammed up.

Tinman figured this was the moment to discuss the beef he had with him regarding Peach. When his brother first returned to Reno, he revealed the new philosophy of life he'd learned in prison. It didn't sit well with Tinman, and he'd been looking for someone to vent on. Now he had the source of the injustice right next to him.

"So you're the guy put this drivel into my brother's head about the benefits of selling his soul to the devil. I ought to rip your innards out just for that."

Shady chuckled low and long. "I did him a favor. After all, it's better to reign in hell, than serve in heaven, as they say."

"They, as in the people that spend most of their lives in prison. You're a crock, Shady. And a liar."

Shady's hand flinched, dying to reach for the gun in his jacket. But there were too many witnesses. And he'd have to time the shot exactly when a batter hit the ball. And it would have to be a really good, loud hit to cover the report. And he was really, really high. He ruled out the notion. "Lying goes with the territory. You are in our business aren't you? Or are you just some poser, trying to hang onto your brother's coattails?"

"You're on the lam, Shady. I know it, and now you know I know. So no matter what this heist is worth, hanging around you is like hanging around a landmine. The feds step on you, my brother and I and the others all go up in smoke."

Shady was so blindsided he couldn't speak for a solid minute. Finally, he said, "Now I see why you're the brains of the outfit. I won't ask how you found out. But the thing is, the feds don't know squat. I got no connections. They'll never trace me here."

"Let's see, they'll start with old cellmates, which means Peach will definitely come on the radar. Then they'll dig into his background and find where he was born. Reno might not be on the top of their list, but it's on the list, guaranteed. Especially since you admitted the cops were aware of your past activities here. These people are not ignoramuses, like some people I know."

"Will you please can the five-dollar words! I get it! And I'm telling you, there's plenty of time if we move fast. We do the heist, make the split, and you never see me again."

"Infinitely appealing."

"Do me a favor, though, and don't tell Peach yet. I want to do it myself."

"I don't keep secrets from my brother."

Shady growled, but Tinman was watching the pitcher throw a rare knuckle curveball. It reminded him of the one "Happy" Hooton used to pitch in the late 70's.

"Okay, guys, it's all set," said Peach retaking his seat with a flourish.

"You mean he's actually interested?" asked Tinman.

"Sure thing! Lucky for us he's right around the corner in Oregon. Take him a couple of days," said Peach, reaching for some of Tinman's dwindling Cracker Jacks.

"I told you!" said Shady. "What did I tell you?"

Tinman shrugged. "Score one for you. Now, either you tell Peach your little secret, or I do. Right now."

"Secret! Oh boy, I love secrets. What is it Shady?" asked Peach.

The batter for the Aces swung hard at a sinker and struck out. He banged his bat on the ground, splitting it in two. The crowd groaned. Shady looked at Peach's glowing face, and groaned along with them.

SIXTEEN

SPECIAL AGENT DEKE WOLFF FIRST SPOTTED THE TAIL his boss Tilston sicced on him when he was boarding his plane at Dulles Airport. He'd never met her, but it made little difference. She looked the part of an FBI agent so much it was laughable. Also, she was not good at tailing, which meant she was some newbie Tilston was grooming to take over his job if he could pin anything on him.

He had a target on his back, but he wasn't particularly concerned. After his one lapse of judgement he had become much better at hiding his favorite vice.

As he flew over the continent he wondered how to play the particular game he was in. First and foremost, he had to catch his fugitive. But that didn't bother him. He was excellent at his job and had no doubt he would run this Shady to ground. His second objective was to try out his poker skills in the Biggest Little City in the World. There were plenty of poker rooms in the various casinos, but he had his sights set on a high-stakes private game, and he'd heard there was no shortage of them in Reno. The problem was how to find one, and not have his tail find out.

By the time he was flying over Kansas, he'd decided the best thing to do was confront the situation head on. Better to keep your enemies close. So, when the plane landed and everyone disembarked, he took his time strolling down the hallway to the luggage claim area, admiring the advertisements for casinos and shows. His tail, who had been at the back of the plane, had to slow down as well so as not to overtake him.

Reno-Tahoe International Airport has a big name that belies its actual size, so it only took a few minutes before he was gliding down the escalator to the concourse where he could retrieve his luggage. His tail was only two people behind, and doing an awful job of being inconspicuous. Deke was a little irked that Tilston would send such a raw rookie to keep an eye on him. Probably wanted to get in her pants.

At the bottom of the escalator, a crowd waited for the late-morning arrivals, with girlfriends running into their boyfriends' arms, and children jockeying to get a better view of their visiting grandparents. Deke reached the bottom, spied the sign for luggage claim and started on his trek.

He noticed right away the difference between this airport and most others. Above him floated a giant neon sign picturing poker players at an upcoming tournament. He paused, and grinned, wishing he was one of them. Slot machines filled whole sections of the concourse. He had no interest, but even the most diehard non-gambler was forced to weave their way past the glowing, flashing bandits.

He was almost clear of them when a tall, elderly man, sporting a walrus mustache, angrily slapped the screen of the machine he was playing, and lunged off his stool directly into his path.

Deke had to stop so abruptly he stumbled backwards a couple of steps and bumped into a body behind him. He glanced back but caught only a shadow disappearing around the row of slots. When he looked forward, the elderly man was back at his machine, manically trying to win back his losings. He said to the man's shoulder, "You'd do better just throwing that money away. It would be a lot quicker."

The man grunted, and continued playing. Deke moved on, wondering about the stupidity of mankind. Everyone knew slots was a losing proposition. Poker was the only game where skill made a difference. A guy that old should know better. He looked behind to see if his tail had managed to lose him, and saw the old man was gone. Maybe he'd actually taken his advice. Good for him.

At the end of the slots, he spotted his tail who was waving a fist at a teenage boy who was scurrying away toward the exits. From the looks of it, the kid must have collided with her because her carry-on bag and purse were on the ground with some of the contents scattered to and fro.

He took it as a sign. He walked back, and stooped next to her as she collected her things. She looked up and gasped. Then tried to cover it, poorly.

He held out his hand, "We haven't been formerly introduced. Special Agent Deke Wolff, as you already know. And you?"

She was tongue-tied, her face slowly turning crimson. He continued, undeterred. "Come on, let's get this over with. Tilston set you on me. Still, there's no reason we can't be friends. We are on the same side. At least I hope so."

He watched as she made her decision. "It wasn't my idea," she said. "In fact, I don't feel right about it at all. It goes against my beliefs. I told the commander that!"

"Name?"

"Oh. Mandy Leadbetter." She grabbed his hand and gave it a surprisingly firm shake. "My father and brothers are cops and they'd have my head if they thought I was spying on another brother."

"Don't worry about it," said Deke, good-naturedly. "Tilston and I have been playing this game for a while."

She smiled in relief and was about to say something when his phone rang. He fished it out of his jacket pocket.

"Well, commander, funny you should call right now," said Deke, with a wink to Mandy. She freaked and waved her hands frantically, begging him to keep their secret. He patted his hand in the air, reassuring her. Then he put a finger to his mouth and switched the phone to speaker.

"Shut up and listen," said Special-Agent-In-Charge, Franklyn Tilston. "We've got some new information. I take it you're in Reno."

"Why, no, sir," said Deke with a grin. "I took your advice and decided to start my search elsewhere."

"Shut up. I know you're there. But you have to leave."

"And why is that?"

"We got a call on Jingles' phone. We triangulated the source and it came from Reno."

"And you want me to leave. Makes sense."

"Shut up! We started tracking the phone, and right after the call it went on the move. Had to be Shady, seeing if the body was discovered yet. When the agent's voice answered, instead of Jingles, he knew we were on to him. It's been moving steadily since early yesterday. Over the mountains into Northern California."

"No more outgoing calls?"

"No."

"And it keeps moving."

"Steadily. I'll give you the latest position. You're going to need to rent a car."

"A train."

"Don't be a smartass!"

"The phone was dumped onto a train," continued Deke. "Probably a freighter. Rather than destroy it, thus stopping the signal and leading us straight to Reno, Shady sends us on a goose chase. He knew we would locate the origin of the call and trace the phone's movements. It was the main purpose for the call, not to see if the body was discovered. No crook in his right mind would do that. It was a ruse, to mess with us."

There was a long pause. Deke yawned.

"Oh."

"Sooo, maybe I should stay in Reno for now?"

"Shut the hell up! Of course I want you to stay. We'll keep looking for Jingles' car. You look up this Peach character. If it's a dead-end. Move on."

"Naturally," said Deke, rubbing the fatigue from his eyes. "Hello?" He stared at the phone, and realized he'd been hung up on. Mandy was gaping. "What?" he asked.

"How did you know about the train?" she asked.

"Because that's what I would do," said Deke, rising to his feet. "Let's get out of here."

They were silent on the way to the luggage claim. Their flight left at an ungodly hour of the morning and with the time change, it was still morning. Deke was starving.

"You hungry?"

Mandy nodded shyly, suddenly feeling foolish next to this pro. He was dressed as a successful businessman, possibly here for a convention. Casual, but classy. No one would ever think he was FBI. She blushed at how obvious she must appear and how foolish in his eyes.

Deke caught her studying him and smiled. He pointed to a food vendor and headed for it. As they stepped up to the counter and perused the small menu, he reached for his wallet. It was gone.

* * *

The first thing Bones did every morning was stretch his fingers. If the creeping arthritis that had overtaken him in recent years was acting up, he would fall asleep for another hour. No work that day. If they felt good, he would immediately rise, his brain clicking away, choosing possible locations for the day's whiz.

This morning, they felt like they did in his heyday. He smiled. He loved his work and would do it every day if he could. He knew, however, there would come a time his fingers would not obey his commands, and he would have to retire. It would be too dangerous to do otherwise. That's why, for the first time in his life, he was actually looking for a big score that would set him up for good.

Most cannons never really think about big scores. They work on the odds, knowing the more pokes they picked, the better the harvest. They worked day to day, wallet to wallet, without ever considering the future. Most died broke. Bones had been like that all his life. Of course, he always stashed away fall dough in the rare case he had to deal with the law. But this was different. Now, he wanted enough money to retire gracefully. And enough for Catfish, as well.

Since the death of the Big Con, his partner relied on his skills as a cannon. But when Catfish was a young man, and a first-class roper steering marks into the big rooms, Bones relied on him. Drifting into Chicago at the age of thirteen, he never imagined he would amount to anything. But Catfish took him under his wing, introduced him to the con, and for a precious time, they were kings, making and spending fortunes like there was no tomorrow.

Bones knew he would never have experienced wealth of any kind if it were not for Catfish. Though the money was long gone, the gratitude for being able to live high just once in a lifetime, would never fade. It's why he privately hoped the heist with Shady would prove to be a go.

As soon as he chose the day's location for the whiz, he dressed accordingly. A pickpocket's protection came from blending in with any crowd, and Bones was a master. His clothes were always well-bought, because people never expected a man of means to be a pickpocket. For today's work, he dressed to look like a well-to-do retiree from a mid-Atlantic state, most likely Virginia, but it could have been Maryland.

As he waited for the water to heat up, he called Catfish and told him the location, and asked him to round up Tek for use as a second stall. Normally, they worked alone, but for two reasons, Bones preferred a second helper today. The first was, Tek had been bothering him for months to take him out on the whiz. Both knew he did not have the skills to be a mechanic, but in practice, he had proved to be a decent stall, especially as the duke man.

The duke man's duty was to take the poke after the touch, turn it out in a safe place, keeping cash only, and immediately dump it where it wouldn't be found quickly. The cannon only kept the wallet in his possession for a split second. This was because if the touch went sour, he was the most likely suspect, being closest to the mark. Tek was a natural duke man. He was young, with strong legs, and could move quickly if pursued.

The second reason he requested two stalls, was due to the day's chosen location: Reno airport, one of the few in the country in which he would work. It was very small. If the mob needed to scoot, it was a quick walk across the drive where passengers were picked up and dropped off, through the bottom floor of the parking garage, across Terminal Way, and they were off the site, lost in the city. Most airports were far from anything else, and it took a shuttle ride or a long hike to get to the perimeter.

The small size did come with a drawback however. The crowds were much smaller than in large airports, and no whiz mob liked working out in the open. A crowd, or crush, was their protection. To counteract the lack of one, Bones liked to have a third person, so the main stall, Catfish, would not have to cover the touch, as well as take the handoff of the poke. With a duke man, this problem disappeared. He handled the poke.

After his regular breakfast of one cup of oolong tea and two pieces of dry toast, he went to the street level of the tenement apartment building. He started walking down the sidewalk to the designated pickup spot three blocks away. He was old school and still maintained the proper code among thieves, that included never telling even your closest associates where you live. The policy was as much for the protection of the partners as it was for yourself. If the cops picked up someone and grilled them, they could honestly say they didn't know where such and such lived. What they didn't know, didn't hurt you.

As he waited for his ride. He thought about the old days when he used to work the railroad stations. They were popular places for pickpockets, and sometimes three or four mobs would work the same one. When two cannons from different mobs spotted the same loaded mark, there were often heated negotiations as to who would get the touch. He grinned at the memory.

Pickpockets were so plentiful back then, the stations used to place signs warning passengers to beware of them. The mobs loved the signs, because the average person when seeing one would immediately check their valuables. This made the cannon's job a lot easier as the mark was essentially showing them exactly where their wallets were placed on their bodies.

Most of the class cannons had died or retired without passing on the skills, so there was no longer a need for warnings to be posted. The advent of video cameras did give Bones pause, but he soon realized the people behind those cameras, especially at airports and other stations, were on the lookout for terrorists and had no experience in spotting pickpockets. After that epiphany, he gave video cameras no further thought. When his hands were properly functioning, his skills were invisible to the naked eye, even from a couple feet away.

Tek pulled up and Bones climbed into the back. Catfish was in the front. As they made the short drive to the airport, Bones went over the day's plan, and detailed Tek's duties. Tek was thrilled, listening to every word with great concentration.

They parked at the Day's Hotel, located on Terminal Way, directly across from the airport's parking garage. They walked across the road and entered the garage, at separate intervals. This level was where people picked up their rental cars, and immediately Bones spotted a mark.

He was referred to as an egg: male, thirty years or younger. He'd just picked up a rental car and was by the trunk, loudly scolding his young wife for forgetting to pack something of his. The woman was on the verge of tears. He was enjoying himself.

Catfish needed no office to know Bones had targeted the young man. He walked directly to the rental car, and claimed it was his. The egg launched into a new tirade, directed at Catfish. Bones hustled by, and without breaking stride, the touch was made.

He immediately handed the poke off to Tek who veered away. He continued across the garage to the airport. Meanwhile, Catfish was playing senile and extricating himself from the situation. Bones chuckled, wondering how the egg would manage to blame the loss of his wallet on his wife.

Inside the airport, he had a few minutes before Tek could empty the wallet, ditch it, and join the mob inside. He took the time to appraise the mood of the place. Several early flights from the East Coast were arriving within the half hour. A small crowd gathered to greet the late-morning arrivals.

The last time they worked the airport, they realized the lack of people could be worked around by using the slot machines as blocks and diversions. Clustered in a heap at the bottom of the escalator where the disembarking passengers were funneled, everyone was forced to walk through the jumble.

He slipped into the maze of machines refreshing his memory of the likely pathways people would take. He spotted Tek taking up his position near the escalator.

Catfish showed right after, and he shot him some non-verbal office, telling him which slot machine he should sit at. The whiz was on.

Bones was a genius at locating loaded marks. He had a list of tells he ran through in his head, almost subconsciously. He studied the rhythm of the stride. People with money walk differently than people without. People with money who can afford to spend it, walk differently than people who have withdrawn their life savings to take one last shot at glory in the casinos.

He watched what they looked at, and how they looked at it. Shop windows, restaurants, advertisements. Could they easily afford to eat in that exclusive restaurant? Were they even considering it? Could they buy that expensive jewelry for their wives, or would it empty their bank accounts?

He studied the overall mood and impression of the person as they moved through space. People with filled wallets carried themselves with a certain self-assurance and lack of concern. Life was good. I can buy whatever I want. Money is not an issue.

He was expert at identifying clothing, and could tell a tailored suit from an off-the-rack at a mere glance. He knew fabric types because some were easier to pick than others. He knew the costs of fabrics in order to identify the financial status of the mark. He watched to see how the person wore their clothes. Were they comfortable in expensive garb, or were they wearing their Sunday best and usually had on Walmart specials?

Locating the poke was the easy part. But no point in pinching a wallet unless it was full. And not just with credit cards. Everybody had them, but they were useless to a pickpocket. He needed a mark that still liked and needed the feel of cold hard cash.

And bingo. There he was. Coming down the escalator. Clothes casual but classy. Moving like he'd been born in them. Experienced traveler. A sense of being above the crowd, but unconcerned in their presence. Good-humored. He watched as he took in his surroundings, choosing specific signs and attractions to look at. Business man. Not corporate upper management. Successful entrepreneur. Yes. That was him.

Bones was as sure as he'd ever been. A few hand movements to Catfish and Tek alerted them to the mark, and the play to be used. As the man moved through the slot machines, Catfish went to work, with Bones directly behind the target, studying his neck, watching for any sign he may turn without warning.

Catfish pulled off the stick perfectly, stopping the mark in his tracks. Unfortunately, as Bones moved in, the man stumbled backwards, bumping into him as he was making the touch. But Tek was shading the play as he was taught, and was right there for the handoff, so Bones decided not to go to the floor with the poke and call it off.

He slipped the wallet into Tek's jacket and they separated. He decided it was a sign they should call it a day, and headed for the exit. As he maneuvered around some slots, he glanced back and saw Tek slam into a very officious looking woman. Law, for sure. Bones swallowed hard. There was nothing to do but hope for the best. It's how the whiz mob functioned and survived. The cannon must be protected at all costs, or the mob went under. He had an obligation to get clear, and with no reservations, he continued out of the building.

He waited for some time at Tek's car before he finally saw him hightailing it out of the garage. Behind, Catfish meandered along without a care in the world. Bones relaxed.

They waited until they were on the road before talking. Then they all erupted at once.

"You're not going to believe what I have to tell you!" cried Tek.

"Hold on now," drawled Bones, trying to bring order. "How about the mark, Catfish? Did he beef gun?"

"Never knew he got hit."

"That's good. Not the prettiest touch I ever pulled. Had my mitt in his prat when he bobbled. Damn near had to go downstairs with the poke."

"Eh, my bad. I crumbed the play," said Catfish. "I stuck him too hard. Startled him."

"Either way, I felt like a rough tool out there."

"Get over it, pal. You're the best and you know it. Now listen, I too have something juicy to spill."

"I called it first!" cried Tek angrily.

"You did," said Bones. "But first, what happened with that lady? You brought attention to us, she could have ranked the play. Weren't you looking where you were going?"

"Come on, you taught me better than that. She came out of nowhere, moving fast, like she was following that guy."

"And she looked like law of some sort," said Bones.

"She was and she is," said Catfish. "At least I think so. After the play while I was waiting to see if the mark would beef gun, he walks right up to her, like he knows her. Well, I maneuver around behind the end of the slots so I could get an ear on them, and turns out they kind of do know each other. And from what I could hear, it makes sense you say they were law. Maybe partners, or were one time. But that's not the best part. While those two are talking the mark gets a call."

"Will you guys please stop!" yelled Tek, abruptly pulling the SUV into a shopping center and screeching to a stop. "We just picked the pocket of an FBI agent! Attached to something called the Fugitive Apprehension Unit."

"You sure?" asked Bones, not wanting to believe he could have been so off in his choice of marks.

Tek looked guilty and nodded. He reached into his jacket and pulled out Deke's wallet. Before the two old guys could freak out, he said, "Look, I know I should have tossed it! But you wouldn't believe me if you didn't see it."

He handed it over and Bones and Catfish did a quick perusal. Tek said excitedly, "Why do you think he's in Reno?"

Catfish leaned back and said, "Chasing a fugitive, what else. Right? Okay, now this starts to make sense. You ready for the kicker boys? So, like I said, the mark gets a call and he's got it on speaker. The guy he's talking to uses a word that's quite familiar to us these days. When I first heard it, I thought it was used in a general sense. What with all the rackets those slots make, it was hard to hear everything."

"What word would that be, pray tell?" asked Bones, his eyes narrowing.

"Shady. And now that I rewind, and piece it together, it was not as in, oh, what a shady park this is, or, this sounds like a shady deal. No sir. They were talking about a guy. Our guy."

The three exchanged looks. Bones drawled, "You know what I'm thinking?"

They all did. It was time to see Tinman.

SEVENTEEN

TINMAN GOT THE CALL AT THE UNCIVILIZED HOUR of 10 a.m.
It came through on the new phone he'd bought after the
ballgame. Peach had bought one too, and as far as he
knew, he was the only one who had his new number, and
vice-versa. So he answered. It was Shady, borrowing
Peach's phone.

"I got a bone to pick with you!"

Tinman did not feel this deserved a response.

"Hey. Hello? Hello!"

After a lengthy pause, Tinman heard Shady tell Peach
the damn phone didn't work.

"Hello?" said Peach.

"Yo," said Tinman.

"There you are! Hey, Shady wants to talk."

"Don't put him back on. What does he want?"

"I stopped over at Dez' for breakfast, and he says he
wants to show you who's boss."

"How exactly would he like to do that?" asked Tinman,
drifting back to sleep.

"Well, I told him it wasn't such a hot idea, but he's
determined."

"Get to the point."

"He wants to shoot pool."

Tinman's eyes popped open. "What does he want to play for?"

"We didn't get that far. But my guess is domination."

Tinman could hear Shady chuckling and a fire lit in his stomach. "Bring him on."

Thirty minutes later, he was doing the last prep on his best cue, using a Willard scuffer to rough up the tip and prevent miscues. He bought it when he was one of the top hustlers in the country. Custom-made by McDermott, one of the best cue manufacturers in the world. Weighing 21 ounces with a shaft diameter of 13mm, the handle was beautifully inlaid with snakewood, turquoise, silver, and ebony.

Twenty-five years ago, it cost him eleven thousand dollars. No matter how bad things got financially he would never sell it. It would be like cutting off one of his limbs. He never used it when working because it scared off the marks. He used his Sneaky Pete. Similar quality, but no fancy woodworking, so it appeared to be a house cue.

He chose his McDermott for today's play, because he would not be hustling Shady. There would be no hiding of his speed. He would play straight up, because he didn't want to merely beat his brains out. He wanted to obliterate him, destroy his nerve. So for the rest of his life he would think twice before picking up a cue with his dirty paws.

He heard yammering outside and knew his prey had arrived. He unscrewed the cue and placed it in it's hard leather case, next to the Sneaky Pete. Opening the door to his apartment, he saw Peach, Shady and Dez outside the Clubhouse. As usual, Dez was in an uproar. As usual, he could care less. When he was shooting, nothing short of an exploding ICBM could distract him.

He walked calmly down the stairs. Dez came running.

"Honey, please don't do this! If you play him, then you won't be friends anymore!"

"We're not friends now. Move," he said. She did, grudgingly, and he walked to the Clubhouse. Peach sidled up as he was unlocking the place.

"I hate to side with Dez, but maybe this isn't such a good idea."

"It was his idea," said Tinman, stepping inside.

"I know. That's the problem. He's more stubborn than you."

Tinman was in the zone and had no interest in idle chatter. He said over his shoulder, "Can you get the cover for me?"

"Sure. Sure thing, champ." Peach went to the table and removed the canvas cover, carefully folding it as he went.

Tinman laid his case on a table and flipped it open. He removed his favorite cue and screwed it together. Shady watched, unimpressed. Tinman took out his Sneaky Pete, and screwed that together.

He held it out to Shady, who said, "You get the good one, huh? Hustling me already."

Tinman held out his McDermott. Shady barked out a laugh. "Oh, I get it. You actually wanted me to have this one. No thanks, buster. I'll take the first one. I know your kind."

"I'll play you with a broom handle if you want," said Tinman, sincerely.

Shady was taken aback, but brushed it off. "Naw, I wouldn't want to be unfair."

"What's your game?" asked Tinman.

"Old school. 14-1 straight. The only game."

"That's the first intelligent thing you've said since I met you."

Dez rushed up between them and faced Shady. "Sweetie, listen! You really don't want to do this. And certainly not 14-1. That's his game! He'll skewer you."

"Go sit down, Dizzy."

"I been meaning to ask, what's up with this, Dizzy?" asked Tinman.

Shady smiled mischievously, and stroked Dez' hair. "Pet name for my lover."

Tinman watched Dez melt, legs quivering. He had never seen her like that. One side of him wanted her to stay this happy forever, and another wanted to punch the lights out of the man who made her feel this way.

"Did you tell her yet?" asked Tinman, unable to stop from bursting her balloon.

"Tell me what?"

Tinman waited, giving Shady the chance, but he shrugged and waved him on. Tinman said, "He wasn't let out, Dez. He walked away."

"Well, yeah! Did you think he was telling the truth? I knew right off. He didn't have to tell me. Course he did last night, but what's the big deal? You can't hold that against him. For crying out loud, it's prison! If you see a chance to blow, you take it."

Tinman should have known, but it still surprised him. Shady gave him a smarmy smile. "Now that's a moll. Am I right, boys?" He hugged Dez, squeezing lovingly tight.

The sight made Tinman queasy, but the glow exuding from Dez was hard to miss, and harder to ignore. She gently pushed herself from the embrace and gave Shady her sternest lover-to-lover look. "Seriously, darling, there are bigger things at stake here. You don't need to do this. In fact, you really don't want to do this."

In a flash, Shady's mien shifted. He pointed to a table and said harshly, "Make yourself scarce." Dez obediently tucked her tail between her legs and shuffled off.

Tinman was forced to admire his ability to shut Dez up. At the same time, he wanted to swing the butt of his cue into his kneecaps so he could never do the tango again.

"So what are the stakes?" asked Shady with a grin.

"You have nothing I want."

"The coin! I lose, you get what the fence gives. I win, you pay the same."

Tinman laughed in his face like he was some idiot who had painted himself into a corner. Shady reddened and said, "What's so funny?"

"You, as always. That coin isn't worth diddly. But I'll tell you what is. If I win, and we decide to go along with the heist after we meet with the fence, I make all the decisions on the operation."

Shady shrugged. "Okay. Is there an, and?"

"And. If we don't decide to do the heist, you leave town, immediately. For good."

"Wait a minute!" croaked Dez from the corner.

"Shut up," hissed Shady.

Tinman noted his tone and knew his second request was not needed. Heist or no heist, Dez be damned, Shady had no intention of hanging around Reno.

Tinman went on. "Lastly, if we do this heist, you will not be there during the job."

"You crazy?! And for giving you my left arm, what do I get if I win?"

Peach involuntarily burst out laughing. He couldn't help himself and he couldn't stop. It was infectious, because Dez started giggling.

"Enough!" yelled Shady, and the room grudgingly went quiet.

"You get to run the heist. And I'll give you this," said Tinman, holding out his McDermott cue.

Peach and Dez gasped, and Shady realized the weight of the bet. "You're on."

"One game to 125, winner take all."

Shady sensed a trap. "Best of three."

Tinman was hoping he'd say that. "Suit yourself. Okay if Peach rack and score?"

"Of course. He's my blood."

Peach grabbed one of the cheap house cues and walked to a line of wire stretched between two hooks mounted on the ceiling. On it hung 100 wooden score beads, with a fixed wooden block dividing them into two sections of 50. As a ball is sunk for a certain player a bead on his side of the wire is slid toward the center using a cue stick. As a player reaches fifty balls, the beads are slid back and the scoring continues at 51. The first player that reaches 125 is the winner.

As Tinman set up two balls for the lag, Shady started talking. Tinman had played thousands of players and knew the type. The talker, using nonstop jabbering—or sharking—designed to throw the opposing player off. He had long ago taught himself not to listen, but Shady was unaware and kept up his patter.

"The nice thing about being a bigtime yegg, you don't have to work all that often. Some hauls lasted a year before I had to get back at it. So, I had a lot of time to kill."

Tinman leaned down to his ball, preparing to lag. As Shady bent to the table he said, "And you know what I did with all my free time?"

They both stroked at the same time, each attempting to have their ball hit the far rail, return to the near rail, and land closer to it than the other shooter's ball.

As the balls traversed the table, Shady continued with his soliloquy. "I shot pool. That's what I did with all that free time. Sometimes from morning to morning."

The balls neared the closest rail and Shady's petered out before it got there, landing a good four inches away. Tinman's rested butt up against it.

"Lucky shot," said Shady. "Your choice."

The winner of the lag has the option of breaking or forcing his opponent to break. Tinman plopped the cue ball in Shady's hand. In his experience very few straight pool shooters understood the first break of the game. He wanted to see if his skill matched his boasting. He didn't doubt he had played a lot of pool in his day. Pool was king when Shady was a young man. But he knew all the practice in the world didn't help if you didn't have the gift.

"Scared of that first break, huh?" Shady scoffed. "Yeah, that first one can be tricky. Or so they tell me. I don't let it bother me. And don't remind me I have to get the cue ball and two balls to a rail or I scratch. I been playing this game long before I crawled into the sack with your mother."

Dez winced. Tinman saw it, and allowed one last thought before he became completely immersed in the battle. Shady needed to be taught a lesson about respect.

Peach removed the wooden rack and Shady dropped the cue ball in the middle of the table. "Uh, Shady," said Peach. "Don't you want it a little off-center so you can hit one of the corner balls?"

"Shut up and learn." He gave the cue ball a mighty whack. It sailed forth, smashing into the rack and scattering the balls. The four ball dropped in the corner pocket.

Dez groaned in horror. Peach hung his head. Shady smiled, misreading their reactions, and said, "See! I don't let that first rack bother me. Everyone's always trying to get so fancy, nick the corner ball, send it and the other corner ball to rails and back into the rack. Play it safe. Leave you with no shot so you have to play a safety. Then I play a safety. Back and forth. What's the point? I got a ball in, and now it's my table. It's a long game. One break makes no difference."

Shady had shown Tinman all he needed. Continuous straight pool is a game of patience, and strategy. Shady had none, and had never played against someone who only needed one false step by the opponent to run out.

Shady took his silence as despair, and leaned down with an air of confidence. He sank six more balls, his cue ball running all over the table to pluck them from the pack. On the next ball, he nearly scratched, leaving the cue ball hanging on a side pocket.

"Tough leave, sucker!" laughed Shady. "Have at it."

Straight pool is unlike other pool games. It is a thinking man's game. It's a game of physics and geometry. The table is the plane where the balls are manipulated, constantly shifting into new patterns, knots to be unraveled. Modern players preferred fast moving games like nine ball, so the game of champions had lost favor. But it was still the most intricate and beautiful of all pool games.

The average player must think five to seven balls out, mapping the correct position after each shot so the cue ball is set for the next shot, and so on. Very good players map out eight to ten. Tinman planned out whole racks, thinking fifteen ahead.

"Experience, that's what it all comes down to," Shady boasted. "Don't matter what you're born with. Age and experience is going to win out every time."

For Tinman to think a rack out, he had to visualize an imaginary triangle on the table, representing the rack. In continuous straight pool, the balls are racked when one ball is still left on the table, leaving fourteen balls in the rack with the head spot empty.

"I don't blame you if you want to walk away. Save a little pride. I have a heart you know. Tell him Dez. She'll tell you. I gotta heart. You just gotta know how to treat me."

The idea is to leave the last ball on the table, or break ball, in a position where the cue ball can sink it and then continue into the new rack, thus disturbing balls and allowing the run to continue. To create a long run, a player must know from the beginning of each rack, what ball should likely be the break ball. Once located it must remain undisturbed throughout the run.

The next most important ball to locate is the key ball, the ball which will be sunk before the break ball. It needs to be sunk in such a way that leaves the cue ball in perfect position to sink the break ball, then ricochet into the rack.

"Come on already! You got squat. Just play a safety and give me back my table."

Most importantly, straight pool is a game of domination. Once a player has the table, he must do everything in his power not to cede it to the other player. If he does, he must shoot a safety which leaves the cue ball in a position that causes the oncoming player to also shoot a safety, thereby relinquishing the table back. Tinman was a master at safeties, and didn't shy away from them out of some misplaced sense of machismo.

"And don't think all my experience came when I was younger. Oh no. In the pen, that's what I did. Sink balls, one after the other. I'll show you how, right after you miss."

Tinman was set, his first shot the most difficult. The cue ball was snookered by the edges of the side pocket so he couldn't shoot any hard angle shots to his left or right. But he had a shot on the one ball sitting to the left of the opposite side pocket. It required a ninety-degree reverse angle hit, which would send his cue ball rolling more than he wanted, but it was the obvious shot.

He leaned down until the cue shaft split his chin. Back perfectly flat, body balanced. He did a few practice strokes and pulled back his cue.

The front door swung open. "Tinman! Guess what we found out!" hollered Tek.

Tinman stroked. The cue ball cut the one ball which plopped in the corner pocket.

Shady spit air. "Too bad, kid. You almost threw him off."

Tinman moved swiftly to his next position. Bones and Catfish placated the excited Tek. Revelations could wait. Tinman was at work. The three quietly moved to seats with a good vantage point.

As Tinman stalked the table, calling out shots and sinking balls, the clicking of the score beads rattled Shady. His running commentary ceased, and he became as transfixed as everyone.

Forty-two minutes later, Peach called, "Game. 125 to 7." Tinman had run out, averaging three balls a minute. He showed no pride or flush of victory. This was his job. He calmly chalked his cue, waiting for the next game.

Shady leapt from his chair and stretched, like it was no big deal. But when he snapped at Peach, "Rack 'em already, will you!" it was clear he was shaken.

Catfish whispered to Dez, "Shady actually got seven?"

"He broke first. Busted the first rack wide open," she muttered, with a mixed look of disgust and desperation.

Bones whistled low. "Must have suicidal tendencies."

Shady was in a rush. He hurried Tinman up for the lag, and he won. No one in the room was surprised. Even when Tinman was playing straight up, the hustler in him couldn't resist. The Posse knew he'd thrown the lag, predicting Shady's next move.

"Your break, smart guy," said Shady slapping the cue ball into Tinman's hand. "Let's see if you learned the lesson I taught you."

Tinman placed the cue ball equidistant from the side rail and the head spot. With an even but firm stroke, he shot. The cue ball nicked the right corner ball, continued to the back rail, ricocheted to the side rail and rolled all the way down and planted itself firmly against the head rail.

Only the two corner balls left the rack, hitting rails and returning almost exactly to the spots they had started. The rack looked like it had barely been disturbed. Textbook.

Shady said, "That kind of game, huh? Okay. But this is gonna take a while." He lined up to the cue ball. Only the top half was visible, the rest hidden up against the rail. He raised the butt of his cue and stroked. The cue ball hit a side rail, then the foot rail and ricocheted into the back of the rack. The two ball and the seven were dislodged, the seven going to a rail. The cue ball remained behind the rest of the rack.

"You're buried punk. Hope you're as good at safeties as me."

The game of pool is largely won by the player who gambles the least. If a certain shot is a possibility and a player attempts it, he's gambling. Winning players wait for shots that are certainties. If there is none, they play a safety. Tinman's only choice was a table-length, thin cut on the two ball, resting three inches from a side rail. He had just enough room to clear the rack and slice the two with the correct angle and spin.

For ninety-five percent of all players this was a gamble. But he had spent countless hours meticulously eliminating chance from even the most difficult shots. Everyone but Shady knew this.

It's why he snickered when Tinman got down for the shot, and why he choked on his breath when the two ball sank in the far corner pocket, and the cue ball bounced off the side rail and back into the waiting rack, dislodging several balls.

He was still catching his breath as Tinman rolled into the rack, picking it apart like a surgeon. The clicking of the score beads as steady as a heartbeat. He cleared the first rack and was starting on the second before Shady could speak. This time his constant sharking was different from the first game. He complimented Tinman on every shot. Trying to make him over-confident and cocky. Look at that shot. What a thing of beauty. Boy you keep shooting like this, and I'm in real trouble. On and on. It didn't make any difference, because the computer in Tinman's brain was oblivious.

To win at straight pool, a player must break up clusters as they're sinking balls. The cue ball is the hammer, and the positioning of it is paramount. When Tinman played, it was never let loose to run. It was always in control, often only moving a matter of inches for the next shot. Unless absolutely necessary, his shots were all straight in or with a minimum of angle. He rarely used combinations, kisses, banks, or anything with an unacceptable amount of chance.

It was unnerving to an opponent and Shady was no exception. As the run went on, he ran out of things to say.

Instead, he paced around the table, trying to avert Tinman's attention. It was no use.

On the fifth rack of the run, he blurted, "Why in the hell they call you Tinman?"

It wasn't as if Tinman didn't hear, but it didn't register. He was isolating his next key and break ball and that was more important. Shady waited for an answer, becoming progressively more unglued.

Tek broke the tension with, "It's because he's got heart."

"Shut up kid! The Tinman don't have no heart!"

"That's the thing, grandpa! When you say a hustler has heart, it really means he hasn't got one. And what that means as far as you're concerned, is he's going to beat you until your grey cells are spilled out all over the floor. No survivors. You got it now?"

Shady's red face held Tek's grinning gaze for as long as he could bear. The clicking of the score beads brought him back to the game. He watched helplessly as Tinman ran rack after rack. The great Willie Mosconi once ran 526 balls. Tinman could regularly run 300 or more. His high run was 486, but his dream was to someday surpass the great Mosconi.

"125 and out," called Peach. sweeping the score beads back to their starting position. "Game and match."

All eyes on Shady. He lifted his cue by the butt and went to snap it on the end of the table. Mid-air, Tinman snatched the end.

"This cost me six large. You can cover that—turn it into kindling. Otherwise, drop it."

"Another game," said Shady, his voice quivering.

"I get more competition when I'm practicing by myself." He took the cue from him and laid it on the table.

As he unscrewed his cue he said to Tek, "So what do you got?"

Tek said, "He's lying. He wasn't released from prison. He walked away."

"We already figured that out," said Tinman.

"Don't make no difference. Nobody's gonna find me."

Catifsh said, "Well, they're sure giving it a go. We just ran into two feds while we were on the whiz in the airport."

Tinman's head snapped up. "You think there's a connection?"

Tek said, "Duh! They're from the Federal Fugitive Apprehension Unit!"

Shady was flustered but was working hard to hide it. "Don't mean a damn thing."

"It wouldn't," said Catfish. "Except for the fact they were talking about you."

Dez yelped. Peach said, "Uh oh."

Shady startled everyone with an incongruous guffaw. "Bull. You're making this all up. Trying to get rid of me." He pointed at Tinman. "You set this up, didn't you? Smart."

"Think again," drawled Bones, and tossed Deke's wallet onto the pool table.

EIGHTEEN

AFTER THE INITIAL SHOCK, AND RESULTING BUZZ, Bones, Catfish and Tek told the tale.

"Why'd you keep the poke, Tek?" asked Tinman.

"Look! I got enough grief already from these guys. So drop it!"

Tinman did, and turned to Bones. "Never known you to pick a bad mark."

"Me either," Bones concurred. "Must be losing my touch."

"Never! But what a stroke of luck!" said Peach. "We'd have never known otherwise."

"Yeah. So now we know," said Catfish. "What now?"

"A slug in the head takes care of the problem," said Shady.

"Shut up!" said Tinman. "You lost. I call the shots, from now until I don't have to look at your ugly face ever again." Shady fumed but backed down, biding his time. Tinman added, "And from what I can see, we don't have to do a damn thing."

Dez cried, "But you have to help him!" He gave her nothing but a blank face. She turned to Peach. "Honey, he's your father! You don't want him to die in prison, do you?"

Peach fidgeted. "Course not, Dez."

"Mom!"

"Right. Mom. But, it's the FBI. I got a record also, you know. Probably me that put 'em on to him. I got worries too."

No answer for that one. She spun to Catfish and Bones. They studied the ceiling.

Shady straightened his jacket and said, "So that's it then. The heist is off. Of course, I'll put together another string, once the heat dies down. But you guys are out."

It was the perfect button to push. For at that moment, Tinman's malaise flared up, causing his left nut to feel like it was on fire. The itching had evolved into pain. Money was needed. Nothing else mattered. Even his loathing of Shady.

"I'll tell you what. If the fence can convince me this heist is worth it, we'll figure out something for the feds. If he can't, then it's off, we're finished, and you're history."

He didn't wait for Shady's reply, and waved Dez away as she came at him, arms open. "Meantime, let's find out what we may be up against. Tek, make a copy of this dick's ID and anything else of interest, then return the wallet to lost and found at the airport. You three follow him when he shows up to claim it. Find out where he and his partner are staying. One of you needs to be on them until our meet with the fence tomorrow. By the way, was he carrying any cash?"

"Funny thing that," said Bones. "He had three grand in crisp Benjamins. Seems strange for a federal agent to have that much scratch on hand."

"Maybe he's got a vice. Doesn't want any record of it. Government is strict with their boys in blue," said Catfish.

"May be useful as a gambit, if need be. Let's put that dough back. See where it goes."

"Nice," said Tinman. "I see the angle."

"Well I sure as hell don't!" yelled Shady. "What he does in his spare time is not going to help me. I say we steer these two into an alley somewhere and—"

"Take off guys," said Tinman over top of him. "Keep in touch."

Catfish, Bones and Tek left without a word. Dez said, "What do you want me to do?"

"Keep him out of sight until tomorrow. After that, I might not care."

"Oh, you'll care!" Shady said, going out the door. "Get me the hell outta here, Peach."

Dez sighed softly and said to Tinman, "Thank you." She kissed him lightly on the cheek. She paused at the door and said, "You really need a better light for the table."

"As you keep telling me."

"Mm. Right. I'll have to look into that." And she left.

Peach slapped Tinman on the back. "Nice shooting, brother. And I really liked how you took command with the fed thing. Shady was impressed too. I could tell."

"O frabjous day. Callooh. Callay."

Peach chuckled. "See you tomorrow. I'll give you a buzz once I hear from Jahllo."

The call came the next morning while Tinman was again in the shower icing down his balls. The gremlin was irritated. It had doubled in size and was ready to explode. He did his best not to look, but it was hard. Like it or not, it was still part of his body. At least until the inevitable castration.

It was increasingly difficult to do certain things, like walk, or sit. So it was more like a hobble that got him to his phone next to the bed. It stopped ringing before he got there.

The voice mail was Peach saying, "Heya! Jahllo is at the River's Edge RV Park. Wants to meet after lunch, around oneish. But look, I need to pick something up before then, so get your guy Garshasp to drive, and pick up Shady at Dez'. I'll meet you at the RV park, near the front entrance. Hasta luego."

Tinman's grumpy mood got grumpier. Being trapped in the same car as Shady was like being stuck in an elevator with a rabid skunk. If the stench didn't get you, the diseased brain cells would. As he pondered this fate, the phone rang again. Catfish.

They talked the night before after the FBI agent claimed his wallet. He and his female partner were staying at the Grand Sierra Resort. The last call came at midnight, reporting the two agents were safely tucked in for the night.

Catfish said, "They're on the move. Just leaving the casino now. They rented a car."

"They'll probably check in with the local dicks first, try and get a fix on Peach, hope he leads them to Shady."

"My thinking, too. Funny thing about this guy. He's hiding something from the chick. Can't place it yet, but I'm working on it."

"Don't work too hard. We may be out from under this in a couple of hours. The meet is at one. I'll call after that."

He hung up and laid on his bed, doing his best to remain absolutely motionless. But the throb between his legs kept reminding him denial was not going to work this time. He had never been so conflicted. He wanted badly to walk (or hobble) away from Shady and the whole mess. He had a bad feeling about it. But if the heist was successful, Shady would prove to be his angel, infusing a much-needed chunk of change just in time to save him before the growth multiplied and swallowed him whole. Just his luck. Having Old Scratch for an angel.

Underlying this was his deep concern over his ability to live up to the lofty expectations set for him. Being the brains and planner for a large heist. He hadn't even graduated burglar school, and now he was expected to be Professor Moriarty. So far, Shady had fallen for the bluff, but Tinman knew a day of reckoning might come. He decided not to worry about it until the job was a confirmed go.

He swung his legs out, and slowly got to his feet. Yoga was out of the question, and this deepened his sour mood. His morning exercise was as important as breathing. Without it, he didn't feel himself. Still, the very thought of doing the Vrikshasana pose was too daunting to consider.

Dressing was difficult but he managed. The tighty-whities helped quite a bit, but he felt stupid wearing them. His stomach was in knots. After twenty minutes of poking at his bowl of five grain cereal and fruit, he dumped the remainder in the garbage.

The call went out to Garshasp at noon. Fifteen minutes later he was in the parking lot. Garshasp, an Iranian émigré, fled his country when his employer, the Shah, went belly-up. All that luscious corruption money from America dried up as well, and he decided to seek out the green pasture where the golden goose resided. He worked as a hack for one of the local cab companies, and found he could make far more money than he ever did as a heavy for the regime rounding up those pesky communist dissenters.

Tinman knew nothing of Garshasp's background but the two had a long, symbiotic, superficial relationship. When Tinman was hustling, Garshasp was his personal driver to and from McCue's. He wasn't needed as much now, but Tinman was loyal, and always contacted him directly when a ride was needed.

He gingerly took the steps down from his apartment and gently slid into the back seat of the cab, leading butt first and swinging both legs in at once.

"Oh ho!" said Garshasp with a knowing grin. "Big night, umh boss? You gots what it takes baby! I thinking maybe lucky whooman walking slow too, you biggest bull you."

For years, Tinman never knew Garshasp spoke any English. Normally, their conversations went like this, "Heya, Garshasp." Garshasp would grunt. After the ride Tinman would say, "Here's your money." Garshasp would grunt again. It was a perfect arrangement. But recently the revelation that he actually could speak English and—heaven forbid—understand more than he could speak, somewhat tainted the relationship for Tinman. But he was a creature of habit, and wasn't about to dump his driver over his ability to mangle the language.

"Yeah, a real humdinger of a night," said Tinman, hoping that would be the end of that. It wasn't.

"Humdinger!" Garshasp squealed, like a kid finding a puppy under the Christmas tree. "I am so very liking this new word!"

Tinman had to spell it, very slowly, while Garshasp jotted it down in a little journal, seemingly unconcerned about driving without seeing where he was going. Once the new word was firmly implanted, Tinman told him their first stop.

As the cab pulled up to the Palladio, Shady was outside looking like he wanted to mug someone. As he slid into the backseat, it was apparent he was equally disgusted with having to ride with Tinman. It was a good five minutes before anyone spoke.

"Looking around, everyone! It is one humdinger of a day! No?"

It was Tinman who told Garshasp the best way to learn a word was to use it in a sentence. In the rearview mirror, he could see him grinning, winking and nodding his head, looking for acclamation, maybe even a gold star.

He forced a smile and said, "It sure is at that." Garshasp beamed and promptly broke into a rousing Arabic folk song. He had a good singing voice, and Tinman caught himself wondering what the song was about. Probably something to do with camels. Or maybe hummus.

"Look what you did now," croaked Shady. "You encouraged him."

Tinman liked the song even more, and hummed along to it. They crossed into Sparks and turned onto Rock Boulevard, where the RV park was located on the edge of the Truckee River. At the entrance, Tinman had Garshasp pull to the side of the drive.

"You are wanting me to go now?"

"No. Keep the meter running. We'll wait for Peach."

"Yeah, and what's up with him?" asked Shady. "I get this mystery call saying he's got an important errand to run before our meet. What could be more important than this?"

Tinman ignored him and got out of the cab. Just down the hill was the river, and it was high with all the runoff from the big winter. Garshasp oohed and aahed, pointing excitedly at the rumbling turbulence. "That is one humdinger of a river, yes, boss?"

Tinman nodded, indulging him, and said, "You can say that again."

"Okay. That is one humdinger of a river, yes, boss!"

"You got that down, Garshasp. Let's work on a new one."

Garshasp nodded seriously. "Sure. I looking for new one," he said, and began his search.

Two minutes staring at the humdinger of a river was all Shady could stand. "I'm not waiting! Let's mosey around. See if we can find this raghead."

"Raghead!" exclaimed Garshasp, hoping this was the new addition to his budding vocabulary.

Tinman shook his head gravely, and Garshasp continued his search. Tinman said to Shady, "What are you going to do, genius, start asking if anyone's seen a fence?"

"No, dumbass. But how many towelheads you really think mingle with these crackers?" And he walked off into the jumbled jungle of motorhomes and travel trailers. Tinman sighed, cocked his head to Garshasp, and they followed.

Many of the RVs were parked semi-permanently, with well-tended little yards and clotheslines. As they meandered along the winding lane, residents eyed them with a mixture of curiosity and distrust. Shady ignored them, his head craning from side to side, on the lookout for anyone who was not pasty white.

The western end of the park was reserved for short-termers. The few people who saw them assumed they must be long-termers from the east end of the park, so they smiled nervously, giving half waves, hoping for acceptance. Tinman and Garshasp obliged them, but Shady was oblivious.

Sprawling over two rental spots, was a gigantic RV, inaptly and inanely dubbed, The Spartan. Forty-five-foot long with a car trailer attached to the rear. Four, count 'em, four hydraulically controlled, super slide out rooms creating a whopping 602 sq. ft. of living space. Two satellite dishes sprouted like mini-Mickey Mouse ears. Sides painted with a splash of interlaced streams: bright colors, flapping and waving in the wind as the monster roared down the byways of bygone America. Tinman thought it was obscene.

Out front, a large, gruff, white man, with a beer belly to match the relative size of the motorhome, was sitting in a lawn chair dutifully expanding his pride and joy with a case of cheap beer. For Tinman, the tacky tableau was complete. Shady saw the man as a likely compatriot and approached.

"Pal, you see any of them Arabs around?" asked Shady. "Besides Muhammed here."

The gruff guy eyed him from head to toe, and let out an enormous belch. He crushed his empty can, tossed it into a growing pile, and said, "Beat it asshole."

Shady wondered if he could off him with a few quick shots, but something told him the neighbors were probably far better armed than he, and he would end up a duck in a shooting gallery. He wasn't going to let the guy just get away with it, though, so he straightened himself up and prepared to fling a bunch of slurs.

He was stopped by the powerful hum of a high-performance sports car heralding the arrival of a neon yellow, Audi R8 Coupe. Tinman recognized it. The driver, more so.

"Hey guys," said Peach. "I thought you were gonna wait at the entrance." He popped out of the car, and waved at the beer drinker. "Yo, Chuck! How's tricks?"

Chuck shrugged, belched mightily, and cracked another beer.

"You know this slob?" asked Shady.

"Sure," said Peach. "He's the cover for our guy."

"He definitely looks the part," said Tinman. "What's with the dentist's car?"

"Yeah, well, I wasn't so sure Jahllo would come if I just told him about the coin, and Thomas didn't appreciate this fine automobile anyway. Hell, there's hardly any miles on it. Let him drive Suzanne's old clunker for a while."

"What the hell are you talking about?" asked Shady.

"A heist we pulled a few days ago. We left this beauty behind for a rainy day, and today's that day."

"I'm talking about my coin! You doubted me?"

"Oh no, not you, the coin. Anyway, he's here and so are we, so let's get to it. Hey Chuck! Jahllo inside?"

"Where else," said Chuck, savoring the last half of his beer.

"Tell him we're here."

Chuck farted as he pulled himself up. After a few needed scratches he climbed inside the RV. After a short wait, he reappeared, followed by what appeared to be an elderly woman, bent over, with a pink shawl draped over head and shoulders. A worn, flowered skirt hung low, scraping the dirt.

When she turned to see the newcomers, however, the thick, dark black mustache dispelled the guise. Jahllo grinned when he saw Peach, frowned slightly at Shady and Tinman, and gaped in horror when he spotted Garshasp. As did Garshasp when he saw what he thought was an old, Arab woman sporting a handsome mustache.

Jahllo's shawl slipped slowly off his head. Garshasp gaped anew, realizing the mustachioed Arab woman was actually an Arab man in drag.

They circled each other, like cats preparing for a brawl. Peach tried to make introductions, but Jahllo impatiently waved him off. The two Arabs tightened their circle until they were almost head to head.

Garshasp said, "Ahlan."

Jahllo recoiled slightly, and responded, "Ahlan wa sahlan."

Garshasp risked sticking his hand out and was rewarded by Jahllo taking it firmly. Jahllo said, "Kayf Haalak?"

"Bi-khayr, al Hamdu lillah."

Suddenly the two men began yakking furiously at each other, their hands gesticulating wildly. Everyone was beginning to worry there might be trouble when they burst into laughter, and fell into a giant bear hug.

Peach said, "You two know each other? Distant cousins, maybe?"

"Oh, certainly not," said Jahllo with a formal British accent. "But we have discovered we are both secularists."

"Say! That's a good thing, no?"

"Very good! Our people are always fighting over religion or tribal loyalty, and we have no such quarrel. We are both non-believers. Loyal only to ourselves. It is an ideal platform for a loving and peaceful relationship. Much like ours, Peach. Thank you for bringing him. It is refreshing to speak to one of my kind who has found comfort, friends, and prosperity in this great and wealthy nation."

"My pleasure!"

"I was the one who called for the ride," said Tinman.

"Indeed!" said Jahllo. "Garshasp has already informed me you are the honorable Tinman, brother of Peach and hustler extraordinaire. He speaks highly of you. I am flattered by your presence."

They shook and Tinman said, "Likewise. And thanks, Garshasp."

"You being quite welcome, boss!"

Jahllo fired off some Arabic. His tone was admonishing and Garshasp bent his head.

Jahllo said, "I told him he must practice harder at his English skills. For if one is to succeed, one must learn the language of the people from who you are stealing money."

"Makes sense to me," said Peach. "Although I did hit a house once that turned out to be owned by some Buddhists. And I can't speak a word of that."

"Merely dumb luck. And you, old man, Garshasp tells me he doesn't know who you are, but he says you are angry inside, and a terrible xenophobe. Which is an occupation of small minds. But since you possess one, you are innately incapable of comprehending this. Are you not?"

Shady was still stuck on xenophobe, so he said with false bravado, "He told you that about me?!"

"Indeed. He says you call people like us ragheads."

Garshasp responded to the shocked looks with an innocent grin and a sly wink. Shady took a step toward him. "Well, maybe I ought to teach him a lesson about talking out of school."

"Not a sound idea," said Jahllo. "We are now blood brothers. If you strike him, it is the same as striking me. If you are so foolish to do so, Chuck here will crush every single teensy bone in each of your feet. Fifty-two to be precise. Then truly, you will be more able to assume the role of the feeble old man, as you hobble to and fro."

For dramatic flair, Chuck crushed his latest can, very, very, slowly. Shady turned red, his eyes watering with rage. "I thought you were only loyal to yourself."

"Ah, well, loyalties change."

Peach, desperate to stay friends with his fence, dove headlong into the fray. "So now everybody knows everybody else! This is good. And so is this honey I told you about, Jahllo. Sweet, huh?"

Jahllo shrugged off Shady's glare and strolled to the Audi like some young sheik wondering if maybe just one more little sports car might complete his fleet.

Chuck ambled Tinman and Shady's way. As he neared, Shady impulsively shied back a half step. Tinman waved away an offered beer, and headed for the safety of Peach and Jahllo. Chuck shoved the beer into Shady's chest.

"Don't take it personal like," he growled. "He's always like this in the morning."

Shady cleared his dry throat and mumbled, "It's afternoon."

"Right? No accountin' for these Arabs." said Chuck, and let go of the can.

Shady grabbed it as it slid down his chest. As Chuck went back to his lawn chair, Shady cracked the beer and drained half, most of it splattering on his shirt.

"It's not the Spyder," said Jahllo.

"I told you that," said Peach. "But the Coupe is almost as good."

Jahllo circled the car, tsk-tsking. "If I take this it will be as a favor. As a rule, I don't deal in automobiles. We've discussed this problem before."

"I know. I know. Cars are a bum deal for both of us. Lots of hassles. Against my policy, as well. But it was so nifty, I knew you'd be interested."

"Six thousand."

Tinman wasn't sure if Peach planned on sharing any of the take on the car, but even if he wasn't, he couldn't stand by and watch a travesty unfold. "Six grand? It's worth a hundred sixty new." Peach waved his hand nervously, trying to get him to shut up.

Jahllo grinned approaching Tinman like an elementary school teacher. "Aha! But it is not new. Second, you clearly are not familiar with the level of difficulty involved these days in recirculating a car such as this. It will need an entire set of clean papers which must match the new VIN that will have to be created once the old is permanently removed. It will need a new paint job. And a buyer will have to be found far from where we are. A costly and time-consuming process. All of this you are asking me to do."

"Even with all that, you stand to make a pile."

Jahllo laughed brightly. "And that is why I am in business! To make piles and piles of money. But this comes with a high level of risk. If you would like to assume that risk then you take the car, and perhaps you will receive a pile of money yourself."

Tinman sighed. "It's only last year's model. Not many miles."

Jahllo propped his chin on a fist. After a moment, he said, "For Peach and his brother I will give you a special price. Seven. This is my offer."

Behind Jahllo's back, Peach nodded his head vigorously. Tinman curled his lip, shrugged and said, "If Peach is okay with that, so am I."

Jahllo smiled wide, like the proverbial cat having eaten the pet parakeet. Tinman's stomach flipped. Now he knew why Peach had called him a horse trader. He'd just swapped his Arabian steed for a llama.

"Chuck, get this car onto the trailer, and cover it up quickly," said Jahllo. "Peach, you did dismantle the GPS and theft-tracking app, did you not?"

Peach was hurt, almost insulted. He spread out his hands, fingers splayed.

Jahllo grinned, patting him gently on the back. "Forgive me. I had momentarily forgotten you are a consummate professional. Step inside and we will complete the transaction. You too, brother of Peach. Come along, Garshasp!"

Tinman held out a palm to Garshasp and huddled Peach and Jahllo. "That may not be a good idea. He doesn't exactly know what we do. Follow?"

"Perfectly," said Jahllo. "But I told him my occupation upon meeting, so I dare say he does now."

Tinman's jaw set hard. Jahllo was perplexed and said, "You fear him? Could it be you do you not know him? You are his friend, how is this possible?"

"Language barrier?"

"Ah. Well, as a young man, your friend worked for the former Shah of his country. This means he is quite familiar with all forms of chicanery, thievery and countless other nefarious activities."

Peach and Tinman's heads pivoted to Garshasp. He waved and showed his teeth. They pivoted back to Jahllo, and Tinman said, "Good to know."

"I would think so. Entrez s'il vous plaît."

"HEY!" bellowed Shady.

"Oh, yeah, right," said Peach. "Mind if he tags along?"

"Must he?" asked Jahllo, like he was being offered pork for dinner.

"Er, kinda. He's my father. Actually our father!" said Peach with an arm over Tinman.

The look of utter dismay and horror that overtook Jahllo and Garshasp was akin to two devout believers being told there were no virgins in heaven.

"Take it easy," said Tinman, feeling their pain. "It's not been officially confirmed."

The relief the two Arabs showed was like finding out the whole no virgins thing was just a practical joke. Jahllo shook the negative vibes off and studied Shady. "Now I see why you are so angry inside. You are in limbo. The bastard father." He nodded slowly and solemnly, like a doctor right after telling someone they have incurable hemorrhoids.

"Also," Peach added, "he has something else you might be interested in. Kind of why we're here, really. That, and we've got something in the cooker we want to discuss."

"That's right," interjected Shady. "A job I brought 'em."

Jahllo could smell money within a five-mile radius, and his whole demeanor changed. When green was involved, he could deal with anyone, even a racist asshole.

He smiled at Shady. One could almost envision a gold tooth catching a sun ray, illuminating the moment. "By all means Peach and Tinman's maybe father, I welcome you into my humble abode. Our initial meeting was, hmm, difficult. Actually there's a better word."

"Ignominious," said Tinman.

"Exactly!" cried Jahllo. "I admire a man who has mastery of the language."

"It's a hobby of mine. I'm up to the I's," said Tinman with a gloating sneer at Shady.

"Well done! Inside everyone!" And they all disappeared inside the land yacht.

NINETEEN

"WHERE DID YOU GET THIS?" asked Jahllo, gazing with paternal love at the silver dollar.

"Does it matter?" asked Shady with a grin. "How much?"

Blast, thought Jahllo. This old heavy was a far better horse trader than either of his supposed sons. After completing the car transaction—knowing full well he stood to make a tidy sum—he thought whatever the bastard father had would be paltry and not worth his time. But instead he had produced this coin. This very special coin. The question was, how much did the pig know about it?

He was seated on a silk upholstered, throne-like ottoman. Peach and Shady looked on from atop large pillows strewn around the floor. Oddly, Peach's brother chose to stand, while Garshasp sat cross-legged in a corner chowing down on a complimentary falafel. Pungent incense wafted through the sumptuous living room. A recording of a five-piece talcht ensemble, consisting of oud, nay, qanun, violin and riq, filled the air with a traditional Arabic melody.

This was Jahllo's kingdom. And of all the valuables he dealt in, only one was personally coveted. Money.

Specifically, coins. It was his passion. As a true numismatist, he knew the very roots of currency, back to the use of lambskins for small change. His collection was large, and secret to all, except Chuck, who could care less.

In his dealings as a fence, he was cunning, cutthroat and chintzy. Coins were his weakness. In the past, he had been stupid, paying too much for pieces simply because he had to have them. Like a drug. Like this 1850 Seated Liberty silver dollar in his hand. No mint mark, so it was from Philadelphia, long before the Comstock bonanza and the Carson City mint. He peered through his magnifying glass. Undoubtedly uncirculated. Condition, hmm. MS-63! The highest rating aside from a Proof. Praise Plutus! (The Greek god of wealth being the only deity Jahllo truly worshipped.)

He eyeballed Shady, it was like finding a diamond in a dung heap. There had only been 1100 of these minted. The last one went for a little over $14,000. Did this hoary creature know that? Or was he just guessing.

"One thousand."

"Give me the coin, ya oily shyster," said Shady.

Blast. He knew something. But how? He had not the intelligence to possess such an avocation. Could it be because of where the coin came from, that he knows it must be valuable because of the source? His brain sifted through his numismatics' files for the answer. There could only be one.

"This is from the Redfield hoard," he said. "How ever did you come by it?"

The shock and awe felt by the others wasn't quite up to Gulf War standards, but close. Shady shot Peach an accusatory look.

"I didn't say a thing! I didn't even mention the coin to him!" cried Peach.

"He speaks the truth," said Jahllo.

"Then how did you know?" asked Tinman.

"Anyone who studies coins, like I, knows about the magnificent LaVere Redfield hoard. My deduction that this coin came from his collection derived from knowing a number of specimens from this year were purportedly lost in a burglary back in 1963."

"61," said Shady with a smirk. Jahllo narrowed his eyes. Shady said, "Hey Peach, your boy is good. He recognizes worth when he sees it." He shot Tinman a glare.

"They are of some small interest," said Jahllo, trying hard to conceal his excitement.

"I'll bet," said Shady, picking up on Jahllo's excitement. "New offer? One that would make me consider doing future business with you?"

Jahllo's heart skipped a beat. "Do you perhaps have more coins such as this?"

Shady chuckled low and long. Jahllo suddenly realized what was going on. He said, "I surmise this coin is in some way related to this possible caper you mentioned earlier."

"You can say that again," said Tinman impatiently. "Show him the picture."

Shady frowned, not liking his thunder stolen, but he slid out the photo of the coin collection and handed it to Jahllo, who immediately began poring over it.

"That's the job. Maybe," said Tinman. "This creep says he knows where we can get our hands on Redfield's special collection. It also went missing during the '61 heist."

Jahllo's hands trembled. There was always speculation this collection existed, but never confirmed. "Oh dear. Excuse me." He wiped sweat from his brow, steadied his hands, and leaned in closer with his magnifying glass.

It was hard to make out each individual coin, but they were pristine. Some he was sure were one-of-a-kind. His mind began a running tally, the numbers spiraling upward. Good god, was that one of the missing 1873-S Seated Liberty dollars? Only 700 minted, none ever discovered. His breath quickened. And there, in the corner, must certainly be an 1838 Gobrecht dollar, arguably the rarest and shortest-lived silver dollar ever minted. Even more exciting were a few coins that seemed out of place. A silver dime tucked in near the bottom. Could it possibly be? The detail was too blurred to be sure, but the chances were good. To possess this would be the crowning point in his numismatics' career. He had to have it.

"Personally," said Tinman. "I don't think it's worth the effort. It's just old coins."

From the reactions of Peach and the old man, Jahllo realized it was Tinman who was holding up the heist. The doubting Thomas. The one who must be convinced.

"I think if you do not make the attempt, you would be fools. It is a once-in-a-lifetime opportunity. It would make all of you rich men."

Shady whooped and pointed at Tinman, who was stunned into silence.

"Gee, Jahllo, I never heard you say that before," said Peach. "That good, huh?"

Blast! Did he have to use the word rich? Now his bargaining position was shot to hell. Still, it was worth it. "Absolutely. Tinman, you should have no doubt about this. I recommend you move on it with all haste."

Tinman stared hard at him. Jahllo knew it was important to appear as sincere as he was. He relaxed his face and nodded with grave assurance.

"And you'll handle the haul?" asked Tinman. "No time payments. Cash on the barrel."

"Naturally, I would have it no other way," said Jahllo. "In fact, I would take it as an affront if you were to seek out another fence. If you could even find one who knows as much as I about such product."

"Oh, we won't go anywhere else, that's for sure," said Peach.

Jahllo breathed a little easier. "Very good. I will be leaving at dawn. I must make arrangements for the Audi."

"Already got a buyer in mind?" asked Peach.

"Yes. The son of a minor emir. He's living in Texas now, studying to be a proctologist. He'll adore it. So I will be unavailable for possibly two weeks. Contact me when you have the collection, and I will arrive posthaste."

"Sounds good," said Tinman. "Thanks for the confirmation."

"Humph," grunted Shady. "Won't listen to his own father, but he'll listen to you."

"A man with a sound mind," said Jahllo. "Now, regarding this particular coin of yours. I'll give you seven thousand, not a penny more."

"That's as much as you gave us for the damn car!" barked Tinman.

"Coins don't have VIN numbers. They are practically untraceable. Small and easy to transport. The marketplace is very secretive and private. And the collectors are rabid. An entirely different situation. So, Mr. Shady, is it a deal?"

Shady got to his feet, reached over and took the coin. "I'll hold onto it for now. Once we have the collection, then we'll see how much you really want it, Mr. Jello."

Damn this old cretin! Where's a sharp scimitar when you need one? He couldn't increase the offer again and risk looking too hungry. It would hurt him when it came time to negotiate the purchase of the collection. Instead he shrugged his shoulders as if he could care less.

"Um, Shady," said Peach. "You sure you don't want to take the deal. Give you a little walking around dough until the job."

"Don't question me, kid. Let's get out of here. That incense is clogging my nose." Without a ta-ta, or adios, he let himself out.

Tinman sputtered in disgust. "Sorry about him."

"Oh, no, I am the one who is deeply sorry for you. May the DNA not be a match."

"Amen."

* * *

Garshasp, still nibbling on the last corner of his pita bread, pulled the car onto Rock. Peach leaned up to the front and dropped half the Audi money in Tinman's lap. "Thanks," said Tinman.

"You earned it," said Peach.

"I need some spending money. Peach, spot me five yards," said Shady.

"But you walked away from seven large, for a dollar coin!"

"Better to keep him hungry 'til the big haul. Come on, fork it over. I'll give you the coin to hold. We all know that's good collateral."

Peach sighed, took the coin, and peeled off $500 from his wad. He handed it to Shady and said to Tinman, "So it's a go, no?"

Tinman's mind was racing. Dollar signs had changed his tune completely. Now there was nothing more pressing than doing the heist, and fast. "Definitely. We need a meet. Today. We have to get the feds out of the picture, at least temporarily. But no matter what we do, it won't stick for long. They're not going to give up."

"You let me worry about that," said Shady. "Just put 'em on ice until after the job. Then I'll take care of the problem, permanently."

Tinman knew what that meant, but he couldn't be bothered. "I'll check in with Catfish." He dialed the number. No answer. He waited for the beep. "When you get this, go to the Clubhouse. Bones should keep the tail, but bring Tek. The thing is on, but we have to move."

* * *

Reno was starting to irk Deke. First, he loses his wallet, which made him look dumb in front of Mandy, which for some reason bothered him. Maybe it was because of the way she was in awe of him. Or maybe it was because he couldn't stop wondering what wonders lay beneath the facade. Either way, she was starting to irk him as well.

After they checked with the local cops, who had nothing on Peach, they started the rounds, hitting bars, strip joints, the one pool hall in town, any place undesirables hung out. Normally, Deke would keep a low profile during his canvassing so suspicions weren't raised. It was never good to let word get around your target was being hunted by the FBI.

At several stops, they found people who knew Peach, but after one look at Mandy and her caricature of a federal agent, they clammed up. Nobody knew where he lived, what he did for a living, or when they might see him again. Or worse—Peach? Oh I thought you said Pete. There was no doubt, however, he was in town. And Deke would find him.

In the afternoon, he decided to scope out the casinos. After the Peppermill where they got no leads, they hit the

Atlantis. Walking past the blackjack tables, just off from the poker room, Mandy suddenly had to pee. She apologized profusely, like it was a disgrace FBI agents actually had bodily functions like everybody else. God forbid if she had to go number two. Deke gently shut her up and she marched off to relieve herself.

It was the first time he'd been out of her sight since they'd gone to bed in separate rooms. He scooted over to the poker room. If there was a private game somewhere in Reno, the regular players would know. A statuesque man, with an old-fashioned imperial mustache was leaving the room. He seemed familiar, which was unlikely, so Deke discounted it. He called out with a little wave, but the man looked like he was not in the mood to be talked to. Probably just lost big. Deke persisted.

"Hold on, friend," said Deke. "I'm new in town. Here for a convention. I hear Reno's got some good poker games. You know what I mean?

"Step right in, partner," said the old-timer. "I just opened up a seat."

Deke looked over his shoulder. No Mandy, yet. But he had to get direct. "I'm not fond of the casino rooms, myself. I was thinking more of—something more private."

The man was initially taken aback, but shortly a small smile appeared buried beneath the flowing mustache. "I just so happen to know of a very private game. Invitation only, though. And you have to be—well-heeled."

"How well-heeled?"

"Two grand to walk in the door."

"Sounds good. How do I get an invite?"

The man looked around, wondering if the casino dicks were setting him up for a fall. He shook his head and said, "I'm not sure about this."

"Sure you are," said Deke. "I'm as harmless as a kitten. Poker's just my way to burn off a little steam."

The man's phone rang as he was studying Deke, but he ignored it. He made a decision, and said, "I'll see what I can do. You have a number?"

Deke only had his official business cards, so he dashed to the closest bar, grabbed a napkin and jotted down his first name and cell number. Still looking for Mandy, he hurried back to the man and shoved it in his hand.

"How long you in town?"

"Not sure. The convention is over tomorrow, but I might hang around a bit, depending on the action."

"I'll look into it. No guarantees. And if you get in, I don't want my name connected. A fellow can get into trouble."

"Got ya. And besides, I don't have your name."

"That's right," said the man, and walked off to the Virginia Street exit.

Deke could practically feel the three grand burning a hole in his wallet. Finally, Reno was starting to look good. He watched Mandy as she high-stepped her way through the throng, a beacon of law and order among the infidels. Now, it was all about the timing. When the call came. When the game was. And how to shake his lovely shadow at the right moment, so he could get down to his real business. Time to deal the cards.

TWENTY

"FIRST TIME EVER I THOUGHT MY COVER WAS BLOWN while tailing a mark," said Catfish.

"And you're sure he didn't make you?" asked Tinman.

"Positive. There was a flicker at first, but he wrote it off. Different mustache than at the airport, and he never really saw my kisser there anyway. But for any play on the guy, I can't be insideman."

"Understood. It was worth it to get the skinny."

"Which confirms what I found out last night," said Tek. "I used his federal ID number and hacked into the employee records on the minimum security database. He already got busted once for online poker. He was playing on the bureau's computers."

"Sounds like he's got criminal tendencies," joked Peach.

"Actually, he does. Used to be a thief. Got busted and skipped bail. Stayed loose for almost three years before they caught him. Did some of his time, until the FBI recruited him for the Fugitive Apprehension Unit."

"So he's a turncoat!" shouted Shady. "Another reason to whack him."

Everyone ignored him. Tek continued. "After they popped him for the poker, he got a written warning. One more screw up, he's back in the can."

"That's great stuff, Tek," said Tinman. "Think we can play him, Catfish?"

"Already got it doped out. Problem is the broad. She was obviously sent to keep an eye on him. Maybe even trip him up. But I'm working on it."

"Work fast. We need them out of our way in the next couple of days. At the same time, we have to locate Chester's house and case it out."

"Already got a lock on it, through the tax records," said Tek. He spun his laptop around, and showed an aerial view of an isolated estate on Lake Tahoe.

"Doesn't look too hard," said Shady. "Hike in through the woods behind."

"Not," said Tek. "These aren't live images, and right now those woods are buried in ten feet of snow. Dork."

"You ever eat a knuckle sandwich, kid?"

Tek blew him air kisses, turned to the others, and said, "And the private drive you see there, has to be impassable as well. Too long and twisty to plow. Whoever's casing is going to need snowshoes, or cross-country skis, to get in close. Then use a drone."

Tinman was impressed, as were the others, except for Shady who thought a drone was a male bee, but was not about to say so.

"You know where to get one of these drones?" asked Tinman.

"Sure. But I'm not going to pay for it. Those things aren't cheap."

"We'll figure it out. Okay, so what if Peach and I take a ride to Tahoe and case the place. Meanwhile, the rest of you work on the feds."

"Sorry, I need Peach," said Catfish, staring off into space. "I just figured how to tie the con together, and take care of both of them at the same time."

"But I need to be there to case the place!" complained Peach. "That's my skill!"

"And you possess another one which I'm going to need for the play."

"Another skill, besides burglary? What would that be?"

"You're a babe magnet."

Peach thought about it. "True. But I wouldn't say it's a skill. It just comes natural. Like breathing in and breathing out."

Shady groaned and rolled his eyes, but the others knew it was true.

"Okay, if you say you need him," said Tinman. "But I don't like going there myself."

"I'll go. No worries," said Shady.

"But there's nobody else left," finished Tinman.

"What? Am I invisible?" blurted Tek. "Besides, I know how to work these drones. And anything it sees, we'll have on tape for Peach to see."

"Sounds good," said Tinman. "When do you think you can play the feds, Catfish?"

"Two nights from now. I'm gonna need a couple of heavies as well. And Dez, if she'll cooperate. She doesn't usually like getting her hands dirty."

"She'll play along! No matter what it is. Trust me," said Shady.

"I'll call her," said Tinman. "She owes me. What about her neighbors for heavies?"

Catfish grinned. "Perfect. Peach, you get along best with them. You make the call."

"Sure thing! I love those two galoots."

"Okay," said Tinman. "Tek, early tomorrow, we'll pick up a drone and some snowshoes. They sound safer than skis. Then off to Tahoe. We'll be back in time for the sting if you need extras."

"I'll keep it in mind," said Catfish.

"So you guys have everything in order, huh?" snarled Shady. "No help needed from me! Guess I'll just twiddle my thumbs and let the whole thing roll along!"

No one had a response for this, so they just stared at him, waiting for something they could respond to. Shady boiled, and shot to his feet.

"I'm out of here!"

Still no response needed.

"Somebody gonna give me a ride?!"

Finally. "Garshasp is waiting outside. He'll take you," said Tinman.

Shady gnashed his teeth and stormed out.

Catfish chuckled. "Pretty cagey of you. Making the bet you did on the pool game. Keeps him right where we want him. Out of the picture."

"Yeah, especially during the heist," said Tinman. "You didn't know that was part of the deal, huh? Well, your story about Imogene hit home, and I figured if he was going to make a cross, that's when he would do it."

Peach smiled. "And that's why you're the brains."

* * *

Shady was so pleased with himself, he could barely contain it. He didn't care if Muhammed was looking at him funny through the rearview mirror. He learned a long time ago, the best way to hijack a heist was after it was pulled. It had worked like a dream before, right here in Reno, and it would work again. The town was lucky for him.

He hatched his little plan by getting the daffy son to tell the pig-headed son he wanted a challenge match on the table. Knowing there would be stakes. If it came down to it, he would have brought up the notion of control over the heist as the bet. Knowing he would lose. And later, feign some old-person illness to bail from the actual job. But the pig-headed son fed it to him without prodding. Free of charge.

While they were out doing his work, he'd be cooling off, waiting for the right moment to get what was his. Maybe having a last little toss with dear old Dizzy.

He flashed his teeth at the bug eyes in the rearview mirror. A reminder payback was due for finking him out. It would have to wait. He needed the ride. And if he offed him now, Jello might not appreciate it. And he needed him. At least until the payoff. Then he and his fat stooge were dispensable. Life was good, and about to get a lot better.

* * *

The last contact from Bones came just before midnight, saying the feds were tucked away. Catfish was not awakened by the call. And did not plan to sleep until every last detail of the con—actually two cons—were worked out.

Of all criminals, conmen are the most intelligent. They have a high level of creative imagination, and an in-depth knowledge of human psychology. The cons they create are like a piece of theater where every player knows the lines, except the mark.

As a roper in the old days, his job was to locate marks for the insidemen to con. He was an expert at it, and at one point in Chicago was working for ten separate mobs, each with their own big room—the stage set, usually made to appear as an illegal gambling club or brokerage firm.

He was good at what he did, because he had an uncanny knack of picking juicy suckers. Any good con relies on the mark having a high amount of native larceny. Intelligence is also a good trait, because the target believes their brains will keep them from harm. Successful men are well-suited, as well, because they carry a certain status which they attribute to their superiority in finance and business. Ripe fruit, because they prefer to forget the part luck may have played on their rise to the top.

Catfish knew every way to locate and entice his likely prey. And just his brief contact with the FBI man, told him he had lucked into a perfect Mr. Bates—an old-time term for a mark. The man was obviously playing a dangerous hand in hiding his vice from his superiors, but his casual confidence in his approach to Catfish showed he believed himself untouchable, and too smart to get caught. A lethal flaw.

It was the unknown female that was bugging him. He had to frame the play in such a way she was compromised in front of her partner, so each had something over the other. The two cancelling each other out. He wished he had more time to get the dope on her, but Tinman made it clear there was a distinct lack of time. So he would have to go on the odds, knowing everyone had some flaw, obsession, deviance, or fetish hidden just below the surface. He would have to trust in Peach to discover what that was, and bring it to light at the right moment. He'd trained him as a kid, and had no doubts he could pull it off on the fly.

For the play on the guy, Dez would be the insideman, of sorts. Bones was the mechanic, which he could do in his sleep. The other players were relatively minor, and not needed until the finale. This included Rudy, Tinman, and

Dez' neighbors—who he'd not worked with, but they looked the part, and had the right blood.

The con needed was quite out of the ordinary. Normally, the play was for money, this time it was to nudge two people out of the scene for an undetermined amount of time. Still, a little reconfiguring of two or three old cons would do the trick.

It'd been years since his extraordinary skills had been called upon. But his brain leapt eagerly to the task. For too long, he'd relied on his partner for his daily bread.

He and Bones were as close as two men could be without being lovers. They depended on each other to remain free. They read each other's thoughts, like soulmates. They laughed at each other's jokes. There was never any contention, doubt or ego wars. And either would take a fall for the other. A true show of devotion.

And it was breaking his heart to see his crony fighting a losing battle with his fingers. Each and every day he fought to keep them working so the two could survive. Catfish was sick of it. Sometimes he believed he could actually feel the throbbing pain in his own fingers, when he watched his pal wince simply picking up a bottle of beer.

Despite his suspicions over Shady, he was praying the heist would come off. This con would be his part in bringing it about. If the payoff was as big as Peach's fence said, it might allow for them to retire comfortably.

Out of the blue, he remembered there was something he'd forgotten to tell Tinman. It was a good thing he arranged to have Shady away from the actual job, but in Catfish's experience, a double cross often came after the heist. He made a note to mention it.

His brain went back to the con, and an idea came regarding Peach's setup. It made him grin, and he jotted it down in his notebook, where the play was taking form. The criminal Shakespeare at work.

Tomorrow he would compile all the props and costumes needed. Locate a temporary room that Peach could use as bait. Round up his actors and do a dress rehearsal. The day after—show time.

* * *

Archie Dunlop was flying the friendly skies in his Father-owned, G650ER Gulfstream at the speed of .85 Mach, and a movie was playing. Not one of the 4000 onboard offerings. This one was in his head. All of Archie's thoughts played out like movies. It's how he saw his life. The cause might have come from an underlying creative bent. But alas, he possessed not a whit.

No, his particular idiosyncratic way of seeing the world came mostly from the excellent Strawberry, Bobblegum Kush he had shipped in regularly from Oregon. A 60/40 indica/sativa strain with the pollen originating from a mix of Strawberry Cough, Razz and East Coast Sour Diesel. Yowza.

His favorite genre of mind movies was the replaying of the rare interviews he had with his obscenely wealthy, tort lawyer extraordinaire, Father. The last one had occurred that very morning and Archie was now loading the reel and waiting in great anticipation. It started exactly as they all did, dating back to when he was just a wee lad.

"You're a loser, Archie," declared Father, posing before his grand oak desk, in the corner office, on the top floor of his Washington based power firm's high-rise. Archie wriggled in his seat, thrilled at the grandeur of the opening shot.

"Gee, dad, thanks!" Archie grinned at his pithy rejoinder.

"You work at it, don't you?" Ooh, the subtext so artfully placed.

"Not too much, no—should I?" Killer comeback.

The visage of dismay, disgust and disdain on Father's face was priceless. Archie shuddered at the brilliance of the performance. He knew the inevitable, scene-stealing monologue was about to be launched. There was always one in any great movie.

Father clasped his hands behind his back and strutted to a floor-to-ceiling window overlooking the Potomac. The lighting was superb, silhouetting him like an avenging angel. With back firmly to Archie, he began in a deep, melodious voice, the kind he used when shaking down the giant companies he regularly fleeced.

"Archie, you are a disgrace. To yourself, to your family, and now, to my alma mater. You have allowed a dangerous criminal to slip from the firm grasp of lawful society. What havoc he may reek on civilization falls squarely on your shoulders. It has always been my greatest hope you would follow in my footsteps, wielding the mighty sword of justice on behalf of the world's helpless and exploited."

Archie hated law. And would much prefer to have a useful job. Like a juggler.

"In your pitiful attempt to become a respected attorney, you have not only failed, you have brought shame upon me, and George Washington University. You were obviously hoodwinked by this malefactor, and therefore you alone are responsible for bringing scorn upon the noble POPS program, developed and heralded by good old GWU. Now, I have been in contact with the chancellor, and despite the uproar by others who demand your expulsion, he has agreed to give you one last chance."

Here comes the really good part, the inciting incident!

"You are hereby assigned to the recapture of this miscreant. I don't care how you do it, but I will settle for nothing less. I'm sure you understand what that means."

Archie hit the pause button and snickered. He wasn't scared of being disowned from all the lovely money the family had amassed. His mother still thought he was nine and doted on him. And old Grandmama, well, god bless her demented mind, thought he walked on water. All sorts of trust funds were in place, and his father couldn't wrench them away even with the entire army of lawyers at his command. And when Grams finally kicked off, he'd been assured her will (which contained a hefty chunk of the old Dunlop tire money) favored him over her son—his Father. Okay, back to the flick.

"I have deep connections within law enforcement. And I have been informed by the commander of the Federal Fugitive Apprehension Unit, that this villain fled to Tucson shortly after he was sent to the halfway house—a decision made based on your fallacious recommendation. So, you will begin your manhunt there. Agent Tillston has promised to keep me updated with any developments, and you will act on them. I don't care how you do it, but I want you to be the one to bring this travesty to a successful conclusion. It is the only way to wipe the blotch from my good name."

Archie bounced excitedly in his seat. The denouement was nigh!

"Naturally, you will have all my resources at your disposal."

Click. End of movie. Party Time!

The problem with trust funds, allowances, and unexecuted wills is they didn't buy you a Gulfstream, yacht, or mansion. All that would have to wait for a couple notable deaths in the family. But for now, he had all the toys he ever wanted for as long as Shady stayed loose. Boy did he love that old guy. He still thought he was harmless, and he felt sorry for him because of the dementia, just like he felt sorry for Grams.

Either way, he didn't feel sorry for himself. He was so happy! He heard a loud snore, and looked over the seat at Chase, his shadow/bodyguard/babysitter, fast asleep.

Now one might think Chase was so tired and slept so much because of carrying out the difficult task of managing Archie. But one would be wrong. The reason he slept so much is because he'd become addicted to Cheeba Chews. Archie had introduced them, and Chase couldn't get enough. What he didn't know is they were infused with 70mg of pure indica THC oil. The tootsie-roll for a new generation!

Archie was so glad Chase liked Cheeba Chews, because they kept him docile and off his back when he wanted to have a good time. Like now! Boy was he happy. Life was good, and about to get a lot better.

TWENTY-ONE

TINMAN WAS UP EARLY PREPARING FOR HIS EXCURSION. He hated snow and any activities that involved being in it. But this was for a worthy cause, so he muscled through his personal angst and did his best to arm himself against the evil white stuff. He began by making a shock absorber for his throbbing nut. Using folded toilet paper, he wrapped it good and tight, then slipped his tighty-whities on. Next went a rather threadbare pair of long johns, covered by jeans that now felt very tight. But tight was good. Crotch firmly anchored with minimal flopping or jiggling.

His upper half was covered in several layers of T-shirts, topped off with a turtleneck sweatshirt that felt like it was throttling him. His one winter coat was a puffy affair, that seemed made mostly of air. He didn't own boots, so he settled on two pairs of socks inside relatively new sneakers. He was sure he owned gloves and a hat, but couldn't find them, so they went on his shopping list.

Tek showed up late, and the first thing Tinman did was scold him. Which was the wrong thing to do between casing partners.

"Put a lid on it!" shouted Tek. "Catfish called after midnight, said he needed me to make a couple of fake IDs.

I just dropped them off. So check it out! I'm tired, I got a headache, and I don't need any guff!"

Tinman slammed a lid on it. Their first stop was on Wells, a funky street with lots of Ma-and-Pa specialty stores, including, CKRC Radio Controlled Hobbies. Once Tek felt like talking civilly, he said the store was the best in Reno for drones and he knew the owner well. He had called ahead the night before with their order, so it would be ready for immediate use.

The specific drone they were picking up was a quadcopter, majestically dubbed the DJI Phantom 4 Pro. All white, with sleek, elegant space age design, a technological tour de force.

Price tag only—"Fifteen hundred dollars! For a dumb kids' toy?!" roared Tinman.

The verbal slap resounded throughout the small store. Several avid hobbyists were ready to physically eject Tinman should they be given the go-ahead by the owner who was purple with rage.

"A toy!" shouted Tek. "It's got a maximum speed of 45mph, 3D vison positioning, visual subject tracking, vertical and horizontal hovering, it takes 4K video and 20 meg photos, and the controller transmits up to four miles! I told you they weren't cheap, and you said you'd cover it. So shell it out so we can get the hell out of here."

Tinman sighed, pulled out his wallet and parted with nearly half the money he'd gotten for the Audi.

"We should get an extra battery. Only a hundred fifty more."

"No extra battery."

"We may need it."

Tinman ignored Tek and walked out. Next stop was Bobo's Mogul Mouse Ski & Patio, where they discovered snowshoes were not a hot ticket a week out from

Memorial Day. As the clerk disappeared to see what he could find, Tinman envisioned the old wood and rawhide kind Grizzly Adams or Jeremiah Johnson used. So he was not prepared when presented with two pairs of MSR Lightning Trail Snowshoes.

Designed for utility and grace on rolling terrain, they featured: ultralight, aerospace-grade aluminum, instep, heel and lateral crampons, DuoFit bindings, 360-degree Traction Frame, cutting edge ballistic fabric, and Modular Flotation tails.

All for the low, low price of—"Two hundred fifty dollars!" bellowed Tinman. "EACH?!"

"What are you gonna do? Carry me on your back!"

With quivering fingers, Tinman peeled off the damage from his dwindling wad. The hat and gloves were now out of the question.

"We should get poles. They're only fifty bucks each."

Tinman jutted his chin in defiance and said, "Poles are for pansies."

The drive to Tahoe was quiet, except when they reached the harrowing switchbacks on Mt. Rose Highway where with every turn the car seemed on the verge of launching off the sheer crags, taking wing into the blue void. But Tinman was well aware the SUV did not possess hidden wings, so he squeaked, squirmed and slammed on his invisible brake pedal with every bend. Tek did his best to keep from head-slapping him. Garshasp taught him to drive, and he knew he could hold his own in any situation.

Until that unexpected icy patch just after the entrance to Mt. Rose ski resort. That was a little hairy. But he followed the proper procedure for regaining control of a rogue vehicle that was coming perilously close to being forced to give its best impersonation of Chitty Chitty Bang Bang, wings or no.

The change in conditions over the thirty-eight-mile drive was dramatic and stark. Halfway up the mountains, snow had begun to appear (and those pesky icy patches), but now as they approached the summit and glimpsed the lake below, it was like they were in the dead of winter. Despite the glaring sun, the air was frigid and the landscape blanketed in heavy snow.

With help from Google Maps, and Garshasp, who had a vast knowledge of the Reno/Tahoe area, Tek had mapped out a route on back roads that would get them to within striking distance of the house. They parked at the edge of a small meadow and suited up. Getting the snowshoes on was a snap. After that, not so much. High-tech snowshoes are designed to be easier to use than old-fashioned ones. If you knew how. Neither of them did.

The problem was the crampons. They were made to provide stability. But if you weren't familiar with them (and you neglected to buy poles) they tended to stick in the thick snow, sending the snowshoer crashing sideways to the ground, like a tree being felled. Therefore, in short order, both were covered in snow, that was slowly finding pathways inside their protective garb, chilling them to the bone.

As Tinman struggled on, his teeth chattering, he rethought his decision not to buy a hat and gloves. The few bills it would have cost him were useless. He couldn't wrap his head or his hands in them. The only one who would benefit was the person who found his frozen body. A morbid reward of sorts. The decision not to buy poles was equally foolhardy, and he was thankful for Tek's silence on the matter. He silently prayed no more grief would come from his rash decisions of the morning.

Two hours later they conquered the meadow (about two hundred yards) and were at the edge of the forest. The snow was not as heavy under the trees so they made better time, despite the occasional mishap where one of them misjudged the height of a low hanging branch, receiving a rude wake-up call to the noggin.

At a small clearing, Tek checked his GPS and found they were only one mile from the house. A mutual decision was made to let the drone do the rest of the work.

Tek explained the controller could be operated by two people, one for the flight controls and one for the camera. Tinman was assigned the camera, and after a short tutorial he was ready to go. The two students of crime were geared up, hoping to make their teacher proud.

Tek turned a couple of knobs and pushed a button and the drone leapt into life, lifting smoothly off the snow and quickly rising above the treetops. A hundred years ago, it would have had to go a lot higher to clear the old age trees that used to tower over the land. But they had all been cut down for use in the Comstock mines, and the growth now was relatively young.

A jiggle of the joystick and it soared out of sight. As Tinman stared at the display screen, he quickly became enamored with his new purchase. He almost, but not wholly, forgot about the hole it burned in his wallet.

The drone lived up to its specs, rapidly covering the distance. As it neared, Tinman began recording. The estate, hewn entirely out of granite, was perched on a steep slope overlooking the lake, with no other houses in view. At the base of the slope sat a large boathouse with a moored yacht. The private drive was mostly invisible, but they could make out how it snaked its way through the trees and down to the lake, ending at the boathouse.

Tek skillfully maneuvered the drone in closer so it was hovering at the backyard. There were no security fences, and no road approached from behind. He flew from one side of the house to the other, and Tinman did a surprisingly good job zooming in and getting detailed shots. The front of the house was odd, with no front door, just an imposing façade peering out at Lake Tahoe, like a mystical moai statue of Easter Island.

"How does he get out for supplies?" wondered Tinman.

"The boat. A lot of people here do that in the winter."

"But how does he get up to the house from the boathouse?"

"Maybe an elevator."

Or a tunnel, thought Tinman. One time when he was a kid, Dez had scored big in a game, and she took him and Peach to Thunderbird Lodge, an estate built in the 30's by the famous playboy, George Whittell. The lodge was named after his 55ft., mahogany speedboat, sporting two supercharged V12 aircraft engines.

Fabulously wealthy, Whittell bought up over 40,000 acres around Tahoe, including 27 miles of shorefront property. During the tour of the lodge, they were shown a 600ft. tunnel he'd had dug through solid granite. It connected different cottages within the complex and even had a private opium den. Chester's house was of the same era, and not far from Thunderbird Lodge. It would make sense whatever tycoon had originally built it might have drawn inspiration—and tried to one-up—the titan of Tahoe.

"Let's get a closer look at the boathouse," said Tinman.

"Better not," said Tek. "We're running out of battery."

"I thought you said it had a range of four miles!"

"That's the range! Not the battery life! Which is why I said we should buy—"

"Okay, okay, spare me the lecture. Just give me one more low pass."

Tek groaned but swung the drone around and dove down to the boathouse. Tinman worked the camera, covering all aspects, including the yacht.

"We have to go!" Tek cried, and pulled back hard on the joystick. The drone shot up, clearing the top of the house, and heading for the woods. Then everything went black.

"What happened?" asked Tinman. Stupid question.

"Come on, let's go. We have all the footage we need."

"What do you mean?! I am not leaving fifteen hundred dollars sitting in the snow!"

"Then you go get it."

"Fine!" said Tinman. "I will!" And he crunched off into the wilderness. Tek sighed, wondering why old people made everything so difficult.

Tinman's pace rapidly quickened. Mostly because he was cascading ass over tin cups down the increasingly steep grade. At one point, he began barrel rolling and the only way to stop was by slamming sidelong into a tree, which he was loath to do. So he just let nature take its course and prayed for the best.

He came to rest face down in the snow. He wasn't sure where he was, and was afraid to look. He wondered if maybe he should just stay like that. He'd heard hypothermia wasn't a bad way to go.

"FREEZE!"

Hmm. Someone was egging him on, agreeing with his plan. But who? Was God tossing in his two cents? If so, it was the first time he'd ever taken an interest.

"GET UP!"

Hmm. A little antithetical to the first statement. A change of heart? Pool hustlers do deserve to live?

Tinman peeked up through the snow and saw what looked like Knobby, the 943-year-old gnome from the Gnome-mobile. As a rule, however, gnomes don't carry .44

Magnum Revolvers. So this couldn't be Knobby, because Tinman was absolutely sure that was the type gun pointed squarely between his eyes.

"Where is he?!" asked the ornery gnome lookalike. "Where's Shady? I know he's close. This is it! It's finally come. Hasn't it? You're part of his mob, aren't you? Uh-huh! One by one. That's my plan. Take all of you out one by one, until only Shady's left, then I'll get him. Payback. That's right. But first you. Hold still."

Tinman didn't have time to act surprised. Hypothermia was an appealing way to go, but a bullet in the head was not. "Hold on just one minute! You've got the wrong idea mister. I don't know who or what you're talking about."

Beady eyes stared down, shaded by scraggly white eyebrows. A long, equally unruly white beard hid the mouth, but Tinman knew it was there because he heard, "I don't believe you. You have to be with Shady. I know he's coming. And soon. Why else would you be here? Aaahhh. Yes. Why indeed?"

The next thing Tinman heard was the cocking of the trigger. Time to come up with something, anything, and fast. But his mind was a blank. He had absolutely no reason to be there, except for the reason he was. Well, one thing about hypothermia is, it takes some time. At least this would be quick.

"Hey dad! Where are you? Did you find the drone?"

Dad? Wait. Good idea! "I'm down here, son! But be careful!"

The gnome said, "Son? I don't buy it. Lying sack of shit. What would the two of you be doing here?"

Tinman had to take the risk. It was now or never. Slowly, he pushed back with his arms until he was crouching. "I was trying to tell you," he said, mostly to the gun barrel than the man, "my kid and I were out playing with his new toy and the battery ran out. I just came down to look for it."

Tek appeared on cue. "I found it! It was right over there. Hey? Who are you? And what's with the gun? You messing with my dad?"

The gun-toting gnome was befuddled. He looked from one to the other, still suspicious. "What's that you got there?"

"It's a remote-control toy," said Tek. "Like a helicopter. It's really fun."

"Oh yeah? Show me."

"Battery's dead."

"You only have one battery? What fun is that? Never mind. Not important. So I guess I was wrong. Damn. You aren't with Shady."

"Shady!" cried Tek.

Tinman knew it was his line, and quick. "Weird name, hey, son? This guy thought we were, I don't know, friends with this guy or something." He began to laugh. But it sounded more like he was choking on a hairball.

Tek's laugh was way more realistic. But the psychopath was not in on the joke, and really didn't seem to appreciate it one bit.

"Shut up, both of you. I mean, okay, so I was wrong." His eyes narrowed, and he swung his gun left and right, seeking out phantoms. "But mark my word, he's coming."

Tinman saw the opening and stood up, shaking off the snow. The old hermit watched as he unfolded to full height, eyes widening.

"Ooh boy, you're a big one! Oh, yeah. Now look, it was an honest mistake. Don't take offence. I still have this gun! But you're not the one I'm after. Oh, no."

Tinman decided to make a full assault on the guy's dwindling facilities. "Look, mister, not to be too forward, but you seem to be taking this Shady guy way too seriously."

"You think so? Hah! Well, let me tell you." Then he clammed up and didn't tell them anything, his eyes skittering to and fro like a frightened rabbit.

"Hey dude, I'm freezing out here," said Tek. "And I really have to take a leak."

It took a while for Knobby to pick up on the tacit request but he worked it out. "A leak. I see. Freezing. Brrr. Say, you two have a little time. Sure you do. I could use the company. Follow me. Carefully. Watch out! That thing. Step over. Good, good. Tripwire. Yep. Blow us all up. Chester's the name. Welcome to my home."

Tinman nodded. "Works for me." He pulled out his phone and dialed.

TWENTY-TWO

CHESTER'S HOME SWEET HOME WAS A FORTRESS. Granite walls, three-foot thick. Bulletproof blinds, all shuttered. Furniture, an afterthought. Strategically placed near windows and outside doors were guns of various designs: revolvers, machine pistols, shotguns, semi-automatic rifles.

After Chester showed Tek the bathroom, Tinman said, "You really are expecting trouble, aren't you?"

"Better believe it. Fifty years. Waiting. Just for him," said Chester.

"I hate to pry, but why does this Shady guy have you so spooked? What's he got against you anyway?"

Behind the beard, a glint of teeth showed. "I beat him to it. That's what. Oh yeah. That's what it is. I saw what he was up to. Right off. See?"

"Uh, no."

Chester was so crestfallen he looked as if he might cry. Then he shook it off and said, "Sorry. Talking in riddles. Being alone all the time. Talk to myself. Don't have to explain things. Used to get out some. Belong to a group, well, more than a group. Tough to explain. We meet in a little bar in Incline. I don't go now. Miss it. Sure do. But my brothers at the bar wouldn't approve of what I'm doing with all the guns, yep. And I can't leave anyway. That's when he'll come. Sure enough. See?"

Tinman shrugged apologetically. Chester's cheeks scrunched in frustration. He looked both ways, and behind, then huddled in close. "Keep a secret, can you? Sure would be nice to tell. Just once. Whaddya say?"

"Fire away."

As quick as a western gunslinger, Chester whipped up his revolver and pointed it at Tinman. Then he cracked up, wheezing and snorting. "Got ya, didn't I? Oh boy, I did. Yep. Okay, I'll tell ya."

"Tell him what?" asked Tek, reappearing.

"AAaiiee!" cried Chester.

"Easy," said Tinman. "Just my boy."

"Right. Boy. Son. Not with Shady. Nope. Okay, I'll tell ya. You won't tell on me will ya? No. Don't matter. Long past. I'm a heister. Was. Just the once. Yep. Only that one time. Hit the jackpot. Not a lucky guy. Just that once. Bought me all this. Used to like it. Now he's out. It's him or me. See?"

"What the hell are you babbling about old man?" asked Tek.

Chester's eyes bugged. "Revenge boy. That's what he wants. Big score. Beautiful thing. All my plan! Believe it. Came off perfect. I held the loot. Three way cut. Me, Newmann and Shady. But Shady wants it all. Before we do the split, Newmann ends up strangled, stuffed in a barrel of cooking oil. That was him. Shady. I was next. I knew it. I went to ground. Now he's out. He's coming. See?"

"But I thought you were the one—"

"I'm beginning to!" said Tinman, shooting Tek a shut-the-hell-up look. "But what could he want? After all this time, the loot must be gone."

Chester chuckled. "Oh no. Not all. One special thing. That's what he wants. Knows I still have it."

"How could he possibly know that?" asked Tek, getting into the swing of things.

"I showed him. Hee-hee. Dumb bastard took a fall. I tracked him down. In the can. Keep an eye on your enemy. Sure. Sent him pictures. All the stuff I bought with the loot. And one special thing. Never sold it. Never."

"Can we see this one special thing?" asked Tek.

"Oh no! No, no. Never. Private. But I will show you where. Hee-hee. My little surprise. Bought it special for Shady. Yes I did. Come on."

Chester skittered away down a hall. Tinman patted the air at Tek—play it cool. At the end of the hall was an elevator door. Chester placed his right thumb on a mounted screen pad, and the door slid open. Tek gave Tinman a sidelong glance.

As they rode the elevator down, Tinman asked the obvious, "If you're so scared of Shady, why in the hell did you send him pictures. Like you were taunting him."

Chester cocked his head like a puppy hearing a new sound for the first time. "Why? Let me see. Hmm. Maybe it was—no. Funny. Why. Not sure."

Tinman knew why. Chester had cheated the devil, knowing payback was inevitable. Sending the pictures was his way to speed up the process. One way or the other, the climax would bring freedom, and put an end to his private torture.

"Where we going?" asked Tek. "To the basement?"

"Basement? I see. No. Half the house is underground. Buried in rock. Spend most time down here. Safer. Somehow. I think."

The door slid open, revealing a richly appointed living room. A walnut bar filling one corner. Leather sectional facing a big screen TV. Stone firewall forming an entire wall. Two passages breaking off left and right. No windows.

At the far end, two giant, ornately carved, wooden doors beckoned. Chester took a bee line for them. "In here. Big surprise, hee-hee." He thrust them open and there was the billiard room. It was everything a diehard player could wish for.

In the middle of the immense room—which could have held three tables—sat a stunning Connelly Catalina pool table, that looked like it had never been played on, the gleaming unused balls racked at one end, looking bored. Tinman was drawn forward, all thoughts of the heist on hold. He ran a loving hand down a rail, stroked the fine cloth, and without thinking picked up the cue ball and lightly tossed it to Chester.

"Up for a game?" he asked with a hopeful look.

Chester was frozen. Gazing curiously at the shiny white ball cradled in his fingers, like he was modelling for M. C. Escher's, Hand with Reflecting Sphere. The trance was broken by Tinman clearing his throat, still anxiously awaiting a reply.

"A game? I see. No. Never play. Bought this for Shady. Heh. Sure I did." He gently placed the cue ball back on the head spot.

"For Shady?!" blurted Tek. "You mean this is his surprise? Are you on crack?"

"Crack! Snap—pop. No. You don't get it. Always bragging. Big pool shark. See? So I got this. Sent him a picture. Har! Dug it in deep. Yep. No! This isn't the surprise. Over here." And he hustled to the far end wall.

Tinman sighed and took a look at the table, knowing he would never have the pleasure to test its merits. The placement, felt, Tiffany-style light overhead, everything laid out professionally. Right down to the string of score beads hanging nearby. He noticed the beads on one side were not pushed back to the end. Instead, they were sectioned in little groupings. Three here, then eleven, seven. Nine groups in all. Like a pool run someone was attempting to master.

"Whoa! Check this bad mo out! Dude, you are something else," cried Tek.

Tinman whirled around to see what was astir. And there it was. The big surprise. And as far as a budding burglar is concerned, just about the meanest, ugliest, most unfair safe that could be imagined.

Chester was leaping from one foot to the other, looking very much like Knobby now. Tinman saw Tek surreptitiously pull out his phone, and assumed he was thinking ahead, photographing the safe for Peach to see. Good idea. Probably get a damn gold star.

"A real beauty!" squealed Chester as he hugged the front of the safe. "Bought special. Just for him. Big-time yegg. Hah! No. The Jaba Master X02. Uncrackable."

Tinman caught the grin Tek shot him, and relaxed. Peach had made it clear to both students, no safe was unbeatable. Hope sprang momentarily.

"So show us how it works," said Tek excitedly. "Open it up. Let us see what's inside."

"Inside?! Oh no. Top secret. Yes siree Bob!" He pushed a button near the safe, and the fake wall panel that hid it slid silently shut.

"That sucks," said Tek. "Well at least tell us about the heist. How did you pull it off?"

"Tunneled. Oh yes. All my plan. Believe it! Dug under the road. Right up to the house. It's why I got this place. Happy memories. Digging, digging. Heigh ho. Heigh ho!"

"You have a tunnel?" asked Tek.

Chester hugged himself, rocking back and forth with silent laughter. "Want to see? Hell yes!"

He sped from the room. Tinman followed.

Fishing a tissue from his pants pocket, Tek moved quickly to the pool table. He carefully picked up the cue ball and stashed it in his jacket. He grabbed another cue ball from a spare rack sitting under a stand holding several cheap house cues. He placed it on the pool table where the other one had been, and quickly left the room.

He found Tinman and Chester at the end of one of the passages leading off from the living room. Chester placed his thumb on a pad like the one at the elevator.

A steel door parted, revealing the entrance to a dark tunnel. A flip of a switch illuminated walls of cold, grey granite.

"To the lake it goes. Down. Steady, steady. Down. Norman Bilitz built it. To show up Whittell. 700ft. long. One hundred more than at Thunderbird. Har."

"You know, Chester I really don't think you have anything to worry about," said Tinman. "You're pretty well-protected here."

"Nothing yet! Oh no. Hee-hee. You want to see something yet? Sure you do."

Off he went again. Tearing down the hall and across the living room to the other hall. Which was empty. No doors. Nothing but another pad with a screen mounted at the end wall. Different from the others.

Chester leaned in close to it with his right eye. Using his fingers, he stretched back sagging skin, and stared unblinking into the black screen. There was a click, and the whole wall slid silently up, disappearing into the ceiling.

"It's a panic room!" cried Tek.

"Panic?! Where? No. Bedroom. Ah! Sure, that's what it is."

Tinman settled on a compromise, deciding it was a panic apartment. The space equaled that of the billiard room and living room, with no walls. Small kitchen area. Cot for Chester's bed. Commode sat open in a corner. It was like a giant prison cell, except for the large console facing a bank of video screens filling an entire wall. The screens displayed multiple views of the house. The boathouse, lake entrance to the tunnel, backyard, front and sides, every interior room. Chester had eyes everywhere.

Tek and Tinman were shell-shocked. They wandered around with Chester lightly clapping his hands, so proud of his accomplishment, and the effect it had on his visitors.

Tinman felt the stroke of luck that got them inside the target's house had only served to prove the heist was impossible. Unless.

"Tell me, Chester, what exactly is your plan for dealing with Shady?"

"Plan? Oh, I see. Yes. Hmm. Shoot him. That's it. Simple. A. B. C."

"Okay. You see him coming on these monitors, you rush upstairs and shoot him before he gets inside."

"Perfect. Ah hah!"

"Uh, huh. And what if he kills you first?"

"The doors! He needs this!" said Chester, holding up his right thumb.

"Let's say he figures that out and gets inside."

"Hah! Jaba Master X02. Never. Never break that. He'll die trying."

"Right. But you'll be dead. That's your plan?"

"Hmm. Good plan. Yes! No. I thought so."

Tinman knew the success of the heist was coming down to this moment. If he couldn't convince Chester to use a different plan, one without guns, there would be no heist. Not on his watch. But how to go about it. What other plan? His mind was blank.

"Well I think your plan is stupid," said Tek.

"Eek! Stupid? Maybe, maybe."

"Hold on, son, I was going to say something."

"First dibs. Now Chester, you know Shady's going to be coming with a mob of guys. He's too old to do this alone. So just bag this old showdown at the OK Corral thing."

"But I have guns. Lots. Lots and lots. Oh yes. Har."

"But you can only fire one at a time. And this mob of heisters are going to have lots of guns and they can fire them all at once."

"Oh."

"Yeah, oh. So I'm thinking you have this cool panic room and nobody, but nobody is getting in here. Right? I mean they'd need your eyeball."

"Can't have it! No sir. My eyeball."

"Wouldn't it be a kick just to sit in here and watch old Shady and his gang fail? That's sweet revenge. And you don't have to die."

"No dying, hmm? Yummy. Good plan. Sweet."

"Damn good idea, son," said Tinman proudly. "I was about to suggest something very similar, but you beat me to it" Yeah, right.

"And while Shady is banging his head on the safe, you just call the cops," said Tek, immediately wishing someone would have shut him up while he was ahead. Tinman's glower told him he was having similar thoughts, or worse.

"Cops! Oh, no. No law. Big mistake. Dangerous. Oh, yeah. None of that."

"You mean none of your security system is tied in with the police, or a security company?" asked Tinman.

Chester didn't seem to understand the question. "Security? That's me. Sure. Safer. Private. No law. No straights. Much better. See?"

"Killer!" said Tek, trying to redeem himself. "Then all you have to do is let Shady's mob take care of him."

This caught Tinman and Chester by surprise. Tek explained. "Well, duh, the only way Shady is going to recruit a gang is by promising a big haul. When he can't produce, how do you think they'll feel?"

Chester's pale face suddenly flushed with color as the truth dawned. "Angry! Very upset. Oh, yes. Maybe, maybe, they want Shady to pay. Ahh. Ooh. I like it."

"Sure," said Tinman, not wanting Tek to get all the credit for this mind manipulation, "bring all the guns in here with you, empty the rest of the house of food. Just hunker down. Wait for the show."

"I see! Come on in, Shady. Water's fine! Hah! I'm ready. Oh boy, am I ready. Bring him on. Put up your dukes. Wait 'em out!" Safe in here. Hah! Gee! Sure am glad you fellas fell in today, er, came in, stopped by. Sure I am."

"Well we are, too, Chester," said Tinman, now desperate to get the hell out of there before the spell wore off. "But we should be going. Mother's waiting."

"Dear old mom. Can't keep her waiting. Oh no!"

Tek said, "Hey, Chester, since you don't play anyway, you mind if we borrow a couple of your cheap house cues for poles. Those snowshoes are a bitch without them."

"No poles! How stupid is that? No fun at all."

TWENTY-THREE

TINMAN WAS SURPRISED WHEN CHESTER AGREED to lend the cues. He was even more taken aback when he dug out an old hat and some gloves for him. They promised to return everything at their next visit. Highly unlikely.

After they bade farewell, they started up the slope behind the house. Tek insisted Tinman carry the drone, so one hand clutched that while the other had a death grip on the cue. Even with the poles, their walk to the car was traumatic. When they reached it, the sun was setting, and their legs were wobbly and unresponsive to commands.

As the car warmed up, the oddity of the day struck both of them as hysterical. They laughed, and hooted, and playfully jabbed each other.

"By the way dude," said Tek, "the thing with Chester and the cue ball was brilliant. I read the office you sent, and snatched it when you two went off to the tunnel."

Tinman hadn't sent him any signals, and he had no idea what he was talking about.

"I never would have thought of it," continued Tek. "Till then I figured we were screwed with the thumbprint locks. But thanks to you, we should be able to lift a pretty good impression. Balls were new, so that'll help."

"And you have the ball," said Tinman. "On you."

"Hello! You'd have been pissed if I blew that."

"Sure. Good job." Tinman finally pieced the mystery together and realized he had unwittingly figured out a way to get into the house. Score!

"And, yo, that was epic tossing me that bone! Letting me be the one to plant Plan B. You were like so slick. Asking him his plan, letting him see how dumbass it was. Just waiting for the right moment to drop a new plan on him to get rid of the guns. And boom! You feed me the ball. Reading each other's minds. Like doubles partners in tennis!"

Tinman sucked at tennis, but he got the drift. He also realized he was getting credit for a lot of stuff he didn't do. But when you're up against the teacher's pet, you don't blab on yourself.

"Yeah, I can really see why Peach says you're the brains. You played that guy clean."

Tinman beamed as Tek pulled out. By the time they were rolling down the mountain on Mt. Rose, however, he was frantic. Tek's driving was erratic, his speed bouncing up and down dramatically.

"Will you knock that off!"

"I can't! My legs feel like they're asleep. I can't control them!"

Tinman saw a sign for a hotel and cried, "Pull over! Right in here! Slow down. STOP!"

Tek managed to slide the car into a parking spot safely, and after some heavy breathing, Tinman said, "We're not needed until tomorrow. We'll stay here tonight."

"Cool! Do I get my own room?"

Tinman snorted and hopped out of the car. His legs buckled as the feet hit the ground, and he sank to his knees. Tek's experience was similar. Like two drunkards they reeled over to the entrance of the boutique lodge.

"You must understand, sir," clucked the pretty receptionist, "we offer the finest in amenities. And our rates are highly competitive with surrounding establishments."

"You call two hundred and fifty dollars a night competitive?!"

"You should feel lucky. Memorial Day weekend, the rooms are double that."

Tinman did not feel lucky, but he was in no position to argue. He slapped the cash on the counter, and grabbed the card key.

When they hit the room, his main concern was his testicle, which had apparently been playing possum throughout the day, but was now an angry ferret, snapping at anything that moved. He called first dibs on the shower and Tek did not put up any resistance. He was starving and said he was going to get food for them at the in-house restaurant. He offered to cover the tab.

Ooh! Big Spender! How magnanimous, thought Tinman. But he didn't dare say it, or refuse the proffer.

Twenty minutes later, Tinman's balls were properly chilled and shrunken to a manageable state. The throbbing was still present, but sufficiently subdued. He suited up and stepped into the room.

Tek was on one of the beds fiddling around on his phone with one hand, while shoving unknown edibles into his mouth with the other. "We got good video. I think it's possible. If we can get in, we both know Peach'll knock that safe off, badda-bing."

Tinman was half-listening while sifting through the remaining food, seeking out something appealing to his discriminating tastes. "Show me the video."

"Hold on, I got a private message. Came in today on the darknet. It's from the webmaster of Crookslist."

"Hmhmummy," said Tinman, discovering a tasty morsel.

"He's dead."

"Hmuh?

"Jingles is toast," said Tek, his voice fluttering. "Oh man, whoa."

Tinman had never seen Tek this way. Always so brash. Fearless. Now it was as if he'd looked into the abyss for the first time, and realized how close we all are to the edge. It wasn't all a lark. His eyes bore into Tinman, needing an answer. Tinman had suspected Jingles' outcome, but it was hard to watch his kid swallow it.

"It was him, wasn't' it? Shady did it."

Tinman nodded and sat down on the opposite bed. "He's old school, Tek. It's the way those dinosaurs are. They feel obligated to cover their tracks. No matter what."

"Well, we're not doing this then! He's too out there. Like some serial killer."

"Not his style. He kills for purpose. Now we know. We still have to go through with it."

Tek sprang to his feet. "Why?! For money? Won't help us if we're dead!"

Tinman thought it ironic he had been pondering the same thing earlier in the day. And the logic was undeniable. But he had a feeling after the day's revelations, he was well-prepared to deal with Shady when the time came. He understood him far better now, and was alerted to the ruthlessness of his resolve.

He was about to say so, when he wondered if his logic was all a self-perpetuated smokescreen, hiding the truth— he needed the money to get his left nut cut off.

Or maybe he was like Chester. He couldn't walk away from it until the final curtain. There could be no surrender. Shady could not, would not, get the last laugh.

"Tek. For a couple of reasons, I'm going through with it. These are my hang-ups, not yours. You walk away, chin up, anytime you want."

Tek shook his head rapidly, not willing to accept the brush off sitting down. "You got reasons, huh?! Okay, well go on! Go ahead and tell me these reasons!"

"First, I can't back down from this. From Shady, actually. It's personal. I don't expect you to get it, or care. But I'm going to tell you something else. You keep this a secret, understood? Nobody else knows, not even my brother."

Then he spilled his guts. From the first time he spotted the red dot to its present grotesque condition. As he talked, Tek—like any sane man thinking the thing might be catching—inched his way backward, creating distance. His eyes, however, told a different story altogether. His idol, mentor and protector was ailing. He was now the one in need. When Tinman got to his plan of action and the decision to part with half his manhood, Tek's breathing quickened, an audible choke sounded, and unabashed tears dribbled out, remaining frozen to his cheeks.

"Like it or not, pal, those are my reasons," said Tinman. "I have to run this thing right to the end. I want to believe it'll turn out okay. But it doesn't really matter, because I'm out of options." Hearing the severity of his situation spoken aloud, caused his face to sag, and shoulders to droop.

Tek quickly closed the gap and grabbed his hand firmly, pulling him back from the edge. "This shit is going down, Tinman. You better believe it is. Shady, Chester, the FBI. The whole stinking thing."

TWENTY-FOUR

DEKE SMELLED A RAT. They could be walking into a trap, but he couldn't be sure. The call had come from the bartender at the one pool hall in town. When they had canvassed the place, Deke left a number where he could be reached if Peach showed up. He had. And he knew the feds were looking for him. He wanted a meet.

All they had was the name of a motel, the Wonder Lodge, a dive near the bus station. And a room number, 310. This could be a setup, with Peach as bait and Shady behind it. Other desperate fugitives had attempted to get the drop on him before. Preferring to shoot it out than go back to prison. Deke was more than happy to oblige, if needed.

Tillston had also called that morning, saying Jingles' car had been discovered at the Boomtown casino in Verdi, a small town just west of Reno. Tillston was convinced this meant Shady was in town, but Deke wasn't so sure. It could be another ruse, designed to throw them off, when in truth, he had stolen another car and headed across the border into California.

Either way, as they climbed the stairs to the third floor of the Wonder Lodge, they approached very carefully.

Deke was surprised to see no sign of nerves from Mandy. She was alert, calm and confident. It struck him as quite alluring.

Both carried their service pistols in shoulder holsters under their jackets. Since it was Nevada, they could have had them out in the open, masquerading as regular citizens, but Deke said it was undignified.

The room was on the corner. They kept a close eye on the rooms they passed. Shady could be in one, waiting to ambush them. Outside 310 was a disorderly stack of empty pizza boxes. The plan was to have Deke enter first, with Mandy remaining outside as backup, should gunfire break out.

They flattened themselves on either side of the door. Deke rapped three times, waited, then once more—the instructions given in the message. They heard a shaky, "Come in."

Deke swung the door open, moving swiftly inside and finding—nothing. There was one bed, and a scarred table in a corner with two chairs. No place to hide. He heard the shaky voice say, "Don't shoot." He wheeled around, dropping to a knee and pulling his gun at the same time. A face peeked out from the bathroom, looking petrified.

"For the love of Pete! Shut the door!" shouted the face.

Mandy stepped inside and shut the door. Troy Harrigan, aka, Peach, stepped out of the bathroom, face dripping with sweat. He collapsed into one of the chairs at the writing table. This was no trap.

"I need your help," said Peach.

"Funny. We need yours," said Deke. "Maybe we can help each other."

"I sure hope so. I know why you're in town. Shady's out."

"Has he been in contact?"

"Hell no! That's why I need the help! Once I heard he was on the loose, I knew he'd come looking for me. Oh man, this is not good. Not one bit."

Deke frowned. "I don't get it. Word is you two were bosom buddies in the pen."

"Hah! What would you do if you were locked in a ten by ten with a lunatic killer? Of course I played nice. I wanted to live out my stint. Look I'm just a burglar."

"Were a burglar, right?" asked Mandy.

"Huh? Oh, sure, that's what I meant. And Shady is way out of my league. But he's on the run. He needs help. And everybody else openly hates him, so he'll come looking for me. Then I get tied into abetting a fugitive. Or worse! Maybe he wants to pull a heist for his retirement fund. I can't be involved in any of that. Like you said, I'm straight now."

Deke had no doubt Peach was still active in his chosen profession, but he could care less. Being a former burglar, he had a soft spot for a fellow thief, and his job was to track down fugitives, not hassle working stiffs. He was, however, surprised at Peach's fear of Shady. "Why are you so scared of him, anyway? He's just an old heavy."

"I don't care if he's a hundred and forty-two in a wheelchair! That guy is poison. Soon as I got wind he was out, I went to ground. I haven't left this stinking room in a week."

"Are you sure he's in Reno?" asked Mandy.

"How could I be? I got you guys all over town asking about me. People call, tell me somebody's looking for me, I don't know if it's him or you! But believe you me, if he isn't here yet, he will be."

Deke holstered his gun and sat next to Peach. As his mind worked on a plan, he scanned the scarred table, filled with carved messages from past lodgers. One scrawl announced, "The New Bonnie and Clyde Slept Here." He snickered. Couple of wannabes. Kids. No doubt harmless.

He studied Peach's nervous face, a tic causing his cheek to flutter uncontrollably. A new addition. He wasn't a guy who would normally have a tic. He did, however, look like the type who could be manipulated. Who would be willing to work on their side, if it meant saving his skin. Deke had joined the other side to stay out of prison, and Peach would do it too, if it was worked right. He was sure of it.

"Peach, I want you to know who you're working with. I'm Special Agent Deke Wolff with the Federal Fugitive Apprehension Unit." Peach shuddered at the official titles. "And this is my partner, Probationary Agent Mandy Leadbetter."

"You're on probation? Did you do something wrong?" asked Peach, giving Mandy a charming puppy dog look.

Mandy blushed and said, "No. It's just a term meaning I'm still in training, sort of."

"Well that won't last long. You sure look the part of an FBI agent."

Deke sighed. That was the problem. "Look, Peach. The only way we can help you is if we can find Shady. And the only way we're going to do that is if you help us."

Peach scrunched up his face in thought, then he caught on. "So you're suggesting what? That I go out of hiding? Hit all the hotspots in town? Carry a big sign saying, Yoo-Hoo. Here I Am Shady! You crazy? No way you're using me to flush him out! I need protection from you guys. That's why I contacted you. Not to be bait."

Deke stood up. "Then I guess we're through here. Good luck, Peach."

As he turned, Peach grabbed his arm. "I just don't like the idea of going this alone."

"We'll be in the shadows, right there when he shows," said Mandy.

"Not good enough," said Peach. "Shady's tricky. He'll figure on you being around, and find a way to separate me out."

Deke knew it was a valid point, but he didn't have an answer. Peach was ripe for the flip, though, if he could only find a way to provide security that would satisfy him. "What if I make like I'm your buddy. We pal around, hit the town."

To his chagrin, Mandy opened her mouth and shot his idea to hell. "If Shady's as smart as Peach says, he won't want to approach him with some unknown man at his side. He'll sniff it out."

"She's right," said Peach. "I'm screwed." He jumped to his feet and paced, hands buried in his pockets, fiddling with whatever was in them.

Deke's criminal instinct told him Mandy was right, but he was still irked. He wanted to take her outside and dress her down, but his phone rang. He answered it and heard, "This Deke?" He said, "Speaking." The somewhat familiar voice said, "You still looking for a game?" Deke's heart skipped a beat. "That's right." The man from the Peppermill said, "Meet me on the footbridge at Wingfield Park. Eight o'clock. You're not there, I leave." Deke heard a click, and closed his phone.

He suddenly could care less about Shady. He wanted to feel the cards. He needed the action. But how to get rid of his partner?

"Okay, what if Agent Leadbetter is the inside person," he said. "I'll shadow, and be there if Shady shows his face."

Both Mandy and Peach stared at him for several moments. Mandy was beside herself with glee, knowing that Deke trusted her with such an important position.

Peach was distraught. "Her?! You kidding? She reeks of federal agent! Shady'll spot her a mile off! No way. I'm not trusting her with my remaining years."

Mandy suddenly felt like crying. She knew she was awful at undercover, but it hurt having a crook tell her so.

"So we dress her up," said Deke, absolutely unwilling to give up on his quickly forming plan. "You help. Make her look like the kind of chick you'd be with."

Peach undressed Mandy with his eyes, surprised to find such wonders hidden beneath. Mandy squirmed under his X-ray vision. Peach said, "It's not going to be easy. Unless she's got some better clothes we'll have to go shopping. And the hair, well, that's gotta go. We're gonna need some serious scratch."

"I'll cover the tab. But we have to jump on it now. Get you two out on the town tonight. Shady may want to get in touch with you, but if he's here, he's not going to hang around forever. What do you say, Peach, you in?"

"And you'll be there, watching all the time?"

"Every second," lied Deke. "You won't see me, but I'll be there, if and when needed."

"Okay, I'm game," said Peach, and he winked at Mandy. "And you sweetheart? Want to be my date tonight?"

Mandy thought of the kudos she would get from the commander if she were the one to lure in Shady. She studied Peach. Damn, he was attractive. Even for a thief. It had something to do with that smile. And the eyes. And the voice. And that cute tush. And—

"Agent Leadbetter!" said Deke. "Are you prepared for this assignment?

"Yes, sir! After all, duty calls."

* * *

291

Three hours and five hundred dollars later, Deke trudged out of the Meadowood Mall. Mandy and Peach skipped after, happily toting the bags with her new outfit. They were giggling and carrying on like two girls getting ready to go to their first junior prom.

Deke paid for the outfit, and the new hairdo, with his own money. He wanted to keep this operation quiet from Tillston—unless it actually worked to flush out Shady. Otherwise, he was sure the commander would not approve of him putting Mandy on the firing line, so to speak. He didn't begrudge the cash outlay, as long as it got rid of his leash for one night. He was feeling good, and expected to make a killing at the game.

It was five o'clock, and at the insistence of Peach, who claimed he'd been eating pizza for a week, they had dinner at a Thai restaurant located on the first floor of a Super 8. The food was so-so. The bill, $100.

By the time they returned to the Grand Sierra, it was well past six. Deke and Peach had some drinks at one of the many bars, while Mandy got dolled up. And what a doll she was when she sashayed into the bar. Hair down, flowing with beachy waves, she was wearing a chiffon party dress, with blue and silver, lightning-stripe print, and flowing angel sleeves. It was cut high in the bottom, showing most of her legs, and low at the top, showing a ton of cleavage. Stiletto heels completed the package.

Deke was floored, never foreseeing such a transformation. Peach, however, was the proud sculptor, never doubting the hunk of clay could be turned into a goddess.

For a fleeting moment, Deke envied his evening with her. It almost might have been worth giving up the poker game to have her on his arm. Almost. He checked his watch. His meeting on the bridge was only forty minutes away. He hustled everyone out of the casino and they took a cab into the heart of downtown.

Deke told them it was time for him to slip into the shadows. Before he slipped away, however, Peach demanded money for the night's activities. "Look, if the bureau wants to find Shady, then they cover the ticket. Not me."

Time was short, so Deke coughed up four C-notes, leaving him exactly enough to get into the game. Mandy and Peach, arm in arm, waved adieu, and off they went. To keep up appearances, Deke tailed them into the Silver Legacy Casino where they entered the Aura Ultra Lounge. It was filled with the young and hip, dancing to old Top 40, egged on by go-go dancers atop small platforms.

Deke slipped away as Mandy and Peach hit the dance floor. He had ten minutes to get to Wingfield Park, an island actually, situated in the middle of the Truckee River. Fittingly, it was named after George Wingfield, a prominent banker in the early 20th century, who originally made his fortune as a poker player.

Deke covered the four blocks to the park in a half-jog. He spotted the man from the Peppermill in the middle of the footbridge over the Truckee. He was impatiently checking his watch. Deke picked up the pace, until he closed in. Then he calmed his breathing and sauntered up like this was no big deal.

"You got the buy-in?" asked the man. No chit-chat here.

"Of course," said Deke.

"You're in luck. One of the regulars is sick, so they're shy a player."

"Where is it being held?"

The man pointed over the river at an imposing ivory tower. Deke was impressed. It was the kind of high-rise only the rich could afford. He could smell the money. The man was skittish as they walked the short distance. At the entrance, he spoke quietly to the doorman, who nodded and let them in.

At the top floor, the man led him to a corner unit and knocked four times quickly. The door was opened by a man-mountain, with island brown skin and a forehead tattoo stating, "Your Worst Nightmare." The monster recognized Deke's chaperone and waved them in. Deke swallowed hard. This was the real deal.

The condo was posh. A beautiful poker table dominated a corner. In another was a bar around which five other people—all dressed to kill—mingled. The only female, of undetermined age but a knockout at any, swooped over.

"So, this is the new blood, huh? Thanks, Pete," she slipped Deke's escort a couple of bills. He nodded deferentially to the others, and took off. Deke felt nervous and alone, and it irked. This was his turf. Just deal the cards and everything will be fine.

"I'm Dominique. This is my game. Do you have a name?" asked the bombshell.

"Deke. Thanks for the invite."

"Oh, it'll be all my pleasure, honey," she cooed. "Hey everybody, this is our fifth for the night. Calls himself Deke. Say hello. And be nice! At least until we start the game."

The others dutifully obeyed the grand dame, clustering around, glad-handing and patting him on the back. There was: Trey, a tall, man with steely, grey eyes; Rudolph, a Napoleon look-alike; Your Worst Nightmare, claiming his name was Mel; and Beauregard, a taciturn old man with a southern drawl.

Dominique quickly lost her patience with introductions and corralled everyone to the poker table. "So, this is dealer's choice, anything goes, no limit to bets or buy-ins, and Beau is designated dealer, just to keep all of you creeps honest. The others have already bought in, so get with it newbie."

Deke was so taken in with the scene, it took him a moment to realize she was referring to him. He looked at everyone's stacks of chips and immediately went for his wallet, fumbling it as he pulled it out. He grinned stupidly and flipped it open. Then everything went dark. At least in his mind.

"My money is gone."

The friendly energy at the table short-circuited. Mel, the walking nightmare, got to his feet, looking like he wanted to eat Deke for a snack. The others shot him angry looks.

Dominique said, "Pete vouched for you mister! Don't mess around. This is no joke."

"I don't know what—Christ, I was sure." Deke ripped open his wallet, looking for a secret hiding spot the money had hidden in, playing a prank on him. "I was at the mall. No, because then the restaurant. God. I don't know. But really, I have more. This is just a mistake. An ATM! Just, just, fifteen minutes. I've got the buy-in. Seriously. I want in!"

Fortunately, the others realized this was no act. They grudgingly granted him his fifteen minutes, pointed him in the direction of a money machine, and he bolted from the room. It took twenty minutes, four cards, and some hefty transaction fees to squeeze the two grand from his accounts. When he got back, it was as if no one had budged. No cards dealt. No funny anecdotes relayed to pass the time. This was a serious game, and Deke knew there could be no more screw-ups, or he was out.

Then the cards started flying, and the sky opened up, raining down pennies from heaven upon his head.

Actually it was chips, and they were landing on his stack, but the effect was the same. And it was so easy. Never before had he had a run of cards like this. High pairs, trips, flushes, straights. In a little over two hours, he was almost two grand up. The other players valiantly attempted to fight back, but it was useless.

After he drew a pair to three of a kind and won with the full house, a five-minute recess was called. Rudolph leaned into Deke and said, "Buddy, you're on fire. If I were you, I'd find another game as soon as you clean this one out. Why blow the streak?"

Deke grinned and glowed. "You know any?"

Rudolph said, "I go over the mountains once a week to play in a game in San Jose. Big money. You'd make a killing. Next game is tomorrow night. You want the address?"

"Is that all I need to get in?"

"That, my name and two grand will get you a seat." He pulled out a pen and jotted an address on a napkin. Sliding it to Deke, he said, "Maybe I'll see you there?"

"Maybe." As Rudolph walked off, Deke checked his watch. He wasn't worried about leaving Mandy on her own. Seeing the way she handled herself at the Wonder Lodge showed him she could take care of herself. Even if she couldn't, he wasn't walking away from a once-in-a-lifetime run of cards.

The players settled back into their seats, and Beauregard started shuffling.

There was banging on the door. Dominique got up, and as she parted it, an Adonis, who could have been Mr. Clean's twin, pushed his way in. He stood over six feet, and had a physique most body builders would sell their souls for. His eyes were pale, with a tinge of pink. He wore a suit. Behind him were two men in police uniforms.

"Nobody move," said the giant, in a high-pitched squeaky voice. With the Spanish accent, it sounded like Speedy Gonzalez, and Deke realized he was an albino. "I'm Agent Alejandro Lopez with the Enforcement Division of the Gaming Control Board. And you, my friends, are busted."

"Now wait just one minute!" shouted Dominique.

"No, you wait, sister. We've been wanting to take you and your game down for a long time. So no excuses, Ms. Dominique. Now these officers are with the Reno Police, they are here to assist me in escorting you all to the pokey."

Mel shot to his feet, ready to make a stink, but Agent Lopez said, "Hey Mr. Nightmare, you know what my nickname is? Angel de la Muerte, so sit down." Mel blanched and obeyed. Lopez said, "Okay, Dominique, hand over the stake money."

Dominique growled, but walked behind the bar and retrieved a metal box. Agent Lopez yanked it away, and said, "You are a bad, bad little girl. The State deserves its taxes. How else are they going to pay my hefty salary? Okay, boys, take them away."

Deke was so upset he didn't even think of the situation he was in. "Wait a minute! I'm big winner here! Most of that money's mine."

"Too bad for you, sucker. Officer, get this loser out of my sight."

When the officer laid a hand on Deke's arm, the reality sank in. He was in deep doo-doo. "Agent Lopez, sir, may I have a moment with you. It's important."

Lopez shrugged and motioned him aside. Deke put his back to the others as they were led out by the local cops. He talked fast and low. "I'm an FBI agent, with the Fugitive Apprehension Unit." He showed his ID. "I was involved in this game because I believed the fugitive I'm after would be one of the players."

"Don't bullshit me, fibbie" said Agent Lopez. "If he was here, you would've already apprehended him. You were here for your own pleasure. I wonder what your commander would think of that. Let's find out. Give me his number. Now."

Deke stopped breathing. This was the moment of truth. If he didn't do something quickly, he'd be back in a cell within the week. "Come on, we're on the same side. And my partner and I really are in Reno chasing a fugitive. I just needed a little relaxation."

"Uh-huh. Illegal relaxation. I thought FBI agents were incorruptible. But you are the exception. Don't you know the rotten apple spoils the barrel?" Deke blushed and Agent Lopez smiled, enjoying the torture. "I'll tell you what, I will not arrest you. Instead, I will personally hand you over to the custody of your partner. They can decide how the bureau wants to handle your indiscretion. Get them on the phone, right now."

Deke wanted to hug him. If he could keep Mandy quiet, he might just get out of this yet. He whipped out his phone and dialed.

Peach answered. There was grinding music in the background. "Hello? Who's this?"

Deke gulped. "Peach, this is Deke. Where's Mandy?"

"Oh, man, it's a good thing you called. Where the hell are you? You're supposed to be in the shadows! You need to get here right now."

"Why? Did Shady show up?"

"Worse! Just get here. We're at the Wild Orchid Gentlemen's Club. Hurry!"

* * *

At long last, Mandy was free. She had discovered the inner woman and embraced her. A little hidden switch in her head had been flipped, releasing all the pent-up desires kept buried for so long. And the person who had shown her the truth was the man out there beaming proudly at her. He was the magic man the band, Heart, was describing right now. A benevolent Svengali. A crook. If her father and brother knew, they'd have her put away. She didn't care. The bondage was over.

It began at the Aura Ultra when all the men were ogling her and she objected. Peach told her she should embrace the adoration. He explained that women like her were meant to be fantasized over. She had that certain thing. That's what he said. And as they tripped the light fantastic in every hot club in Reno, she became a believer. Somewhere along the way, as the drinks flowed, she told him things. Forbidden secrets. Private obsessions. None of it flustered him, as if it was the most natural thing in the world to have a secret life. But he chastised her, saying it was her duty to throw off the shackles and release the tigress.

That's when she told him about the pole dancing. He was intrigued, but doubtful. He kept probing, prodding, daring her to prove herself. She saw him waving excitedly, and wanted to wave back, but in her current position she was not able, so she tossed her hair to and fro, her beachy waves sending back a fond hello. She completed the Bendy Diva Dive, and smoothly segued into the Dangerous Bird pose. The crowd erupted.

Peach's goading had led them to the Wild Orchid, where Open Pole Night was in full swing. She was on her fourth encore, and giving it her all. She swung her legs over her head, nailing the Extended Pencil, fully aware her panties were on open display. Had been for quite some time. In fact, she was very tempted to lose the dress and bare the boobs like the professionals at the club. She knew she could outdo any of them on the pole, but what really made the whole thing work was skin.

If she only had the guts, her transformation would be complete. She moved from the Rainbow to the Extended Brass Monkey. Then it dawned on her. If she went from the Crucifix Climb to Banana Splits, she'd be in a position to slip her dress up and over her head. Her mentor, and savior, was out there, urging her on.

So that's what she did.

* * *

Despite the uproar in the upscale strip club, Deke spotted Peach immediately, waving frantically from a table in a corner. He and Lopez walked over.

"For crying out loud, where you been?" asked Peach.

"Who are you?" asked Agent Lopez.

"Who am I? Who are you? Don't tell me. I don't want to know. But Deke! You leave me here with her? How is she supposed to protect me up there?"

Deke and Lopez looked at the stage just as Mandy's dress wafted out over the rabid audience. They were both transfixed. Deke more, because now he knew two things: he had something over her which would save his neck; and his imagination had not prepared him for the wonders that Mandy had to offer. Yipes.

"You know what? Deals off. You and your nutty partner find Shady on your own. I'm finding myself a hole in the wall and disappearing until you do." Then he left.

Deke could care less. He'd never seen anyone pull off a Teddy Cleaver into a Funky Monkey so effortlessly. Mandy. Wow.

Agent Lopez said, "You kidding me? That's your partner? Oh, man, you fibbies are something else. All high and mighty, when really you're a bunch of lowlifes."

Bada-bada-bada-bada-boom-boom ended the song. Mandy was a hit. It took two bouncers to get her, and all the money the audience had thrown, off the stage and safely back to her table. She clutched her flimsy dress and the pile of bills between her breasts as she ran up, expecting Peach. Who had been replaced by Deke. In the grips of rebirth, she had completely forgotten about him, lurking in the shadows. Buzz kill.

Agent Lopez broke into their frozen stare. "So you are Agent Mandy Leadbetter. I'm here to deliver your wayward partner who was caught playing in an illegal poker game. My hope was that you would do the right thing and report this immediately to your superiors. Now, I don't really give a damn, because you are as despicable as he. So here's what's going to happen, that guy was obviously your lead to your fugitive and you spooked him. He's out of the picture, for good. So I strongly suggest you look elsewhere for your man. Outside of Reno. Understood?"

Deke and Mandy hadn't budged. Agent Lopez shook his head, mumbled some Spanish curse words, and stormed out.

"Deke, I can explain," said Mandy, breathlessly.

"Don't. I like the memory just as it is." He said with a wolfish look.

Mandy blushed and rubbed her dress and money excitedly over her sweaty bust. Perhaps Deke and her could be friends after all! She looked up at him, batting her eyes, "You were playing poker."

"Yes. The commander won't be happy about it. Could put me back in the can."

That's right, thought Mandy. Deke was once a crook, just like Peach. Maybe he's got that same kind of magic! "Why would he find out? About any of this."

Deke grinned wide, "You're something else."

Mandy moved just a wee bit closer so nipples were grazing. "Were you winning?"

"Actually I was. I'm on a roll. Best ever in my life."

"Isn't there another game you could try?" she asked, glancing at her handfuls of money. "Always a shame to waste good luck."

"There's one in San Jose tomorrow night," said Deke, a glint in his eye.

"Hmm. I'll bet that's where Shady is hiding."

"Odds are good," said Deke slipping an arm around her oily waist. "Let's find out."

TWENTY-FIVE

HERE'S HOW IT WENT DOWN. The call to Deke with Peach's request for a meet came from Amber, at McCue's. She'd never really worked with the Posse before, but she was deemed trustworthy by Catfish because she was an official member of the Clubhouse, and she really had no idea what they were up to anyway.

Catfish was in Room 309 during the meeting. A lot hinged on having Deke be the one to suggest Mandy be the one to act as bait with Peach. It was therefore up to Peach to signal Catfish to make the call to Deke when the time was ripe, figuring the chance of a poker game would force his hand. When Mandy shot down Deke's idea of him being part of the bait, Peach knew it was the right time, and sent the signal via a pager he had in his pocket. Catfish made the call and the plan was hatched.

The whole runaround getting Mandy a new outfit was diversion, to keep Deke hooked and stop him from thinking about what he was about to do. Forcing him to spend money made him divest in the plan, solidifying it before he could change his mind. Once he left Peach and Mandy at the Aura Ultra and met up with Catfish on the footbridge, both cons went into play.

Dez' condo worked perfectly as a stage set for the game. The players were: Tinman as Trey; Rudy, Tinman's tenant, as Rudolph; Bones as Beauregard; Dez as Dominique; and Malice as Mel.

Malice, and Angel (an albino from Guatemala and the one who played Agent Lopez), were Dez' next door neighbors. They had a cottage industry in illegal drugs. Not selling them. They hated drugs. Instead they made a nice living shaking down the local drug dealers for protection money. Not protection from other dealers or the law, but rather themselves. Few dealers were willing to take on the two giants, and eagerly paid their dues. They had become friends with Tinman and Peach during the basket disaster, and were honorary members of the Clubhouse, having aided Peach in stealing the pool table he gave to Tinman.

Okay, so originally, Catfish figured the con to be more about getting rid of the feds, but his natural inclination demanded any good grift involve the extraction of cash from the mark. So when Deke showed up at the game and was introduced to the others, Bones picked the cash from his wallet without removing it—a signature move he could only pull off when the fingers were feeling fine, and they were feeling swell.

Putting Deke in a sticky spot with all his money gone served two purposes. He was immediately put on the defense, assuring he would not attempt to see through the set dressing and spot the ruse. Also, the need in the con to have him win could be done without any monetary outlay on the gang's part. It was easy for him to win with Bones dealing. He was as good a card mechanic as he was a cannon.

The need to have Deke be big winner was essential for Rudy's job—the most important in the con—to work. By making Deke believe in his lucky streak and by having Rudy give him the address to a fictional game, he now had an out after the bust, and a personal reason to leave Reno. The "send" to San Jose was felt to be enough to keep the feds at bay while the caper was pulled off.

When Angel, as Agent Lopez, busted in, the two cops were part of Rudy's can-collecting gang, recruited at the last minute when Catfish knew to lend an air of authenticity, he was shy a couple of local bulls. They were more than happy to oblige for a generous daily rate. Their uniforms were obtained from the RPD, which had recently revamped their look and disposed of the old uniforms. Rudy had discovered a couple of them when dumpster diving and donated them to the cause.

Angel and the fake cops waited in the hallway until they got a call from Catfish who, after dropping Deke off at the game, immediately contacted Peach who told him where he and Mandy were. Catfish watched and waited until Peach had maneuvered Mandy into a compromising situation. Then he called Angel and the bust went down.

The stake money Dez handed over to Angel was all Deke's. The game was using chips, and he was the only one who bought any. When the two cops marched the other players off to jail, they sauntered down the hall to Angel and Malice's apartment and waited until Deke and Angel left. The call to Mandy was legit, but Peach had absconded with her phone as soon as she hit the stage so he was able to answer.

Peach had the most difficult role, since he was working single-o. But Catfish's trust in him was well-placed. Few women can resist his charms, and more than one had revealed their innermost secrets.

Throughout, Garshasp acted as wheelman, shuffling Catfish to various locations, and picking up Peach and

Angel when they left the strip club. To make sure the con stuck, Garshasp, with Peach, Angel and Catfish, followed Deke and Mandy to their hotel, and waited until they checked out that very night. They tailed them onto the interstate and out to the state line. At that point, Catfish knew the sting was successful, and he sent a text to Tek, who's unfortunate job had been to keep Shady on ice at the Clubhouse. Tek drove Shady to Dez' condo where the rest of the mob had converged.

And that's why at the cast party everyone was congratulating themselves, because Catfish's play had been performed exactly as written.

"Oh, my god, Angel, when you said you were going to haul us off to the pokey, I thought I was going to lose it!" squealed Dez.

"What is wrong with pokey?" asked Angel.

"It's a little dated," said Bones with a chuckle. "Same with fibbie."

"It's all good, Angel," said Catfish. "He fell for you all the way." Angel's pout turned to a wide smile receiving such high praise from the director. He'd nailed his role, despite the archaic argot.

"So, Catfish, once the mark finds there's no game in San Jose, won't he come right back here?" asked Rudy.

Catfish, grinning, with the knowledge of a thousand cons under his belt, said, "No chance. He'll keep looking for a game until he finds one. He's got the bug. And he thinks he's on a streak. He's not gonna get off that pony until he beats it dead. But not in Reno. Like I said, Angel put the fear into him."

Angel leapt to his feet, and parted his shirt, displaying his magnificent chest tattoo of an ascending angel. At the top, arched across his pectorals in flowing script, read,

"Angel de la Muerte." He roared in his squeaky voice, "Beware the Angel of Death!"

Everyone broke up. And the celebration continued anew.

Tinman's role had been small, and though he was happy over the success of the con, he was anxious to tell the others about he and Tek's coup at Chester's. But that had to wait, because the rest of the cast was too pumped up, and needed to crow before letting go of the post-performance high. One thing that did bother him was the fact his excursion cost him almost all the cash he had, where Peach and the others hadn't laid out a cent, in fact had made money. But he kept it to himself. No need to whine and bring everybody down over his own irritation. He knew his glorious moment in the spotlight—shared by Tek, partly—was coming.

Shady remained very quiet. Despite Catfish and the others saving his butt, he was not a fan of the con game, and secretly wished he'd been able to get rid of the feds his own way. The permanent way.

After Peach had relayed his run with Mandy for the fifth time, becoming more salacious with each telling, the party started to wind down. Using Deke's money, Catfish paid off Rudy and his two mates for their roles. Thrilled with the windfall, they hit the streets in search of aluminum. But not before receiving a firm promise from Catfish that if he ever pulled off another con he would keep them in mind. Garshasp also received his healthy wage for the evening, then took off, hoping to pick up some late-night fares.

Catfish tried to pay off Angel and Malice, but they refused, saying they were only doing it to help Dez and her boyfriend. They had had little contact with Shady so they didn't know the kind of creep they had just helped. They only knew how happy Dez was now he was back in her life. Despite being shakedown artists, they were hopeless romantics. They said their farewells and went off to their apartment.

With only Dez, Shady and the Posse left, Tinman felt ready to unveil the epic casing episode. He was waiting for the right moment when Shady growled, "Now that all you hustlers are done loving yourselves, I want to know what happened at Chester's."

Despite his boorish manner of bringing the topic up, everyone else was in agreement. Tinman took the stage, but shortly into his recitation, Tek cried foul, saying he was not being completely truthful. The audience booed Tinman off the stage and Tek took over.

His description of the pain and suffering Tinman went through buying the drone and skis, brought hoots and guffaws. As did the horrific trek into the wilderness with no ski poles, hat, or gloves. Groans were elicited when he told of the downing of the drone, and Tinman's decision to retrieve it.

But when the part came about Chester getting the drop on him and the ensuing father/son scam to get into the house, there was a hush in the audience. Even Shady was impressed. He looked at Tinman and said, "You really are one smart cookie."

"Dough," added Peach.

"Huh?"

"Well you said one smart cookie, and I said dough. So it's one smart cookie dough. Before and after. You remember. We used to watch the show in the pen."

Shady suddenly remembered Peach's habit. "Don't tell me you're still doing that."

Peach looked curiously at him. "Show's still on. Why not?"

Shady groaned and waved Tek on. The audience was in a silent state of awe and disbelief as he detailed how Chester offered to show them his defenses and plan, including the panic room and the tunnel. As he described how he and Tinman (graciously giving Tinman most of the credit) had manipulated Chester into a different, safer plan which would benefit them all, every jaw in the crowd dropped. But it was nothing compared to the reaction when he told them about Tinman's idea to snatch the cue ball, and how he had pulled it off, giving them access to the thumbprint locks.

Tek and Tinman, realizing the profound effect their story was having, winked at each other. Tinman wondered if he should mention the cue ball thing was not his idea, but he couldn't bring himself to do it. He'd never gotten a gold star before.

Tek said, "And get this, I have video of this supposed uncrackable safe."

Everyone gathered around. He first played the video the drone took, and then played the indoor footage taken with his phone.

As it played, Peach asked, "What kind of safe was this?"

"Something, something, X, something," said Tek. "I forget. It's coming up soon."

They all watched as Chester revealed the safe from behind the wall panel. And they chuckled a little as he leaped back and forth on his toes like Knobby. Shady growled and spit air at the image of his nemesis.

They all listened intently as Chester said, "Bought special. Just for him. Big-time yegg. Hah! No. The Jaba Master Xo2!"

"Pause it," said Peach abruptly. "Rewind five seconds."

Tinman rarely heard such a serious tone from his brother, and he leaned into the laptop, wondering what had caused it.

"Jaba Master X02! Uncrackable," shouted Chester.

"Stop it," said Peach, and he shot to his feet and paced.

"What the hell's your problem?" asked Shady gruffly.

"It is," said Peach, his back to the others.

"It is what?" asked Tinman.

"Uncrackable."

TWENTY-SIX

"THAT'S BULL!" BARKED SHADY. "No jug in the world that can't be beat."

"I wish," said Peach, wheeling around. "You've been in too long. They've gotten better. I've read about this one. It's not pretty. And it can't be cracked. Guaranteed."

Dez moaned. Bones and Catfish couldn't even look at each other, dreams of retirement fading away into stark reality. Tinman and Tek were struck dumb. They simply could not believe the words coming out of their esteemed, beloved professor. Somehow, they felt cheated. Like they'd been led astray by their hero.

"The Jaba Master X02 is the most advanced locking system for a safe ever designed," explained Peach. "They're so expensive it's rare to run into one. Especially in a home. I never saw it coming. I'm sorry fellas. It's a wash."

"Wait a minute!" cried Shady. "I been a peterman a helluva lot longer than you kid. I'll say it's sour once you prove to me what you say. Not before."

Oddly, everyone in the room shared his sentiments. The expectant eyes unsettled Peach. "You don't believe it!"

he shouted, so out of character. "You think I'm just not good enough? Tek. Bring it up!"

Tek, hands shaking, found the company's website and description of the awful thing on the first search. He spun the laptop around, but Peach angrily waved it away. "Read it. Nice and slow. So it all makes sense to the slower people in the room." And he glowered at Shady.

"The lock is user-powered. Turning the dial charges the generator. A Zener diode prevents the dial from being turned at high speed, stopping thieves from using a Robot Dialer. When entering the correct combination, the user turns the dial to the left for the first two digits, then to the right for two digits, then back to the left for the last two. The dial position is not proportional to the previous number dialed. If you turn to the right and land on ten, when you then turn to the left, the numbers completely reset themselves. There are a true one million possible combinations. If you dial continuously for one and one-third turns without a pause of .25 seconds, the lock shuts down for 24 hours. In addition, if you dial the entire combination in less than fifteen seconds, or continuously dial for more than five minutes, or dial ten incorrect sequences the lock will shut down for 24 hours. Oh man, this sucks. I can't read anymore."

"Keep going," said Peach. "It gets better."

"The CPU, designed by Intel, comes with a random number generator. Data representation of the number sequence is changed each time the dial direction is changed. Now that is not fair! The random number generator seed is encrypted and the "key" is changed each time the dial is turned. Are you kidding me? A free-running counter in the CPU is re-encrypted at each opening. The algorithm seed and its memory location is changed at each re-programming. Ouch. These guys are good, and anal, which is very bad. The lock serial number is used to generate a new seed, thereby allowing access if the combination has been lost. Huh, weird. There are nine data lines going to the display, more than any other locking system on the market. A thief is therefore not able to perform a differential power analysis on the data lines to get information. Damn. They thought of everything."

Aside from Peach, and to some degree Tek, nobody in the room knew what any of that meant; they only knew it was a death knell. Even Shady looked like he'd taken a Quaalude. Still he rallied, going back to old school.

"Blow the damn thing."

"Tek," said Peach.

"The particular model safe on which the Jaba Master X02 is installed is the Super Platinum Monolith TXTL 60. The safe boasts the highest security rating issued by the Underwriters' Laboratories. Meaning it can withstand at least an hour-long attempt to open it using hand tools, picking tools, electric tools, grinders, jack hammers, carbine or diamond-tipped drills, thermal lances and cutting torches. It is also able to resist for more than an hour, repeated attacks with explosives, including nitroglycerin and C-4."

"Christ all mighty," howled Shady. "What do they expect us to do?"

"The safe also possesses the Brown Safe's M rating, meaning it is encased with eight inches of ballistic armor developed in partnership with the US military. Tests were done where 50 caliber bullets were fired at close range, leaving no visible sign."

"It didn't even scratch the paint?" asked Catfish.

"The walls are also reinforced with a layer of specially designed silicone to prevent heat attacks. It successfully survived an impact test where it was heated in a furnace to

1100 degrees Celsius, and dropped from a three-story building onto a pile of bricks."

"For crying out loud!" wailed Dez. "Who's gonna drop a safe off a building anyway?"

"It also features a glass relock system that activates large relockers should someone attempt to get in." Tek sighed and looked to Peach. "And who would be stupid enough to do that?"

"Check," said Peach sadly.

"Aw, you're looking at this all wrong," said Shady, rising up. "Pay attention. We get our hands on Chester and torture the combination out of him. Easy."

"We already told you, he's planning on holing up in that panic room," said Tinman.

"Yeah, and who was the bright one who planted that idea?" asked Shady. "Anyway, it's not my problem. I'm out of the picture, right, brains? This is your baby. So get to it. Otherwise, we're gonna be neighbors for a long time. Course, no sweat here. I love the digs. Fact, I'm off to bed children. Keep me posted." And he sauntered to the bedroom.

"Hey! You can't just walk away!" shouted Dez. "Get back here!" She raced after him. There was a brief spat, then the door slammed shut.

Tinman looked at his brother who was crumbling. "Peach, this is not your fault."

"Huh? Oh. Yeah, sure. Sure thing. Just got a little cocky. I guess. Hey, I'll be seeing you guys around. I need to—" He shook his head and left in a daze. Tek started to follow, but Tinman waved him back.

Bones got to his feet, smiled wanly at the others and said, "Think I need a little air as well. See you later fellas."

"I'll join you," said Catfish, draping an arm around his pal as they shuffled out.

Tinman looked to Tek who was intently examining the carpet, looking for an answer to the enigma amid the woven pile. "Let's go, buddy," said Tinman, reaching out and ruffling his hair.

The drive to the motel was quiet until they pulled into the parking lot and Tek said, "So what are we going to do, Tinman?! This can't be it! What about—you know."

Tinman gingerly swung his legs out of the car and said, "Not sure about anybody else. But Iike I told you. I'm out of options. One way or the other, I'm getting in that safe. You can take that to the bank."

TWENTY-SEVEN

ARCHIE WAS SO GLAD TO BE RID OF TUCSON. Ugh. Reno, now that was the place to be! So close to Tahoe, and the Memorial Day weekend just around the corner. There would be all kinds of ways to spend money and have fun, while of course keeping up his diligent search for the elusive Shady. Agent Tillston had finally fessed up to Father and told him the official search was actually happening in The Biggest Little City in the World. Oh boy, oh boy, oh boy!

Chase had arranged to have a limousine waiting for them at the Reno airport. He was supposed to be acting as the driver, but there had been quite a bit of turbulence on the flight from Tucson, so his mid-flight nap was most unsatisfactory. He was now sprawled out in the back of the limo, blissfully snoring. And Archie had the wheel. Which, in a way, was a good thing. Chase was not a fan of sightseeing and that's exactly what Archie felt like doing.

They hadn't arranged for lodging accommodations, but that wasn't out of the ordinary. Archie normally preferred to wing it. Letting the vagaries of the world determine where they land. As he tooled around the city, admiring the buildings and the flickering neon lights, he became enamored with Reno. It was so colorful and raw in a seductive sort of way.

The TV was playing in the back, and Archie heard a section of the news begin, entitled, Crime Wave. "Good evening, ladies and gentlemen! This is Scott Frenley, coming at you with all the crime you can stomach. Tonight, we have a special report. Some of you may remember last year we featured two separate stories about a couple of local security guards who went loony tunes within weeks of each other. One was a male campus guard at UNR, and the other a female guard at the Nevada Museum of Art. Both were wanted by the Reno police, but neither were ever apprehended. Well, as luck would have it, it appears these two nutcases managed to form a partnership of sorts, dubbing themselves, The New Bonnie and Clyde!

"That's right. And after eluding local authorities, the two banditos went on a crime spree stretching from Utah to Alabama. Unlike their namesakes, however, their heists did not include vaults and armored cars. No, they preferred mini-marts, laundromats and an occasional food bank. We're talking world class criminals here folks!

"Their reign of terror came to a screeching halt when they attempted to rob an evangelical church in Tuscaloosa. Unaware of the firepower possessed by the congregation, the dynamic duo of crime found themselves outgunned. They managed to escape the bloodthirsty worshippers long enough to turn themselves over to the relative safety of the local police. The nation can rest easy.

"Reno, however, has the dubious distinction of spawning these mental midgets. Not exactly the best goodwill ambassadors for our fair city, don't you think? Maybe we'll produce our very own Ma Barker gang, or another Baby Face Nelson! Wouldn't that be something?

Don't laugh, people. As local historians know, those hoodlums hung out here back in the day."

Archie turned off the TV. He was all aflutter. Reno was such a lusty, bad boy sort of town. Just the mood he was in.

A movie began to roll. He was a gangster on the lam, looking to lay low, wait out the law. But where? A seedy motel, yes. He leaned low and pulled the imaginary brim of his fedora over his eyes. There was the All Inn Motel. A perfect hideout. No. Closed for business. Hmm. The Sandman Motel! It'd be perfect, but the cool neon sign was broken. Boo. Hiss.

The Hi Ho Motor Lodge. Eh. Ho-hum.

Wait! Is that a black and white approaching? Okay, green and white, a county mountie, but still, The Heat. Take it easy. Play it cool. They don't know nothing from nothing. And there they go. And so do several other cool dives. Damn. Make a U-ey? No. Don't draw attention. Take a right up here on Lake, turn around in this parking lot. Which belongs to the Wonder Lodge. Wait a minute. That sounds pretty darn good for a hideout. But maybe he'd missed a better one when the fuzz went by. Best to check.

Okay, bus station, and uh-oh, what do we have here. Brick period piece. 1930's. Better for the noir ambience. Morris Burner Hotel. Perfect.

No G-men in sight. Slip out nice and easy and get to the front door quickly, but not hurriedly. Two knocks. A pretty face appears at the door. Waving excitedly like she knows him. Been waiting for him. Was this a setup? But nobody knew he was here.

Door opening. Large bare breasts. Tie-dye tutu. All belonging to Pretty Face.

"Hi! I'm Sirius!"

Click. End of movie.

"I'm definitely not," said Archie with a goofy grin.

"Get in here silly. I've been waiting light years for a man like you."

TWENTY-EIGHT

THE OBVIOUS AND MOST LOGICAL SOLUTION to open the safe was the one Shady originally suggested. Using the father/son guise, Tinman and Tek would be the bait. By claiming they were there to return the cues, gloves, and hat, they would lure Chester out of his panic room. The rest of the gang would be in hiding and when he appeared, they'd grab him. Then he'd be tortured into telling the combination. Easy.

Except Tinman had ruled out the possibility the first time it came up, and every time after. It was not fair play, he kept saying. Not something he could condone, he insisted. Period. The problem was, it kept coming up. Because there was no other solution.

For the past three days, Tinman and Tek had been attached at the hip. Neither willing to accept the inevitable. Peach had been a no-show, and they were unwilling to call, knowing he was in a bad state. Bones and Catfish also kept a low profile, with only an occasional call to see if there was any progress. Shady had called repeatedly, trying to harangue them, but they shrugged him off.

Sequestered in the Clubhouse, Tinman and Tek thought. And thought. And thought. Along the way, Tek, ever the optimist, managed to lift a perfect thumbprint from the cue ball. He now had two copies, imprinted onto flexible silicone film that could open all the locks but the panic room.

Tinman spent some of his time shooting pool, his mind working on unraveling the mystery. The rest of the time he pored over the Jaba Master X02 website. He felt he'd learned more about safes in the last three days than he had in all the time under Peach's tutelage. And still, he was no closer to opening it. He learned how only a six-digit combination could create a million different possibilities. He discovered the magic of a random number generator and how the seed it created was encrypted. He learned how the locking system was reprogrammed using a nine-digit serial number, which had well over a million different possible combinations. Tek explained about the data lines and how a differential power analysis would help them if they were able to perform one, which they couldn't because of the system configuration and number of lines.

The whole thing was hopeless, but neither would admit defeat. When one succumbed to despair, the other would gently bring them back into the fold. At this moment, it was Tek who was ready to snap.

"Let's leave it for a few minutes," said Tinman, laying a hand on Tek's shoulder which was quivering with frustration. "I forgot to ask. What did you and Shady do all that time during the con?"

Tek shook his head to clear the cobwebs. "We started out playing pool. I was kicking his ass at nine ball, but he said it was a pussy game, so he quit. Then he asked to see the video of the house again, and wanted to know why we didn't just come down the private drive. I reminded him it wasn't kept plowed, but the roads Garshasp showed me were. And then he asked how I was going to get a print off the cue ball. Stuff like that. What I really wanted to do was smash a cue stick over his head for bumping off Jingles."

Tinman said, "Don't worry. Guys like that always get their due."

The door swung open and Amber stumbled in, carrying a heavy cardboard box. "Help!"

Tek ran over and grabbed the box and placed it on the bar.

"What are you doing here?" asked Tinman, sort of forgetting there still was an outside world with people in it.

"I'm a member! Remember?" Amber shot back. "The bar needs restocking. That is my job here, as you pointed out." From out of the box, she started pulling half-full bottles of booze, pilfered from her regular job.

"We're a little busy here," said Tinman, pacing—more like hobbling—idly around the room.

"Tough. I haven't seen you or anybody else since I made that call to the Fed. Is anyone going to tell me what that was all about?" No clues were offered, so she prattled on. "Hey, why are you walking so funny?"

Tinman froze, one foot still dangling in space.

Amber closed in, wearing a knowing look. "Hemorrhoids, huh? God, I hate those things. You know what I use? Apple cider vinegar."

"You drink it?" asked Tinman.

Amber head slapped him. "You rinse your butt with it, you knuck."

"Oh."

"But most importantly—and I know it's tough—don't spend too long sitting on the can. Do your movement, and move along. See?"

"Makes sense."

"You bet your bum, buster. Okay, gotta get back to the hall. Just wanted to see if you two were still alive. Don't be strangers." She whacked his ass, and then she was gone.

Tinman asked, "Is it really that noticeable?"

"Uh-huh. I didn't want to say anything," said Tek. "It's getting bad, isn't it?"

"I just need another shower."

"Fourth one today."

"Who's counting," said Tinman. "I'll be back."

After he left, Tek laid his forehead on the table, his giant of a mind limp with fatigue. He had never encountered a wormhole he couldn't hack, or a system he couldn't infiltrate. His brain was a force—creative, expansive and brilliant—but this thing was too much.

He rocked his forehead back and forth. Defeat was not an option. Tinman was relying on him, and he knew it. With an effort he hefted his head to a somewhat normal position and checked his phone. Almost nine. No food since lunch. That's what he needed. Sustenance. Something he often denied himself, believing, as Sherlock Holmes, that food slowed down the mental faculties.

He was forced to concede, however, the lack of it was causing his stomach to growl so loudly, it was blocking out any lucid thoughts his mind might have. He hoisted himself to his feet, and plodded to the door.

As he climbed the stairs to the apartment, he decided Tinman needed a break. He had been doing the cooking for the two of them and it was time someone else did. Tek wasn't a good cook by any stretch, but he could manage sandwiches and cereal. One would suffice.

He walked inside and started for the refrigerator. A loud anguished croak from inside the bathroom stopped him short. He turned just as Tinman stepped out, a towel wrapped around his waist. A wad of tissues in his hand. Bloody tissues. Tinman looked up, his eyes not really seeing. Shower water mixed with flowing sweat, ran freely down his face and neck.

"Tinman!" cried Tek. "What happened?"

"My ball sprang a leak." Then he sank to the bed.

"That's it! Get dressed! I've had enough! You're going to Urgent Care, and I'll drag you all the way if I have to. So don't argue!"

Tinman didn't. He was beaten. His destiny as a eunuch written in the stars. Might as well get to it. Gently, he dressed and they headed out.

Halfway down the stairs, Peach's car came barreling up, kicking up gravel as it slid to a stop, Peach jumping out right after.

"What's wrong, brother?!" he shouted.

Despite his pain and fear, Tinman grinned. It was the Feeling that had brought his brother here. He had known without knowing. "Nothing much," said Tinman. "Just need to get something checked out."

"Oh, sure! No biggie. Just a little boo-boo. Slap on a Band-Aid," ranted Tek.

"What in the hell's going on?" asked Peach.

"I'm telling him! Promise be damned," shouted Tek. "He's got a rotted ball."

"Ball?" wondered Peach.

"Nut! Gonad! Testicle! Your balls, man! His left ball just exploded! He could die from testicular death. I looked it up!"

"You did?" asked Tinman. "I could?" he asked without waiting for the answer to the first question, because he figured the answer to the second question was just a teensy bit more important than the first.

"Holy moly! We need to get you to Urgent Care! Pronto!" cried Peach, clutching Tinman's waist, like he was a wounded soldier on the front lines.

"Why didn't you tell me?" he asked, desperately. "What can they do for this?" he asked, figuring along the lines as Tinman that the second answer was more important.

Both Tek and Tinman studied their feet. It was as if Peach hadn't posed a question, and it was answer enough. "Oh, geez, oh, man."

They decided on Tek's SUV as the transportation, but as they were pulling out of the parking lot, Garshasp's cab suddenly blocked their path on its way in. Bones was in the front, with Catfish in the back.

Peach jumped out and ran over. "We got an emergency! Tinman's got a bum sack!"

"A bum sack?" asked Bones.

"His family jewels are diseased! His nut just blew a gasket!" Peach cried.

"Oh, my!" said Bones, shuddering.

"That's awful!" shouted Catfish.

"Family jewels?" asked Garshasp.

"They'll explain on the way! Just follow us to Urgent Care!"

* * *

Normally, Marlena loved being the one to work late and close up the clinic with the Doctor. It gave her a chance to be close to the person who she had been secretly in love with for almost a year. With all the other nurses and receptionists gone, she had the opportunity to make her love known, in private. She had yet to take the leap, but earlier that day, she'd decided tonight was the night.

And now this. When the motley crew she was now staring at appeared at the front door just as she was locking up, and practically muscled their way in, she thought they might be crooks looking to steal whatever drugs were on hand. But no, it was just your normal run-of-the-mill emergency where the ailing person and friends and family demanded immediate attention from the poor overworked healthcare specialists.

If it were up to her, she would have had these cretins hauled off to jail. But it wasn't her decision, and naturally, the Doctor had agreed to see the patient. It was irritating because it threw off her plans to bare her soul—and other things. On the other hand, it was exactly why she so adored the Doctor. So conscientious and selfless. One of the few left who took the Hippocratic Oath to heart.

Still, she was feeling very uncomfortable out here alone. The patient was already in an examining room, waiting for the Doctor, but his entourage were firmly planted in the waiting area, watching her every move, somehow making her feel it was her fault their friend was suffering from some mysterious ailment. An affliction the patient and his friends flat out refused to reveal when they so rudely demanded assistance. Only the Doctor could be allowed to know. How silly is that? Like they think their malady is somehow special. Never before seen in the history of humankind! Piss ants.

What was more disturbing was the friends of the patient, all male, were unabashedly cradling their crotches. And they all looked like they'd seen a ghost. Normally, people waiting would chat quietly, read magazines, or take a nap. But, no, this gang just sat there clutching their balls and gaping at her. Men can be so gross.

* * *

Tinman sat in the small, sterile cell called an examining room and waited. He felt like he was in The Prison of Infirmity. The lady who had showed him to his cell, told him to strip down and get into the embarrassing paper-thin gown that he now wore. He had never felt so exposed, particularly because the damn thing had little ties in the back, that were impossible to tie without help, so his mostly bare butt was perched on a raised stretcher-like thing, and it was cold.

It was the first time he had ever been forced to see a doctor and he was almost as petrified over that as he was the prospect of becoming half a man. He wondered how the process would go. What sort of tools would be used for the operation. Were saws still used for amputations? It would seem like overkill, given the size of what had to be removed. A hatchet? Tough to be accurate. Maybe pruning shears. That would be more fitting. Just a little snip here and a snip there. Like a haircut.

The image nearly made him swoon. He rallied, reminding himself, he could still live a relatively normal life sans one gonad. He was not planning on having any children, and really what else did they do? Surely the lack of one wouldn't affect his game.

The door opened and a short, Asian lady in a white jacket stepped in. Tinman looked behind and saw no one else. This must be the nurse, prepping him for the grand arrival of his savior.

"Mr. Harrigan," said the lady.

"That's me," said Tinman, weakly. "Just waiting for the doctor."

The woman smirked, shut the door, sat down on a low stool with wheels, and said, "You're looking at her, sweetheart."

"Huh?!"

"Huh?!" aped the Doctor, mockingly. "You know they do make lady ones at the big doctor factory. Special order only."

"Well, yeah, I kind of figured that. But—"

"But you would prefer a man."

"If you have one handy, that'd be swell. No offence. It's just this particular problem I have is a little, er, delicate."

"Uh-huh. Tough. I'm it. So spill it."

Tinman gulped audibly which made the Doctor grin sadistically. There was no way out. He either worked with this person, or figured out how to perform self-castration. Without yet knowing what tools would be required, he capitulated.

He said, "It's down there. The problem."

"I see. Um, the foot? No. Okay. Ankle? Nope. Knee? Shoot. Am I getting warm? Ooh. I am. Oh! You mean down there! Oh goody. Let's have a gander!"

"Isn't there another way?!"

"Well, I could just shove a hand down there, feel my way around, try and figure out what's going on in the blind. Could be interesting."

"Uh."

"Look, I've seen plenty. And I'm not personally interested. Hint, hint."

Tinman frowned, then he got the riddle. "Oh. You're that kind."

"Yep. They make those, too, in the factory. Now, spread 'em!"

Tinman did. The Doctor lifted the flimsy gown and began a close examination, while he stared at the ceiling and jabbered.

"I hardly ever use it. That's what's so weird. I mean, I have used it. For—uh—fornication!"

"Sex," the Doctor clarified, her gloved hand twisting his nut like a tiny door handle.

"Better word. When I used to do that, it was the normal kind—not that there's anything wrong with the abnormal kind! And that isn't the word. Different, that's it. The different kind. But I don't even do that. Not even with myself! Well, hardly ever. But not enough to be a problem! Look, I know what has to happen. I'm just curious what kind of implement you're going to use to, um, detach the thing. I'm sure you've done lots of these, so I'm not worried. Now that we know each other better, I have a lot of trust in you. Of course, it would be nice to know how many you've done. But you might feel put upon, and that wouldn't be good. We want you to have a steady hand, because I'm sure you can see, it's really only the one. And I'd kind of like to keep the other. For old times' sake, you know. I mean who wouldn't?"

The Doctor stood up and said, "It's a good thing it burst."

"That my ball blew up!" shouted Tinman. "What kind of crackpot are you?"

The Doctor let that one slide and said, "It relieved all the built-up puss and pressure."

"Come to think of it, it is feeling a little better since it did that. But I thought it was just because it had died."

The Doctor scratched something out on a pad and handed a slip to him. "Antibiotics. Take all of them. If you have any more discomfort, apply a warm poultice. Now get the hell out of here."

"Huh? Wait a minute. What's wrong with it?"

"Ingrown pubic hair."

Tinman stared at her widening grin, tinged with playful malice. He began cackling insanely, like a hyena on a bender, or better, a mad scientist having discovered the secret to eternal erection. He had foiled the Grim Reaper. The crazed laughter increased in volume and intensity. He pounded his fists on the stretcher-like thing and rocked it back and forth. The Doctor retreated to a corner.

Tears of joy sprang from Tinman's eyes, making everything in the white cell blurry. Walls, tongue depressors, gay Asian Doctor, all swirling in a watery hallucination.

In that moment of ecstasy, a bright light appeared, penetrating the deepest, darkest caverns of his mind. And all was suddenly clear. He knew how to get into the safe.

TWENTY-NINE

"WE NEED A BOAT. I'm not going through any more snow," said Tinman.

"They have plenty up there," said Peach. "But does anybody know how to drive one?"

"I do," said Tek. "My dad used to let me drive his off Long Island."

"Good. We're also going to need the two heavies, for the part with Chester," continued Tinman.

"I'm sure they'll be happy to oblige, for a cut of the action," said Catfish.

"Equal shares for everyone," said Tinman. "It's no longer about the money."

"It is to Shady," said Bones. "Even with your pool bet, you don't think he's just going to sit on his hands during the caper, now that we have an angle."

"I have that worked out. But it'll take you, Catfish, Garshasp, and help from Dez," said Tinman, sliding four balls in front of a corner pocket.

"You sure you trust her alliances?" asked Catfish.

"I guess we'll find out," said Tinman. "We line up the boat tomorrow, stay in a hotel overnight, and move on

Saturday. The crowds will be out for the holiday. Better cover."

"You learn quick," said Peach proudly.

"So that's it. What does everybody think?" asked Tinman.

"I think it's damn near brilliant!" said Peach. "And that's why you're the planner."

"It all makes sense to me," said Tek. "If nothing's changed since we were in there."

"No reason it should have," said Tinman. "You heard him. He never uses it. But if he did, then we pack up, go home, and call it a wash. At least we tried."

Everyone was quiet, digesting the plan.

"I gotta admit, it sure looks sweet. For a while there, I thought we were done for," said Catfish. "And it all came to you in a flash, huh?"

"A true epiphany," said Tinman. "Nothing like almost having a ball cut off to make you see the light."

THIRTY

SHADY WAS IN A FOUL MOOD. It had been five days since Peach declared the safe uncrackable, and despite his threats and cajoling, his worthless sons hadn't come up with anything. Also, he hadn't been sleeping well. In old age, Dizzy had developed a bad habit of snoring and it was drowning out his own. To make matters worse, it was raining. Had been for two days. It started out light, but now, late Saturday morning, it was coming down in buckets.

Dizzy was also being strange. Never one to care much about the weather, all morning she had been watching the skies over the mountains and silently fretting. At first, the knock on the door was a welcome diversion, but when he saw it was the old pickpocket and grifter, he was less than pleased. Even more disturbing was Dizzy claimed she invited them over.

"What better way to spend a rainy day than playing the Game of Life with some dear old friends?" she had said.

So here he was, sitting around with three old farts playing a game about living when they were all on borrowed time. The conman's spin earned him a PH. D, while Shady had to Pay Travel Expenses to the tune of twenty large. Stupid game. Fitting name.

"So the kids are still stumped, huh?" asked Shady.

"Painfully so," said Bones. "Life's a bitch."

"We should have done it my way. Torture is a surefire cure."

"But it hurts!" squealed Dizzy.

Shady snorted, and proceeded to regale them with a quaint anecdote. "Pain is a fact of life. First pain I remember, I was like four, running around the yard, barefoot, like kids do. And, boom, I pick up a rusty nail. Straight up through this foot. Top sticking out three inches. Ugly thing. My pa, he plops me on the porch. Calls ma for cotton and a jug of his special brew. Then he just grabs that sucker and yanks her out."

"Eeew!" shrieked Dizzy.

Shady grinned. "Then he shoves a hunk of cotton into the hole, spills some hooch over it and reams it out with a wooden matchstick. Never even got a scar. Helluva thing." His chest heaved up and down as he wheezed out a gurgling chuckle.

"But didn't it hurt?" asked Dizzy.

"Of course it hurt! That's the point of the story."

The others didn't seem to get it. Sitting there, looking at him like he was weird or something. "For Christ's sake, just spin, Dizzy."

She did. "Oooh! Look at that. I just got twins! Is that too funny?"

The dip and the shyster thought so. Shady, not so much. "Yeah, those two you already got were a real gift from above. They just worship you."

"Hah! Very funny. Do you know they walked out on me when they were kids? Right after Christmas. Gave me some baskets as consolation prizes and left. Went on the road with these two!"

The two old guys held up their hands in surrender. Dizzy grinned and waved it off. "I'm over it. Hell they're no different than you," she said, and playfully slapped Shady.

It was a revelation. And it hit home. The only reason he had decided on hijacking the heist afterwards, was his belief the two boys would never take a powder on their mom. He was wrong. This could all be a setup.

"You know, this game would be a lot more fun if we had more people," he growled. "Let's give the children a break from thinking and have 'em over."

A small silence. But telling.

"Good idea," said the flimflammer, "But they already decided to take a break. They're at the movies."

"Uh-huh," said Shady. "How about your two fat neighbors?"

"They are not fat!" declared Dizzy, then hesitated. "And they went away for the holiday weekend."

"Uh-huh," said Shady. As the cannon did his spin, it all came together. These guys were here to keep him on ice. Did Dizzy know about it? He doubted it. The boys wouldn't trust her. Thinking she was allied with him.

But the caper was on. Right now. They figured an angle for the safe. And when they had the loot, they'd contact these guys, meet up, and blow. Leaving dear old mom and dad with nothing. That was the plan. Time for a new one.

"This game is dull. Let's hit the town. Get some lunch, a few drinks, some laughs. Adult entertainment."

Long pause. Come on. Whose line in the script is it?

"It's raining," said Dizzy, retreating to the damn patio again, looking at the rain—in the mountains! At Tahoe! So that's why she's doing that. She is in on it. Ungrateful moll.

"Not inside it's not. Let's go. My treat. I insist," said Shady. "Any other arguments?"

The old guys didn't yet know the gig was up, but they were suspicious, and were in a box. No options but to play along. See what happens. They shrugged and nodded.

"Good deal," said Shady. "Call Muhammed. He can be our ride."

When Dizzy hung up the phone and said the raghead happened to be right around the corner, Shady had no more doubts. He was being played for a sap. He wondered if he should just off the two old guys. He couldn't afford to leave them behind because they would no doubt tip off the boys. If he killed them here, Dizzy would throw a fit. And he couldn't waste her. He might need her, for negotiations. He decided to take them all.

When they stepped out of the Palladio, Shady escorted everyone to the cab. He waited until the three got in the back, then slid in next to the Arab.

"I don't want to go too far," whined Dizzy.

"Too bad," said Shady. "We're going to Tahoe."

"In this weather?" Are you crazy!"

"It seems to be the happening spot today," said Shady.

"What are you talking about," asked the grifter.

"I'm talking about a cross," said Shady, pulling out his gun and showing it around. "And don't deny it. You all cooked this up together. Pull the heist when I'm not looking, then split town, leaving me high and dry."

"That's not what's going on!" yelled Dizzy. "And where did you get the piece?"

"Fellow enthusiast. I knew I couldn't trust any of you. Protection was needed."

"No one's trying to cross you, Shady," drawled the pickpocket. "You'll get your cut. We were just trying to protect ourselves from you."

"I got no time to listen to your lies. I was going to play this straight up. But now you forced my hand. And everybody's gonna pay. Listen up, Muhammed. You were the one that mapped out the route the first time. So, what's the fastest way to that house."

Garshasp stared at the gun, wishing he could get his own out of the glovebox. No chance. "Fastest? Mt. Rose Highway, of course. But you no wanting to go this way. No, sir. Very much raining, causing so much mud. Very dangerous."

Shady poked the barrel in his nose. "No, camel jockey, this is dangerous. Drive."

THIRTY-ONE

CHESTER, NOW DEFINITELY RESEMBLING KNOBBY, capered around his panic room. He was dressed for war. He had on his lucky red shirt, and vest covered with all his medals and badges, a black hat perched jauntily on his head. Oh, boy, was he ready. It had been a week since Dad and Son had dropped in. After they left, his keen but addled mind replayed every moment of the visit, and their suggestion for fending off Shady.

In retrospect, he liked the plan even more. That's why all his guns were piled up near the door of his underground fortress, and every speck of food in the house now filled his private refrigerator. He could wait out even the longest siege.

He skipped to his video monitors and studied the outside. A wild and wooly morning. Raining. Windy. The lake dotted with whitecaps. This was the day. He could feel it. Shady's presence closing in. His focus switched to the inside cameras and he perused every corner, ending in the billiard room. This is where, soon, the culmination of all his years of waiting would take place.

He chuckled. Thanks so much to Dad and Son he had a perfect plan. Shady couldn't penetrate the Jaba Master

Xo2, and he couldn't get to him. Even if Shady did manage to break into the panic room, no amount of torture would get the combination out of him.

Because he didn't know what it was! There was no combination. The safe had never been programmed. Har! A stroke of genius. The thought of Shady torturing the combination out of him, had long scared him. Not the pain. And he wasn't afraid of dying. He just had to be sure Shady never got his hands on the coin collection. He'd take the secret of the Jaba Master Xo2 to the grave before letting him win the day.

Of course, his mischievous sense of humor, could not be suppressed. So, he had left one clue. The purloined letter. The way in. There it was in the monitor. He snickered. What a perfect little prank to pull on his nemesis. After Shady failed, then he would find him, wherever he was, and let him know the solution was right there in front of him. Oh, what fun! Just imagining him chewing his tongue off when he found out how close he had been, and how stupid he was.

"Cry Havoc!" cried Chester doing his best Marc Antony impersonation. "And let slip the dogs of war."

THIRTY-TWO

As TINMAN WAS KNOCKED FROM HIS FEET for the umpteenth time he wondered who first said, "The best laid schemes of mice and men, oft go awry." He figured it had to be Shakespeare, since he had dibs on almost all the good quotes. But he had a feeling it was someone else who predicted the demise of his master plan.

It had started out okay. Surprisingly, Dez accepted the need for the subterfuge regarding Shady. And, earlier, Catfish sent a message, saying he and Bones had successfully planted themselves in the condo, and were busy Shadysitting. So, at least Tinman knew he didn't have to worry about him.

They were fully staffed, because Angel and Malice readily accepted the offer to be in the mob. So far so good.

Everything else had gone awry. First, it was raining, which wouldn't have been so bad, except for the mudslides that made the approach to the lake treacherous. Knowing Mt. Rose Highway and the eastern approach would be hit the worst, they chose to come in via the interstate, through the town of Truckee, and down Route 267. They did avoid most of the mud, but so did the thousands of other people who were coming to the lake for the Memorial Day holiday and decided on the same, safer route.

The road was bumper to bumper, and it took most of the morning to drive the twelve miles and finally arrive at King's Beach. Oddly, when they had crossed into California, Peach asked to stop so he could buy a lottery ticket, Nevada ironically being one of the few states that didn't have a lottery. Tinman secretly believed he was hedging his bet should the heist go sour, but he wouldn't give his reason. Once they reached the lake, the search for a boat began. With all the people creeping around Lake Blvd., it took several more hours for Peach to locate one they could borrow for the next day's caper.

It was moored on a private pier near Moon Dune Beach, and after some soggy casing it became clear the house it belonged to was unoccupied. The boat was a Sunseeker Portofino. Forty-eight feet long, with a capacity of ten people, and boasting two powerful engines. Peach easily bypassed the ignition system, making sure there would be no delay the next morning. So, granted, that was a good thing.

Then they decided it was time to find accommodations for the evening. No problem. It was only a holiday weekend at one of America's premier destinations. Take your pick.

Bzzz. There was no room at the inn. Or the stable. Or any hotel, motel, hostel or cabin, for that matter. And if they thought it was raining earlier, they were mistaken. Visibility was nil, and the snow from the surrounding mountains was melting rapidly, causing washouts.

Peach suggested they return to the boat and sleep there. There was plenty of room, and it came with TVs, stereo, and full kitchen! The vote was unanimous, and they muscled their way through the storm until they reached the pier and the boat. Once inside, everyone dried up, chose digs, and settled in. Until the wind started. Then the rocking. And the seasickness.

First it was Angel, which was a sight to see, or rather, avoid. Then Tek, which was even more disturbing since he was The Captain. And finally, Peach succumbed. The three retreated to the safety of the land-based SUV. Around midnight, Tinman felt the first tremors in his stomach, but the car was full, so he was forced to ride out the storm and keep down the bile. Only Malice, with Samoan island blood, slept peacefully, letting the rocking of the waves lull him into pleasant dreams of copra and roasted taro.

When dawn finally broke, the rain had subsided, only to be replaced by sustained 60mph wind gusts. Most people, including Tinman and the others, had no idea, that with certain conditions such as these, Lake Tahoe could do a damn good impersonation of a raging ocean. Just like now.

Everyone was glad they had Tek along to do the piloting, until he actually started piloting. They were only a short distance from the shore when the boat began its imitation of a bucking bronco, rearing up headlong into the seven-foot wave crests, briefly going aloft, then slamming nose-first into the water, only to pitch backwards again, ready to take on the next mount.

Tinman struggled to his feet and was promptly tossed back down. Deciding crawling was safer, he slithered to the cockpit where Tek was clutching the steering wheel like Odysseus returning from the Trojan Wars. Everyone else was below, most likely praying to whatever deity they worshipped. Tinman, with no such allegiance, decided he'd stick to praying for Tek's piloting ability.

"I thought you knew how to drive this thing!" he bellowed over the roar of the wind.

"I didn't think we'd be in a tsunami! So back off! And get your life jacket on!"

Life jacket. Right. Like ski poles, but more important. Tahoe was the second deepest lake in the country, and all kinds of mysteries surrounded it. It was even rumored Jacques Cousteau had emerged from a diving expedition with the cryptic words, "The world is not ready for what I have seen." Condescending perhaps, urban legend or not, Tinman was certain he was not ready. As the boat reeled, he let gravity slide him to the rear where he found an unused life jacket lashed to the side.

With effort, he returned to Tek. "Do you have to go straight over the waves? Why not come at them from the side?"

"Brilliant! Then a big one comes along, hits us broadside and capsizes this thing!"

Good rational thinking, thought Tinman. Then he kept his mouth firmly shut. He found himself looking fondly back on his idyllic trek through the snow on their first visit to Chester. Like going to grandmother's house in a sleigh. But he didn't regret the decision to approach by water. With all the rain, the snow was now mostly mud, and being swallowed by mud had to be a lot worse than drowning. Okay, marginally, but still.

The only good thing was there were no other boats on the lake. Mostly because the people who owned boats knew about Tahoe's ocean impersonation and believed only insane people would tackle it in these conditions. It made Tinman smile. "No great mind has ever existed without a touch of madness." Shakespeare? Nope. Aristotle.

"There it is!" cried Tek.

And it was. Like the Goddess Circe beckoning from her mystical island, Chester's boathouse loomed ahead.

Tinman became more impressed with Tek's captaining as he maneuvered the boat to the dock and pulled it in across from Chester's boat.

"Tie us off! Quick!" shouted Tek.

Huh? Thought Tinman. That was supposed to be Peach's job. He was more lithe. But he was below, probably barfing. So it was up to him. The boat rocked back and forth, banging angrily into the side of the dock. He slid to the side and grabbed a dockline. He spotted a cleat and leaned out, trying to lasso it.

But he was no cowboy and after the third try, Tek yelled, "I can't hold it much longer! Get onto the dock! Tie it off from up there! Hurry!"

On the dock? But there was water in between. First a little as the boat swung in and hit the dock, then a lot as it swung the other way. It would take perfect timing, and an acrobat's leap. Swing in, swing out. Swing in, and jump, and slip, and fall, legs dangling in water, pull up before you drown or the boat crushes you, boat swings out, rope almost pulls you off the dock, and boat swings in, lash the sucker with whatever knot you didn't learn in the Boy Scouts, and ta-da. Really?

"You did it!" cried Tek.

Whew. Now collapse face down onto dock. Give thanks to whatever God you think might be listening, even if you don't necessarily believe in them. Gain composure and say, "Piece of cake! Tell the guys to suit up. I'll tie off the back one."

Despite Tinman's urging for speed, it took thirty minutes before his gang could regain their composure, courage, and land legs enough to climb off the boat. Tinman had Tek leave it idling to help with a quick getaway. As they hustled into the boathouse, they were all wearing black ski masks. Tinman knew the plan hinged on

Chester still believing Shady was one of the heisters, and hoped the masks would throw him off.

He also didn't want him to know how they had mastered the thumbprint locks. The old man was crazy but not stupid. He would realize the father/son visit had been a ruse. And it would be enough to make him do something irrational, and change the plan he'd been fed. So when they entered the boathouse, Peach quickly located the video camera mounted in a corner over the tunnel entrance. Angel hoisted Tek up and he sprayed the plexiglass cover with black spray paint.

Tek then pulled out a small plastic packet and removed one of the thumbprint impressions. He gave Peach the silicone film, and he placed it over his thumb and planted it on the panel above the lock. The door clicked open and he pulled it wide. The gang switched on their flashlights and filed into the tunnel.

Peach was last. As he turned to pull the door shut, Tinman stopped him. "Leave it open. There's nobody around. And if we have to hightail it, we don't want to be worrying about opening doors."

Peach grinned, and they disappeared into the tunnel, Tinman hoping the earlier bad luck would result in good karma, and everything was unchanged in the house.

* * *

Garshasp didn't know it, because the word was not yet entered into his English vocabulary notebook, but the drive to Tahoe so far had been harrowing. They had narrowly avoided rockslides, flooded out washes, and gale strength winds. One good thing was there was almost no traffic. Mostly because only insane or hijacked people would venture into such a weather hell. Throughout the drive, Shady, the pig, had been manic, forcing Garshasp to perform feats never before attempted in a cab. Everyone had tried to reason with him, but he silenced them with a flashing of the gun.

When they left the main road and ventured onto the back roads, the way become even more treacherous. Whole trees were felled by the moving earth, and several times, Garshasp had to swerve to avoid them. They finally reached the entrance to Chester's private drive. A one-lane dirt path weaving its way among towering Ponderosa pines and dropping down to the lake at a steep grade.

It looked like it was moving on its own. Garshasp leaned out his window and realized the lava-like substance creeping slowly down the drive was a river of mud. He was already very upset at the damage his beloved cab had sustained, but this was too much. If it weren't for the fact Tinman's mother and friends were in the car, he would have taken his chances trying to disarm the pig, and get to his gun in the glovebox to finish him off. But perhaps there was still a way.

"We must be walking from now. Very dangerous. Taxi not capable."

"Don't be such a namby-pamby. Just a little mud. Drive on."

"You're insane, Shady," cried Tinman's mother. "We'll all die!"

"Not me sister. But you shut up, or I'll give you the two and one."

"What the hell's that?" asked Tinman's mother.

"Two in the heart, and one in the head," the pig cackled. "Tried and true, never fails to get the job done. Okay, Muhammed, move along."

Garshasp was fuming. He knew a threat when he heard it, even if he didn't know all the words. He had been an expert at making threats in his job with the Shah, and he clenched his jaw, knowing there was nothing he could do. He put the cab in gear and crept into the oozing earthen magma.

The first ten yards went really well. Then they all saw it. Half the hill to their right had broken free and a wall of mud was moving to envelop them. Garshasp, not caring about the consequences, slammed the car into reverse, but the tires slurped up the mud, spinning uselessly. They were in the grips of the slide. The slow-moving chocolate river lifted the car up and carried it along on its pre-destined path to the lake. The sensation was so surreal, nobody could utter a word. Okay, there was lots of screaming, but all of it nonsensical.

Down they went, speed never changing, the car bobbing around like a pilotless canoe, so that sometimes they were traveling backwards, which was most unpleasant. But by the time they approached the lake, they were facing forward, able to see their fate, which made going backwards seem a lot better.

If it hadn't been for Chester's boathouse they would have surely tumbled into the water, as the mud was doing. Instead, the front right bumper of the cab hooked the edge of the pier and spun inward, flattening the car against the end of the boathouse.

Garshasp nearly fainted. Dez almost peed herself. Bones and Catfish finally exhaled.

The pig said, "Good driving, Ahab. Let's go. Out the windows. Your boys must already be inside. And I don't want to miss the party."

* * *

Chester ran back and forth in front of his bank of video monitors. What was going on here? He'd seen Shady's mob land on the boat, and one of them tying it off, but his

347

camera was too far away to make out any face. After what seemed like an eternity, the gang got off the boat and ran into the boathouse, but they were hidden by masks. But he knew they were professionals when they sprayed the camera over the tunnel entrance. He couldn't see how they were attempting to break in, but he thought the thumbprint lock would stop them cold.

He was wrong. After only a few seconds, a buzzer went off, telling him they'd gotten through! Shady must have compiled a group of master criminals. And heavies. The two big guys together would outsize a VW bus. There were three others. Two, about the same height, and one much smaller. But which one was Shady?

Wait. What is this? A taxi cab? Now? Here? Riding in on mud? It's going into the lake! Hah! No. It's hung up on the pier. It's stopped. Someone's climbing through the window. He's got a gun. It's him. No amount of years could hide the cruel face. But why didn't he come on the boat with the others?

More people climbing out of the window. A dark-skinned man, two old guys and a dame? What's a woman doing here? Ooh! Good looking too. Va-va-voom! Been a while. Uh huh! Yum, yum, yum, yum. Stop it! This is serious. Shady's pointing a gun at them, directing them into the boathouse. What's going on? Is he up to his old tricks?

Chester's head spun to another monitor, the one showing the inner tunnel door. He knew if they got through the entrance so quickly, he should soon see the first group appear. This was the moment when everything would become clear.

* * *

Tinman and the others stood outside the inner door, making last minute preparations. The whole plan relied on speed. He looked into the eyes of each member of his crew. No fear or hesitation. They were ready.

"Angel, remember, you and Malice don't be shy with the props. It's key that Chester sees you packing. Wave them around if you have to."

Angel and Malice grinned, holding up their mean-looking handguns. Tinman was not above a little deception, and the two pieces were actually realistic-looking pellet guns they'd picked up at Walmart the day before. Unloaded.

"Okay, if everything is the same as it was, we should be in and out in under ten minutes," said Tinman. He motioned to Peach, who placed the thumbprint impression on the panel and the door clicked open.

Everyone raced in. Only dim accent lights lit the place. They ran down the hall and into the living room. Angel and Malice with guns held high ran forward into the hallway leading to the panic room.

They both flattened to the ground, guns pointed at the base of the door. Tinman had remembered it rose upwards. If Chester considered escape, he would see in his monitors that his guards would be able to shoot his legs out from under him.

Tinman, Peach and Tek moved quickly through the living room. Tinman swung open one of the large doors leading to the billiard room and they stepped in. All three swept their flashlights to the row of score beads hanging over the pool table.

And there they were. Unmoved. All nine groupings of beads exactly the way they'd been when Tinman first noticed them. They all grinned. Tek swung around and pointed out the locations of the cameras. A minute later, all four had been painted over. Tinman knew as soon as Chester saw they opened the safe, he would throw caution to the wind and come out blazing. They had to delay him for as long as possible, so that if they got the collection, the first he would know is when they ran through the living room and into the tunnel. By then, it should be too late for him to do anything about it.

"Let's get to it," said Tinman. No need for masks anymore, so they removed them.

Tek pushed the button to open the fake wall panel and reveal the safe. Peach stood silently, grudgingly admiring his nemesis. Then he knelt in front of the dial. "Ten turns to the left to power the lock," he said mostly to himself. As he turned, a display screen began to slowly glow.

When finished, he said, "You know the rules, brother, I need the numbers in exact order, with only a short delay between, so feed them to me every five seconds."

"Got it," said Tinman. He grabbed a cue stick and held it up to the string of score beads. He wanted to make sure he did this right. There would only be one chance, so his idea was to use the cue to mark off each grouping, then slide it to the left after he'd called it out, ensuring he wouldn't miss any, or count any twice.

"I still can't believe Chester would leave the serial number out in the open," said Tek. "Let's hope this isn't just a coincidence."

In Tinman's vision at Urgent Care, the score beads had flashed into view, and he knew, or at least thought he knew, the nine groupings of beads represented the nine numbers of the serial number. "Probably had trouble remembering the combination," he said. "He wanted to make sure he could still get in if he forgot. Who would ever think to look here, and then make the connection to the safe?"

"You, brother," said Peach with a grin. "That's why you're the brains."

"Indeed, indeed," said Shady, appearing at the open door, gun in hand. "So that's what your angle was. Very nice. I never would have figured it out. Thanks so much."

"Where did you come from?!" shouted Tek.

"Just thought I'd drop by. Nice of you to leave the door open. Made it a lot easier. Now, don't let me stop you. Just go ahead and get me my collection."

Tinman's eyes narrowed. He couldn't do it. He would not let Shady win. With a broad movement, he swept the beads to one side. Peach and Tek gasped.

Shady roared and thrust his gun at Tinman. "That was very stupid. Now, you're going to have to remember every number or I'm going to blow you away. Dumbass."

"Do it," said Tinman. "And you'll never get your precious coins."

Shady grinned. "You think you have me, huh? Alright everybody, get in here." From behind the door, Dez, Garshasp, Catfish and Bones appeared and shuffled into the room, heads hung low.

"See? I don't need to shoot you. Now who should I begin with? Maybe hurry your pickpocket's retirement along. Pop one right through this hand here. No more arthritis. Or maybe one in the grifter's knee, take away a little swagger. The cabbie, eh, who cares. But mommy dearest, that's another story," he said pressing the gun into Dez's temple. "Oh wait, you don't really like her all that much do ya. So, no great loss."

"Don't let him do it," said Peach, faintly, for the first time in his life not sure of his brother's thoughts.

Tinman and Dez locked eyes. He was surprised to see she had little fear in them, and was not pleading. She would not bow to Shady, and would accept Tinman's decision. It hit hard. She had taught him how to be tough. She had taught him a lot of things. More than he admitted, until now. He knew the moment would come when he would forgive her for lying and hiding the truth about who she was. This was the time.

Without looking at Shady, he whirled to the table and said, "You ready, brother?"

Peach sighed and wiped the sweat and threatening tears from his eyes. "Anytime."

Tinman removed the wooden rack from around the balls, and quickly lined them against a rail. He closed his eyes, remembering what he originally thought was a pool run. He began to shoot it out in his mind's eye. As he did, he pulled balls from the line and slapped them on the table. Peach dialed in the numbers as he called them out, using the exact procedure for using the serial number, as detailed in the online .pdf manual, which differed from simply dialing in the combination.

"Three. Eleven. Seven. Two. Five. Eight."

Everyone waited. Seconds ticked. Peach needed the next number, and yet he didn't want to break in to Tinman's thoughts. But soon the lock would shut down.

"One. Four." Then he stopped again. He'd lost the run. His mind blank.

"You better remember, brains," said Shady, cocking the gun.

Tinman spun around, his eyes meeting Tek, who was chewing his lips, silently egging him on. Tinman shook his head, begging for help.

"Were all the beads on the one side used for the nine groups?" blurted Tek.

Tinman nodded. Not sure where he was going. Tek ran to the table, studied the eight balls, and did the math. "Nine! It has to be nine!" he yelled.

Peach spun the dial, grabbed the handle and yanked. The safe door swung open.

THIRTY-THREE

THE LEATHER CASE LOOKED EXACTLY AS IT HAD in the picture Shady had shown them what seemed like so long ago. Peach pulled it out.

"Don't fall in love with it," said Shady. "On the pool table. Good deal. Now open it and everyone over there."

Peach did as told, and joined the others against a wall. Shady's face grew into a grotesque formation of lust and greed, like the alpha wolf claiming the pack's kill for his own. "I knew I could count on all of you. So that's it then. I'll be moving along."

As he went to shut the case, Peach said, "Dad. This isn't right. You gotta give us something. We're blood."

Shady flinched. First time ever. An emotional tremor. He didn't like it. And he was afraid of it. It was primal. "I'll tell you what, kid," he said, reaching into the case and retrieving a stray dime in a plastic holder. He flipped it to Peach and said, "I'm in a generous mood. Go buy you and your brother some penny candy. I'm out of here."

"That isn't like you, Shady," said Tinman. "Leaving loose strings behind. I figured you to cover your tracks."

Shady said, "Yeah, this is an eight shot, so I could take care of all of you. But it's easier to let Chester do that job.

Once he finds out he's been tricked, he'll be less than pleased. Which reminds me. Peach, take that film off your thumb and tear it up."

Peach sighed and removed the thumbprint impression and shredded it. Shady looked to Tek. "And you, hand over the backup."

"I don't have one!" declared Tek.

"Sure you do. You're a real up-and-comer. Think of everything. Now hand it over."

Tek cursed under his breath then pulled out the small packet with the second impression. He tossed it at Shady, who opened it and wrapped the film over his thumb.

"And now I will say my farewells. Thanks to one and all for your help. I noticed you kept your boat running as a favor to me. But of course, that's what family is for."

As they all watched, he backed out of the room.

* * *

Angel and Malice were in a quandary. Tinman told them to remain at their stations no matter what. They had been lucky when Shady arrived. Their positions on the floor and the dim lighting had hidden them. They would have leapt into action right then, but were afraid Chester would get out and the gang would have even more troubles.

They decided Malice would creep to the end of the hall so they could at least get a peek at what was going on. That's how they found out Shady had hijacked the heist. And that's when they decided to act. As Shady backed into the living room, they slipped out of the hall and drew their guns.

"Drop it, Shady," said Angel.

Shady wheeled around, his face gaping. "Damn it! How could I be so stupid."

"Easy for you," said Malice. "Now do as my friend says, or else."

Shady started to lower his gun, his expert eyes planted on the two pieces pointed at him, wondering what chance he might have in a shootout. Then his eyes popped with recognition and he started laughing. "What are you gonna do? Fill me with pellets? Or is that one of those paint guns you're gonna splatter me with? Oh, boy, you almost had me fellas. I gotta hand it to you. Good try."

The others in the billiard room had moved to the doorway and were watching, crestfallen. Shady smiled, "Don't cry. I'm supposed to win this one. Gotta move."

He hustled through the living room and down the hall to the tunnel entrance. He spied a camera overtop the door. He grinned at it, waved and mouthed, "Thanks, Chester." Then he disappeared into the black, slamming the door behind.

* * *

Chester was losing whatever was left of his befuddled mind. He hadn't counted on the gang blocking his vision from the billiard room, so he had no idea what was going on. And the two thugs lying outside his door were preventing him from escape. He was almost certain Shady was up to no good, but he couldn't be sure. His face remained planted in front of the monitor with the view of the living room.

When he saw Shady backing out with the gun and his coin collection, he nearly fainted. Somehow he'd beaten the Jaba Master Xo2! And he had done it again! He hijacked his own gang just the way he'd done it to him and Newmann!

But wait. Hurray! The two heavies had the drop on him. Oh, no. Why's he laughing? Why aren't they shooting him. Shoot him! Kill him! NO! The guns must be fake! He's leaving. Stop him!

Chester followed his path as he made his way to the tunnel door. He watched in the monitor as Shady taunted him, mocked him. And something snapped.

He became like Gollum, having had his precious ring stolen by the burglar, Bilbo. He became part animal. Rabid. Tortured. Blood thirsty. He grabbed a machine pistol from his arsenal, activated the door and charged outside.

* * *

When Chester burst onto the scene, everyone froze. His eyes were wild and the gun looked equally demonic. "After him! Come on! He's getting away!" Then he froze as well, his eyes flitting back and forth between Tinman and Tek. His madness making room for a remnant of rational thought.

Tinman could see the moment he figured it all out, and he was worried. Chester was a live wire. At this moment, he could be more dangerous than Shady.

"Dad—son," mumbled Chester. Then with a roar, "A nest of traitors!" (Finally, a little Shakespeare.)

"Take it easy, Chester," said Tinman.

"You did this! When you were first here. You discovered my secret over the pool table! And you helped the devil! And now you're all going to pay! Yep!" He took aim squarely at Tinman's head. Then things got a tad strange.

Peach suddenly started hopping around on one leg, with an arm outstretched over his head, and hooting like an owl. Chester's eyes glazed. "The Symbol of the Ill Jackass," he muttered. "The distress signal."

He closed in on Peach who stopped his antics. Their eyes met. Chester placed his thumbs in his ears and waggled his hands, the gun wobbling back and forth. Peach made a fist and thumped his chest.

"The Hewgag brays," said Chester, solemnly.

"Before or after the full moon," intoned Peach.

"Credo Quia Absurdum," bellowed Chester.

"Dorkus Malorkus!" cried Peach.

The two fell into each other's arms and hugged like old war buddies. Everyone else stood around wondering if the insanity was contagious.

"Brother Chester," said Peach. "I'm Brother Peach."

With tears of joy, Chester asked, "How did you know I was a Clamper?"

"The red shirt! And the vest and badges. I have mine on under all this stuff."

"Of course! Hah! And these? Are they also Brothers?"

"Uh, not yet, they're still PBC's, everyone except the woman, she's my mom," said Peach. "Thanks for coming to our rescue—from you! How funny is that?"

Chester bobbed his head up and down happily. "Very funny! Oh, yes. Tee-hee. I save you from me. Hah!" He abruptly stopped. "Brother Peach, I came to your rescue but now I am in distress! Shady! He's taken it!"

"I know, Chester, it's a real drag, and you're right, we will help. But you're forgetting a cardinal Clamper rule, no guns, remember?"

Chester looked at his gun. "You're right. The Brothers at the bar wouldn't like it. Oh, no. But then we have no power against Shady. Ooh."

"Sure we do," said Peach, waving his arms around. "Power in numbers."

Chester looked at the others. He cackled, dropped his gun and took off running, shouting, "Once more unto the breach!"

"What the hell was that?" asked Tinman.

"Must be Shakespeare," said Peach.

"No! The whole Clamper thing. What is that?" asked Tinman.

"I'll explain later. Let's go," said Peach.

"Shady still has a gun," said Tek.

"Eh, he's long gone. But Chester has the way out of here. He's the only one with the right thumb."

The logic sank in quickly and everyone dashed after Chester. When they reached the tunnel door, it was open, but he was out of sight. They all scooted inside.

When they clambered into the boathouse, they heard a gunshot. They peeked outside. Chester was on the deck, apparently having dodged Shady's first shot. Shady was at the wheel of the stolen boat and was gunning the engines trying to free it from the surrounding mud. He let off another round, but the rocking of the boat caused the shot to go wide.

"I know you think guns are for cowards, Tinman," said Dez. "But I sure wish Chester had one now. He doesn't have a chance."

"Well, you see," said Garshasp. "I am very much a coward. And liking guns so much! Go USA. And just happen to be having one in my glovebox. I being not so very fond of Shady, and with your humble permission—"

"You were packing all this time?!" screeched Dez. "Why didn't you use it?"

"But, but—"

"Mama Bear gives you humble permission. Now, go, go!"

Despite the familial hierarchy, Garshasp looked to Tinman, who, after watching another of Shady's shots nearly hit Chester, nodded, and said, "But don't kill him. It's not the way. Just even the sides."

Garshasp grinned, got into a commando crouch and bolted out of the boathouse. Shady took a potshot, but missed. Garshasp shimmied across the pier and slid into his cab, precariously perched on a mound of mud. He retrieved his pistol, and made a sharpshooter's shot at Shady, nicking his hand and sending his gun into the water.

Chester looked back and waved. Garshasp reciprocated, so happy to be of assistance. Americans are so friendly! The others burst out of the boathouse and raced down the pier.

But they were too late. Shady freed the boat and started pulling out into the lake. Chester pierced the air with a howl, sending shivers down everyone's spines. He jumped to his feet and sprinted down the remaining section of pier. With a mighty leap he flew through the air and caught the end of the boat.

He scrambled aboard. Shady was oblivious as he battled the incoming waves. But as Chester neared, he slipped, and Shady heard. He turned and the two grappled. Shady clutching the leather case with one hand, and fighting off Chester with the other.

* * *

Archie was so happy. He and Sirius were getting on like gangbusters. He was sure Grandmama would adore her. She had once told him she'd gone swimming nude in the Ganges, and survived without nary a touch of typhoid, cholera, or amoebic dysentery! So she would certainly appreciate Sirius' free spirit. As would mother. He was equally certain Father would not approve. Oh glorious day. And his new family, the Burners, were everything he had always wanted in a family. Many of them didn't have much money, but all of them had wonderful ideas on how to spend it.

After Sirius had discovered his secret passion to be a juggler she suggested they construct a giant juggler for this year's Burning Man. It would have glowing giant balls that actually flew through the air. And the hands and arms would move, catching them. The vision was breathtakingly spiritual, and though they hadn't figured out how to build it, Archie knew it would happen. Because that's what life is. Making your own reality.

Take this weekend. He had no idea what everyone was celebrating, but he knew he wanted to participate. But how? That's when his new family suggested a fun-filled weekend at lovely Lake Tahoe. And what better place to begin? The Thunderbird Lodge, naturally. Built by a man even wealthier than Father, and yet one who knew how to have a good time. Archie paid for the whole tribe to have a private tour of the estate. After lolling around the private opium den smoking spleefs with the guide, they were shown the Thunderbird, George Whittell's magnificent speedboat.

Archie was instantly enamored. And it was for rent! Cheap! Only five thousand dollars of Father's easy-earned money per hour! So, he had rented it for the weekend. The rain and wind and waves were no deterrent for Archie, because at this moment, he was starring in one of his movies.

Originally, he was James Bond, flying around the canals of Venice, but then Sirius and the Burners didn't quite work as supporting characters. So he'd switched to Our Man Flint. It was a much better fit for his cast.

So here he was, pounding through the waves. The provided crew of three for the boat were happily crashed below, having discovered the wonders of Cheeba Chews. Chase was joining them in their slumber. His family was scattered around the boat, enjoying the wind in their hair, and Sirius was wrapped around his waist.

What's that? Aha! It's a boat carrying his current foe. Another nasty Evil Villain that must be eradicated from this blissful Eden by, Our Man Flint.

Wait! There was a fight going on. The Evil Villain is holding some kind of case. It must be the secret plans stolen from the Pentagon. And another man is trying to wrest the valuable documents from him. It must be an Ally In Need! Flint to the rescue!

He cranked hard on the wheel, spinning the boat around. Then he tromped on the gas and the V12 supercharged 1100 H.P. airplane engines erupted. As he sped toward the other craft like an asteroid hell-bent on destruction, he reached up and yanked on the cord activating the bank of horns which had come off a steam locomotive.

The sound was deafening and he could see it affected the ongoing battle on the enemy boat. His Ally In Need was now balancing precariously on the edge, a leg and an arm dangling over water. His other hand grasped to the attaché case. The Evil Villain had both hands clasped to the case. It was now or never.

With just enough room to spare before crashing into the other boat, he jerked the wheel and the Thunderbird swung sideways. Like sliding into second base, water sprayed over the other boat and a large wake kicked into its side.

The Evil Villain strained. The Ally In Need pulled valiantly, willing to risk his life for the safety of the free world. The boat pitched violently and they both toppled over the side and sank. Mankind was saved. All because of Our Man Flint.

Archie smiled down at Sirius' bloodshot eyes and peaceful smile. He looked around. All his family was having the best of times. Wouldn't it be wonderful if poor old Shady was never found. Then he would have to go on searching and searching, and spending and spending.

Ain't life grand.

THIRTY-FOUR

"WELL, THERE THEY GO, SAID PEACH.

"Yeah. And the coins," said Tek.

"What did you think I was talking about?" asked Peach, perplexed.

"I sort of feel bad for that Chester guy," said Dez.

"I don't," said Tinman. "He won."

"And we most certainly did not," said Bones.

"Check," said Catfish.

"Excusing me, boss," said Garshasp. "That man, Shady, he was a pig, no? I just want to checking my English."

Tinman smiled and said, "Your English is spot on."

"Oh very good," said Garshasp, pulling out his English journal.

"So how are we going to get out of here?" asked Angel.

"I don't like mud," said Malice.

"We'll take Chester's boat," said Peach. "It can't be any more difficult than the other one to start. I'm sure he won't mind. In fact, I think it'd be okay if we poke around his place a bit before we go. Have to be a few knickknacks we can pick up to make this caper worthwhile."

"Let's do it!" cried Tek. "Dibs on the eyeball recognition lock to the panic room!" He ran back into the boathouse with everyone following but Dez, Peach and Tinman.

Side by side, they looked out at the lake as the Sunseeker Portofino drifted on the waves, moving farther away, like the Flying Dutchman, doomed to an eternal search for a port that would never come.

"Sorry, Dez," said Tinman.

"Oh, please. I'm the only idiot standing here. For a lot of reasons. And I want you to know I'm going to be different. More like a mother. Like I should've been."

"Please don't," said Tinman.

"I'd appreciate that as well," said Peach.

"What do you mean?!" cried Dez. "You both deserve a mother!"

"The problem is, see, we're just not used to it," said Peach. "It's better if we just go along as we were. And I promise not to call you mom anymore. I know you don't like it."

Dez pursed her lips and welled up.

Peach put an arm around her and said, "We love you just the way you are, Dez. We have no beef with you."

Dez looked hopefully over at Tinman and he nodded and smiled. She sighed and laid her head on his shoulder.

Tinman said, "I do have one question, though. What was this craps dealer like?"

"Like?" she asked, then smiled in remembrance. "He was a real character. Fun-loving. Goofy. Life was a lark. The complete opposite of Shady."

"Oh," said Tinman, quietly.

"Say! I just thought of something Chester has that would fit in perfectly at your Clubhouse. Come on!" She said, heading to the boathouse.

"Be right there," said Peach. When she was gone, he turned to Tinman and said, "Why the interest in the craps dealer?"

"No reason."

Bull. Peach tapped into their psychic connection and he realized what it was. "Now hold on one second. You're not thinking maybe we had different fathers are you? With the same mother? Is that even possible?"

"It's possible. Superfecundation."

"Well, that's super silly! And you know it. And would it really make a difference?"

Tinman shrugged. They stood silently. Each trying to keep the bonds between them from fraying. For Tinman, the question was, would he ever know the real truth? And was it all that important, like Peach said?

"Well I'm going to tell you what," said Peach, "and you can put it in the book. You and I only have one brother each. That's enough for me. It's all I'll ever need."

Tinman looked at him. At times like this, he liked to remember the beauty of being human is the ability to remain in denial. To simply stop searching for the truth and accept the bliss that comes in the fog of ignorance.

"That's good, because it's all we got," said Tinman.

He threw an arm around his brother and they walked to the boathouse. Along the way, Peach said, "You never know. That dime might be worth something."

THIRTY-FIVE

WELL, FOLKS, IT TURNS OUT THAT LITTLE, OLD DIME was worth enough to buy a lot more than penny candy—for everybody. Jahllo bawled like an infant when he heard the coin collection now resided at the bottom of Lake Tahoe. His spirits were revived, however, when he learned Shady had gone down with the coins. He became further elated when he found out about the dime.

It turns out that coin was a bone of contention between LaVere Redfield and Norman Bilitz, the man who built Chester's house and had an ongoing rivalry with George Whittell of Thunderbird Lodge. Seems Bilitz spent years trying to put together a complete collection of coins minted at the Carson City Mint, spanning its twenty-one years of existence.

As an avid coin collector himself, Redfield knew of Bilitz' aspiration and approached him to buy the still incomplete collection. Bilitz flat-out refused, and being the kind of man Redfield was, he determined if he couldn't have the whole collection, then he would prevent Bilitz from completing it.

And he just happened to have a Carson City silver dime, minted in 1885, the only one known, and missing from Bilitz' nearly complete collection. Poor Shady had given away the most important and valuable piece.

Jahllo was beside himself, and made his way to Reno posthaste, arriving on Father's Day, just two weeks after the heist. All the participants of the caper—minus Tek who was mysteriously missing, and not returning calls—gathered in the Clubhouse for the showdown. And it was there a high-stakes game of haggling commenced. Tinman on one side, representing the Posse, and Jahllo on the other, representing himself.

A little preliminary research on the coin had made Tinman a much harder nut to crack than he was with the Audi. This time, he wasn't giving up without a fight. He knew Jahllo wanted the coin for himself—badly. And it gave him the edge. Back and forth they went. Offer. Counter. Debate. Offer. Counter.

"Come on, Jahllo, look at the size of the family I've got to feed," said Tinman, gesturing at his gang, each due an equal share of the take.

"Are you aware you are breaking my back, good man?" asked Jahllo.

"Boo-hoo. You're breaking my balls. Both of them," countered Tinman.

On and on it went. Hustler vs Horse Trader. Sweat poured. Tempers flared. Until finally, Jahllo caved.

When the dust settled, the price for the dime came to $270,000, and the silver dollar Shady had given Peach for collateral, went for $9,000. Five less than market value, but two more than offered Shady. Each heister, Bones, Catfish, Dez, Tek, Angel, Malice, Garshasp, Peach and Tinman, received $31,000. Not enough to retire on, but it was a nice shot in the arm for all concerned.

Despite Jahllo's whining, he'd made a killing. The Bilitz collection was now housed in a special vault at the Nevada

State Museum in Carson City. Should he ever decide to part with the coin, the state would gladly pay twice what he had paid for it. But for now, he was thrilled just to have it in his possession. The prize of his personal collection.

It would be a couple weeks before he could arrange for all the monies to be transferred, as he rarely kept that kind of cash on hand. Who did? At first, Tinman balked, saying he had promised to pay on the barrelhead, but after firm assurances, the deal was consecrated with a handshake. That was good enough to seal the deal. Straights might think of breaking such a sacred contract, but crooks knew the wronged party would never stop seeking revenge. And that was bad for business. Thus resulted a fragile, but reliable form of honor among thieves.

So now, everyone was celebrating. Drinks flowed, music blasted, Dez took turns dancing with Jahllo, Bones and Catfish. And Chuck, Jahllo's driver, had enticed Garshasp, Angel and Malice into a rousing game of beer pong.

Tinman sat at the bar, taking it all in. His eyes wandered to his pool table and he admired the Tiffany-style light hanging over it. A gift from Dez after they removed it from Chester's house.

Peach approached, and said, "See, brother, I told you we were due for a big score? Didn't I tell you? Huh, huh?"

Tinman laughed. "You did at that."

"Hey, it's time for the late news. I need to see Channel 11, the Bay Area." Peach clicked on the small TV just in time to see the drawing of the CA state lottery. He pulled out a piece of paper from his wallet, where he'd written down the numbers on the ticket he'd bought on the way to Tahoe. "Holy guacamole! He actually won!"

"Who won?" asked Tinman.

"Mr. Clarkson, who else? The guy who's house we were going to heist until we found out he was busted flat and going to lose it. Remember? I told you then I wish there was a way I could help him out. No reason anyone should lose their home. So I mailed the ticket to him, anonymously. Said it was from a guardian angel. And look there, he won ten G's. That should be enough to keep the taxman off his back for a while."

Tinman got goosebumps. Peach was a gem among men, and he hoped someday he might learn the secret way into his enchanted world where everything was what you made of it.

Into this festive scene burst Tek, looking like he'd seen a phantom. He was greeted loudly by the others, but he ignored it all, making a beeline for Tinman.

"Where you been, buddy?" asked Tinman. "We scored big tonight. Payoff comes to a little over thirty large a piece."

"That's great. Look, I got a problem. Or maybe you do. I'm not sure which, but either way, I need your help."

"Calm down now. How bad could it be?"

"It's not how bad, but how good."

"Huh?"

"It's this chick," said Tek, obviously agitated.

Peach grinned. "Chicks are no problem. Once you know what they're after."

"Well this one is after Tinman," said Tek.

"Huh?"

"I was at McCue's, practicing my game before coming here for the meet, when in walks this girl. She asks if I'm looking for a game. I figure it would be an easy score. Then she beat the pants off me in nine ball. Eleven games straight."

"What did you lose?" asked Tinman.

"That's the thing. Nothing. While we were playing, she starts asking if I know you. I don't think anything of it, so I say, sure. After she whipped my ass, she says she doesn't want the stake money. She just wants to meet you. Actually she's been looking to play you for a long time. She's gunning for you, I'm telling you."

Peach grinned at Tinman. "Your reputation proceeds you."

Tinman smiled contentedly, his ego stroked. "So where is she?"

"Outside," said Tek. "I'm sorry, but she kind of hijacked me."

"How? She packing heat or something?"

"No," said Tek, blushing. "Boobs."

"Aha! Do it every time," said Peach.

"So what do you want me to do with her, Tinman?"

"Bring her on. Humor the little girl. Should be fun."

Tek dashed outside and a moment later returned with a lanky, somewhat awkward girl in her early teens. She was wearying boy's jeans, a size too large, denim work shirt, and carrying a battered cue case.

Her sandy hair was cropped like a young boy, and the boobs Tek was so in awe of were just budding. Her grey eyes, however, were that of a much older, hardened person. They quickly scanned the scene, looking for danger, and settling on Tinman, piercing him with a coldness that he couldn't explain.

"You Tinman?" she asked with a husky, gravelly voice.

"And you are?" asked Tinman.

"She won't say!" said Tek.

"Does it matter," said the girl. "I came here to shoot pool. You up for that, old man?"

"I wouldn't have let you in if I wasn't, small fry," said Tinman, rising. He walked back to the pool table and removed the cover. The girl, all business, prepared her cue. He noticed it was in better shape than its case, and must have set her back a pretty penny.

As Tinman screwed his cue together, Peach rounded up the others and let them know what was going on. They all hustled into the pool room for the entertainment.

"What's your game?" asked Tinman.

"The only one. 14-1 straight."

"What are we playing for?"

"I'll let you know when I win."

"That's what she did to me!" cried Tek.

Tinman chuckled and shrugged. "Okay. To what?"

"Shootout to fifty," said the girl.

It was an unusual number. Straight pool was always a longer game, for good reason. Normally, Tinman would not have gone for the bait. But he was cocksure and nodded, knowing the game would be over quickly.

They lagged for break and he won. He chose to go first and pulled off a near perfect break, leaving only one possible shot to get out of the jam and continue a run.

He smirked, and said, "Didn't leave you much."

And that was his mistake. The girl set her jaw and marched up to him. "You think you're cute huh? Well, I've seen that movie too."

"What movie?"

"Don't mess around!"

"The Hustler," murmured Tinman, knowing he'd been busted.

"Bingo," spat the girl. "Fast Eddie shoots a safety in their first matchup. And he says, 'Didn't leave you much.' And what does Minnesota Fats say? Come on, Tinman, what the hell does he say!"

"You left enough."

"That's right," said the girl. "And so did you." All the awkwardness of her motions suddenly became graceful as she fired into the hanging ball, sank it, and proceeded to run out the rack. Then another. And another. And halfway into another.

Everyone was stunned into silence. Especially Tinman. As he watched her shoot, she reminded him of the great Willie Mosconi. Her stance, stroke, the methodical way of picking apart the racks, like a dancer. She was his reincarnation. Tinman was shaken.

"Fifty and out," called Tek, sliding the last score bead across.

"You lose," said the girl, and she started unscrewing her cue.

"And what do I lose?"

The girl zipped shut her case and looked up at him. "First of all your freedom."

It was the way she said it. A remembrance of another voice he'd known in his past. "What's your name?"

"Sarah."

"Sarah what?"

A sly grin crept on her face. "McGillicuddy."

Uh-oh. Phoenix. Fifteen, sixteen years ago. The one time he'd thought he'd dodged a bullet. "Your mom is Rebecca."

"Was. She's dead."

"And my freedom?"

"Gone. Daddy."

A collective gasp. Tinman propped himself up on the side of the table.

The girl, relishing the shock and awe, said, "So, here's what happens next. I'm moving in. Where's my room?"

Tinman was having trouble focusing, and breathing. His mind was frozen in time as he stared at her, seeing the color eyes and hair for the first time. The line of the jaw. The lanky build. It was true. He felt his life melting away.

Peach appeared at his side, a wide beaming smile as he looked at his newfound niece. He slapped Tinman on the back.

"Congratulations! Happy Father's Day, brother!"

To Fans of Tinman and the Posse

I personally want to thank you for reading this second book in the Tinman series. I hope you enjoyed it and welcome your comments. They can be sent to marc@crookbooks.site. If you'd like to spread the laughs, no better way than to post a review at the site where you bought the book.

The third book of the series, *Calling the Shots*, is coming soon. I know you'll get a kick out of watching Tinman deal with a new, unexpected member to his family, while attempting to pull off another impossible heist. You can find upcoming release dates for future books on my website, **www.crookbooks.site**.

Newly released on Amazon, two collections of short stories featuring Tinman and the Posse, *By Cook or By Crook*, and *Real Crooks Do Eat Quiche*. Companion recipes are in *Thieves Recipes*.

Additional articles can be found on my blog at **crookbooks.site/blog**. Narrated short stories are on my podcast, Crookbooks Radio, on the website.

See you on the flip side. Peace to all and long live laughter.

About the Author

Marc J. Reilly began entertaining people as a child actor. He graduated to directing and producing, and successfully founded two theater companies. He has worked in film as a cameraman, and director. For over two decades, he has worked as a freelance writer, while also writing several plays and screenplays. He now concentrates all his efforts to the writing of novels, specifically comedy/capers. He lives in Reno with the apple of his eye, Peg.

Made in the USA
Middletown, DE
23 June 2020